The RED ADMIRAL'S SECRET

Mark Poynter – No. 2

MATTHEW ROSS

RED DOG
UK

Published by RED DOG PRESS 2021

ISBN 978-1-913331-43-6

www.reddogpress.co.uk

PRAISE FOR DEATH OF A PAINTER:

"A chaotic comic caper that's as funny as it is brutal" – **The Sun**

"Matthew Ross's darkly comic debut novel, Death of a Painter, is a true delight. With a cast of colourful characters and a riveting plot, Ross breathes new life into a classic genre. A must for TV. I loved the cover too!" – **Julie Wassmer**, author of *The Whitstable Pearl Mysteries*

"The story has everything – **excitement, edge of your seat action and a lot of humour.** It is fantastically well written, definitely a 'just one more chapter' type of book… It is **darkly comic and thrilling to the last page**... Death of a Painter is a fantastic read from an author who is going places." – **Chris McDonald**, author of the D.I. Erika Piper mysteries: *A Wash Of Black* and *Whispers In The Dark*

"A **rip-roaring blackly comic crime caper** that had me turning the pages extra-sharpish" – **Rob Parker**, author of the *Ben Bracken* series and *Far from the Tree.*

"I was humbled, honoured and above all else flabbergasted (in the nicest possible way) to be asked to provide an author quote for 'Death of a Painter' but it's easy when you're reading something as **funny, dark and touching** as this. Enjoy!" – **Jonathan Whitelaw**, author of *Banking on Murder* and the *Hellcorp* series

"Do yourselves a favour and buy this book!" – **Evan Baldock**, author of *Bang, Bang, You're Dead!*

For J & S

-1-

MY UNCLE BERN wore his old bottle green suit the way most people wear a hangover. The skewiff flowery tie didn't brighten his mood either.

'You're not ready yet?'

He'd adopted that tone people in suits like to use; the one that says their words carry more importance because they come in a Marks and Sparks two-piece.

'Come in, Bern.' I left the door open behind me and sloped off back to the table, 'Why are you dressed like an Abbey National deputy manager?'

He scrunched up his nose to push his glasses back up his face. It made his eyes blink and his bald head crinkle in the way of a confused mole. 'The Abbey National disappeared at least twenty years ago.'

'Exactly,' I said, and returned to my toast which, like my uncle, had turned dry and stiff.

'The press launch…' he missed off the *durrr, stupid* from the end of his sentence, considering it unnecessary, judging from the attitude he was giving me. I hadn't forgotten. I was ready to go, but was enjoying winding him up more than I'd expected. I left him to fidget from foot to foot and tug his too-tight shirt collar while I finished my breakfast. After several minutes' amusement watching Bern constrict himself in a tie he'd never worn before and would never wear again, I dropped my plate and mug in the sink to deal with later and reached for my jacket.

'Come on then,' I said to the flush-faced Bern. 'Let's go.'

Actually, I'm getting a bit ahead of myself with the press launch and Bern dressed like a door-stepping Lib-Dem local councillor. Let me take you back a little while, back to when it all began…

THINGS WERE GOING good for me, very good indeed. I'd got in with Danny Kidd—yes, that Danny Kidd, Premier League bad boy, Danny Kidd. Never a world-class superstar, never won the FA Cup, no major silverware, in fact not even a single international cap, but one of those players you'd love if he played for your team and hate if he didn't: a crafty elbow when the ref's not looking here, a theatrical tumble to win a foul there, and a cheeky wink to the home crowd to say he'd got away with it again. Like many in the modern game, he'd made a lot of money through football, but unlike many he'd managed to keep most of it. That was thanks entirely to his older brother Stuart: a self-taught commercial whizz who'd taken care of all Danny's contracts and many endorsements for shampoo, skincare, sportswear and other paraphernalia no handsome man about town should be without. Stuart's shrewd investments had created a sizeable property portfolio, Kidd Properties. And that's where I come in.

It began as a few landlord tests and certificates but, as is often the way, because I know lots of different trades, it's easier for me to manage them all. Before you know it, it'd grown to me doing all their maintenance across the entire portfolio. Nice, easy work: good rates; prompt payments; and enough to keep me, Disco and Uncle Bern busy. I even had Fiery Jac on first refusal for whenever we needed an extra pair of hands. Things were sweet; I hadn't chased a new lead for ages.

During all that time Danny had been a vague presence in the background—like Jesus—we never saw him, only occasionally referred to him by name, but knew he would provide for us all. Now he was here constantly, and Christ, he was a nuisance!

He'd recently announced his retirement. In typical swagger, he'd told the back pages that he was too good to drop down the leagues: Danny was going out on top, Danny was going places, Danny had big plans for after he'd hung up his boots. As I found myself facing directly down his deep, dark yawn, tugging my paperwork from under his heels on the table, I couldn't help thinking those grand plans probably didn't amount to sitting around a small desk with me and his brother, debating whether or not to renew a clapped-out extractor fan.

A former Premier League star—Palace, Reading, and Tottenham—I'd never met anyone so bored and unfulfilled. At least he'd had his house refurbishment to occupy him; the local boy done good, retiring back to the area. And man alive was he returning in style.

He'd bought himself a magnificent Georgian manor house—the word 'impressive' simply wouldn't do it justice. Approached by a long, sweeping gravel drive, the first thing you see are the two double-storey bays as straight and upright as sentries either side of the portico entrance. The Gothic tracery to the tall sash windows brings elegance from an age long since. And its location couldn't have been any more perfect, set in the heart of Bearsted—a picture-postcard Kentish village so ridiculously quaint that if you saw it in a movie, you'd complain places like that don't exist anymore. But for people like Danny Kidd, the young celebrity rich, it most certainly does.

The house had been lovingly preserved by the old couple he bought it from, but Danny, being Danny, wanted his own stamp on it: the height of luxury, full automation. I'd had a happy, and by happy I of course mean highly profitable, three months remodelling it for him including a fabulous home cinema in the cellar; a huge, handmade kitchen with every appliance you can think of, plus plenty of others you couldn't even dream of, built into swathes of quartz countertops; luxury bathrooms with TV screens in the shower and changing LED mood lighting in the bathtubs; not to mention the walk-in wardrobes bigger than most people's bedrooms, housing more clothes than a department store, all gladly given for free by eager brands and designers. The place is breath-taking. Behind an ornate walled garden comes a further five acres with outbuildings, some of which we sensitively renovated. The first being the original groundsman's cottage, modernised as a high-spec, rent-free home for Stuart. Next the ramshackle old barn: once a tatty dilapidated specimen on a serious lean, now a four-berth garage for Danny's collection of luxury cars.

Above it, the old hayloft was transformed into an impressive state-of-the-art gym, fully kitted out with top of the range specifications from Danny's Premier League fitness coach. Danny, at thirty-six, still maintained the trim, toned body of an athlete and even in his retirement retained the stardust privileges of celebrity: bronzed, tanned skin; teeth—capped, perfect and gleaming; intricate tattoos by Europe's finest artists; his short, blond hair, despite beginning to recede and thin slightly, was expertly coloured and styled by the best salon in London. You could see the family resemblance in Stuart, like a real-life 'before and after' makeover: the square jaw, the wide nose, the blue eyes. But despite Stuart's daily punishment in their hayloft gym, he'd never be mistaken for his famous younger sibling, nor Danny for a civilian slob like the rest of us.

We did face an obstacle with the rickety old stable block, though. Stuart wanted to make it the self-contained head office for Kidd Properties. At first the local planning officer was resistant. Located, as it is, adjacent to the main house, the planning officer insisted the Grade Two listing extended to the stables as well. He met the famous new occupant, got star-struck and a compromise solution was quickly found: so long as we kept the external cabling to a minimum, forgot about installing air-conditioning and he got a selfie and an autographed shirt for his boy, he was happy with the office proposal. And it turned out nice in the end. It was small, but had a neat professional look. Two stylish desks in a pale wood veneer butted each other head-to-head, a brand-new, top of the range Apple computer sat on each with the largest thinnest screens you've ever seen. Huge padded leather swivel chairs that'd make Donald Trump green with envy behind each desk. A four-person circular meeting table and chairs to one corner, refreshments in the other, including a frothy coffee machine and a glass-fronted fridge always packed full of bottled water and energy drinks. A glass-doored bookcase took up half a wall but didn't contain many books. Instead it sparkled with the souvenirs and memorabilia of a celebrated career: engraved glass player of the season awards, silver cups and trophies, a couple of huge champagne jeroboams with logos celebrating the man of the match, a bronze football boot on a mount, and plenty of photos of Danny Kidd with legends past and present. Around the walls, mounted in identical black square-edged frames, were signed shirts and magazine covers. Should anyone be in any doubt, this was the house that Danny Kidd built, and this was his shrine.

Everything had been plain sailing so far; my client's happy, the neighbours are happy, the council's happy, and I'm getting paid, so I'm happy too. Happy days all round. And in the self-contained office suite, headquarters to Kidd Properties, approved by our friendly planning officer, is where we begin.

-2-

'MARK, WHAT'RE YOU doing tomorrow?' Danny took his feet off the table and sat upright. He looked across at me. 'There's a property in next week's auction I quite fancy seeing. Need your advice. I'm looking at doing a development, a bit of building.'

Stuart's face of alarm told me Danny hadn't spoken to him about this. I know better than to get caught in the middle of an argument. I held my silence.

'You don't know the first thing about building,' said Stuart.

Danny gestured towards me, 'No, but Mark does.' Great, now I'm slap-bang in the middle of it, and appear to have picked sides, just what I don't need.

I really didn't want to piss Stuart off, he was the one who brought me in to begin with. He was a lifesaver. He'd come at just the right time. I was struggling for work after the events of last year: I'd lost a lot of money when a client dropped dead on me before he could get his chequebook out, and I'd upset a lot of people when I couldn't pay them. It was fair to say my reputation throughout the Medway Towns was in tatters. And it certainly wasn't helped by adding in several months of national lockdown when none of us could earn. Every penny I had was disappearing down the gurgler, so getting off the usual patch and in with Stuart had been a godsend. I had absolutely no intention of messing up the good thing I had with the Kidds. That's why I'd been forced to restrict Uncle Bern's time around Danny. He was starting to annoy him, forever whipping out pieces of tat he'd stick under his nose for him to sign for his new little venture: flogging genuine autographed Danny Kidd memorabilia online.

'What's the scheme, what do you think Stuart?' I said in an attempt to bring him back on board. He gave a slight shrug of the shoulders and looked towards Danny.

Danny opened the auctioneer's glossy brochure and jabbed a finger at lot number fourteen, 'Here. Former public house. Scheme for six one-bedroom flats. Lower Gillingham, down your way, know it?'

Twisting the brochure round the right way up, I could see it was a solid-looking two-storey Victorian pub. Quite a wide frontage: three large, square windows with two entrance doors set alternately between them. Its sad neglect was plain: painted brickwork, the colour of sour milk; external joinery a faded and flaking ghost of once-glossy verdant green; rusted brackets bled orange tears beside the doors where vibrant flower baskets once hung. I recognised the pub right away. It'd closed at least ten years ago, maybe even longer. There's no sadder sight than a dead pub.

'The Admiral Guthrie, yeah I know it, used to be popular when I was a kid.' I immediately pictured it on Dockyard Open Days and Gillingham home games, the baskets in bloom and happy drinkers congregated on the grass out front.

Stuart gave a dramatic sigh and pointed to the auctioneer's sales blurb, 'Says the planning permission lapsed six months ago.'

'It's not a big problem,' I said. 'So many projects got put on ice by the Coronavirus, and the developer might have gone under during the shut-down. Many have. Maybe that's why it's being auctioned off now for a quick sale. But properties in that area of Lower Gillingham near the Dockyard have been hot ever since they opened the university campus down there. I wouldn't have thought it too hard to get permission granted again.'

'Great. That's sorted then,' said Danny, rising to his feet. 'Give them a call, will you? Book us a viewing.'

Danny stepped outside, did a few stretches, then, as Stuart called the auctioneer, began his daily jog: three times round the perimeter of his grounds. Half an hour later he returned to Stuart's smug mug: 'Bad news. It's sold.'

Danny threw his headphones on the table-top and reached for a bottle of water, 'What do you mean it's sold?' he twisted the cap off with more force than necessary. 'It's in the brochure for next week's sale.'

'They've received an offer the seller likes, and they've decided to withdraw it,' I said. 'It happens sometimes.'

Danny's chin dropped to his chest. He looked to the floor, only for a breath, and when he looked up there was a curl to his lip. 'Not to me it doesn't.'

He grabbed the brochure from the table and quickly found the auctioneer's number. He dialled it, deliberately muttering in a whisper loud enough to be heard, '*want something doing* …'

The call was answered very quickly, and he asked to be put through. Danny introduced himself, which by the sound of it caused some confusion. 'Danny Kidd, yes… no… not *like* the footballer… I am Danny Kidd… yes… that's me, hello.'

He chatted for a few minutes, said what he wanted, dropped a few famous names in for good measure, and then with a cheery goodbye ended the call.

'All sorted. He'll meet us at eleven tomorrow. Right, quick shower and then I'm off.'

STUART AND I were planning out the week ahead's work when the sound of crunching gravel made us both look up, just in time to see Danny's beautiful Mercedes AMG disappear from view.

'He's off to meet his agent,' Stuart offered without me asking. 'He was convinced he could just walk straight into a pundit role on the telly but… well, it's not as easy at that.'

I gave a non-committal 'Uh-huh.' There's a time and place for gossip, and it's definitely not stuck between the two brothers that pay my wages.

'I mean, look at this prick,' Stuart twisted his computer screen round to face me. *'Not Kidding About'*: the bold banner headline above a photo of a snarling, dishevelled Danny restrained by a massive bouncer. Just a few feet from him a young mixed-race man was also held back by an equal behemoth, the tattoos up the young man's neck contorted into blurs in his struggle to reach Danny. I'd seen the photo earlier that morning but hadn't mentioned it. It was in all the papers and on the breakfast telly: Danny squaring off against a rising young grime hip-hop star who went by the name of Muzzkett. I'd never heard of him, but that shouldn't come as any surprise—if it happened after Britpop, I'm not interested. According to the papers, being known as a gangster and a criminal was this Muzzkett's thing. Apparently, they fell out over some reality TV bimbo I'd also never heard of, but who seemed to be famous for being famous.

'Fighting in nightclubs, the nobhead.' There was no mistaking the disappointment in Stuart's voice. 'I tell him he's mad expecting a pundit job. The whole boo-hiss pantomime villain thing was fine as a player, made him stand out, got his name known. But a TV pundit is different, they want experienced guys who command respect. They've got World Cup winners lining up for these jobs. He's got no chance. Give me time, I tell him, I'll get you some commercials, a guest spot on a quiz show, get you ballroom dancing or stick you in the jungle. But what's the point? Even they won't touch him with headlines like that. You've got to be squeaky clean. I think he's finally realised he needs to lay low for a while. Probably why he's now suddenly decided to play at being a property developer.'

I gave another non-committal uh-huh, but Stuart hadn't finished. 'There's one journalist, if that's what you call them, anyway, there's one been round here making a nuisance of herself, Rachel… something. Been calling, door-stepping, even pretended to be a prospective tenant wanting to look around one of our flats just to get close to Danny.' The contempt was obvious, it was clearly an aspect of Danny's celebrity lifestyle impacting adversely on his. 'Listen Mark, I hope I don't need to say it, but never ever talk to any tabloid hacks about Danny. If you do…'

I gave yet another non-committal uh-huh, then managed to steer the subject back to our original discussion: refurbing a pair of shabby one-bed flats.

LIKE I SAY, it was a nice number I'd got myself. Things were good, except… Uncle Bern. He'd now been back in town for almost six months, and to say he'd outstayed his welcome was an understatement. Bern had perfected the semi-retired, semi-itinerant lifestyle, spending the winter months in his apartment in Spain which he'd then rent out during the Summer and come back here to pick up whatever work he could, usually from me and his other contacts to fund his next few months on the Costa. The rest of the year he'd flit back and forth whenever the money or Auntie Val's patience ran out, whichever came sooner, and the answer to that conundrum—Val's patience. After months cooped up, enduring each other in a one-bed apartment on the Costa del Covid, Val threw him out as soon as she could legally open the door again: hasta la vista Bernie! So he made his way home and made himself my problem. To be fair, he'd been alright on the work we'd been doing for the Kidds—apart from giving Danny the hump with his online sales shenanigans.

Other than that, things were good. Until…

THE PHONE RANG. I'd just pulled away from Danny's. The name displayed on the screen in capital letters—shit, just what I need. I knew I had to take the call, I pressed accept.

'Where the bloody hell are you?' the voice filled the van and bounced off the walls in an angry echo.

'Hello Sweetness—'

'Don't you give me any of your sweetness bullshit, you were meant to be home over an hour ago, where are you?'

'I'm on my way now, I'll be fifteen minutes tops,' I said, knowing full well it'd be at least twice that but seeing as it looked like I was in line for a fight, I might as well put it off a bit longer.

'Make sure you are,' she said, and cut the call without even a goodbye. With the confidence you only get when on your own, I blew a raspberry and flicked the Vs towards the phone. Then immediately regretted it and found myself saying sorry out loud. I knew it wasn't Perry's fault, but I knew it wasn't mine either.

About a year ago, Perry had rented the house next door, and we'd got together very quickly thereafter. Within weeks, she'd ended up more or less living at mine. However, things recently had started feeling a bit fraught. It's that big milestone; you hit the first anniversary and then you must decide whether you're in it for the long haul or not.

It actually took me almost an hour to get home. Traffic problems on Boxley Hill. In the Middle Ages, the true believers came through here on foot as part of the Pilgrims Way, I bet they climbed it bloody quicker than I did.

'*Welcome to Medway*', announced the blue sign from behind overgrown hedgerows just past the Harrow Inn. I'd crossed the threshold, Maidstone back to Medway. Back to home.

The Medway Towns: the catch-all description for the three towns of Chatham, Gillingham and Rochester. Already ancient by the time the Romans came to stay, they'd long ago melted into one another, the boundaries blurred and indistinct over centuries.

My whole life story lay in Gillingham and as I crossed that invisible boundary, I thought of home, and more importantly I thought of family: times past and faces gone. I don't know why, but the prospect of coming home always made them feel just a little bit closer. Everything I could see around me reminded me of my father, but I'd moved on from every connection making me sad, and instead I found reassurance and legacy.

LEGACY, NOW THERE'S poncey word, you'd have given me a sideways look if I'd said that to you, wouldn't you, Dad? And as for Gillingham, your dad knew it all. If I can correctly remember what Granddad told me: once upon a time many, many centuries ago there lived a chieftain called Gylla, said with a J. And the Anglo-Saxon word for family was 'inga', so put it together and you get Gyll-inga or home to Gylla's tribe, and over the aeons it became Gillingham. I don't recall where he said the 'ham' came from. Sainsburys, probably.

Granddad loved his local history, didn't he? Do you remember how he had so many stories, myths and legends about the area? Tell you the truth, I wish I'd paid a bit more attention to them now, maybe written them down, could've given me something to do when I was stuck at home. I even thought about starting the family tree again, but didn't. I always remember though, when he'd drive me home, sitting low in his red Mini, we'd pass The Avenue nightclub and he'd tap the window on his side. 'Saxon king buried there, Mark,' every single time—got annoyed with it in the end to be honest. Turns out it's true. I looked it up once. A complete Saxon skeleton and his burial treasures. Some unsuspecting matey was grubbing out the foundations of The Avenue nightclub in the nineteen-thirties, although—as you always liked to remind me—back in your day it was called The Central, and ta-da, he discovers possibly Gylla's last resting place. The jammy sod. The only buried treasure I've ever found on a job was two hundred Silk Cut and half a bottle of gin under the floorboards of a girls' dorm when I rewired that expensive boarding school over towards Cuxton. Just goes to show though, if poor old Gylla can't rest in peace, then nothing can stay hidden forever. Not in a town like this. I haven't given up hope yet, Dad. I know I don't talk about him much these days, but I haven't given up—Adam will come back one day, I promise.

Anyway, old Gylla, by all accounts, he was one scary dude. He'd lead the tribe into battle screaming and hollering—hence the town motto, 'Domus Clamantium', translation 'the home of the shouting men'. Ironic really, seeing as I now seem to live in the home of the shouting woman. No, I take that back. It's not fair. We're both as guilty as each other, we shouldn't be picking fights and trying to score points, not when we've got things going so well for us now—the money's finally good again, it's coming in regular, I've not had to chase a lead in months, why spoil a good thing? Do us a favour Dad, next time it happens, give me a tap on the shoulder, whisper in my ear, something. Remind me to take a breath and calm things down. Thanks, mate.

I DREW UP outside my little terraced house: a modern starter home built in the Eighties but only now looking mature and part of the landscape. It takes a while for a property to bed in and look established, and no amount of trees or planting can hurry the process. You can always spot a new build in the same way you can always spot a wig across a crowded room.

Perry waited for me in the window with a look that ought to have been registered as a weapon of mass destruction. The way her eyes drilled into me, I was sure I could feel the breeze whistling through the holes in my chest. Those beautiful eyes, they used to shine with happiness once. Now they shone with steel.

She wore a silky orange crew-neck top, it looked new. I'm breathless every time I see her. I love how she blends her Indian heritage with modern fashion, and aside from her fierce face of fury she looked amazing. I'd totally forgotten we were meant to be going to a birthday dinner, one of her friends off the ward, I'd probably met them before but couldn't remember. I got changed double quick. Carried by a speeding taxi and a cloud of mutual resentment, we made it just in time. We managed to ruin everyone's evening without even speaking.

Other than that, things were good…

-3-

'HEY HEY HEY!' hollered Danny, announcing his approach. I'd arrived at eleven o'clock as requested to find Stuart already waiting, but as usual, Danny breezed in fifteen minutes late. No apologies, just bags of confidence and swagger.

'What do you think then?' he leaned back, feet wide apart and arms outstretched, adopting his famous goal-scoring pose to face the boarded-up frontage.

Stuart lacked the same level of enthusiasm. 'Looks alright, I suppose.'

I'D EXPECTED A junior from the auctioneer's office to open up for us, but it was the top man himself—and my, wasn't he keen for a few selfies with his midfield hero? Stuart and I left Danny with the auctioneer discussing Tottenham's prospects this season and began looking around.

I wasn't particularly interested in the sad, dilapidated state of it internally. I couldn't care less about the damp smelling carpets or the torn wallpaper. And I could see beyond the unpleasant yellow stains and the dead flies that crunched under my feet. None of that mattered, it'd all be grubbed out. All I cared about was the structure, and it seemed sound enough. No nasty cracks. Anything else that might need a costly fix? The old water tank was made of asbestos, and some of the pipe lagging looked like asbestos too. Thankfully all intact though, it shouldn't be too expensive to get someone sensible to remove it.

Stuart and I turned towards the cellar. A low, narrow door leading from the main bar area had been formed in the spandrel under the stairs, so small and tight it'd be illegal now. I groped around the edge of the doorway and found the light switch, not a knobbly old Bakelite titty type but not much newer, it was a smooth pearlescent plate with an elegant, long central switch from Britain's jet-age fifties, yellowed through time like ivory. It didn't matter, it didn't work, no power. Using the torchlight from our phones we crouched in the confined staircase as it wound a quarter-turn then doglegged another turn. With such low headroom it was one of those staircases you had to walk down backwards—if you were to maintain the crouch going forwards you'd be at risk of toppling over.

Like all good plans, it went wrong. Too concerned at watching my step as I walked backwards, I cracked the back of my head on a low beam at the bottom of the staircase. Luckily, my swears warned Stuart of the danger ahead. New access to the cellar was a definite requirement, unless things have changed and the average first-time buyer now finds a daily dose of mild concussion acceptable.

I led the expedition, Stuart gamely made up the rear. At the bottom, I stretched back to my full height and took in the surroundings. It smelt dusty and musty, but I didn't smell any damp or the sweet pungent fragrance of dry rot, so that was good. And aside from there being more cobwebs than around Uncle Bern's wallet, the main thing I saw was the cellar didn't have a lot of headroom. There was still air above my ears, but not as much as you'd like in your new apartment. The floor would need to be broken out and dug down if it was to be turned into a habitable space. That could be pricey.

We measured the existing head height, then clambered back up the stairs in our crouching chimp-walk. Back in the bar, back in the daylight, back in the fresh air, I shook out my stiff spine and dusted a few webs from my hair. Stuart hadn't unrolled from his crouch. He rubbed his lower right leg and winced: 'Are you okay, Stuart?'

'I'm fine,' he assured me, but kept rubbing his shin, 'I broke my ankle years ago, never set properly, every now and then if I step awkwardly it'll flare up and hurt like a bastard. I'll be okay in a minute, don't worry.'

I left him to recover and continued my walk-through survey, checking where the gas, water and electric came in and where the drains went out. Nothing seemed amiss. In fact, the more I looked at it, the more convinced I became that if Danny and Stuart could get this at the right price, they could have a good scheme on their hands.

'THERE'S BEEN A lot of interest in this property.' The auctioneer had broken himself away from worshipping Danny for a moment to talk to us. 'In fact, we'd already received an offer for it pre-auction, which our client had accepted. But—'

'I've just bought it!' interrupted Danny. 'He shoots, he scores!'

I don't think either Stuart or I actually believed what we'd heard, and both stared at the auctioneer.

'Yes. Congratulations,' he raised his hand, hoping for a high five, but Danny hadn't noticed and was engrossed in his phone, leaving the auctioneer hanging. 'I've been doing this for twenty-five years, never had a day like this before.'

'How can he have bought it, just like that?' Stuart had that accusing tone I imagine my dad used a lot at school parents' evenings: *and you're his teacher, you just watched him do it, did you?*

'He asked to speak to the client, so I put him in touch,' began the auctioneer. The wobble in his voice suggested he'd only just realised what he'd done wasn't strictly ethical. But then, he was so lovestruck he'd have done anything Danny had asked. 'They did a deal.'

'A deal?'

Danny glanced up from his phone, 'Yeah, a deal. Geezer said what the other lot were paying him, I topped it and offered the deal done in forty-eight hours. Nice bloke. For a Man United fan.'

'Forty-eight hours, is that even possible?' I asked.

'Very much so.' The auctioneer's voice had more confidence. He was back on firmer ground now. 'We have to have all the particulars ready as a pack for the auction, and the vendor had unfortunately had a failed purchase in the past so he's provided all the searches et cetera from that, and Danny…' he blushed saying his name—his new best friend. I could tell he'll be talking about this morning for weeks. '…Danny said it's a cash purchase, no finance required, and you're doing your survey now. So, it is literally a case of producing the money and signing the contract.'

Danny draped an arm around the neck of the auctioneer—sportsmen tend to be very touchy feely, have you noticed? It's all man-hugs and high fives. I don't like it personally. Social distancing that was more to my liking, but clearly that's just me, because the auctioneer looked ready to mess himself, especially when Danny squeezed him even tighter and announced triumphantly, 'Kidd Properties is in the development business.'

THE BROTHERS AND I huddled around a white melamine table in the coffee shop over the road. It had a nasty stickiness that pulled on my forearms every time I moved. A surly waitress with a European accent had delivered us three bland-tasting coffees in tapered glass mugs. When she failed to recognise her famous customer, I detected a smirk crinkling around Stuart's eyes: to her, he was just another annoying punter trying to chat her up, to Stuart it was a small victory.

The price Danny had offered was more than I would have; his money, I guess, not for me to comment, but I do know it'll make it hard for them to turn a profit now. Savings will have to be wrung out of everything right the way through from start to finish, including my time. I concluded our impromptu meeting with the promise of a budget estimate for the conversion within the next day or two. They seemed happy with that.

'Can you get me a chandelier?' said Danny, completely out of the blue, the surprise knocking us both into silence. 'I want one for home.'

AFTER LEAVING THE Kidd brothers, I headed down to my favourite merchants, Thorpe Timber and Building Supplies, to get some price books. There's plenty of the national big boy chains locally, but there's something nice about an independent family firm, and the something nice was serving on the trade counter.

'Hey, Goldenballs, got me any tickets for the FA Cup yet?' said the magnificent Maria Thorpe.

'I told you, learn the offside rule and I'll take you.'

'Funny. What do you want?' she said, pretending to be annoyed. We had history—just a dabble, a long time ago. I've often wondered whether there could have been a rematch, I'd heard her latest engagement was off, but I was with Perry now. Maybe that was it? Maybe that was what was behind the heightened flirting between us these days, I pondered as I walked back to the van with a pile of brochures and a slight feeling of arousal from the innuendo-laden chatter. I was trying to get better discounts, but I think she was having fun embarrassing me. I still don't know if she was mocking me or coming on to me.

I placed the brochures on the bonnet and fished around in my pockets, looking for the keys. Lost in my daydream of playtimes with Magnificent Maria, I didn't notice him until he reached the van. Next thing I knew, he was up in my face. I could feel his fetid coffee breath warm against me, his pockmarked cheeks were flushed red and although shorter than me, his dark eyes were locked on to mine.

'I want a friendly chat with you,' he said. His accent was out of place, he wasn't local. 'I saw you outside the Admiral Guthrie today. Tell me you don't want to buy it… go on, tell me.'

'No, I don't,' I said truthfully. I couldn't speak for my clients though. I resented his aggression, but knew better than to react: he was the one bringing hostility to the younger, bigger man—he must fancy himself as pretty handy. He could be any kind of nutter, he could be armed, better not to provoke him. 'Why? Do you want to buy it?'

'I represent some very important men,' he said. Scottish, I'm certain of it, the way he said the R sounds, 'And we want that building. We will have that building. Understand?'

I didn't answer. The Scotsman moved back one step, the way he kept his eyes locked on mine made an ice-cold slurry churn around my guts. Idiots mouthing off is something I can take any day of the week, but there was a darkness in his eyes, an undercurrent showing he meant business. It shook me.

'Understand?' he said once more, then got into a black Range Rover and accelerated away in a fury of speed and noise. His taillights disappeared from view. I became aware of the prickly rush of adrenalin, my heart pounded faster than the pistons on a runaway train. I took a few deep, slow breaths and looked skywards, following the flight of a lone seagull overhead. It glided a slow arc out across the river and back in again. My panic receded. It's fair to say that wasn't the usual encounter you'd expect at the builder's merchant. I wondered whether to say anything to Danny and Stuart, then decided not to, not until I'd made some enquiries.

Feeling normal, appearances restored, I ventured back into Thorpe's. Maria was serving a lusty joiner in a lumberjack shirt I vaguely knew. He was giving her his best seduction. I gave him a nod of recognition and leant across him.

'Maria, quick one, some guy outside, Scottish fella, black Range Rover, bit of a bad attitude. Know who he is?'

'Scottish?' Maria looked thoughtful, Lumberjack turned and stared at me for cramping his style. 'No, we've not had anyone Scotch in here today, can't help, sorry, don't know him.'

'Scotsman, attitude? Wasn't Andy Murray, was it?' quipped Lumberjack, soon realising he was laughing on his own. Maria and I stared at him, stoney-faced.

'Anyway, if he comes in again, will you let me know?' I said and turned to leave. Lumberjack preened, ready to resume his patter. 'Andy Murray, that's funny… and to think, your wife says you don't have a sense of humour… Hide the gold ring next time, dumbass!'

-4-

I'D FOUND DISCO later that day in the Golden Lamb, not that it was a major international manhunt. Some things are set in stone: the sun will rise every morning, tea never tastes as good in a coloured mug as it does in a white one, and if the clock's struck four, Disco's in the Lamb. He ordered us a couple of pints and rolled himself a fag whilst they were being poured, poking it behind his ear for later. I wanted to find out about my new Scottish friend and David 'Disco' Dancer was the best place to start. Nothing gets past Disco. He's like the building trade's air traffic control: he knows exactly where everyone is, exactly what they're up to, who's flying high and who's about to crash and burn.

'Remember the Admiral Guthrie?'

'Down near the Dockyard? Yeah, used to be a nice boozer once upon a time.'

'It's up for sale, as a scheme for six flats. I was down there today with Danny Kidd. Know if anyone else is looking at it?'

'I did hear the Tombliboos were keen, even got as far as asking people for quotes.'

The Tombliboos? Made sense, exactly their kind of project. Brothers George and Wesley Tomblin, known to the Revenue as Tomblin Groundworks, known to everybody else as the Tombliboos—but never in their hearing, unless you wanted a shovel wrapped round the back of your head. They were proving '*where there's muck there's money*', they'd done very nicely out of their excavations and their earthworks and had recently branched into property. They'd built a couple of houses over on the Isle of Sheppey, by all accounts done a nice job. I could see this scheme being right up their street: relatively straightforward, not too big, but enough money in it to be worthwhile.

'Did they put in an offer, before the auction?'

'No. From what I heard, they were all set to, but now don't have the time for anything like that. They've just picked up a massive job, they're having to call in people from all over to cope with it.'

'Oh yeah?'

'They've got all the groundworks and concrete on all phases of an enormous housing development over the other side of Gravesend: eighteen hundred units, all the estate roads, basement car parks, drainage, everything. For Fielder Homes.'

That I found intriguing. If they could make it work it'd set them up for life, put them up in the big boy league but, 'How'd they get that then?'

'No idea. I don't think it even went out to tender because John Healy's livid. Having worked for Fielder's for ages, he was hoping to get at least a piece of it. Friends in the right places, who knows?'

Disco promised to keep an ear to the ground in case he heard any more about the Admiral Guthrie, and then loudly, probably more loudly than was necessary, informed me and the rest of the bar he was going for a dump.

I stood idly leaning, back to the bar, gazing up at the silent TV screen: a golfer in red potted a ball, don't ask me who, I don't know—I don't understand golf at all, but he seemed very excited by it, and so did the crowd who all mobbed him. Nope, don't get it at all.

'Hello Mark,' said a familiar voice. Harpo, for it was he, pulled a stool towards him and sat beside me. 'How goes it with you?'

Harpo was into what he exotically referred to as architectural salvage but everyone else called old shit. He fancied himself as an expert and had recently built his own website that grandly declared him to be "Medway's leader in the field" which was true, but only if the field in question looked like a flytipper's big day out. Still, the truth was, if you needed a weathered Kent peg tile or a Victorian sash weight, he was the man to see. I told him about my special request.

'I take it by chandelier you don't mean a little three-armed thing from a DIY store, fake wood, plastic drippy candles, do you?' The thing about Harpo is that he can be a pompous old fart when he wants to, which happens to be most of the time. 'I'm guessing your flash footballer wants something like you'd see in the Palace of Versailles? Eight feet wide, lead crystal droppers, the full bifta?'

By his empty-handed lingering, I could tell this information was going to cost me. Being fluent in publican sign language, I caught the barmaid's eye, raised a finger and pointed at Harpo. A freshly poured pint swiftly arrived in front of him.

'Cheers Lyn.' I offered a ten-pound note. 'And take one for yourself.' She thanked me with the lusty smile only barmaids of a certain age can get away with. I knew I wouldn't see any change from it but then I've always found buying the occasional thank-you drink goes a long way and looked at it as a long-term investment, a queue-jump token for the next busy match day.

Harpo took it hungrily and necked a slurp, the damp bedraggled patch of facial hair around his mouth reminding me of an Alsatian that used to live down our road growing up: stupid thing, always running off, always coming back soaking wet, bugger only knows where it went. Anyway…

'The thing about chandeliers is you're better off buying one second-hand,' he said. As he spoke, his revolting beard rolled and rippled, and it occurred to me that it'd been some time since I last took the van through the car wash.

'And I suppose that's because you happen to have a second-hand one you're trying to shift?'

'Far from it. In fact, I wish. Believe it or not, you're at least the third person in the past fortnight to ask me about them, all these people building big houses, seems they've become the must-have thing. Brand new chandeliers are well expensive. They charge you for the privilege of being the first owner, like a new car. Then when they're taken down, second-hand, the price drops big time. But that was because there weren't many places to fit them—all the places that could take a chandelier already had one. But now there's more money about and people are building bigger and bigger gaffs, they want something for you to stand under so you can gawp up at how rich they are. You're probably looking at just the right time as I imagine the second-hand prices are going to start rocketing soon.'

Very convenient, I thought, not believing a word of it. I could sense he was making mental notes to add at least twenty-five percent on top of any old tat he finds to offer up to me as his 'special customer'.

'As well as being mega expensive, new ones come in kit form. You need to get your hanger fixed securely and then you build the frame and hang all the droppers on one by one. It's like hanging off the ceiling to build an upside-down Christmas tree. It's a long fiddly pain-in-the-arse job.'

I gave an understanding nod, but I'd done plenty of fiddly pain-in-the-arse jobs in my time, that didn't faze me.

'An old one however is taken down whole. You need to be careful and protect it in transport, but it's a whole heap easier. You get your hanging point securely fixed and then three, probably four of you, because they're bloody heavy, raise it up and drop it on. Make the connection, and job done. Like I say, much easier. But I haven't heard of one being available for a few months now. If I do hear of one, want me to give you a shout?'

I LEFT THE Golden Lamb feeling it had been a successful diversion: firstly I'd got my name down for a chandelier—although God only knows how much Harpo will try to spank me for it now he knows I'm in the market for one; and secondly, thanks to Disco's encyclopedic knowledge, I managed to track down the Tombliboos just as their day was coming to an end at a nearby primary school.

'Hello chaps, what's going in here then?' I asked the two big brutes pulling together steel mesh fence panels.

'Alright Mark. New music block,' said George Tombliboo: the muscles in his biceps bulging, as big and black as cannon balls and probably as deadly if on the wrong end of them. 'Lottery funding, apparently.' He snaked a thick metal chain through the mesh panels and secured it in place with an enormous cruiser padlock. 'You're a bit late though if you're after work, I think they've got all the subbies in place already.'

'That's a shame.' I tried to sound convincing, but I knew the main contractor from bitter experience. I asked who'd got the electrical package and tried to hide my smugness when they told me, knowing the problems he'd face getting paid. Groundworkers never seem to have any problems getting paid. Maybe that's because they come in right at the start of the job when the main contractor is desperate to get going and protect his programme. Or maybe because groundworkers tend to be big, strong men wielding heavy tools. Who knows?

'The reason I'm here boys is the Admiral Guthrie. I've got a client very interested in it, and I understand you were too. But changed your mind, is that right?'

'Yeah, we were, Wes went to have a look at it, didn't you?'

'That's right,' said his brother, rubbing his massive hand over his buzzcut. 'Nice little scheme, got potential, but the time just wasn't right for us, so we dropped it.'

'So, there'd be no hard feelings then if my guy went for it?'

'No, don't be silly, there'll be another one along in a year or two, there always is, you know that Mark.'

I nodded my agreement, 'Thanks boys.'

'In fact, if your guy gets it, bear us in mind for the demolitions and grubbing out, we'll give you a good price for it,' said George.

'What happened about your big job for Fielder's? I'd heard you were going to be flat out on that for the next couple of years?'

'We will be, but they're still finalising whatever it is they have to do, we've been told to expect a start date in about six months from now, so we could easily drop onto your little pub conversion and be in and out way before then.'

'George no. No, we can't. You'll have to forgive my brother, he's mistaken. We can't commit to any work, I'm afraid, we've a full order book. Sorry Mark.'

George stared at his sibling, hands apart and eyebrows knitted together in confusion.

'We'll talk about it later,' said Wesley.

I bid them farewell and walked away with no idea what was going on, other than it wasn't them that had made the offer, so my logic told me it wasn't them that the Scotsman was working for.

-5-

IT HAD JUST gone half six by the time I got home. I decanted my tools from the van to the garage, a task I do every day without fail - there's no worse feeling than wanting to crack on and get earning only to find some scumbag has broken in to your van and robbed it overnight. My garage has a nice sturdy padlock on it, it's dry and it's fully racked out floor to ceiling. It's the ideal space to store everything I could ever need to run my business, that and three transparent plastic boxes sitting in a row: the full extent of my Dad's estate. One contained legal-looking paperwork, certificates, policies and the like. One contained nick-nacks and assorted bits-and-bobs. And the third contained all the family photos, some neatly stuck into padded leatherette albums, most piled an inch thick into the wallet envelopes they came back from the shop in. A print had worked its way free and pressed itself up against the wall of the clear plastic box; an old photo of Mum and Dad one Christmas morning, back when I was still small enough to get excited by the thought of Santa. They looked out of the box every day at me, and it had become a recent habit to kiss the pad of my first finger then pass the kiss on by pressing my finger against their faces, and it's a habit I was happy to carry on today. They looked happy, and that made me happy. It made me want to look favourably to the future—the days were beginning to stretch out again and it wasn't quite dark yet. There was still a nip in the air: these were sunglasses and long-sleeve days, and the thought that summer would soon be here cheered me up even further. I found myself smiling as I unlocked the front door.

'I don't know what you're bloody laughing at,' she said, anger darkening her face.

'I… what… I… but…' I hadn't even shut the front door and was already in trouble. 'Perry? What? Who's laughing? What's the matter, what have I done now?'

'He called the house Mark. The landline. I didn't know who it was, I just answered. He called our house.' The fury in Perry's voice was all too clear, but I could also detect something else, fear perhaps? 'You promised me. You bloody promised me. Liar!'

'Who?'

'You swore you were done with him.'

'Who?' I said once more, even though by then I suspected who, but I wanted her to say it. I'm in enough trouble already, so I certainly wasn't going to go dropping the H-bomb in case I was wrong.

'Hamlet,' she said quietly.

Not wrong. I'd guessed correctly.

'He called here? But why? Honestly Perry, honestly, it's nothing to do with me.'

PERRY ACCEPTED MY open-armed offer for a hug. It was good to hold her close. Her gentle sobbing burrowed against my shoulder. I smoothed my hand against her back in an attempt to soothe her, as though trying to brush away her memories of last year. We'd got caught in a web with Hamlet at the centre; an entanglement that very nearly got her killed. Since then I'd kept my promise to her, I'd cut off all contact, hadn't even mentioned his name once. I had absolutely no idea why he would have called now.

I reassured her once again and she seemed to accept I was telling the truth. She looked up at me from our embrace and smiled. 'I need to be going. Night shift cover, see you in the morning.' She gave me a soft kiss and left.

I remained rooted to the spot watching her go and, as she turned to pull the door closed behind her, she looked me straight in the eyes, 'Don't get involved Mark, whatever it is, don't get involved.'

From the window I watched her get in her little white Fiat. She saw me looking and gave a small wave. I waved back until she'd driven out of view then I headed to the kitchen—I was famished. The phone began to ring.

IT RANG, AND it continued to ring. It's so rare to get a landline call nowadays, we never bothered setting up an answerphone. I deliberated: I could try and ignore it, but it'd just ring all night. I could pull the cable out of the wall, but that'd cut off my wi-fi and as I'm tied into a long contract with a shitty provider, it'd be more trouble than it's worth getting it rebooted later on. Nothing else for it, I lifted the handset off the coffee table and pressed answer.

'You took your bloody time. What, were you on the khazi?' said an all-too-familiar voice. 'You going to let me in?'

'Sorry,' I replied. 'Not a good time, got visitors, talk another time maybe?'

'Marky Mark. Don't tell me no porkies. Look, I done you a favour by hanging back, as I could tell she was becoming emotional. I'm getting cold out here, I thought we was done with standing out in the street for the nurses. Come on, open up.'

Before I could even think of a response, I heard the tap-tap-tap of metal against glass—a ring or a key against my window. I looked round and there, smiling through the glass, Hamlet—his face as big, beaten and brazen as an Easter Island statue that's discovered hair dye.

I opened the door—what else could I do?— and ushered him in quickly before anyone saw.

'Come on Marky, get the kettle on, it's taters out there.' He marched through my house as though he owned the place. Hamlet had that aura. He'd own the place, no matter where he was. 'You've finished the kitchen, I like it.'

HE LOOKED BIGGER than since I saw him last. His white designer polo shirt clung tightly to his chest, the little horseman logo rode a pectoral as big and solid as a dinner plate and the short sleeves strained over biceps as wide as your thigh. Back on the 'roids probably. Even more volatile. I needed to tread carefully. We sat facing each other, mugs of tea in hand. He held his mug back-to-front having slipped the handle over his knuckles and rolled it across his palm to study the decoration: *I love Belgrade.*

'Belgrade, where's that then? Hungary?'

'Serbia.'

'Serbia, is it? When did you go to Serbia?'

'I didn't,' I replied, then trying to remain polite, 'Why are you here? What do you want?'

'Marky Mark is that any way to talk to an old friend?' His mocking tone was proof he knew perfectly well our friendship—if that's what it ever was—was dead and buried.

Hamlet, the presentable face at least, owned the region's hottest nightclub, a sizeable investment property portfolio and also ran a number of successful pubs. The real Hamlet was at the head of the food chain in Medway's black market and underworld, the apex predator, the king of the plains. A smiling damned villain. And he was sitting in my front room sipping tea making small talk about bloody Belgrade.

When we were young there was something glamorous, something adventurous about hanging around with Hamlet, being in his orbit, hoping to catch some of his stardust. When we were young. When we were stupid. Even last year, when I thought I was old enough and wise enough to handle him, he still wrongfooted me. He still caught me out. He still short-changed me and left me wanting. He won't do it again. I'm not that stupid any more.

'YOU'VE BLOODY WELL agreed to work for him?' Perry was cross with me. Correction. Perry was furious with me.

'You know what he's like.'

'Yes, I know what he's like. That's the problem Mark.'

'No, I don't mean that. I mean he's… what's the word…'

'A crook? Criminal? Gangster? Villain? Am I getting warm?'

'Persuasive. He's very persuasive, he's promised there's nothing dodgy, it's all above board, it's a legitimate business venture.'

'Oh, for God's sake Mark, listen to yourself.'

'No, you listen. Instead of going off on one, just listen. He's got himself a couple of shop units, and he wants them refurbed into tanning salons.'

'Mark…'

'No, listen, please. It makes sense. At the moment all my work, every penny I earn, is coming from Danny Kidd and his brother. What happens if one day they decide they don't want me anymore, we fall out, or they find someone cheaper? Then it's "So long, sayonara and don't let the door bang your arse on the way out," and I'm left with nothing—no work, no money, no nothing. It's not a good idea to have a single source of income.'

'I suppose…'

'Look, it's a quick and easy job. There's me, Bern and Disco, plus we've got Fiery Jac coming free on her downshift next week, we'll crack it out in no time at all, then it'll all be over and done with.'

'I suppose…' she said, mulling it over, 'And I suppose it makes good business sense to spread the risk…'

'Yeah, I thought that when he said it too.'

'When he…? Fuck you, Mark, you're an idiot!' she shouted, stomping up the stairs, slamming the bedroom door.

IN DISGRACE WITH Perry again. She'll come around I'm sure of it. In Hamlet's grasp again, but I can handle him this time. Time to start work again. I slipped on my jacket, lifted the morning's post off the mat and let myself out of the house without saying goodbye. I tried to convince myself I was over the worst of it, nothing else could go wrong, and very nearly succeeded.

I flopped into the van and dropped the small bundle of post on the passenger seat. A quick sift sorted the junk from the proper mail. Circulars and promotional rubbish in clear polythene wraps fell to the footwell. I flicked through the envelopes, recognising the logos and franking stamps; all bills and invoices, they can wait until later. Only the last one needed to be opened right away: a slim brown envelope, the big black bold letters, 'HMRC' gave it the welcome urgency of a kick in the balls. The taxman wanted me, again.

Dear Mr Poynter, it began, *we write to give you notice...* This didn't bode well. I skimmed through it quickly, words like *notice*, *investigation*, *unpaid tax*, and *penalties* sprang from the page. Shit. I read it again slowly, trying to take it all in. I was being given notice of an impending investigation into my accounts for the past five years because they believed I'd underpaid tax of close to twenty thousand pounds. Twenty bags! And if proven, I had twenty-eight days to pay it or I'd incur penalties for late payment. What a nice way to start the day! To be honest I strongly suspected I owed more than that so the last thing I needed was them crawling through my books. God only knows where that'd lead.

Maybe Hamlet had done me a favour, thrown me a lifeline. He'd pay me in cash, he always does, and I can forward it on the Revenue, pay them off before any investigation.

No need to worry Perry about it, I thought, stuffing it back in its envelope and then sliding it under the sun visor overhead.

-6-

SO… I THINK that's us up to speed now… work's good, relationship's in crisis, Hamlet's back on the scene, the taxman wants to take chunks out of me… and… what else? Oh yes, Bern's wearing a suit. Everything is SNAFU.

WHILST IT WAS true Danny and Stuart had decided to announce their development ambitions with a press launch, I'm sorry to say it didn't match Uncle Bern's expectations. The suit and tie had come with dreams of being on a long table like a latter-day Brian Clough facing down hordes of eager journalists barking questions. Instead, we met a young man called Shane from the local paper. Shane was a very fat boy with thick glasses, scarlet cheeks and an ear that looked like the dog had had a chew on it. He cast a quick glance at the sheet of notes Stuart gave him, muttered, 'Seems fine, it'll go in the next edition,' then used his phone to take a couple of photos of Danny and Stuart in front of the pub, then a couple of Danny by himself.

'Do you want one of me?' asked Danny, 'You and me?'

Shane looked as though it was the stupidest question he'd ever heard. 'No.'

Stuart couldn't hide his amusement, 'Not a football fan Shane?'

'No.'

'What's your sport then, what are you into?'

'Minecraft,' replied Shane.

'That figures,' grumbled Danny, walking away.

My phone rang. Not recognising the number, I ignored it and let it run to voicemail. I moved away to listen to the message and, with a dismissive hand gesture, I declined Shane's offer of a free copy of the current edition of the paper.

Hello, hello right back, *this is a message for Mark Poynter*, well you've come to the right place, *my name is Michael Unwin*, how do you do Michael, *I'm calling from Fielder Homes, I'd like to talk to you about a piece of work*, oh would you now? *Can you call me back please?* nope, don't think so.

I cut off midway through him reciting his numbers. Not interested. Not calling him back.

Some might ask why turn away work, isn't a job offer arriving out of the blue like a gift from God? Am I being too hasty? The answer is no. Let me tell you about your residential developers—speak as you find, this is just my opinion, but you need to be super sharp and super disciplined on these projects, and between you and me, I'm neither. Everything gets scrutinised to the last ha'penny, every nut and bolt is accounted for and when the costs are creeping up, the subbies are under the microscope. I had a bad experience working for a developer many years ago when I was first starting out—turned out when it came to the fine print of the contract, they were much hotter than me and I got my fingers burnt. Never been tempted back to that corner of the industry. I hope Mr… I've already forgotten what his name was… isn't waiting in for my call, as it ain't coming.

It did make me think though: am I a hypocrite? Am I becoming something I hate by sticking with the Kidds? If their development is to turn a profit after the hefty purchase price Danny paid on impulse, I'll have to make every penny count and play the blame game to the max. If I wield the big subbie-bashing stick, am I waving goodbye to my principles?

I HEADED BACK to the group, noticing Shane had gone, but someone else, someone familiar was heading towards Danny and Stuart. As I got closer, it came rushing back to me… it was the angry Scotsman who'd threatened me. As I drew up to them, he began to speak.

'Congratulations on your new acquisition, gentlemen' he said, although his expression didn't look very congratulatory. 'Perhaps I was a little… let's say off-hand with you when we met before Mr Poynter. I apologise.'

He placed a hand on his chest as he spoke and even gave a little bow. Stuart gave me a confused look that was searching for an explanation, but before I could say anything our new companion began again.

'My name is Donaldson and I am what you might call a freelance consultant…' He might call it that, but I'd seen enough rich man's goons to recognise one when I saw one. 'And my employer, as you already know Mr Poynter, was very keen on the Admiral Guthrie.'

'Oh, was he?' Danny seemed a little bit uncomfortable and a big bit irritated by the intrusion.

'He had been led to believe he'd as good as purchased it, but clearly it wasn't to be. I have just come off the phone after updating him on the situation.'

Stuart and I exchanged a glance, neither of us knowing where this was leading, neither of us very keen to find out.

'Needless to say, lawyers will be consulted, and actions will be brought against the auctioneer. Nevertheless, we remain very keen on buying the property.'

'What a shame.' Danny's tone had the expectation of laughter from us to back up his sarcasm. His face fell and looked quizzical when it didn't come. He turned back to Donaldson, taking him seriously this time.

'As I was saying, I have spoken with my employer and…' Donaldson coughed into his fist, rolled his neck to chase out a faint cracking noise and then looked straight at Danny. 'My employer has instructed me to offer you the sum paid for the property plus fifteen percent, for your inconvenience. Cash. I can have it here within an hour.'

Stuart looked at Danny with eyebrows in danger of altitude sickness. Donaldson grinned at the brothers' looks of disbelief.

'That means,' said Donaldson, 'we can call the auctioneer's office—they won't have finalised the documents with the Land Registry yet. We just tell them there's been a change of plan, they tear up the piece of paper with your name on it and we get them to write it out in our name. If we do it today, here, now, you've got no stamp duty, no capital gains tax, just a nice fat profit from having this friendly chat. So, what do you say?'

'Go fuck yourself!'

-7-

DONALDSON DISPLAYED NO visible reaction. 'In that case, I'll say goodbye. You'll be hearing from us again soon.'

He turned and didn't look back. By the time his black Range Rover had sped away, Stuart was ready to explode.

'What did you say that for? Are you bloody insane?'

'He was Billy Bullshit. He's a dreamer,' said Danny.

Stuart clearly didn't think so. He looked to me for comment. I gave a small shake of my head, I didn't think so either. Like I say, I know a rich man's goon when I see one.

Danny gave a gormless *'what am I like?'* grin, only further angering Stuart.

'Laugh it up, dickhead! Thanks to you, we've lost money before we've even started.' Stuart lingered on each word for effect. 'That would've made us more money than if you'd bought the bloody thing for the budget, we agreed in the first place.'

This was awkward, stuck in the middle of this. I looked about, trying to find where Bern had got to, but he'd wandered off out of sight.

'So, on your first day as a property developer, you've bust us! Nice work, numbnuts. You've screwed up any chance on getting on TV, and now you've screwed the business. Loser.'

'I just thought—'

'No Danny, you don't think, that's your problem. You're always given every opportunity, and you chuck them all away.'

'Boys, come on, let's cool it down, can we?' I felt obliged to break this up before things got out of hand, but neither one was listening to me.

'You piss all over every chance you're given, you don't value anything.'

'Here we go again.' Danny's passive aggressive tone spoke volumes. 'Look, it's not my fault I made it. Get over it.'

'Shut up, Danny.'

'No Stuart. I'm bloody sick of this, all my life you've been jealous. Blaming me.'

Silence. The brothers stared at each other. Motionless. They wore that expression you only find in bickering families: part wanting to fight, part wanting to cry, part wanting to laugh—but too mixed up to do any of them.

Stuart blew out a sigh, flapped a dissenting hand towards Danny, then stormed off. Danny smiled and smoothed his shirt and trousers: looking sharp. He sauntered off without a care in the world. The Mercedes roared, and he was gone.

Bern wandered back again, tightly clutching the free newspaper he'd blagged from Shane under his arm, 'Where's everyone gone?'

We stood orphaned outside the building, not quite sure what to do next. After a little consideration, we decided a spot of lunch was in order.

IT WAS A largely uneventful, but slow-moving journey across town from lower Gillingham to the Golden Lamb, although twice on Woodlands Road I was forced to slam on the brakes when herds of secondary school kids stepped out without bothering to look. The second time Bern yelled, 'You got a bloody death wish?' and got a V-sign in reply from a girl no older than twelve—ah, they grow up so fast.

Disco didn't need much persuading, and soon enough strode through the door to find us at a corner table. 'Looking smart Bern, getting married?' he said, admiring the bottle green suit. Bern pretended to be busy reading his free local paper and only grunted in response. I went to the bar to order us all something to eat and by the time I came back both were studying the paper intently, looking at the property pages.

'Can you believe anyone would pay that much to live there?' said Bern.

Disco shook his head, 'World's gone mad, Bern.'

Either they hadn't noticed me or, more likely, they didn't care. They scanned all the photographs and tutted. Bern licked his finger and turned the page. The left-hand side was covered by a grid of small square photos with a big blue and yellow agents' logo splashed across the top. The right-hand side was a full-page advert. I pointed at it: 'He offered me a job today.' A man in a light blue suit, white shirt, no tie, smiled genially from the page with his arms folded. Behind him an artist's impression showed happy families playing in mature gardens with tranquil water features twinkling between modern apartment blocks.

'Who? Ron Fielder?' asked Disco.

'Yeah, well, one of his surveyors anyway,' I replied, still looking at the face in the advert. His benevolent smile promised the dream: shared ownership, help to buy, no stamp duty, whatever you needed to make it happen, Uncle Ron could sort it.

'Wouldn't have thought it's for this scheme, though' said Disco. 'It's not even out the ground yet. This is the one the Tombliboos are doing.'

'You taking it? The job?' Bern asked, with an edge of caution in his voice. I assumed, for once, he'd actually listened to me and knew my reservations about working for high-volume house builders.

'No. Not interested.'

'Good,' said Bern, 'I've heard he's a right tough bastard.'

'To be fair, to get on like he has you'd need to be pretty tough. Every penny counts in that game,' I replied. 'You can't go wasting materials or slacking off on a rezzy dev.' Bern did that scrunched-up mole look he does when confused. 'Residential development,' I explained.

'He can't be that bad, Bern.' Disco flicked backwards towards the front few pages of the paper, scanning the news articles until he jabbed a blackened nail at something, 'Here, take a look at this. He doesn't look that much of a bastard.'

From under Disco's grubby digit, Ron Fielder again smiled genially: his blue eyes twinkled. It worked well with his slightly rabbit teeth, busted nose and short cropped white hair; it made him look a bit roguish.

'It's the white hair,' Bern informed us, as though imparting great wisdom. 'People always think well of someone with white hair, they think they're nice, reminds them of Father Christmas.'

'Anyway...' a clearly unimpressed Disco began to read the article aloud, '*Fielder in Line for New Year's Honour.* Chatham-born Ron Fielder, fifty-eight, founder and chief executive of Fielder Homes, is to be knighted in Her Majesty's New Year's Honours list for his services to industry. Fielder started his housebuilding company in 1983... blah blah blah... largest independent residential developer in the South of England... blah blah blah... and employs over one thousand staff... except for MP Electrical who told him to poke his job up his arse!'

Disco relished the laughter his news bulletin received and started to ad-lib. 'But despite missing out on MP Electrical, they've got the Tombliboos. A spokesman for Fielder Homes said surely those two big muckers count for at least six normal people.'

'And Bob Matthews,' added Bern.

'Bob Matthews?' I was surprised to hear that, 'Really? Last time I saw him, he said he was done with contracting. Him and his son were happy working for themselves, doing up old houses.'

'Straight up,' replied Disco, confirming Bern's news. 'He said he'd got all the second fix carpentry on a new build of twenty-four flats, asked me if I wanted to fit the kitchens for him.'

I was more annoyed at someone trying to poach my staff than thinking about anything else, but was floored when Bern further chipped in, 'And Dag Chatterjee. He's now working for Fielders.'

Chatterjee was a plumbing and heating engineer, and a very good one too. Trouble is, he knew it, and when they know it, they start charging the superstar rates they think they deserve. He never struck me as the sort to go over to the housebuilders, simply because the margin wasn't there for him. Anyway, he'd moved away from plumbing and heating recently.

'Dag's back on the tools?' I asked my fonts of all knowledge. 'I'd heard he'd got in with someone in one of the coffee-shop chains?'

'That's right,' said Disco. 'He'd been driving about all over the county finding old banks and supermarkets, showrooms, pubs, anything like that to offer to the coffee-shop. His family, they've got a bit of money, his brothers are doctors, they'd buy the property, the coffee-shop lease the ground floor off them, and Dag converts the upper floors to flats for the family rental business.'

'Nice,' I said. 'So why would he give that up?'

'Who knows, maybe he's fallen out with the coffee-shop, maybe other people have cottoned on to it, maybe he took too much of a hit in the Pandemic. Who knows?' said Disco.

'Shedloads of money. That's what he told me.' Bern sounded delighted to have the gossip before Disco. 'He said the rates couldn't be turned down, so he accepted before they realised or changed their minds.'

Maybe, if Fielder Homes are throwing money at people to get them on their jobs, I was a bit too hasty? Perhaps I should speak with them after all?

-8-

I LEFT BERN on the pavement outside his flat, still dressed for success in his bottle green suit. He yanked his tie loose and looked relieved as the blood flowed back into his head. He went inside without a goodbye. Realising I had nothing else to do and grateful for the chance to get ahead of myself for once, I decided to swing past Hamlet's shop unit, do a drive-by survey of what's required.

Hamlet had given me the address. He'd told me it was on the High Street. Technically that was true, although only just hanging on by its fingernails. A tatty vacant unit under the shadow of Luton Arches, it looked as if it had stood empty for a very long time. The roller shutter had been raised about two-thirds off the ground, enough to open the front door—someone was home. I gave the grubby glazed door a light knock and stepped inside. 'Hello, anyone here?' I called out, wiping the grime from my fingers on my jeans as I did so.

'Marky Mark, fancy seeing you here,' boomed a voice from the shadows. Hamlet stepped forwards to the edge of the daylight, 'And just at the right time too. Come and help us, can you?'

I followed him through the darkness to a small and dingy store room that smelled damp, as though it had been sealed up and then forgotten. Daylight struggled, and failed, to peek through a small square stippled window mounted high in the right-hand corner of the wall like a stamp.

He wasn't alone in the gloom, one of his dumb muscle-brigade was with him: by day fetching and carrying, by night door security. He did have a name, I'm sure I was told it once but didn't care enough to learn it. He looked like a greyhound: lean, with a rangy walk and long bony face, and I called him Dunlop for reasons I no longer remember. Dunlop was fiddling with a prehistoric fuse board that had probably been installed by Edison himself. Hamlet helpfully used the torch on his phone to throw some light on it, but it was clear they had no idea what they were doing. I moved Dunlop out of the way and examined the very basic and totally unsuitable set of tools he'd brought. Seeing as I'm allergic to blowing myself up, I fetched my toolbox from the van that was still blinking away on double yellows. Ten minutes later we had light. The neglected old shop flickered awake again.

'So, what do you reckon Marky Mark?' Hamlet had his arms open and was slowly rotating, marking his territory. 'Soon to be Sunny Daze, tanning salon to the stars. Hey, you could ask your mate the footballer to do the grand opening, there'll be a good drink in it for him.'

Remembering Stuart's complaints about Danny's reckless spending, I figured if Danny carried on like that, he'd probably have no choice other than to do crappy little store openings to earn a living. 'I'll mention it to him,' I said, with no intention of the sort. Hamlet seemed pleased.

He walked me around. He told me what he wanted. I took notes. It was all relatively straightforward. I told him we could start it next week, which also pleased him. I felt the time was right to take advantage of his good mood and told him about my run-ins with Donaldson, first at the builders' merchant and then this morning.

'Scotsman, small and ratty, called Donaldson? No, don't recognise the name,' he said, 'You?'

Dunlop shook his head.

'I'll keep an ear open, if I hear anything, I'll let you know.' Hamlet extended his hand to shake, letting me know our meeting was over, finishing with, 'That's the best I can do.'

I thought about that phrase as I drove home: 'the best I can do'—he was making it very clear he was doing me a favour, that I'm beholden to him. Yet again.

PERRY WAS IN a very buoyant mood when I got home, taking me a little by surprise given how we left things this morning. She's so unlike me, I dwell on things and let petty resentments fester, whereas she can live in the moment and enjoy the day for what it is. She was just like when we first got together: happy, carefree, confident. Seeing her like this melted me inside; this was why I fell for her. She asked about my day, then told me about hers. It had been good, leading to her happy mood now—I guess saving lives in the direst situation can do that for you. She made me laugh, made me feel wanted. I felt, no, I knew, we had something worth saving. The euphoria lasted all evening, and we headed upstairs, both of us knowing this was our opportunity to re-affirm our feelings to each other.

'Mark,' she said, 'what are we doing?'

'I thought that was pretty obvious.'

She moved away from me, her face showed she was unimpressed.

'No, what are we doing about us?' She pulled the duvet up over her shoulders, keeping in the warmth, keeping me at a distance.

This was a conversation I didn't want. Things were fine as far as I was concerned. We get along, we have fun, why try to fix what's not broken? I tried to assemble all of that into words, particularly words that would sound diplomatic and positive, but Perry took my thinking time as hesitation.

'I need to know where we're going, Mark. Are you committed to this? To me?'

What a question? Of course I was. Why else would I work the long hours if it wasn't to earn, if it wasn't to provide? But I had the impression that would be the wrong answer, by that point any answer would be the wrong answer. Thoughts of playtimes and happy ever after vanished instantly.

-9-

THE BAD ATMOSPHERE carried through to the next morning. We got dressed, barely speaking, and ate breakfast separately: Perry on the sofa, her legs folded underneath, watching a soap recorded the night before, and me in the kitchen gazing out the window.

Force of habit made my eyes scan the fence tops and shed roofs for the cat that'd never return. When Perry and I first got together, she adopted an old stray that would sometimes visit, scavenging for food. A scrawny old chap called Mr Skinner. It hated me but adored her, and his last few months were happy ones weaving figures of eight around her ankles. Poor old Mr Skinner, it was his kidneys that did for him in the end. It came on suddenly and the vet said it was incurable. One day he was there and the next he wasn't. It was the cat that finally got to her.

For weeks, months even, she'd been battling on, bottling it up. Shift after shift, days running into nights running into days, she worked tirelessly, fearlessly. The worst public health crisis in living memory, they called it. A global, viral pandemic. And there she was manning the front line. As the weeks wore on, as the fatalities grew, she nursed them and she comforted them and she saw them pass lonely and afraid. Meanwhile, the neighbour's children pushed their drawings of rainbows through the letterbox and people would applaud her every time she set foot outside the door. On the very rare occasions she got a night off, drained and exhausted, she'd feel compelled to join in with the street cheering and rattling pots and pans, and give them a papal wave of solidarity: we're all in this together! The day I told her the cat was gone was the point she broke. All that emotion, all that stress, it needed an outlet—and that outlet happened to be a mangy old ginger tom with a bent ear and a crooked tail who she loved dearly.

The memory of it made me shudder and my mind made a leap: it was then, during that period, that was the root cause for where we are now. We're allowed back out again, life's getting back to normal again, but something was seeded back then that's grown like a bindweed to choke our relationship.

I looked out the window at nothing in particular and thought back to those days, watching her leave and watching her arrive: the hero's fanfare. All the while I'm trapped by these four walls, forbidden from going out, unable to earn. When things started to ease, it didn't help: nobody wanted strangers working in their homes, then the small scratches of work I could pick up it was nigh on impossible to get any materials, and then if I did get the work and did get the material, I couldn't get the labour because nobody wanted to commit to anything fearing they wouldn't get paid. I've worked all my life, I've paid my way and then all of a sudden it stopped.

You must be so proud, they'd say to me; *she's a star*, they'd coo; *we're so lucky to have her*, they'd remind me. And I'd nod and agree—and they were right, one hundred percent, it'd be churlish of me to suggest any different. But it didn't make it any easier—watching her go, sharing her, worrying about her—being forced to impotently sit there doing nothing of any use to anyone.

It has to be the root cause of our tension: the reason why I'm working every hour I can, filling every available second. It's my turn now, she's done her bit, now I need to provide, I need to take care of us—and the only way I know how to do that is through work: if I don't work I don't earn, if I don't earn, I can't provide. It's that simple… isn't it?

I shook my head, chasing the thoughts out. It was too complicated to think about this early in the morning. I took a mouthful of tea and grimaced. It had turned cold in my hand, too much time spent pondering. I tipped it down the sink along with the what-ifs that had been filing my head. I knew I should talk to Perry, explain, put matters right. But not now, not yet. Luckily, I had a diversion and an excuse to get out of the house.

HARPO, MUCH TO my amazement, had found me a chandelier and Disco, Fiery Jac and I were on our way to go and get it.

'I had a call, Mark,' Harpo told me. 'Some fella down near Rye, stripping out an old house, selling various bits and pieces of architectural salvage, phoning around trying to offload it, and called me. He was rattling off everything he had and I'm thinking Rye? I'm not schlepping all the way down to Rye, but then he mentioned he had a chandelier, and I immediately thought of you.'

Very generous of him, you'd think. Well, you'd think wrong. Harpo's not daft. He tempted me with the photo the guy sent him then fleeced me of a hundred pounds for the guy's phone number. 'Finder's fee,' he said, trying to justify this extortion. 'It's very common.' My response was very common too.

'THIS MUST BE the place,' said Fiery Jac, drawing up alongside some very fine stone gate posts. The lions atop the pillars were green with lichen, decades of sea air had weathered their features smooth, but they added a certain grandeur, nonetheless. Fiery Jac took the gravel approach to the house slowly and respectfully.

She's used to throwing thirteen-tonne fire engines down narrow, double-parked back streets, so we decided she was best suited to drive the shitty old box van Bern had cadged from a friend of his for the day. A good result all round. Because I didn't fancy being at the wheel of this death-trap, Bern hadn't bothered getting out of bed on time to join us, and Disco doesn't drive. He got a twelve-month ban about fifteen years ago, and when he was given the choice to drive again or keep on drinking, the breweries' shares hit a record high.

Jac was on her down time: four days off after four days on, and like a lot of firefighters had dropped on to her second job. She was quite handy to have about: a tidy decorator, a terrific wall-tiler, not a bad carpenter and keen to learn just about anything else by helping out. Some say—idiots say—the building trade is no place for a woman., I disagree. Jac was, by far, head and shoulders better than a lot of loafers and clock-watchers I'd had the misfortune to come across in my time. Brought up by a single dad and with three brothers, Jac was more than capable of shutting down any numbskull mouthing off. She'd proven herself time and again in the Fire Brigade, been awarded some medals too. And she'd developed some impressive site skills in her bid to fund her true passion: Harley Davidsons.

With two gleaming chrome monsters at home to support, and a Route 66 trip with her biker buddies planned for the Summer, Jac was keen to earn when and wherever she could. Gripping the wide wheel, the veins in her lean forearms stood out against the intricate ink she wore in sleeves. Reflex made me breathe in with a gasp as we shot through an impossibly narrow gap, and looking across at me from under her short-cropped hair, she gave me an amused wink. She threw the van around like a go-kart, laughing at mine and Disco's squeals.

'Look at that!' Jac sounded impressed. The place was spectacular: a beautiful Regency red brick mansion house that was positioned just right to catch the sunlight and to enjoy the views out across the Channel. It radiated an old-fashioned noble warmth. Jac rolled the van slowly up to the front door.

The man had clearly been waiting for us, watching us approach. He galloped out the door before the engine had even spluttered its dying wheezes. He looked late twenties to me, with the build and gait of a long-distance runner. His clothes looked expensive but casual, the heavy watch he wore sparkled in the sunlight, and bare skin exposed itself around the ankles; too fashionable for socks. His well-groomed, warm caramel complexion suggested Arabic heritage, or perhaps Mediterranean? I wasn't sure.

'Are you Matt?' I asked, stepping down from the passenger seat.

'That's me,' he replied. 'And you must be Mark. Good journey?'

We all got out of the van, trying to stretch out knees and backs that were as stiff and jagged as our attempts at small talk. I think he sensed it was a struggle too, and he quickly ushered us into the house. We followed, leaving Disco single-handedly bringing down the tone of the place, loitering outside for a smoke. As I stepped through the tall, pillared entrance, I looked back to see him extract a roll-up from his back pocket that he'd been sitting on all morning: crumpled and question-mark shaped. In less than a second, he'd expertly straightened it and plumped it back into shape and got it lit between his lips.

Another man was inside the house: younger, heavier, shorter, scruffier. He spoke to Matt in a rapid-paced language I didn't recognise, and Matt responded equally as fast.

'Sorry, my cousin, he's only recently arrived from Nicosia. He doesn't speak much English yet. He's lending me a hand stripping this place.'

'Right-ho, shall we get started, Matthew?' I asked, knowing the sooner we began the sooner we get home.

'Mehmet,' he said, 'Matt is short for Mehmet, not Matthew.'

I began to apologise but was interrupted by Fiery Jac, 'Lovely house. Is it yours?' she asked, running her hand over an ornate mahogany newel post. We'd congregated in a grand hall at the foot of a wide and sweeping staircase. Matt led us towards an imposing double doorway: 'I wish,' he replied.

The parquet beneath our feet bloomed a warming sunburnt orange, and we stepped into what must once have been a ballroom back when the homeowner wore a powdered wig and fretted about the loss of the Americas. 'The old chap who lived here died. I'm doing the house clearance. My job's to empty it out, and if I can sell any of it for antiques or salvage, well, that's my bonus.'

'What's the plan for this place when you're done?' asked Jac.

'From what I hear they're going to turn it into a fancy restaurant, wedding venue, that sort of thing. Anyway, I believe this is why you're here,' Matt extended his long skinny arms heavenward. We looked up to see a magnificent crystal chandelier, exactly what Danny Kidd wanted.

'Fuck me, that's enormous,' said Disco re-joining the group.

IT TOOK THE three of us, plus Matt and his cousin, whose name I never did learn, nearly three hours to carefully take it down, wrap it, protect it and get it in the van.

Matt shook all our hands firmly. Flexing out the squeeze in my right hand, I used my left to pass him the thick bundle of cash I'd got from Danny. 'It's all there, as agreed.'

'It's okay, I trust you,' he laughed, then, 'I hope Mr Kidd appreciates it. It's a thing of beauty.'

Fiery Jac started our long and arduous journey home. It was clear from the sluggish way the van began to move, and how much play was now in the steering, that the weight in the back was immense. I knew Jac would be fighting against it all the way home, I steeled myself, it was going to be a long uncomfortable trip; the vinyl seat was hot and sticky and smelled distinctly of sour milk.

'NICE BLOKES,' SAID Fiery Jac, when we were back on the open road.

'They were nice blokes,' I agreed.

'How'd they know it was for Danny Kidd?' asked Disco. 'I don't remember hearing you mention it.'

I tried casting my mind back, but failed. 'Don't know. I expect Harpo told him,' I replied and made a mental note to ask him when I got home, which I promptly forgot.

DANNY CAME BOUNDING out to greet us. He snatched and tugged at the van's handles, desperate to see his new purchase. We let him fling up the roller shutter, and he clambered aboard the truck. He couldn't see much of it under all the protective wrapping, but it didn't dampen his excitement any.

Danny and the late-arriving Uncle Bern made five of us and, with great care and concentration, we removed it gently from the confines of the van—honestly, Tutankhamun was probably whipped out quicker than this thing. Carrying it between us, we got it safely inside the house, and it must have taken us another two hours to get it raised up and securely fixed in position.

Danny was absolutely thrilled with it: high fives all round, and handouts of cash tips to the crew, all gratefully received.

And to my greatest surprise, Danny had actually been pretty useful. No prima donna antics. Certainly not the same spoilt kid I'd seen before. He'd been happy to get stuck in, be part of the team, and get his hands dirty. Maybe there is a future for him in the building and property game after all?

-10-

EARLY NEXT MORNING, Fiery Jac, Disco, Bern and I assembled outside Hamlet's shop unit. Disco safely guided the landing of a skip on to a small patch of spalled concrete to the side of the shop, and the demolitions began in earnest.

By the end of the day, the place had been stripped back to a bare shell. The reception counter and a few other bits that Hamlet wanted saved had been carefully dismantled and wrapped in heavy protection outside. Tomorrow Disco, with Fiery Jac's help, would be stud partitioning to create a new staff room. This is the bit I love most, the big kick-off, a whirring blurring buzz of activity. I live for the start of a job, it never fails to take me back to my first time: fifteen, a holiday job labouring on a small project close to home. An old Irish foreman with a face like a burst football gave me a scuffed blue hard hat, a broom, and told to get on with it. Since that day I've loved the smell of fresh sawdust, and grit grinding between my teeth. It reminds me of when I earned money for the first time ever, when I was treated like a man. When I had my whole life ahead of me.

I left them to lock up, went outside and called Maria at Thorpe's to order materials. After a little cajoling, she promised me first drop tomorrow.

A car pulled up to the kerb, a black Range Rover. I knew who was in it even before the blacked-out window began to fall. His ratty face leered at me.

'What, so you're following me now, are you?'

'Just passing,' he said. 'And I thought to myself, there's a familiar face, must say hello.'

Of course I didn't buy it, he was here on purpose, he had a message. I waited for it, keeping my silence.

'So glad to see you're gainfully employed—you're better off without those Kidd brothers. Amateurs.'

I said nothing.

'Between you and me, you're better off finding work elsewhere.'

'Is that right?'

'That's right. Danny Kidd's getting out of the property game. He'll realise that soon enough. And then where will you be?'

'I'll be fine.'

'Really? I hear you were on your knees not so long ago, didn't have a pot to piss in. You don't want to be back there again do you, when the Kidds kick you into touch?'

He was trying to rile me, but it wouldn't work. My cash flow difficulties last year were hardly state secrets, every bugger and their brother across the Medway Towns knew about it.

'Take this as friendly advice, drop the Kidds, drop the job. If you know what's good for you, you'll see it makes sense.'

I didn't want him to see he'd annoyed me. I said nothing, I did nothing other than set my eyes in a sullen stare at him.

'Be seeing you.' His window rose back into place, masking the rodent. He sped away from the kerb aggressively.

Bern came up behind me. 'Who's that, son?' His hand rested on my shoulder. 'You okay?'

'Fine, all good.' I needed to change the subject before he saw through my lie. 'Fancy a pint?'

WE ALL RETIRED to the Ship Inn for a change of scenery: a nice pub that I occasionally visited, it sat snugly at the crest of a gentle hill. The table Bern had secured us gave a wide view across the River Medway and beyond. Silently in my head, I counted the dinosaurs gathered on the horizon, like I do every time I'm close to the river.

'Do you remember as a little boy you used to think those were dinosaurs?' asked Bern, trying to get a laugh from the others. They duly responded. Bern pointed towards the many derrick cranes with their long straight necks and broad backs at the far-away Kingsnorth power station. 'Dinosaurs. Kids, eh?'

A couple of pints later and we'd temporarily misplaced Disco. He'd gone outside for a smoke and got talking to a bathroom fitter we knew. Bern, after cadging some money from me, had finally offered to buy me a drink and was at the bar, leaving just Fiery Jac and me at the table alone.

She leaned across to me, there was a look about her, excited. 'So, tell me,' she said. 'What's Hamlet like?'

Something the size and weight of a bowling ball dropped in my chest. I hate these conversations; the hero-worship for Hamlet. But then, once upon a long-ago, I'd been there among the star-struck. Then I was there among the hangers-on, and in time I graduated to the inner circle. Now I'm trying to break free of him once and for all and still he's all people want to talk about.

'I told a couple of the lads back at the station I'd be working for him.' Jac actually sounded more star-struck about the possibility of meeting Hamlet than she did about Danny Kidd. I will never understand this fascination for a thug with charisma and a bit of patter. *One may smile and smile and be a villain*—that's how Perry describes Hamlet. one of her sayings, she collects sayings and quotes. Not one of her best though admittedly, I suspect she made it up herself.

I NEEDED A moment to check my loyalties: I know better than to gossip about Hamlet, but Jac's a good mate and should know what she's letting herself in for.

'Hamlet,' I began, 'is like a ticking time bomb, and when it goes off, it takes everything with it.'

Jac grinned her big wide smile, this was exactly what she wanted to hear. I looked back towards the herd of steel dinosaurs frozen on the horizon and a memory sprang to the forefront of my mind, I leaned closer towards Jac making sure no one was listening in.

'Imagine Hamlet's a bear,' I began. 'He might look fun. He might look friendly. He might buy you a drink and be your mate but—' I snapped my fingers for added drama, 'just like that he could rip your head off. Let me tell you a story, then you can make your own mind up about him.'

This is the tale I told Jac: a few years back, Hamlet had somehow got hold of a box at Arsenal. A dozen or so of us got invited for an afternoon of wining, dining and the beautiful game. Afterwards the others went in to town to hit the bright lights, but it wasn't long after Dad's diagnosis, so I just wanted to get home to him. Anyway, it turned out Hamlet had something on at his club that he had to get back for.

The train from Victoria wasn't particularly busy. We easily found seats. Hamlet took one beside the window, his back to the direction of travel. I sat opposite.

The doors started beeping and were sliding closed, when I saw some bloke dart through. They whooshed shut behind, almost nipping him. The train began moving. For some reason, I kept watching this guy coming along the aisle. I don't know why I was watching, but there was something about him I instantly didn't like. He was too in love with himself. He'd cultivated a hipster arty look: long swept back hair and a well-manicured beard, round glasses, a long coat and a wafty scarf. Over his shoulder hung a school satchel—a satchel I ask you, he must have been mid-thirties.

Anyway, the train was probably a third empty, but he decided to plonk himself next to me. But before he does, he yanks open the window. Before he's even seated, Hamlet shot his arm up and slammed the window shut. The hipster starts pulling a '*what the fuck*' gesture that he'd obviously seen in a movie and thought gave him attitude, but Hamlet looked straight through him.

'Hey, Arsehole. I just opened that,' said the Hipster rising to his feet.

'And I just closed it,' replied Hamlet.

'Why?' demanded the Hipster. 'Why'd you do that?'

'You didn't ask.'

'Oh, excuse me.' The Hipster had a sarcastic edge to his voice; if I'd noticed, I'm certain Hamlet had too. 'I didn't realise you owned the window. I didn't see the sign saying I needed your permission.'

Hamlet's left hand came up to stroke his chin, one of his tells, the Hipster was getting to him.

'Look mate,' I said, trying to defuse the situation, 'there's plenty of other seats, why don't you go and sit over there, eh?'

So much for my good idea, he started on me: 'So, so, your ticket's better than mine is it? Or do you run the railway or something, choosing who sits where? Fuck you!' He leaned forwards and yanked the window open again.

'You're on your own now mate, I tried to help you out,' I thought, turning my face to see the chimney pots shooting past the window, we'd soon be arriving at Bromley South.

I heard the slam of the window above my head, no need to look up, I knew what had happened.

Hamlet locked eyes on to the Hipster, and this made the Hipster's self-righteousness even greater. In a graceful movement, not breaking eye contact for a second, Hamlet popped the clasp of his chunky Rolex. The Hipster didn't notice as Hamlet transferred it across to his right hand. He pressed the big watch face into his palm and folded his fingers over it to form a fist. The steel bracelet lay across the back of his hand. Click, the clasp locked shut.

In the blink of an eye, Hamlet was on his feet and swinging. His makeshift knuckleduster driven firmly into the jaw of the Hipster, who toppled backwards onto the seat. Hamlet was on him—one, two, three—jabs busted his nose, burst open an eyebrow and ripped his cheek. And then Hamlet stopped, stood and returned the Rolex to his left wrist. He patted down the Hipster and ripped his wallet from his coat pocket. Brandishing his driving licence, Hamlet got up into the Hipster's face, 'I'm keeping this, you hear me? I… am… keeping… this.'

Blood streamed from the Hipster's burst eyebrow, he tried blinking it away. Then foolishly raised a hand to wipe his face—foolish because Hamlet thought he was trying to snatch back the licence.

'No, no, no,' Hamlet slapped his hand away, 'Mine. And now… I know where you live. You *will* see me again.'

Hamlet sat back down again. To the world at large, he looked calm and at peace with himself. The Hipster, on the other hand, hauled himself to his feet and shuffled to the other end of the carriage, collapsing on an empty seat. A couple of minutes later, we pulled into Bromley South. The doors automatically hissed open to an empty platform. Hamlet leaped up and charged towards his terrified victim. He grabbed his long hair and dragged him out of his seat. As the warning beeps sounded and the doors began to slide closed Hamlet launched the Hipster out onto the platform. He hit the tarmac hard and only as the train began pulling away did he move again.

Hamlet was watching from his seat, laughing. He reached up and opened the window.

'But I thought he wanted it closed?' interrupted Jac, who'd been hanging on every word until now.

'Open, closed, the thing is he didn't care one way or the other.'

'But, why?'

'Simply because the guy didn't ask him first,' I replied.

Jac sat wide-eyed and open-mouthed for a second, and so I decided to drop in another nugget for her to process.

'I know for a fact he did see him again, one of his guys told me,' I added. 'Seven o'clock next morning, Hamlet and three others turned up at the Hipster's house and dragged him and his girlfriend out of bed to tell them it'd be very silly reporting the matter. Apparently, his girlfriend kept yelling "*Told you so*" at him. Turns out it was the first thing he did when he got home.'

'And?'

'I never heard any more about it, so I'm guessing he was scared enough to tell the police it was all a misunderstanding. But the point I'm making is, for all the charisma and all the bonhomie, it's equally matched by extreme rage and violence, and you can never second-guess what side up the coin will land.'

Jac grinned her agreement, but I don't think she got my point. I counted more dinosaurs on the horizon and waited for Bern to return with the beers.

-11-

WE WERE WELL underway at the salon the next morning when I received the message, *'Want to talk to you about pub conversion. Be at mine 3pm. DK.'* The royal summons from Danny Kidd himself.

All the way there, I wondered what I'd say to Danny. I didn't know whether Stuart would be there. Had they made up? Should I contact Stuart to see if he'd be there, just in case he wasn't aware of it? But then would Danny see that as being disloyal to him; but if I didn't call Stuart, am I being just as disloyal to *him*? I hated being piggy in the middle, but knew that pissing either one of them off would be a major mistake. Couple that with one more of Bern's dog-eared matchday programmes shoved under Danny's nose and I'm sure I'd be out on my ear.

My crisis of conscience took over my entire thoughts. So much so, I arrived at Danny's without any memory of the journey and the vague feeling I'd got there sooner than expected. I still didn't know how to earn back his approval after siding with Stuart earlier. I was seriously considering making an excuse and putting this off to another day when a woman's voice called my name from the pavement, 'Mr Poynter?'

She was a striking young woman in an edgy, urban kind of way: deep brown African skin; long glossy black hair, dip-dyed red ends; a black hoodie under a green flight jacket; and black Converse all-stars. Hanging against her hip was a large leather bag with a lot of fringing. Too cool. For school.

'Can I have a word please Mr Poynter? Just a minute.'

I dithered, but I still wasn't ready to face him. 'Okay,' I said. 'Just a minute. What do you want?'

'Mr Poynter, my name's Rachel Ridder...' she introduced herself like it was supposed to mean something to me. It didn't. Unfazed, she continued, 'I'm a journalist—'

'No thanks.' I began to walk away. 'I have nothing to say to the tabloids.'

'Mr Poynter…'

I was halfway up the driveway. She was beside me, matching me step for step. 'Look,' I said, 'this is private property, you'd better go, you can't be here.' I turned back towards the road and escorted her away from the house.

'I'm not a hack from a tabloid, I'm not here looking for scandal.'

'They all say that.'

'It's true. Here, take this,' she forced a stiff white business card into my hand. 'Look me up on-line, check my stuff out, you'll see I'm genuine.'

'Yeah, yeah, yeah. Bye-bye,' I stuffed the card in the back pocket of my jeans and waited until she had driven away before I stopped watching the road. I looked back at the house. I'd been summoned, I couldn't put it off any longer. I began a slow trudge towards it.

I saw the explosion before I heard it.

It only lasted a second, maybe less, but a sun appeared to the edge of my vision. Then the rumble caught up. Reflexes took over. Before I knew what I was doing, I was running towards it.

The garage was on fire. We'd spent months converting the derelict barn into a four-bay garage for Danny's luxury cars, and it looked great. We'd fitted a reclaimed wrought iron staircase, courtesy of Harpo, to the gable end wall to access the door to the old hayloft above, now Danny's state-of-the-art gym.

In the centre bay, his beautiful Mercedes AMG was ablaze, and it had spread across to the G-Wagon. Soon it'd reach his mint 1966 MGB and they'd all be destroyed. The heat was intense. It forced me to take a step back and turn my face away.

'Fire brigade please,' I said to the operator and gave the address. They confirmed firefighters were dispatched and I promised to listen out for them on the road to guide them in.

It broke my heart to see the MGB engulfed by fire. I heard its screams as the metal buckled under the extreme heat. I choked: burning plastics had created an oily black smoke that filled the air. Another explosion, smaller this time, but an explosion all the same, dropped me to my knees in shock. Another small explosion, and another. Pressurised containers, aerosol cleaners and the like were succumbing to the heat and popping like bombs.

Then I realised… the house was in darkness. The office was locked up. But Danny had invited me over, and all his cars were being cremated. Danny's here, somewhere. The gym?

I looked towards the upper level: the smoke was too great, the heat too intense, the flames too bright. My eyes streamed. I looked away and blinked out the sensation.

He's in the gym, he must be. I couldn't hear anything over the fury of the fire. If there were any cries from upstairs they were lost. I ran towards the road, but couldn't hear any sirens. If the fire brigade was coming it wasn't soon enough. I realised then I was alone. It was down to me.

The physical wave of heat blocked my approach, like a big hairy-arsed rugby prop forward, it tried to push me back. I struggled through to the metal staircase. I grabbed the handrail and immediately snatched my hand back at the feel of the burn. I climbed the stairs, each step sticky as my trainers peeled off the treads. I reached the square chequer-plate landing platform at the top. Smoke snaked up the face of the building and in through the door, slightly ajar. I kicked it wide open, my eyes stinging, my lungs bursting. I pulled my T-shirt high up across my face and went inside.

Danny was lying face down on the floor, not moving. I ran to him and grabbed him, somehow hoiking one flaccid arm around my shoulders. I dragged him towards the door. Still the smoke tumbled in, each breath was heavy and cloying. My knees buckled near the door and I fell. I grabbed Danny under each arm and struggled to my feet. Walking backwards, I hauled him towards the door; not far now.

More by dumb luck and determination than anything else, I got us to the landing of the staircase, but the sudden brightness of day disoriented me. Short of breath and unable to fill my lungs, my knees collapsed. I was still conscious enough to know the fall down the metal staircase was going to hurt. I braced myself for it… but I didn't drop.

I DIDN'T UNDERSTAND until later. By then I was sat on the grass, I had a mask over my face and my brain fizzed with the pure oxygen. I'd been caught just before I fell by a trio of firefighters sent up to retrieve us.

Danny was with a medic checking him out for damage. He saw me looking and gave a thumbs-up in my direction, I returned the gesture.

The firefighters had made short work of the fire and were now tidying away their equipment. The garage looked like it had taken a direct hit from a hellfire missile. The cars were unrecognisable, just the blackened metal shells remained, dropped low on the axles.

I sat there looking, thinking, wondering. I recognised a voice behind me and snapped out of my thoughts. I turned to see Stuart checking Danny over, making sure he was okay. I wasn't ready to get up or be sociable. I stayed put and enjoyed the sensation of cold oxygen on my face and the chill trickling down inside me with each breath.

The lead firefighter approached Stuart and introduced himself. They walked together talking, I wasn't close enough to hear what was said but from the way he used his hands to point at different areas of the garage, I guessed he was telling Stuart how he thought the fire had started—*please don't say it was the electrics, please don't, please don't blame the electrics.*

Stuart had his hand to his mouth, his eyes fixed on the spot indicated by the fireman. I looked in the same direction. Concentrating my gaze made my eyes tingle and moisten again. I needed to blink it away. As the tears fell I saw it, in letters about two feet high, painted on the wall in white capital letters: '*GAME OVER DANNY KIDD*'.

-12-

I DON'T KNOW how long I'd been sitting on the grass, all I knew was a numbness had set in: to both my lower back and my mind.

A familiar voice called me from somewhere distant, but by then I was on autopilot. The sudden embrace around my neck and shoulders, that familiar smell, the soft skin against my cheek: my absent mind and tired body crashed back together as one in an instant.

'Are you okay? Let me see.' Perry released me and reached around to take my hands in hers. Straight away she was in her professional nursing mode. She looked me over, checked me out and made her diagnosis.

'I'm fine.' I hadn't spoken for a while and my words came out in a dry croak. I looked at her and saw Uncle Bern approaching close behind.

'Well done, son,' he said. 'You're quite the hero, proud of you.' He gave my shoulder a squeeze and ruffled my hair, then instantly regretted it. 'Oh arseholes, look what you've made me go and do,' and wiped his hand on his shirt, leaving a sooty grey smear.

Perry knelt in front of me now and looked straight into my eyes. I wasn't sure if it was compassion or checking my vitals—knowing her, probably both.

'Stuart called Bern, told him what happened, he called me, and we came straight away.' She spoke in her professional healthcare voice: the slow, gentle one that tries to penetrate people's trauma when they need to understand what's happening to them. 'I've spoken with the paramedic, told him I'm a nurse, he's happy for me to take you home. Can you stand?'

Bern held out both hands. I reached for them. He pulled me to my feet. I gripped hold of him, waiting for my knees and hips to thaw. When my balance restored itself, I let go of Bern, only to feel Perry's hand had quickly taken its place.

'Come on, let's get you home.'

THE FIRST JET of the shower struck my hair and released the smell of smoke; it lingered on the air for a few seconds, then washed away. With both hands and forehead flat against the cool tiled wall, the spray massaged my back, melting my stiff, aching joints and detangling knotted muscles.

Perry had whisked away my clothes as soon as I stepped out of them, *'I don't want them stinking the house out,'* and I heard the washing machine chundering away when I came downstairs quarter of an hour later.

'I think these will have to be chucked out…' she waved my trainers: the soles were melted and deformed from the heat. 'Go and sit down, I'll get you a drink.'

But rather than obey, I followed her to the kitchen. She opened the fridge and passed me a bottle of beer. I turned towards the special drawer for bottle openers, corkscrews, egg whisks and other kitchen paraphernalia and noticed a small treasure trove on the counter top. Perry noticed me noticing.

'I emptied your pockets before I put everything in the wash,' she explained unnecessarily. 'You've got eighteen pounds sixty-three, half a packet of chewing gum, some small cross-head screws and a business card.'

I recognised her curiosity in the way she said, *'business card'* and it took me a moment or two to recall where I'd got it from… Oh no, don't say suspicion and jealousy, I really could do without an argument today of all days.

She reached across and picked it up as though she was examining it. 'Rachel Ridder: journalist.' She gripped a corner in each hand, ever so dainty and walked to the opposite side of the room. 'Where did you get this from?'

Shit, I wasn't in the mood for a fight. 'She gave it to me today.'

'I love her,' said Perry. That totally wrong-footed me: I didn't expect that response. 'She's great, I love her writing.'

'But you don't read the tabloids… do you?'

Perry shot me a look that could wither slugs. 'Course I don't. She's not a tabloid hack, Rachel Ridder's a proper journalist, investigative, she writes big features, she's brilliant.'

I didn't have a clue what she was talking about. I resorted to the standard 'uh-huh'.

'She wrote a fantastic piece about the NHS PPE crisis, best story I've ever seen on it, got loads of awards for it. Have you honestly never heard of her?'

'No. Who's she write for?'

'You're useless. Most of her stuff goes online. She's a blogger and writes for a couple of the web-based news outlets. The NHS piece got picked up by the *Guardian* and she's done features for *The Times* too.'

Oh right, I thought. It meant nothing to me.

'She's got a massive following,' continued Perry. 'All the young, politically active people know who she is, hell, even *I* subscribe to her blog and follow her on social media.'

That got another uh-huh from me in lieu of anything useful to say, but then a thought had clearly occurred to Perry as I was given her quizzical face, 'Why've you got her card?'

I explained I'd shooed her off for sniffing around Danny's house looking for a bit of scandal.

'She doesn't do celebrity gossip, I told you that.'

I gave my final uh-huh and headed to the sofa to enjoy my beer. I'd deserved it.

-13-

THE RADIO NEWS said quietly in the background it was nine thirty a.m. Disco and Jac were pushing on with Hamlet's salon, and Bern was out and about picking up materials for them. I, meanwhile, was ensconced with Stuart in the Kidd's converted stable block office. We were supposed to be wringing out even more savings from the pub conversion estimate, but for the past forty minutes, Stuart had been moaning about Danny taking himself off to London for the day, leaving him to sort out the insurance claim for the fire.

Stuart sifted the day's post. Most were bills, and tossed straight into an awaiting tray on the corner of his desk with a cursory glance. He slit open a stiff white envelope and extracted a glossy page. 'Might be interesting.' He laid it on the small pile on his desk for further action. From where I sat I could see it was a charity newsletter: big money donors were being invited to buy tickets for a forthcoming gala ball: the Cantium Invicta Awards. Colour photos on both sides from last year's event showed all the great and good in their tuxedos and gowns looking fancy.

Bored of watching Stuart reading mail, my eyes wandered the room, scanning across Danny's many trophies, trinkets and magazine covers. No matter how many times I'd been in that room, I could always find something new, another star-dusted souvenir to catch my eye. This time my attention rested on an autographed white shirt. It read *"To my friend Danny"* and was signed by Zidane. I found myself wondering how they would have ever met, being of slightly different ages and extremely different career paths. I was about to lean over for a closer view when Stuart spoke out, alarmed, 'Who's that?'

I followed his eyes and saw a young man, younger than me anyway: cropped scruffy brown hair running into an equally scruffy brown beard. His hands pushed deep into the pockets of his navy Barbour, elongating the diamond padding. He saw us watching, and the hands came out to point at us. From behind him, previously obscured by buildings, came three uniformed policemen. The four of them walked in an awkward formation, like the world's worst boyband.

'What's this all about?' I asked, but Stuart was beyond hopeless, sitting there staring, 'Stuart?'

I called his name again, and he snapped back to life. 'I don't know. Do you think it's about the fire? Probably the fire. Must be here to follow it up.'

The man with the beard let himself in to the office without even the courtesy of a knock. Bit rude, I thought. He stood quietly beside us, not saying a word, just looking, as if examining us. Even ruder. Stuart and I both waited for him to speak.

'Which one of you is Mark Poynter?' he eventually said, although I suspected he already knew. I raised my hand. 'Mark Poynter, I am arresting you for burglary, theft and sale of stolen goods.'

'Say what?'

'Okay then,' he had an accent from not round here, Yorkshire maybe. 'If you want to play stupid, I'll make it simple. That chandelier. You stole it. You sold it. You're nicked.'

Struck dumb, I looked across to Stuart, who was equally agog. Our visitor gave a come-hither gesture to one of the uniforms outside, who obediently joined us. Without a word, he pointed at me. The uniform understood. Before I could work out what was happening, the uniform was raising me from my seat and within seconds I was wearing handcuffs.

'Is that really necessary?' protested Stuart

'Are you the homeowner, sir?'

Stuart shook his head and explained his brother's absence, then asked for identification.

'I am Detective Sergeant Lawrence,' said the visitor. 'Now, could you please open up the premises for us? I could come back with a warrant, but it'll be a colossal waste of everyone's time because we know you've got it, you can see it from the road, it's bloody enormous.'

The meat wagon doors were open to their widest. The last thing I saw was Stuart fumbling with the house keys before a hard shove in the back pushed me to the floor of the van.

MAIDSTONE POLICE STATION: well and truly off my patch. I didn't know anyone here, and when offered the chance to call a lawyer, I accepted. Only problem is, the last lawyer I hired was a returning-to-work mum to do my conveyancing when I bought my house many years ago. I couldn't remember the name of the firm, much less hers. I didn't know any lawyers. Luckily, I knew someone that did.

I dialled the number from memory. And true to his word, Hamlet had someone there within half an hour: a fat, pompous man with a posh voice and a loose and ample chin that spilled over his mauve silk tie. His first words to me were that he's three hundred pounds an hour. I told him, in that case, he'd better get a move on.

'James Capel, representing Mr Poynter,' he informed DS Lawrence. I liked the superior tone of voice he used. I liked how Lawrence bristled against it. 'What evidence do you have against my client?'

'Plenty,' Lawrence's Yorkshire accent sounded stronger by comparison, especially the T sounds. 'Shall we begin?'

Capel flipped open a yellow pad and unscrewed the cap of an expensive-looking fountain pen, his heavy gemstone cufflinks tapped against the table top as he did so. 'Please do,' he replied, without looking up at Lawrence. His arrogance was annoying and unsettling Lawrence, I was enjoying this.

'Okay, so Sir Eammon Reams comes back from Cape Town only to find his ancestral home stripped bare. Everything gone: furniture, fireplaces, wood panelling, carpets… chandeliers. We've got CCTV of a shabby box Luton van arriving at the house and then leaving several hours later. We've traced the van to its owner, who provided us with a statement that he'd lent the vehicle to a friend for the day in question, namely yourself Mr Poynter. We've also got a Lewis fifteen crystal chandelier, circa 1850—'

'Louis quinze,' interrupted Capel without looking up from his pad.

A sigh, then: 'We've also got a Loo-ee Cans crystal chandelier, circa 1850, matching the homeowner's one hanging up at Danny Kidd's house, sold to him by your client.'

'Firstly, how do you know it's the same one? Mr Kidd is a very wealthy individual, and could no doubt have his pick of any light fitting. Secondly, my client doesn't deny visiting the premises and buying a chandelier in the very best of good faith. I suggest my client is equally as much a victim in this instance as the homeowner, as he has been defrauded of a considerable sum of money.'

Lawrence fidgeted. He tapped the tips of his index fingers together but didn't speak. He wore the resigned look of someone who'd accepted their sandcastle was in the path of the incoming tide.

'You say the house was stripped bare, but then that my client was only on the premises for a matter of hours. Are you seriously suggesting he managed to strip a substantial house in its entirety in that time, and clear it all away in a single trip in a small van?'

Lawrence flicked through the loose-leaf pages in front of him but didn't appear to be looking for anything in particular. We knew, and he knew we knew, it was just a distraction to buy him some thinking time and that rattled him even more.

'I suggest you release my client without charge immediately, as he clearly is an innocent party caught in the deception of others. He will of course be willing to co-operate in apprehending the real perpetrators by answering any questions you may have about how he came to acquire the item. At a later date. By appointment.'

Lawrence announced the interview was suspended and left the room. Capel placed his hand over my wrist. 'Soon be out, old man,' then went back to doodling on his pad.

Lawrence returned about ten minutes later. 'You're free to go, Mr Poynter. But please make yourself available should we need you to help us with further enquiries.' He jerked his head towards the door. 'See them out.'

Capel gathered his things, then gestured for me to lead the way with a grand sweep of the arm. A uniformed policewoman waited on the other side of the interview room door. She escorted us through the police station to the front entrance. The police station faced onto a busy main road. It was a modern and ugly structure: a squat, dark frontage squashed between two historic grey stone buildings.

'Thanks.' I shook Capel's hand. The claustrophobia of my wrongful incarceration fell from me like a heavy winter coat in the heat of summer.

'No problem, they didn't have anything, and they knew it,' he replied.

'Other than the CCTV. But if I'm on camera, why isn't anyone else, it must have taken them days to strip that place.'

'Who knows? Who cares? It's nothing to do with you now. You're in the clear,' Capel tore the polythene wrap from a brand-new packet of cigarettes with his teeth. He offered one to me. 'I don't,' I muttered. He lit one and took a long, satisfying drag.

'Look, for all I know it could have been the gang that stripped the place that gave the police the footage.' He was one of those people that had the knack of speaking while exhaling smoke through their nostrils. 'Set you up as the scapegoat. Wouldn't be the first time someone's tried to cover their tracks that way. Anyway, it's over now, so forget about it. Right, I must go.'

'Wait, so, what, you'll invoice me, will you?'

'Mr Hamlet's taken care of it, told me to add it to his account. Lovely to have met you. Goodbye.' As I watched him waddle away in the direction of a pay and display car park, I wondered how much this favour from Hamlet would ultimately cost me.

I needed to call Bern to get him to come and pick me up. My belongings had been returned in a clear plastic bag on the way out. I switched my phone on, and as it powered up, I slipped on my watch and snapped the buckle closed. The phone chimed and vibrated as it caught up with all the messages from that morning.

Looking for a space in the busy traffic, I crossed the road towards the car dealer opposite. The reflected sunlight from their acreage of highly polished cars had been giving me a headache, so I sat on their low stone wall with my back to them.

I raised the handset to call Bern when a message from Danny Kidd arrived. *'You fucking idiot! What kind of muppet cowboy are you? Any idea of the shit you've caused? You're sacked. And forget about any more money!'* Great, just what I needed. He'd attached a web link, a long blue line of jumbled letters and numbers. I tapped on it, it led to a tabloid website, *'Stolen? You're Kidding!'* Half a dozen photos showed policemen swarming all over Danny's house, one showed the chandelier being brought out by several burly coppers, an old one showed Danny being jumped on by team mates in a goal celebration and of course there was the familiar one of him fighting in the street. Colourful block capitals declared the short article beneath to be *'breaking news'* and *'exclusive'*. The first paragraph brazenly accused Danny Kidd of dealing in stolen antiques, but the remaining three merely reheated the old news about his public spat with Muzzkett. I called Stuart and told him about the message from Danny.

'Don't worry about it,' Stuart said. 'He's just venting. He's just worried it'll affect his TV prospects, but I've told him it wasn't your fault, you're as much a victim as he is.'

The traffic had become heavy and I struggled to hear over the noise. I got up and headed in the direction of the town centre. A salesman who'd been hovering close by looked crestfallen at my departure. Maybe I'd been his big hope of selling a car this week. Oh well, not your day either, mate.

'Look, I run Kidd Properties, I decide who works and who gets paid. So, don't worry, you're still on the team,' said Stuart. 'Must have been a bad morning for you, so get yourself home and we'll catch up later.'

I JUST WANTED to get home, get showered, scrub the sour stench of the custody suite from me. The powerful jet cleaned my skin and cleared my head, and I was finally back in a good mood when I headed downstairs.

I found Perry in her usual spot: always the same end of the sofa, her legs folded underneath her. She had her computer on her lap, surfing websites, and a chat show jabbered away in the background.

'Oh my god,' she squealed, 'says here your footballer's been dealing in stolen goods.'

'Has he?' I hoped I sounded convincing.

'Says he bought an antique chandelier stolen from a stately home… do you know anything about that?'

'Me?' I said, but my protests weren't necessary as she'd already moved on, keen to share something else with me.

'He's a bit of a lad, your Danny Kidd, look,' she patted the arm of the sofa. I perched and looked at what she was so keen to show me: the familiar photo of him outside the nightclub.

'That's not the only one,' she clicked on the next link to an article about their feud, then another, then another. 'They seem to have a real grudge, these two. They've been hurling insults and abuse at each other on social media for weeks now.'

'Well, that's not real life, is it?' I said, despite knowing nothing about it at all.

'This Muzzkett guy, he's got over a million and half followers, so real or not he's got the attention of a hell of a lot of people.'

'But these rappers, it's all make-believe, they're all posh stage-school boys playing gangsters, but as soon as they've made a few quid it's all big houses in the country and wanting to be taken as a serious actor.'

'What a lazy stereotype! You might want to read this.' She brought up a Wikipedia page, 'it sounds like he's the real deal. You should warn Danny to cool things down a bit.'

I read the webpage she'd displayed:

Mustafa Ketay[1] (born 3 September 1990)[2], better known by his stage name Muzzkett, is an English singer, grime rapper and MC[3]. His father, a Turkish Cypriot who came to England in the 1970s, left the family home shortly after Ketay's birth[4]. His mother is English. Ketay grew up in a poverty-stricken household in Edmonton, North London[5][6]. Ketay had no contact with his father during his youth, and to this day has no relationship with him[4]. Ketay's step-father was violent to both him and his mother who divorced him in

1995 citing domestic abuse[7]. *Ketay became involved with criminal and gang-related activities from the age of twelve and was expelled from secondary school aged fourteen for violent and intimidating behaviour. Whilst placed within a Secure Children's Home he resumed his education to GCSE level*[8][9].

Ketay was accepted on a trial Home Office initiative[10] *to divert young men of disadvantaged backgrounds from criminal lifestyles through music and the creative arts. Ketay showed early promise as a DJ*[citation needed] *and adopted the name Muzzkett, a contraction of his own name but also a play on the word Musket, based on gang life and gun culture*[11]. *He began rapping and drew inspiration from the North London criminal gangs he has maintained an association with*[citation needed], *incorporating garage music and drum and bass into his sound. His debut album 'Scimitar Bites' was shortlisted for the 2014 Mercury Prize and best debut album at the 2014 MOBO Awards*[3][12][13][14][15].

In 2016 Ketay, whilst in the company of at least eight others, was involved in a confrontation between rival gang members in which 19-year-old Emmanuel Azikiwe was stabbed and later died from his injuries[16][17][18]. *Despite the police not bringing charges against Ketay*[19] *he was dropped by his record label following the incident*[20][21]. *Ketay signed for RFLI Music three months later*[22].

It appears I was wrong. The real deal, indeed.

-14-

STUART WANTED TO meet me at lunchtime to find out how I was getting on with the revised estimate. Given the choice of getting a colonoscopy or going to this meeting, I'd happily bend over and touch my toes. It's fair to say, I wasn't looking forward to this at all.

I'm normally pretty good with my quotes and get them back to the client when promised, but I was struggling on this. It annoyed me because it was such a simple job, all things considered. Stuart wanted to go ahead with the scheme that had previously been approved at Planning, thinking it would be easier to get it re-approved than start again from scratch.

This meant I had a set of detailed designs to work from, and it was a very thorough design too. Someone had spent an awful lot of money getting these produced. My eyes rested on the drawing title block, against 'Client' it read 'Philip Hopkins Holdings'. Out of curiosity, I fed that into the internet. The search engine immediately came back with the name, address and smiling photo of a man in the motor trade. I didn't recognise the name or face, but when I clicked on the website I immediately recognised the dealership, having driven past it every time I go through Chatham town centre.

But all of this was a distraction and didn't help me any. My problem was that I simply couldn't find anyone to price the job. Guys I'd worked with for years had either declined, said they were too busy, or simply not bothered to respond. I'd never known anything like it. The only quote I'd received was so ludicrously expensive, I could never in a million years accept it. I was worried if I told Stuart I couldn't give him any kind of cost certainty, he'd think I wasn't up to the job and bin me for someone else.

STUART WANTED TO meet at a businessman's hotel-cum-golf club off the M20 close to Leeds Castle. For some reason it was very busy. Recent arrivals ignored '*Keep off the grass*' signs and parked on verges and anywhere else they could find space. A noticeboard in the hotel foyer welcomed a computer software company for their annual conference, a firm so big even I'd heard of it: *that'd explain the busy car park*, I thought.

I found Stuart and Danny in the bar: a huge glazed area overlooking the first tee on a wide flat fairway. Both dressed in designer golfing casuals with half-drunk beers in front of them. The pair of them, sat at a table for four, beckoned me over.

They'd just competed in a tournament for a local children's charity: 'Kidds for Kids?' I said, but neither of them got it. Danny asked if I played. I replied I didn't have the patience or the interest. 'Shame,' and then he gave me a blow-by-blow account of the game he'd just played, trying both my patience and my interest. I let it fade over me and took in the surroundings. I quite liked the old-fashioned style of the bar: thrupenny bit shaped in footprint, it gave wide panoramic views of the golf course; the high, timber-panelled vaulted ceiling and painted joinery gave it an American Cape Cod feel.

'I said, how does it affect you?' Stuart's words snapped me out of my trance. 'With the land cost so high, how does it affect your estimate?'

'Well, err…' I frantically tried to engage my brain. 'My estimate was pretty tight to begin with, there's not a lot of fat on the prices at all.'

'So, by buying it for this stupid price…'

It was left to me to put into words what he feared, 'You've basically spent any profit in the job.'

'We'll need to do more sums, you and me, but I guess the obvious solution is we have to keep the flats.'

'That's an option. Keep them for rental, lower the specification of fittings to save a bit of the build cost,' was my suggestion.

'True, I suppose in a few years, if the market's gone up we could look at refitting them as and when the tenants move out and then start selling them on.' Stuart paused as though pondering this option in greater detail before adding, 'Beer?' He held up three fingers to a passing waiter.

'Do you mind if I sit down, gentlemen?' asked a voice from behind us. We all turned back from the waiter to find Donaldson sliding himself into the fourth seat. He gave the most insincere smile, his ratty dark eyes locked on to Danny's. 'I wonder whether you've had the chance to re-consider my offer yet?'

'Consider this, mate,' Danny leaned towards him. 'Fuck off. We're not interested.'

'Danny…' Stuart sounded parental, warning the naughty boy to behave.

'No,' said Danny. 'He can fuck right off! I was right about that place. I knew it was a little goldmine, there's a good profit in it. That's why this prick's trying to get hold of it.'

Danny was getting agitated. His voice was getting louder. People had started to look in our direction.

'Hardly,' Donaldson's voice as smooth and calm as a country vicar's. 'You won't be getting much return out of that scheme, in fact I'm willing to bet you'll lose money.'

'Oh, shut up and leave us alone.'

'You'll probably lose quite a significant amount, Danny, what with the reckless price you paid for it. Plus, you can't get anyone to do the work for you… isn't that right Marky Mark? It does seem quite the most annoying coincidence, doesn't it, that everyone is just too busy at the moment to help you out of this predicament? What's your solution, pay through the nose for expensive out-of-towners to help you out? That sounds costly.'

'Whatever. Just fuck off,' Danny answered on my behalf. Danny's voice was too loud now, it had drawn a lot of attention our way. I spotted a phone held up to record us. I readjusted my chair to block their view of Danny.

But Donaldson hadn't finished with me. 'I hear you've been offered a sweet opportunity on a new housing project. You might want to think about taking that, what with that nasty tax bill to clear. You don't think your pretty little nursey will hang around for long once the money runs out, do you?'

A burning flare erupted from somewhere deep within me. Both Kidds looked at me for an explanation. Donaldson had riled me. How did he know about my business, my accounts, my relationship? He'd done his homework, but more importantly, he was letting everyone know he'd done it.

'I've told you already, fuck off,' Danny jabbed an angry finger in Donaldson' direction as he spoke.

'That's a bad attitude you've got there.' Donaldson' voice carried a laugh in its tone. 'Is that why someone tried to burn your house down? I hope you've got good insurance.'

Danny leapt out his seat to grab Donaldson, but Stuart held him back. Donaldson brushed an invisible crumb from his thigh, then stood. A nasty smirk spread across his face. If his objective had been to goad Danny, mission accomplished.

'Be seeing you,' Donaldson used the same calm tone and walked away. Danny writhed in Stuart's grip. I didn't like the interest they were attracting. People had drifted into the bar to gawp, a few more phones out. I felt obliged to break this up before anything got posted on the internet for the world to see.

I failed.

THE NEXT MORNING the tabloids went to town on Danny. They all had the grainy camera-phone photos enlarged and Danny's blurred low-resolution face was everywhere. They all offered online the shaky handheld camera-phone video recordings of Danny restrained by his brother and shouting obscenities. They all made the same appalling puns about how badly behaved kids shouldn't be allowed in restaurants. And without fail, they all made reference to Danny's feud with Muzzkett and yet again showed the photo of the pair of them being restrained.

If Danny's TV ambitions weren't already dead, they were now cold, dry ashes in the urn with the lid screwed down tight. Meanwhile, Muzzkett earned another thirteen thousand likes on social media (whatever that means).

-15-

JIM AND LINDA... Barry and Sue... Phil and Jackie... Nigel and Marilyn...

Names, names, names. I'd struggled putting faces to them and had already given up trying, but if I'm totally honest, I was more taken with the handwriting. I enjoyed the familiarity and felt instantly transported. Immediately recognisable, I'd know it anywhere.

Dad's old address book was exactly where I thought. I'd gone through it just the once before. I'd let people know the funeral arrangements and then it laid it to rest in the drawer, untouched for years. Holding it now, seeing his handwriting, something permanent left behind, made him closer all of a sudden. I could hear his voice through the distinctive handwriting. The letters leaned impossibly forwards as though they were about to topple over. My eyes traced the straight backs and flowing curves remembering all the birthday cards, the same handwriting, the same message every year, '*Happy days Mark, love, your Dad.*' My eyes began to prickle and sting. I blinked away the moisture before it became tears. Silly, eh?

It was Disco's fault for this emotional relapse. Donaldson had got inside my head. He'd done his homework. I realised it was time to do mine. First question: why did he want the pub so much? Disco knows every pub in the area by the smell of the carpets alone, so I figured he must know something about it.

'The Admiral Guthrie? It was alright as a pub.'

'But what's so special about it?'

'I don't know. To be honest, its heyday was way before my time. It was popular with the Dockyard mateys back in the late seventies, early eighties, when the Dockyard was at its height. How many worked there, ten thousand men?'

'Something like that,'

'It was probably one of the first pubs out of Gillingham Gate.'

'And what's that meant to mean?'

'Your dad never told you about the Gate crawls?' Disco sounded genuinely surprised, 'You'd get the Navy coming out through the Pembroke Gate heading into Chatham, but the mateys would come out the Gillingham Gate towards Gillingham, obviously.'

'Obviously.'

'The route would go from the Dockyard to Gillingham Town Centre, pub to pub.' Disco closed his eyes, dredging long-forgotten memories. 'Royal Marine… The Cannon… Admiral Guthrie… Jolly Sailor… gah, what was it? Bridge House… Bricklayer's Arms… Countryman… The Monarch.'

'Well done, that's quite a talent you've got there, Disco.'

'I've probably forgotten a few and got some of them the wrong way 'round, but the Admiral Guthrie was definitely one of the first on the route.'

'Yeah, you said that.'

'I mean the place, as I remember, was always packed, so they either went straight there or they gave up on the crawl by the time they reached it.'

'But what's so special about it? It's no different to any of the others.'

'That's what I'm coming to. Someone like your Uncle Bern might know better than me, him being the right age, but I seem to recall stories of a pub on the Gillingham crawl offering the red light, you know what I mean?'

'A knocking shop, brothel? And you think it may have been the Admiral Guthrie?'

'Maybe… I don't know. It's an urban legend from donkey's years ago. Tell you what, do you know any of your dad's old workmates? They'd have been around at the time, they'd have heard the stories.'

And so, it was thanks to Disco's suggestion that I'd fished out Dad's address book. It sounded a good idea, but now the thought of contacting old men out of the blue to ask if they knew of a house of ill repute thirty or forty years ago seemed ridiculous. Besides, it didn't answer why Donaldson wants it now. I decided to put the address book back in its drawer and forget about the whole thing but couldn't resist one more flick through to hear Dad's voice again: *Ian and Marion… Pat and Maureen… Pete and Brenda… do your homework Mark, don't let him beat you.*

THE LUNACY OF the whole thing slapped me around the face: I knew it'd be a total waste of time, but I also knew I wouldn't be able to live with myself if I didn't at least try. I selected three names more or less at random, hoping they'd remember Dad well enough to talk with me: *Come on Dad, help me out here, please.*

I figured turning up on the doorstep unannounced would make me more awkward to get rid of than a simple telephone call. I made my first visit. He was the one I remembered most fondly. I'd not seen him since my early teens, but as kids he made us laugh a lot. Things like that stick in your mind forever, don't they?

The man who answered the door looked like a melted version of the man in my memories. The once sleek, hawk-like features had been replaced by folds, jowls and eyes as saggy as an elephant's ballbag. It took a second or two to reconcile the effect twenty-five years has on a man.

'Pete?' I asked with caution, 'Pete Kramer?'

'Yes?' his voice also carried uncertainty, 'I'm sorry, I don't buy at the door.' He pointed a twisted, arthritic finger towards a faded Neighbourhood Watch label stuck to his porch window.

'No, I'm not selling anything. I'm Eric Poynter's son, Mark.'

He said nothing. An outcrop of coarse silver hair stuck up on one side, suggesting I'd woken him from a nap. He peered at me through his smudged and smeared glasses, then a yellowed smile broke across his face, 'Of course you are, of course, my goodness there's no mistaking you, you look just like him, come in, come in.'

I followed him along a chintzy hallway to a chintzy living room and was offered a chintzy tasselled armchair. The house had been decorated to a high standard many years ago when chintz was the in-thing, probably his keeping-busy project when he first retired.

Everything still looked new. It had all been very well maintained but was so out of date I felt as though I was wandering through a museum exhibit; it could just as easily have been a mock-up Edwardian parlour for all the connection it had with the here and now.

Pete was very welcoming. He apologised that his wife wasn't there and said she'd have loved to have seen me, although I'd swear I only ever met her once or twice. It was an easy-going conversation, as though I'd last seen him only a few weeks ago rather than a quarter of a century. He was keen to learn about Perry and my work, and out of politeness I only told him the best bits. In return he told me about his son, who I vaguely recalled meeting one Christmas a long time ago. Apparently, he's in insurance and living in Sevenoaks with his second wife and her children.

With a throaty chuckle, he remembered Uncle Bern and asked if he still played the piano. Bern had more or less stopped playing after Dad died. I told Pete I wasn't aware of him performing in public any more.

'Shame,' Pete muttered, 'Eric and Bernie. I used to enjoy watching them play. They were good together.'

Pete leaned forwards. He placed a light hand on my knee and drew in a breath, 'I was so sorry to miss your dad's funeral. You know I wanted to be there, don't you?' I murmured pleasantries to assure him it didn't matter. 'We were in Cyprus you see, ruby wedding anniversary, it had all been booked a long time before, forty years married…' Pete's words trailed off, as though distracted. I again murmured pleasantries but don't think he heard. He sat back in his armchair and slumped into his own thoughts and conflicts. I let the silence hang a little while, before I roused him from his daydream by broaching my reason for being there. His rheumy eyes fixed on me as he listened. They remained on me as he thought things over.

'The Admiral Guthrie? That takes me back. But I don't think I can help you Mark.' He polished his glasses with the corner of his shirt, 'I only ever went in there a few times, people's birthdays or leaving dos, but never out of choice, you know, socially. It was a bit too rough and rowdy for my liking. As you recall, me and your dad used to prefer The Countryman.'

I nodded that I did, even though I didn't. I knew this'd be a wild goose chase, and I quickly ran out of things to say. I remained passive and let him lead the conversation, nodding at the correct moments. Judging the time right, I excused myself, saying I had another appointment to get to.

At the door he told me how pleased he was to have seen me, and again how sorry his wife would be to have missed me. He shook my hand firmly and I felt guilty promising to drop by again, knowing I never would.

MY SECOND VISIT took me to Lower Gillingham, near the river. To a utilitarian-looking block of flats that resembled a wafer biscuit: long, narrow but squat; three concrete slabs sandwiched a storey of living space between each one. Built by and for the council, but all privately owned by now, I imagine. I pressed a door number on a large push pad, spoke my introduction into the voice box, waited for the buzz to release the heavy entrance door, then started to climb. Up on the top landing a door opened to greet me. 'Hello Ginger,' I said.

'No one's called me that in a long while, can you guess why?' laughed the man in the doorway pointing at his short, polar-white hair. He was small and fat and round. His T-shirt didn't quite reach his waistband, and a doughy quadrant of belly grinned at me. Clive 'Ginger' Gordon: another of Dad's old workmates. The only thing I remembered about him was he was widowed very young, moved back in with his elderly mum and never left. I'd picked him on the assumption that no wife and no kids meant more likely to spend more time down the pub.

'I haven't seen you since you was a nipper,' Ginger sounded just as keen to see me as Pete before; a tribute to Dad, I guess, holding him in such high regard, it cascaded down to me. 'And your brother, Adam, was it? How's he?'

'He's fine.' I hoped that'd be enough to cut off any conversation in that direction. 'So, how's you, Ginger?'

'Mustn't grumble,' he replied. I've normally found that phrase a warning signal that a tidal wave of complaints are inbound and coming at you, but, 'Like I say, I've not been called Ginger in a long time. They should call me Snowy now instead.' I smiled, but he hadn't finished. 'It's the curse of the redheaded man. We never go bald, instead we go pure white. I'm like one of those albinos.'

I couldn't be bothered to correct him, so I gave a weak smile. He beckoned me in. Even with his back against the wall of the narrow passageway, it was a squeeze getting past the curvature of his belly. He gestured towards the kitchen at the back of the flat then closed the door, pulling a small security chain across, 'Can't be too careful round here anymore, you know how it is.'

I've worked in so many houses and flats that, without even stopping to take in the decorations and fripperies, I knew he lived alone simply by the smell of the place: a pungent fragrance of BO, bad diet, filled ashtrays, and the sweet, rancid tang of stale beer. The unmistakable flavour of the long-term single man was thick and sticky in the air and led me to assume Old Mother Ginger had passed away some time ago.

The small kitchen was your typical domestic biohazard. Dirty, crusty crockery stacked beside a small lime-scaled sink, in which a very old floral-patterned saucepan languished in a grey swamp of cold stagnant water. Several pint glasses bearing beer logos, all purloined from public houses, stood on the countertop, each with varying amounts of pale brown dregs. An overflowing rigid green recycling box belched cheap supermarket own-brand bitter cans onto the floor.

'Excuse the mess,' said Ginger, without a trace of shame. 'My butler's day off.'

I declined the offer of a cup of tea, preferring a dry thirst to cholera. I followed him to the equally squalid living room. I was offered a pastel pink velour armchair to sit in. I perched on the front lip so as to avoid coming into contact with the greasy grey patches across the headrest. It took every ounce of effort not to scratch myself. Above me, the ceiling was yellowed from a permanent nicotine cloud. Below me, the once pink carpet had smooth dark paths mapping out the regular walking routes. The flat hadn't seen a hoover since Gazza's tears in Turin.

And yet, in amongst the squalor and the filth, standing out like a diamond in the shit, a brand-new television, and boy it was a whopper, at least a fifty-inch. Its hi-gloss framing sparkled in testament to the rabid popular-press stereotype of the modern poor: living on the poverty line, unable to feed themselves properly but tripping over every latest gadget. Ginger spotted it had caught my attention: 'A treat to myself. And why not? It's great for the football. Want me to switch it on, watch a bit?'

'Not on my account.' I stood up, convinced I would catch scabies if I sat any longer in that chair. To change the subject, I walked across to the window and looked out, 'I bet you get a nice view of the river from up here Ginger.'

'Yeah, life's terrific up here in the penthouse.'

He wasn't wrong. The view took in a wide section of the river; I could just about make out Otterham Quay in one direction, the Dockyard buildings in the other, and my dinosaurs standing on the far horizon. Yet it was what was up close that caught my eye. I'd reached Ginger's block following side turning after side turning on a series of estate roads. Of course, it was obvious now: the architects had put the entrances, staircases and landings on the blind side so that the living accommodation could benefit from these river views on this side. And there, front and centre, about five hundred metres away at the bottom of the hill—the Admiral Guthrie.

'That pub there,' I pointed towards it, 'isn't that the one Danny Kidd the footballer has just bought?'

'Yeah, so I hear. That's the one. I used to like him, good player.'

'What do you know about the place?'

'What do you mean?' Ginger's voice changed, it was only subtle, but I still heard the suspicion.

'I just remember my dad saying it had a reputation back in the day.' I hoped I sounded on the right side of conversational.

'Reputation for what?'

'Well, you know, it was a naughty boys' pub?'

'No, I don't know,' Ginger's tone had firmed up even further.

'Ever go in there?'

'Me, no,' he shook his head. 'There used to be so many pubs around here, some nearer, and all much nicer. They've all closed now, of course. Not that I go out any more if I can help it, not with my condition.'

'Oh yeah, what's that then?' I felt out of politeness I should show interest, even though the last thing I wanted to hear about was someone else's ailments.

'Agoraphobia.'

As soon as he said it, certain things made sense, such as the rapid bolting of the door and keeping it locked even when home, as though under house arrest.

'I was diagnosed eight or nine years back. Doctor said it was as a result of Mum passing so suddenly. Anyhow, if I was to go to a pub these days, I'd need a taxi on account of my ankles, and pub prices are so expensive, and you can't smoke any more. It's not like it used to be. No, I stay at home these days. Buy my own beers, have a smoke, and watch my big telly. Perfect.'

'Yeah, perfect,' I agreed for simplicity's sake. I'd heard enough. It was time to go. I began showing myself out.

'What was it you came for again?' asked Ginger, holding the door open for me.

'Oh, I was just interested in Dad, I'm thinking of writing a book,' came my response, before I could think of anything better to say.

'Great. Nice one, more than happy to help,' Ginger offered a weak floppy handshake. He closed the door behind me and I heard the rattle of the chain sliding back into position: can't be too careful round here anymore, you know how it is.

MY THIRD, AND I'd decided definitely my final, visit was to a tidy little bungalow in nearby Lordswood. The small lawn was neatly mowed, and a little red hatchback gleamed in the sunlight. The doorbell chimed the peal of Big Ben and through the stippled glass I saw a tall thin man approach from within. Standing there in a polo shirt embroidered for an under-elevens football tour two years previous, Ray Doyle recognised me immediately, 'Mark, isn't it? Eric's lad?'

I was promptly invited in and ushered towards a spotless circular pine table in a clean and tidy kitchen. I scanned the room, not a single thing looked out of place. My eyes settled on a fixture list stuck to the fridge, upright and parallel to the edges of the door. It showed a team photo of youngsters wearing red and blue kit. They'd taken the traditional formation: one row standing, one kneeling. Below the picture, printed in the same red and blue, were the season's match dates and opponents. A spidery handwriting filled in the scores for games played already. It looked as though the team were having a good season so far. Ray followed my eye and realised I was looking at it: 'Yes, I'm still coaching the boys' team.' I had no idea what he was talking about, what had actually caught my eye was the logo of one of my competitors, a fellow electrical contractor, on the boys' shirts and at the head of the list. He appeared to be their principal sponsor. I wondered how he afforded it seeing as he was always moaning how little work he was getting.

'I'd half expected to have hung my boots up by now, but people don't volunteer any more do they, so what can I do,' Ray gave the team photo an affectionate tap, before pulling open the fridge door, 'Still, keeps me active I suppose. Tea or coffee?' Through the window I could see the lady of the house busy at the bottom of the garden. Ray took out the milk and clicked the kettle on.

I opted for tea and, as he went about it, we exchanged small talk, mostly about his predictions for Gillingham in the league this season; like most of the town, he didn't have high hopes. Then he surprised me: 'Does Adam still follow football? He was always keen.'

'You know Adam?'

Ray laughed, 'Don't you remember? He used to play for us, a couple of seasons, then your dad told me he'd joined the school team.' Something drew me to a cupboard far back in the attic of my mind, stuffed full of things put away and forgotten. The cupboard door opened and passed down a memory of pride for my big brother, aged about eight or nine, muddy knees and gappy smile, in a red-and-blue striped football kit and Dad dancing round the kitchen, 'Adam scored a goal, Adam scored a goal, ee eye add ee oh Adam scored a goal.'

I spotted a way to get to the purpose of my visit that was certainly more plausible than writing a bloody book. 'Do you know Danny Kidd? I'm working for him. In fact, it's why I'm here.'

'Danny? Of course, I know Danny, he was one of our kids too,' said Ray. 'And his brother. Only for a season though. They were way too good for us. Didn't take long for the scouts to spot them, then the professional clubs moved in.'

'His brother? Stuart?'

'Stuart, yes. He was the one the professional clubs wanted, he had so much promise, a very talented player. It was their dad made the clubs take Danny too. Part of the deal for getting Stuart.' Ray wiggled an empty mug towards his wife in the garden. She shook her head with a smile and got back to her borders. 'If you'd asked me back then, I'd have said Stuart was the one who'd reach the big time, he played everyone else off the park. Played for England schoolboys, did you know? Such a shame he didn't make it.'

'Why not, what happened?'

'Same reasons ninety-nine-point-nine-nine-nine-nine percent of them don't make it: birds, booze and bad behaviour.' Ray sounded more saddened than disapproving, 'They become teenagers, young men, their focus changes. From what I heard, he was fifteen and got pissed on a pre-season tour somewhere. First time abroad, first time away from home. It happens all the time. He fell down some steps, broke his ankle, never recovered properly. He never got his form back.'

Mention of a broken ankle brought back a conversation from a few days ago, and it felt like a circle had been squared. Ray looked out across the garden, out across the years, to see two young brothers starting their respective journeys, then almost as quickly he was back in the here and now. 'Anyway, what's Danny got to do with things? What made you look me up?'

'The Admiral Guthrie. Danny's bought it. He wants to turn it into six flats but thinks there might be a problem getting planning permission. I remember Dad saying it had a reputation, so I thought

I'd ask some of his old Dockyard mates to see if they remembered anything about it.'

Ray ran his whitish tongue over his brownish teeth, a thought process had begun. I further prompted him with, 'I've just been to see Pete Kramer,' a comment dropped in to judge his reaction. 'He sends his regards,' I lied, but it got an appreciative smile.

'Good old Pete, is he well?'

'He is, yes.'

'Good, good,' Ray's voice trailed off, as though still thinking of Pete, then, 'It was as rough as arseholes that place. I'd have thought the council would be grateful for someone to do something with it.'

'What was so bad about it?'

'You name it. There was drugs, fights. They say they used to hang the old red light outside, you know, prostitutes. They didn't call it the Red Admiral for nothing,' he chuckled at his own turn of phrase. He gave a sniff, 'And there'd be all sorts nicked from the docks being bought and sold through there.'

'So why wasn't anything done about it?'

'Rumour was it was run by gangsters, I wouldn't be surprised if they'd bought the police off.' Ray's comments only confirmed everything I already knew. I doubted he'd know much else.

'You're wasting your time talking to Pete Kramer about it though,' Ray pushed a mug in front of me, '*Number One Coach*', and gave a bashful smile: 'Secret Santa gift from the team.' He took a seat beside me. 'I'd be amazed if Pete ever went there, he was far too straitlaced. Plus, I'm sure Brenda would never have approved of him going to places like that.'

I drew a cautious sip of the deep mahogany-coloured tea. Ray liked it strong, it seemed.

'Shame about poor old Brenda,' he said, then read my blank look. 'Didn't you know? She died, pancreatic cancer, about eight months ago. It was ever so quick, she was diagnosed just before Christmas and gone by February. Nasty business.'

All of a sudden I saw Pete differently, how could I have missed it: the loneliness, the delight of a visitor, the desperation for a return. My sympathies and thoughts were with Pete when Ray spoke again. 'Ginger Gordon is the one you want to speak to. He worked there for a while.'

'He did what?'

'Just after his wife died, he moved back in with his mum. She got fed up with him moping about and got him a job down there. He was only the pot man collecting glasses and tidying up, but it was more to get him out meeting people.'

'I didn't know that,' I replied. 'How long was he there for?'

'I know he was still doing it after the Dockyard closed in eighty-four when we all got laid off. It was a difficult time, some blokes moved away to find work in other dockyards round the country, other blokes like me and your dad took up new careers, but there was a lot of men out of work. Ginger pissed plenty of them off bragging he was sorted when the Dockyard finally closed its gates, saying he already had another job to go to. To tell you the truth, I wouldn't be surprised if he was pot man until the day the pub shut down. Why not? It was free beer for him, he lived rent-free with his mum and he had his Dockyard severance and pension coming in. Easy life for a loafer like him.'

I drank Ray's bitter tea to show my gratitude, but even as I drove away it clung to my teeth like scales.

-16-

AN HOUR LATER, shaved, showered, and in my best going-out-out shirt, I waited outside an exceedingly intimidating pub in Lower Gillingham: a large grey building reminiscent of a medieval castle and just about as welcoming. I've never found cream walls, pine floors and the feeling I'm about to get my head kicked in the most appealing features when choosing a pub, but it wasn't my choice. It was Perry's. Date night!

She'd called me earlier in the day, said we should meet for a drink after her shift at the hospital. It'd been ages since we'd been for a drink, just the two of us, like we used to. Things had been a little difficult between us, as you know, but her tenderness and compassion at Danny's after the fire showed she's still there for me. I appreciated her making the effort today by suggesting this. I took it that she still wants it too, and I'd resolved, tonight was the night I'd tell her what she wanted to hear.

I'd only been loitering outside for a few minutes when I saw Perry approach. She looked amazing in a cute little dress: short with long loose sleeves, deep blue but with vibrant cuffs and hem in bold red and purple paisley patterns.

'Why, Nurse Parminder, don't you look mighty pretty,' I said. She bashfully dropped her head and flicked her eyes upwards to me, giving me the full treatment: wow! She put a slight skip and swagger in her walk as she came up and kissed me.

'What made you choose this place?' I asked when her hand was on the pitted brass door plate, my question halting her from pushing it open.

'I thought it made a change, somewhere different,' she said, 'And I asked Disco about it. He said it was a *Star Wars* bar. Sounds fun.'

'I don't think he meant what you think he meant…' but my words of caution were too late. She'd gone inside. From my experience, a *Star Wars* bar is Disco shorthand for full of roughnecks and monsters.

Before the door had sprung shut on its heavy closer, Perry was back out. 'Maybe not here,' she said. Hopping back in the van I suggested the Star up on the top road as an alternative. Perry texted for the whole short drive but for once I didn't mind, I was more distracted by her amazing smooth pale brown thighs where her dress rode up slightly getting in the van. And knew I'd be mad to jeopardise what we had.

IT WASN'T TOO busy inside. We got served quickly and took a seat by a window. From where I sat, I looked out to the deserted children's play area outside while Perry faced the room. I told her about Dad's address book, how his handwriting affected me. She made sympathetic noises, but I could tell she was distracted by something over my shoulder: 'Wait there a second.' She left the table with a bit of urgency in her step.

I took a sip from the neck of my bottled beer, creating a satisfying pop as I removed it from my mouth. Outside, a couple of heavy lads, both in the purple-and-black jerseys of the nearby rugby team, plonked themselves on the tiny kids' swings for a smoke. Perry returned to the table, but she wasn't alone: Rachel Ridder, the journalist that door-stepped me outside Danny's house.

What?

'Mark, this is Rachel,' Perry used her nurse voice, the level, sensible, calming one. I muttered that'd we'd already met. Perry continued in the same tone, 'Don't be cross, but I invited Rachel to join us.'

I knew then it wasn't a chance encounter, she hadn't happened to have bumped into her in the Ladies', she'd pre-arranged it. I'd been set up. A hot, acidic rush passed through me. My hands trembled. The way Perry looked at me indicated she could see exactly how I felt about this ambush.

'Calm down,' the soothing caregiving voice said. 'I just want you to listen to what she has to say, that's all. Can you do that?'

What happened to Date Night? What happened to Perry and Mark talking things through? Is this who she was texting on the drive here? What would happen if the Kidds found out I'm meeting with journalists? I'd be finished, that's what, out on my ear, no money, no work. I looked up at the ceiling and drew a long, deep breath through my nose in the hope it would calm me down. Fat chance. The two women sat across the table observing me, then Perry gave a prompting nod in my direction.

'Mark…' Ridder placed both hands flat on the table as she spoke; her fingers long and widely spaced made me think of stars. 'Mark, I'm sorry if you're angry or you feel duped in any way, it wasn't our intention to upset you.'

I shrugged my shoulders, 'meh', and immediately regretted it, knowing how petty it must have looked.

'I contacted her Mark,' said Perry. 'I wanted to find out what she wanted with you. And I think you should hear her out. Please, for me.'

I looked at Ridder. She took it as her cue. With the back of her hand she brushed her hair from her face, and began to speak: 'When we last met I explained I wasn't a tabloid hack. Have you had the chance to check out my work?' she paused long enough for me to shake my head. She didn't seem to take offence and pressed on, 'I know talking to Perry that she's familiar with it—hopefully she'll vouch for me when I say I'm not interested in showbiz gossip, I'm not looking for kiss-and-tell scandals and I'm not a rent-a-gob to spout opinions at the drop of a hat. I write features, I look for the bigger picture and how it influences and impacts on society.'

'So why are you chasing Danny Kidd?'

'Because of Muzzkett, you've heard of him? What do you know about him?'

'Not a lot. I don't follow modern music.'

'Okay grandpa,' Perry teased, 'I bet you remember when all this was trees.'

It was a well-timed quip. I smiled. Ridder smiled too, then continued, 'I'm interested in the Grime music scene. Its roots are planted squarely in the heart of deprived "Broken Britain". Some of these guys now topping the charts have had childhoods of the most heart-breaking neglect. We're talking poverty, violence, sexual abuse, drugs, prison, gangs, murder even. They found their outlet through music. Except, now it's being hijacked by privileged middle-class wankers to sell new cars and luxury holidays. That's what's fascinates me.'

I looked at Perry. She gave a reassuring nod. Ridder's passion was impressive and sounded genuine.

'I've been shadowing several Grime musicians, including Muzzkett, and earned a degree of trust with him, he's quite a character. He's the real deal. He's from a very deprived, fractured background. He's unlike the others I've seen. Most use their music as their escape ladder out of the estates to leave all that behind them. Muzzkett is still very much a part of his community. He still hangs with the Turkish Cypriot gang he grew up with. I've gained a credibility with them, gained a little access. They're tough and they're vicious, no mistake.'

'That's all very interesting, I'll be sure to let Danny Kidd know,' I said. 'That is what you want, isn't it?'

'Yes,' she replied. Pause, 'And no.'

I looked across to Perry, but she was focussed on Ridder, completely transfixed by every word she said.

'To be honest with you, I'd never heard of Danny Kidd until a month ago,' Ridder again moved her hair away from her eyes with the backs of her long fingers, 'I had no interest in football. But this feud between them has fascinated me. Can you see, it's the clash of two totally different strands of popular culture, the old and the new. I want to explore this juxtaposition.'

I nodded along as she spoke and made a mental note to ask Perry what *juxtaposition* means as soon as we're alone. Ridder slid a tablet device across the table towards me.

'See, for how different they appear, both fields are very tribal and very masculine,' she offered the tablet to me, 'and they are both extremely aggressive to outsiders.'

Her tablet displayed a comments page from an internet forum for Grime music fans. My finger, using the lightest of touches, scrolled up and down. Dozens if not hundreds of abusive insults and threats against Danny Kidd; one followed another followed another, it was relentless. A particularly unpleasant one caught my eye, formed from a series of little emojis, emoticons or whatever you call them—little cartoons, only they weren't funny: 'gun knife hammer bomb flame skull gravestone RIP DANNY KIDD'. When it's someone you've personally hauled from a burning building, you don't see the joke, you only see the threat. And there were plenty more like that.

Ridder reached over and navigated to a different page, this one for football supporters, but again packed with hateful comments only this time directed at Muzzkett. I scrolled down, whizzing through them. The hate grew stronger the further it went on, the threats more lurid, eventually giving rise to vile far-right filth. I'd seen enough and pushed the tablet back to Ridder. She slipped it back into her cavernous fringed bag.

'I would be so grateful if you could introduce me to Danny. I'd love to get his take on it, see if his personality and his motivations are the same as Muzzkett's, or how they compare. I think it'd be fascinating.'

This was all very thought provoking, but it was never going to happen. It was time to close this down: 'Danny doesn't like journalists.'

'So I gather,' Ridder replied with a knowing tone. 'But look, I know, we all know, he's desperate to get himself a telly job. Surely it'd be in Danny's best interests to get favourable press for a change? That is if he's serious about his TV ambitions?'

'I know what you're saying, but—'

'You know I'm right. I can help him. I've got good friends who work on the morning chat shows. I could pull in favours, get him an interview on something cosy and family friendly, let him showcase his good side. Perhaps there's a charity he supports, he could talk about that.'

I was mulling things over when Perry voiced my concerns perfectly: 'I think Mark's worried in case it backfires. He's got his livelihood to consider, and that of others. The Kidds have very strong views on journalists, and I think Mark's worried that if he tells them about you, they'll get the hump and sack him. So, basically, to put it bluntly, what's in it for him?' She's amazing, this girl.

Ridder thought for a moment, twisting a tendril of her long, glossy hair between two fingers, brushing a pillar box red tip across her lips. Then she spoke, 'Look, I cannot swear to this, but…'

She paused, gave it some more thought, then continued, 'As I say, I've been shadowing Muzzkett and gained a certain amount of trust with his Turkish Cypriot gang associates. They were talking the other day, and I have absolutely nothing concrete to back this up, and I will deny this conversation ever happened, but I strongly suspect from what I overheard, they set Danny up with the stolen chandelier. Apparently, he hadn't been subtle in saying he wanted one: rich flash footballer with money to burn. They put the word out through London fences and others dealing in stolen goods, and sure enough Danny Kidd took the bait.'

Of course, now she said it, it all made sense: Matt who was really Mehmet, the lad from Nicosia, the CCTV footage of our van coming and going. What was it Hamlet's lawyer said—being made the scapegoat for someone else?

I felt avenged for having this information, but absolutely no idea what to do with it, not yet anyway; I'll plant it out back and see if anything ferments.

But in the meantime, the idea of a cosy sofa mid-morning interview for charity sounded tempting. Perhaps I'll mention it to Stuart first, test the water.

RIDDER LEFT US shortly after that, 'Let me know how you get on,' her parting words. Then it was back to just Perry and me, but it didn't feel like Date Night any more. An awkward silence hovered over us. I swigged the last mouthful from my bottle, the beer tasted sour and flat, it made my neck twitch going down.

I placed the bottle on the table, 'Home?', she gave a cursory glance towards her own empty glass then nodded.

WE STARTED THE drive home. Neither of us spoke. Hanging like a bad smell above our heads was the expectation of a massive argument: a ticking time bomb neither of us wanted to trigger. This was wrong, I knew by prolonging the silence, I was only tormenting the poor woman. But I wasn't going to be the one to go first.

Eventually Perry broke the stand-off. 'Mark, I'm sorry, and you've every right to be angry.' I looked across, but she didn't notice, she'd turned her face to the window to talk. 'I wanted to find out why she was trying to speak to you, that's all. If it had been silly showbiz tittle-tattle, that'd have been the end of it. But when she told me, I thought it was important you heard for yourself.'

'Okay,' I heard myself saying in the absence of anything else to say.

Perry gave my thigh a gentle squeeze, 'Thanks.'

I knew we had a lot to talk about, but I put it off again, it can wait until tomorrow. In my experience all problems tend to shrink away by the morning.

-17-

I WOKE TO find the sun prying through a gap in the curtains. All felt right with the world. Any problems had faded away with the night-time stars.

I wiped mist from the mirror above the basin and began to shave. Perry turned the radio up loud and sang along to a cheery, bouncy pop song in the shower, I had to smile. She's not the best singer in the world but was probably the most enthusiastic, and it made me laugh out loud. Perry poked her head out of the shower. 'Are you mocking me, Poynter?'

In a grave and severe voice, I told her yes, I was. A snowball of coconut scented soap suds hit me squarely on the side of the head in response. 'Well, are you going to come in here with me or what?' teased the voice behind the steamed-up glass. I'd arranged to meet Danny and Stuart at eight o'clock this morning… I can't be late… does it matter? I know I shouldn't… but does it really matter? We're only talking twenty minutes.

I decided I could always blame the traffic, what's twenty minutes after all?

I ARRIVED AT Danny's house just before half-eight with a good apology to excuse my tardiness. It sounded plausible, *Sorry, slow going on Boxley Hill.* But when I arrived, the office was locked up and in darkness. No sign of Stuart either. I walked back towards the house to see whether Danny was around. As I got close, I saw the kitchen door ajar. I turned on the balls of my feet and walked backwards: approaching the house but scanning the grounds in case Danny had gone for an early run, but no.

'Hello. Danny? Stuart? Hello?' No sounds came back from the house to greet me.

I stepped through into the kitchen, still calling out their names. A half-drunk glass of red wine from the night before stood alone on the counter-top. A purplish crescent moon stain orbited it where a fallen drip ponded around its base. And still I couldn't hear a thing: no voices, no television, no radio, no shower, no bath taps. The place seemed deserted. Then I saw it.

Danny Kidd was dead.

IN THE ENTRANCE hall. Flat on his back. His dry, cloudy eyes stared up at the bare cables where the chandelier had once hung. His arms outstretched either side of him in a crude likeness of his goal-scoring celebration. His white shirt clung to him, slashed all over, drenched in blood, his face rinsed red and his hair matted. The blood ponded around him, just like the wine glass in the kitchen. Macabre scarlet sprays decorated the staircase and walls. I stepped nearer, slowly. Through gaps in the torn fabric, grey and purple organs lay still, deep in the gaping wound across his stomach.

I didn't get too close, but retreated and called the police immediately. I tried Stuart next, but straight through to voicemail, tried again, voicemail, tried again. I ran towards his cottage, but found it dark and locked up. When I got connected to his voicemail for the third time, I could see no alternative than to leave a message: 'Stuart, it's Mark. I'm at Danny's house. Call me as soon as you pick this up.'

As I spoke, I remembered Danny's arms. I guess he must have raised them to fend off his attacker, his sleeves were slashed and blood-soaked, but it was his left hand: the little finger was all but sliced off, hanging on a whisper-thin tendril of skin and cartilage.

I TOOK MYSELF to the terrace outside the kitchen. I pulled a heavy cast iron chair from under a matching table. It sent vibrations up my arm as it scraped over the flagstones. I sat. As I waited, I rolled a coin across my knuckles, popped it up beside my thumb, rolled it back down knuckle to knuckle, slid it across and repeated on a loop.

A magic trick Dad taught me, a good distraction to switch my mind off. I did it until the police came, however long that was, any concept of time had been lost.

PLENTY OF PEOPLE came to Danny's house that morning, just not in the order you'd have expected. First came the police, then came the coroner, then came men with the white paper suits, then came a mortuary ambulance, then came the Media and then, only then, came Stuart.

-18-

'WHERE THE BLOODY hell have you been? I've been calling you all morning.'

'I'm sorry.' Stuart looked rough, his eyes were red, his face grey. 'We were out last night. Big black-tie charity ball. The Cantium Invicta Awards, no less. All got a bit messy.'

Maybe I have a macabre sense of humour, but I immediately thought it ironic, he could have been talking about what had happened here at Danny's, but at least I had the self-control to stop myself from pointing it out.

'Didn't get in until late, too much to drink, I needed a lie-in this morning. I should've cancelled our meeting. I forgot, sorry.'

From the way he spoke I would have wondered if he'd known about Danny's demise, but I'd seen a uniformed policewoman pounding on his door, finally rousing him from his drunken coma and escorting him over to the lead investigator. Perhaps this was how he dealt with his grief? I decided to stay quiet, let him go where he wanted to go.

'Good night at the Cantium Invictas,' said Stuart, 'Good laugh. We—Danny and me—we had your mate on our table, the builder who's getting knighted, you know who I mean?'

'Ron Fielder?'

'Fielder, that's it. Danny kept taking the piss out of the knighthood thing, calling him Lord Snooty.'

'Did he now?'

'He looked like he was about to get right annoyed at one point, but Danny kept telling him it was just banter. It's what footballers are all about, you've got to take a bit of stick now and again.'

'So, Ron Fielder wasn't amused?'

'You'd think not, but by the end of the night they were laughing like old mates. I think Danny won him round when he told him to watch out, Kidd Properties are in the development business now. Told him we're the competition to look out for.'

I knew Stuart had been asked to identify Danny as soon as he got here. I knew from experience how difficult it is to get your head straight and reconcile the person so full of energy last time you saw them with the hacked apart shell before you. I let him talk without interruption. If this was how he dealt with the situation, then what else could I do?

'Anyway, it all got a bit daft later on. I got put in a taxi home and… and… and…' Stuart burst in to tears, '… when I woke up my brother was dead.'

People bustled around all over the place but to a man they halted their activities and stared at Stuart; big fat tears ran down his face, his nose snotty and glistening.

'Come on,' I helped him off the patio chair. The house was a hive of activity, I couldn't take him there, so I led him towards the office suite. I thought we'd get some privacy there. A policeman with a grey beard stopped us and told us to stay where we were. Above us, the noise of a low-flying helicopter became louder and louder.

'TV crew,' said Stuart. 'Didn't take them long, did it?'

It's been said I'm emotionally stunted. I probably am, but even I could see Stuart was in pieces. 'Stuart, my van's just over there, come on, let's get out of here.' We headed towards it. That was when they arrested Stuart.

ONE EMPLOYER DEAD, the other one arrested. And this was all before nine thirty in the morning. I think I deserved the day off. I called Disco, but his mum answered. He hadn't crawled out of his pit yet. I asked her to wake him up and tell him I'd be there in the next half hour to take him out for breakfast. Being a nice old girl, she of course agreed to do so, but was then very apologetic when I arrived, having no doubt been on the receiving end of a torrent of profanity and farts from under the blanket. She fussed and fretted and I reassured her it was fine: he wasn't in trouble and neither was she, and yes, I'd love a cup of tea, thanks for asking.

She pottered away in her kitchen with that warm claustrophobic smell of constant tumble-drying and I took myself upstairs. I threw open his curtains to let the daylight in, but it didn't want to come, probably worried it'd catch something. Old underpants and overflowing ashtrays lay all over the place, Disco's finishing touches. I yanked the duvet off Disco. I manhandled him to the bathroom and tipped him into the bath tub. I grabbed the shower hose attachment and twisted the cold tap to full bore. Disco woke up.

'Morning,' I said cheerfully, shouting over the sound of the spraying water and the colourful swearing. 'Hurry up and get dressed, I need to talk to you. Breakfast, my treat.'

Disco looked up at me like one of those old dogs you see on TV appeals, the mangy mutts that are brought in and cleaned up for the first time. His dark eyes had a sense of bewilderment, unable to tell if you're there to help or torture, his dark and grey muzzle snapped up and down, too angry to make any noise, his stringy dark hair clung all over his face. 'Some treat!' he finally managed to say as I was closing the door.

DISCO WAS DRESSED. His hair was still damp, but he looked reasonably presentable. He needed a shave but then he had the kind of face that always needs a shave.

'Do you think he did it—seriously?'

I had taken him for breakfast to a charming little gastro-cabin outside a crinkly tin warehouse. All the other cafes in the area had decided unanimously one day to dedicate themselves to the Yummy Mummy market. We didn't want to sit listening to babies moan, and they didn't want to listen to workmen moan, so we decided to part ways. An enterprising grease-monger by the name of Dave The Manc had traded in his burger van in a layby for a twenty-four-foot portacabin on an industrial estate and will probably be a millionaire this time next year. With two sweet teas and an inch-thick slab of crusty white bread inside him soaking up last night's excess of hops and barley, Disco began to function again. As we awaited our breakfasts, I told Disco about finding Danny, and Stuart's subsequent arrest.

'Do you think he did it, seriously?' Disco asked again.

My mind flashed with Donaldson' dark, evil eyes, and I could hear Perry's warning about Muzzkett. Danny Kidd had enemies he should have been fearful of. 'No, I don't,' I said.

'With Hamlet's tanning shop finished, where's that leave us? Are we still working for the Kidds?'

'I don't know,' I'd been pondering the same question myself, 'We'll need to see what happens next.'

'THERE'S SOMETHING DIFFERENT about you,' said Disco. 'Don't you reckon, Marky? There's something different about him.'

We both sat and stared at Uncle Bern who'd come to join us—of course he did, if there was a chance of a free meal, you try and stop him. We stared some more, and when he started to feel uncomfortable, we stared some more. Great fun though it was, I couldn't see anything different. I stared some more.

'What? What?' demanded Bern.

Disco raised a finger, as though he had an answer. 'Have you had a haircut? A Chatham Bogs special?'

I knew Bern—in a second or two he'd flounce off, and then we'd have to spend the rest of the day coaxing him back. 'He's just winding you up, ignore him,' I said.

Disco scrutinised Bern, up close and personal, giving him a full inspection. Bern tried to look dignified and stared straight ahead, but his resolve cracked when the tip of Disco's nose touched his, 'Piss off with you! Leave me alone.'

'I've got it,' Disco clapped his hands. 'You look healthy. Why do you look healthy?'

Bern tried swatting Disco away with a flap of the hand, 'Pah.'

'Last time I saw you, you were a pasty-faced little twat.'

'None taken' replied Bern, after a long slurp of tea.

'Now you're tanned and healthy looking,' Disco also took a satisfying slurp, 'Still a little twat though!'

'I've been down Hamlet's, on the sunbeds,' Bern began to tell us, 'Thought I'd top up the tan. It's started to fade after—'

'She dinged you out.'

'No. *It's started to fade after six months back here,* is what I was going to say. It's six months today… since she dinged me out.'

'So how much is that costing you then? Can't be cheap.'

'Nothing. Nitto. Nish,' Bern seemed very smug. 'It's never busy in there. I just tell the girl I'm there to do a bit of maintenance, sort out some defects. She don't care. I go out the back and get twenty minutes of sun.'

Seemed odd: it didn't sound like Hamlet to open a business for it to struggle, it'd have to be a guaranteed success before he'd commit his money to anything.

'Now you mention it, there was no one in there when I had to go in yesterday,' added Disco. This was sounding odder and odder. He continued, 'Did the girl keep turning the machines on even though there was no one there?'

'Yeah,' said Bern, 'I thought that a bit weird. I remember thinking—no customers, machines on all the time—must be costing a fortune for all that electric.'

Something smelled fishy to me, and it wasn't Disco. The pair of them wittered on but then—*ching*—the penny had taken a long time to fall a very long way, but it finally dropped.

'It's a front, isn't it?' I said, interrupting their nonsense. 'For laundering money. It's a front, isn't it?'

They both stared at me with that expression cats give their owners when they talk to them in funny voices.

'Hamlet's records will show the machines are working all day and there'll be lots of cash in the till from non-existent walk-in clients. He's found a way to wash a lot of cash through legitimate accounts.'

The pair of them made murmuring appreciative noises, seeming to approve and admire the scam. Me, I kept my humiliation quiet and to myself. I shivered and rubbed a hand over my forearm, it felt ice-cold to the touch, a sickening electric pulse fired through me, my shoulders heaved in reaction. Perry was right, and I knew I simply couldn't tell her: Hamlet had tricked me again.

Bern raised a fork, and flicking egg and bean juice across the table, pointed at the small silent television screen behind the counter. 'You seen that, Mark?'

It was impossible to miss. It had been going on ever since we'd arrived. A reporter stood outside Danny's house mouthing muted updates, all the while a rolling tickertape trundled across the bottom of the screen: '*BREAKING NEWS: FORMER FOOTBALLER DANNY KIDD KILLED, BROTHER SUSPECTED.*' Every few minutes it would replay the same footage: the helicopter I'd heard had caught a perfect view of Stuart in handcuffs being marched into the back of a police van.

'I knew he was a wrong 'un. From the moment I met him, I knew he was bad,' said Bern, then after a pause, 'Where's that leave us?'

'I don't know mate, I don't know.'

-19-

I HUNTED THROUGH my phone for an old message. I found it, listened to it again, then pressed the call-back option. It began to ring.

In hindsight, with one employer dead, another prime suspect for his murder and my third and final employer having tricked me into his shady nasty world yet again, perhaps I'd been too hasty rejecting the job opportunity from Fielder Homes.

It rang once, it rang twice, it rang a third time. I hung up. No, I was right to begin with. It's not the job for me. It's not what I'm about. I'd get through this, I always do.

The phone rang and buzzed in my hand. It was the number calling me back. I pressed answer and prepared to apologise.

'Hello, this is Michael Unwin, Fielder Homes, I've had a missed call from this number.'

'Yes, I'm sorry about that, my mistake, pressed call-back instead of delete. Sorry to have troubled you,' I said.

'Is that Mark Poynter, MP Electrical?' he asked. I replied that it was. 'Why were you deleting my message, do you not want the work? You don't even know what it is yet.'

'I'm sorry, I don't do residential developments. I'm sure plenty of other people do, so you'll have no trouble letting it, good luck.'

'I was told to get you. You're the one they want for it.'

I was flattered. It's always nice to be recommended, but then most of my work is through recommendation. I've never had to advertise or chase work too hard—most good tradesmen don't need to.

'Like I say, I'll pass, but thanks. And please pass on my thanks to whoever put me forward.'

'Put you forward?' Unwin's voice carried the same sound of surprise as if I'd just told him I'd not only been sleeping with his mother, but I wanted him to call me poppa and buy me slippers. 'We don't work on subbies recommending their mates. We don't give out work on a subbie's say-so, we have a rigid procurement process.'

'*Here we go,*' I thought. '*I don't even work for you and I'm getting a lecture. That's it, put the sub-contractor in their place, let me know how wonderful you are and what a privilege it is to work for you.*' I let what he was saying drift past and waited for a gap when I could cut the call and be done with him.

'But in this instance…' Jeez, he was still going on, '…the instruction came down from on high, we will use you.'

'Is that right?' I was near the end of my patience now, but politeness matters—stay professional, Poynter.

'It's not for me to question Mr Fielder's motives,' said Unwin. 'But he suggested you, and a few other sub-contractors, for packages of work. Maybe in his special year, to celebrate his knighthood, he's chosen to give something back, create some opportunities for small businesses back in his hometown, boost the local economy after the lockdown, that kind of thing.'

His sanctimonious tone had given me the right hump by now. 'Well be sure to thank Mr Fielder for me,' I cut the call, 'Next time you're bent over kissing his arse,' I added, and hoped the call had indeed been cut in time as I'm always polite and professional, mostly.

OVER THE NEXT couple of days, hundreds of pages were devoted to the death of Danny Kidd. Thousands of words were written about his sporting achievements. Even more words on his tabloid-fodder celebrity lifestyle: the romps with glamour models, the nightclubbing party boy, and of course the feud with Muzzkett. But the press had moved on from the celebrity gossip. They had Stuart squarely in their sights and they were shooting to kill.

They'd become Stuart Kidd's judge, jury, and executioner. They reprinted the photos of Danny and Stuart arguing in public at the golf club, but edited them to make it look like a heated row between themselves. And from somewhere they found quotes from people who'd heard Stuart moan about Danny not appreciating him. They'd delved so far back they'd even found old Ray Doyle and got his account of Stuart being the more gifted player: tragic he never recovered his form, I always thought he was the one that'd make it. Worst of all, they'd managed to dredge up some old former girlfriend of Stuart's to give her story about him getting prescribed anti-depressants when he was released from the football academy after being told he'd never make pro.

If the tabloids wanted to paint Stuart as bitter, twisted and jealous with mental health issues, they'd succeeded. As far as the tabloids, and no doubt their readers, were concerned Stuart should be locked up right away. Therefore, the last person I expected to get a call from that morning was the man himself.

'Mark, I'm sorry, I didn't know who else to call,' he sounded on the verge of tears, 'They're letting me go, can you please pick me up?'

So, I did.

I DROVE OUT of the police station gates with Bern in the passenger seat. Hordes of photographers waiting for Stuart's impending release didn't give us a second look. Before they'd figured out he'd gone, Stuart would be miles away, perched on the wheel arch in the back of my van.

'Thanks Mark, Bern. I didn't know who else to ask.'

'That's alright, we always had faith in you,' said Bern, forcing me to bite my tongue against such lies. 'So, have they properly let you go?'

'It was horrible, the way they kept trying to trick me and make me implicate myself, but gradually, one by one, my lawyer managed to knock back all their claims. He'd got the taxi driver to confirm he'd taken me straight home after the charity dinner. We could prove I was at a meeting with the accountants when the garage was set on fire. And all the stuff, the allegations in the paper, we batted each of them back. They've let me go, but I'm still under caution.'

'Don't worry mate, we've got somewhere nice and quiet lined up for you,' said Bern. He was right, the police may have seen sense and let him go, but the tabloids had him tagged as Public Enemy Number One. I knew, from what I'd seen on TV, we couldn't go back to Danny's house. Every news outlet had a reporter outside. The mountain of flowers and scarves and football shirts grew day by day, although I suspected Bern would find a use for all of them given half the chance. I assumed Stuart's cottage on the grounds would also be under siege. For his own safety, we needed somewhere under the radar. I knew just the place; nice and convenient.

'Here we are.' I drew the van to a smooth halt. 'Home away from home.'

Stuart stepped down from the back of the van. He blinked against the daylight and stretched the journey out of his spine. Before him stood a row of yellow bricked terraced houses, thirty-or-so years old.

'That one there is mine,' I pointed towards my front door. 'And the one next to it on the right, that's where you're staying. It's my girlfriend's house.'

'Next door to you?'

'Yes, she lives with me, but rents that house.'

'Oh?'

'It's complicated,' I added, suspecting the addition was probably unnecessary. He didn't ask any further. If he thought it extravagant to keep the house next door empty, he didn't say, and I had no intention of explaining. As it happens, Perry had looked at giving up the tenancy, but then the pandemic arrived. She put herself on the front line, treating the very worst affected, and decided to keep the house. It became an airlock or a decontamination zone, depending on what kind of disaster movies you watch. She kept some clothes there. After every shift she'd come in through the front door, get undressed, showered and changed, then leave by the back door and come home to me. Always thinking of others, she'd kept me safe by not bringing the virus home.

I unlocked the door for him. 'Nobody knows you're here apart from you, me, Bern and my girlfriend Perry, and I've got you a brand-new pay-as-you-go burner in case anyone's hacked your phone. It should grant you a few days' peace and quiet. If you want anything, just give me a knock.'

Stuart genuinely seemed touched by the gesture. Bern stepped forward and gave him a hug. I stepped back and looked away. I'm not good at things like that.

-20-

UNFORTUNATELY, IT WAS a slow news week, meaning Danny, and in particular Stuart, stayed on the front pages. He chose to seal himself away and didn't emerge from Perry's house. On her advice we didn't pester him, instead leaving him to deal with things his own way.

I was an idiot. Thanks to keeping in with the Kidds and wanting to stay so close to them at the expense of anyone else, I'd ended up cast adrift with no work. Perry didn't say I told you so, no one said I told you so, but I bet they all wanted to. All I had was Hamlet's other tanning salon to make a start on, but knowing it was all a sham and he'd tricked me again, I'd lost the appetite for it. However, with Bern to pay and the risk of losing Disco to a rival with a full work book, I knew I had no alternative other than to press on with it. I called Hamlet and told him I'd start in the morning. I ended the call swiftly, not wanting the obligation of small-talk.

THE DOORBELL RANG around eight o'clock. I was home alone, with just the last scrapings of a microwaved shepherd's pie for company. It rang again… Whoever it was, they were impatient. It was dark, but they'd triggered the infrared sensor to the security lamp. Brilliant white light floodlit the path. The obscured glass panel in the door acted like an x-ray and offered up a grey shadowy silhouette of the caller's head dead centre. I opened the door and was confronted by the unwelcome appearance of Donaldson.

'House calls now, is it?'

'I've not interrupted your supper, have I?'

'What do you want?'

'Can I come in?'

I leant against the doorjamb, using my body to fill the space, 'No.'

'Very well. I'll be brief in that case—'

'Please do.'

'I've been unable to find Stuart Kidd… to pass on my condolences and the like. He appears to be keeping a low profile.' He bowed in to me as though sharing a secret and tapped his temple. 'But then I thought, he's got a pal. If anyone could get a message to him, it'll be Mark Poynter.'

'I've no idea where he is, I've not spoken to him since it happened.'

'Aye, course not. That's very admirable, loyalty to your pals, well done.' He took a step back to deliver his message, the real reason he was there, 'Tell Stuart Kidd, I want that pub. The offer still stands.'

'PURCHASE PRICE, PLUS fifteen percent?' queried Stuart.

'That's what he said, the offer still stands, but he wants a response and contracts exchanged in forty-eight hours or that's it.'

'That's what?'

'*That's it*, those were his exact words, *forty-eight hours, or that's it.* I took it to mean the offer expires and any deal's off but...'

Stuart rubbed the back of his neck and paced up and down. 'But what?'

'You don't think he meant *that's it*… as in it'll be the same fate for you as what happened to Danny, do you?'

Stuart stopped pacing, and turned to stare at me open mouthed, 'I hadn't, no. But thanks for putting that thought in my head.'

'No, it's probably nothing,' I said trying to backtrack, but from the faraway look in his eyes I suspected that my attempt at reassurance wasn't working. 'I'm sure he was talking about his offer, forty-eight hours or the deal's off, that's all.'

I wasn't sure if he was listening to me, he seemed lost in his thoughts. I assumed it was one shock after another beginning when he'd heard voices outside the window. He'd recognised Donaldson when he peered out. As soon as Donaldson had gone, he was banging on the door, demanding to find out what had been said.

'Forty-eight hours? Well, that's the end of that then,' Stuart finally said when he came back from wherever his head had been. 'Everything's in probate with the lawyers, there's nothing I can do until it's all sorted out and released.'

'Probate?'

'Yep. You know what Danny was like,' Stuart sounded frustrated by Danny, even now. 'He refused to make a will, refused even to speak about it. Any attempt to would lead to an argument, and so now we're left waiting for the lawyers.'

'What happens now?'

'We'll have to tell him it can't be done. Have you got a number for him?'

I hadn't. Donaldson' last words were he'd contact me. Stuart looked disappointed at this.

THE FOLLOWING MORNING, bright and early, I headed for Strood: an unexceptional suburb hanging off of the edge of Rochester by the Medway Bridge. I soon found Hamlet's second shop unit. It was set within a cluster of shops that town planners have done their best to decimate by ploughing a busy ring-road straight through the middle of it, and then for good measure some busy A-roads spinning off in various directions. Any unfortunate shop stranded on the wrong side of the road got practically no passing footfall. Hamlet had chosen his location wisely. Hamlet's place was a long-forgotten unit tucked far enough away to ever be bothered by genuine passers-by, but the fact it carried the words "high street" in its address would justify the turnover should any faceless civil servant in a faraway office ever glance at the annual return. The shopfront said it was a ladies' fashion store; I guessed from the faded posters in the window, the fashion was back when Kylie Minogue was the look—the first time round. When the keyholder hadn't arrived by nine, I knew it was time to call Hamlet: '*Why do I have to do every bloody thing myself?*' he boomed loud and clear through the van's hands-free.

HAMLET'S OFFICE, twenty-five minutes later. Last time I was there he burst some idiot's nose across his face; blood, goo and bodily fluids everywhere. Now, as he rummaged in his wall safe, I ran my eyes across the carpet, wondering how thorough his cleaners had been.

'Here you go, don't lose them,' a flash of silver caught my attention just in time to realise a bunch of keys was hurtling towards my face. I raised my hands. Something hard and painful struck my thumb; cue fairly imaginative and medieval swears from me. The keys began to tumble, my arms swept around wildly in all directions, but still the keys hit the floor. Proof positive why I've never played cricket—can't catch to save my life. With a stretch, I got them and slipped them in my jacket pocket. Hamlet looked amused by my awkwardness.

'You found anything out about Donaldson yet?' I asked, thinking if he wants awkward, I'll put him on the spot, see how he likes it.

'Not really.' Hamlet seemed unfazed by the question, which to be honest annoyed me. 'I asked around, but the only Donaldson with a Scottish accent I can think of was a guy who used to be a proper handful back in the day, you wouldn't mess with him. He'd take you down along with all your mates and the room you're standing in. A proper scorched earth merchant.'

A lifetime like that, that'd explain why he had no fear bringing hostility and threats to a bigger, younger man he'd never met before. But Hamlet's description was all very much past tense.

'Who's he work for?'

'No idea, mate,' replied Hamlet. 'Ever thought about asking him?' He held his palms out in front of his face and widened his eyes: a gesture that said, 'That's all you're getting. Push it if you dare.' I knew better than to push it.

'Well, what about the Admiral Guthrie pub? What do you know about that?' I asked.

'Not much. It was a Flint family pub. Heard of them?'

I nodded. I'd heard of the Flint family alright, most people had: an old established criminal firm from Lewisham. They'd had a stranglehold on the South East long before the Krays were even born.

'The Flints had control of that pub since the War when the old man, Ken, used it to control the black market. It was their staging post for contraband smuggled in and out the dockyard off the Atlantic convoys. All sorts of stuff went through there. Later, in the sixties, seventies, eighties, they still used it to move stuff in and out of the dockyard. It was also used as a knocking shop for all those sailors on shore leave. The Red Admiral, they called it, because of the lamp in the window, did you know that?'

I did. I'd heard it mentioned somewhere before, but I gave him an amused smile out of politeness. There was still something on my mind that needed to be explained: 'But how did they get away with it, if it was such an open secret?'

'I don't know,' started Hamlet. 'Rumour has it, they had a pet copper who diverted any attention away, but who knows? Anyway, that was thirty or forty years back, when the dockyard was at its busiest. I've honestly no idea why anyone would want it now, other than for the development potential, but didn't you say there's no money in the job anymore?'

'And you knew all this, did you?'

'Look, the Flints may be South London, but they've had business in and around Medway going back generations, long before the War even. But it's fine, as long as I keep out of their way, and they mine, then all's good, there's enough to go round for everyone.'

I was beginning to feel this conversation was a bit pointless. He'd put a bit more meat on the bones of what I'd already learned elsewhere, but not given me much else. He must have read my thoughts, because:

'Look, that's all I've got, sorry if it's not much or not what you want to hear, but that's all I can give you, okay?'

There's not much happens around here without Hamlet knowing about it. I believed him. I don't know why. Perhaps it's easier than accepting you're being fed a bald-faced lie.

BY NOON, WE'D made a good start in the shop unit, clearing out all the old junk. I'd been tagging and tracing the cabling that tumbled out of the meter cupboard like spilled guts and had suggested Bern and Disco take half an hour for lunch. They headed to the nearby McDonalds, promising to bring me something back. I pressed on with the task in hand. As is always the way: so many cables crammed in, no idea what's redundant or essential, and absolutely no way to identify what's what. Sometimes the quickest thing is just to cut them all one by one to see what turns off and what goes bang.

'Keeping busy?' said Donaldson. I spun round, my heart pounding at the surprise. I hadn't heard him come up behind me, the creepy little bastard.

'What did Mr Kidd say to my offer?' Donaldson continued, dropping any pretence that I hadn't been in touch with Stuart.

'He said no.'

Donaldson tilted his head and narrowed his eyes. It emphasised his ratty features. 'No? Is that all he said?'

'I told him the terms you told me.' I figured there was no point antagonising him, so I gave him the truth, I just wanted him to go away. 'Stuart said he can't do it.'

'That's a pity,' Donaldson sounded disappointed rather than angry. 'I guess that's the end of that then.'

'I guess so.'

'I'll let you get on with…' his hand made a lazy circle towards the cables, 'this. Be seeing you.'

Donaldson turned and headed for the street door. I watched him leave, then got back to trying to decrypt the mystery of the cable spaghetti.

A hand on the back of my head drove my face into the wall at speed. The taste of iron and earth filled my mouth. I saw a smear of blood on the plaster and realised I'd split my lip. My tongue flicked out to survey the damage.

Donaldson, the creepy little bastard, had snuck up on me again. I turned to face him just as he swung a length of timber at me screaming 'You fucker.'

Through luck more than anything else, I flinched in time and the timber glanced off my shoulder. A flare of pain went off inside me, but I knew it would have been a lot worse had it connected with my head.

Donaldson raised the timber to swing again but before he could bring it down Disco was behind him, pinning his arms. He wriggled, but very quickly composed himself. He dropped the timber and kicked it away from him, which I read as a sign he wasn't a threat any more. I nodded to Disco to release him.

'I apologise, I lost my head in the heat of the moment.' He placed his hand on his chest and did the same peculiar little bowing gesture he did the first time he apologised to me.

'Listen…' I tried to maintain my calm. I wasn't prepared to give him the high ground of maintaining his composure while I lost mine. 'You asked me to pass him a message, I passed it. You've had your reply. After that, it's nothing more to do with me. I'm out, leave me alone.'

'My mistake,' Donaldson smoothed his sleeves as he spoke and shot out his cuffs. 'I should have realised you have no influence in this matter. I will leave you in peace, providing you leave me and my business partners alone too.'

'Fine.' I had no idea what he was talking about, all I knew was I wanted him gone.

For the second time Donaldson turned and left. At the doorway he barged past the returning Uncle Bern, causing him to drop his brown paper bag, the golden arches tumbling to the ground.

'Who's the arsehole in a hurry?' he asked, scooping my spilled dinner off the floor and back into the bag.

AWAY FROM DISCO and Bern, I made the call. Stuart was angry. I didn't understand why.

'What did you tell him that for?' he demanded.

'Because you told me to. Your exact words were *no, it can't be done.*'

'In forty-eight hours. I couldn't sell it *in forty-eight hours,*' said Stuart, 'because of the probate.'

'Oh. I thought you were sentimental about it. Are you saying you did want to sell it?

'Yes, I want rid of it, the bloody thing.'

'Why didn't you say that then?'

'I thought I did.'

'No, all you said was you can't sell it.'

'In forty-eight hours. But if he was prepared to have been reasonable, we could have come to an agreement and done the deal once probate is over.'

'Oh, sorry, you should have been clearer,' I said, somehow apologising for taking a beating over something that wasn't my fault. 'What happens now?'

'The next auction's not for another two months, I'll stick it in that, but in the meantime, I'll get on to the council and try to fast-track re-approval of the planning permission. And if you can go in there and strip it out, back to the bare shell, hopefully the combination of the two will add some value and it'll cover its costs in the next auction.'

Sounded like a plan to me.

-21-

'STUART, WE'VE GOT a problem,' I said, aware of the understatement, but to be honest it sounded better than the truth: *'Stuart, there's a mountain of trouble teetering above us, and I think I've triggered an avalanche.'*

STUART'S IDEA TO put it in the next auction had made some sense to me, so I'd left Disco and Fiery Jac to get on with Hamlet's second salon, and over the next few days, Uncle Bern and I stripped out the Admiral Guthrie with a demolition team from the Isle of Sheppey Disco had put me in touch with. They'd bring their eight-wheeler in every morning, drop the sides, load it up and take it all away at the end of the day to tip somewhere. So far, so good.

Harpo had already snooped around to see if anything was of value to him and actually gave over the odds for some Victorian panelled doors. I think he knew he'd overpaid, but was attempting to make amends for the chandelier incident. Years of unimaginative refurbishments had already stripped the place of any other interesting period features, leaving nothing else worth preserving. This let us tear through it like a hurricane. The ceilings came down, the carpets taken up, bathrooms and toilets stripped out: all straight to landfill. Next, out came the stainless-steel kitchen and the copper piping; Bern sold it all for scrap and conveniently forgot to share the proceeds with the rest of us. The Sheppey demo crew made very short work of the non-loadbearing partitions, smashing them to pieces and removing every last trace. Stuart had asked for the place grubbed out completely hoping to add value to any prospective buyer, and we'd succeeded in doing that in under a week. Needless to say, I was feeling quite smug.

'Seeing as you've got the demolition crew on site and you're ahead of time, you might as well break out the cellar floor while you're at it,' said Stuart, upon hearing my progress. 'Take it down to the correct level while you've got the right men and machinery there.'

I wasn't too keen on that idea, and not because I wanted to slope off early. I had other, more significant concerns. 'Are you sure you don't want to get a structural engineer to take a look at it first? You've no idea what's holding the building up. I don't think you should go poking around, undermining the walls.'

Stuart was silent for a moment, I heard a couple of deep breaths blown into the phone, and then he was back, 'Fair point. Tell you what, leave a metre's margin from the external walls untouched before breaking out, we can clear the middle to the correct level and leave it to whoever buys it to do the rest once they've got their engineer's report. So, can we get on with that?'

I agreed. I didn't comment on the '*we*' even though I knew that '*we*' wouldn't include him hauling buckets of broken concrete up through the pavement cellar flaps. Perversely though, I could picture Danny getting stuck in, he'd have enjoyed this past week being part of a crew.

And so, on Stuart's instruction, we began breaking out the floor to reduce the levels.

'STUART, WE'VE GOT a problem,' I said, aware of the understatement, my phone sweaty against my ear, the dust clinging to my face and hair.

'What?' It was the first time I'd spoken to him for a couple of days and he instantly sounded scared. 'Oh balls, it's the foundations isn't it. I said we needed a structural engineer. Have the cellar walls burst, is anyone hurt?'

'It's not the walls, everyone's fine. But I think you should get down here now.'

STUART ARRIVED AT the Admiral Guthrie within half an hour. Very quick time. He must have had the fear of God in him and triggered a few speed cameras getting here that quickly. I sat on the grass outside, waiting for him to arrive. He looked around for the rest of the workforce, his hands outstretched either side, speechless. I told him I'd asked Bern to take the Sheppey demo crew to the nearby café for an early lunch, and to stress to them to keep this completely top secret. Stuart nodded agreement vigorously despite clearly having no idea what was happening.

I handed him a yellow safety helmet. He adjusted the strapping at the back to a comfortable fit and put it on. He donned the safety gloves offered but declined the paper-cup face mask. The dust from the breaking out had mostly settled, so I wasn't going to argue with him, but I pulled mine back over my nose and mouth all the same and told him to follow me down to the cellar.

A rolling breeze hit us squarely in the face: a cooling jet brought down through the open cellar flaps then escaping back up the staircase behind us. The concrete slab directly in front of me dropped as sharply as a cliff face, and with great care I stepped down the six hundred millimetres—two feet in old money—to the reduced level. Stuart stepped down to join me, declining my offer of a helping hand.

A lorry thundered past on the road above us, making Stuart jump. A tinge of pink flared on his cheeks and, in an attempt to hide my guilt at laughing at him, I blamed it on the cellar flaps.

'This is where they used to drop the beer barrels down to the cellar,' I pointed at the square opening in the ceiling above us, 'The dray wagon would drop them down from the road outside rather than manhandling full barrels through the pub and down those stairs.'

Stuart looked up at the daylight overhead, the rumble from the traffic above echoed around the empty cellar shaking us to our boots. 'We had to open it, and leave it open because of all the dust we were creating gunning out the concrete.'

Stuart nodded his understanding. He seemed less jumpy now. He gazed up towards the underside of the exposed ceiling, at the hefty timber joists. An asbestos-like board had been tacked over the existing ceiling to add fire resistance, but that came down on day one. We found the original ceiling behind it, so that came down too. Behind Stuart's head I noticed a tack puncturing a joist, pinning the last remnants of a chestnut lathe in place. Knowing it'd annoy me if it stayed in, I reached up and plucked it out.

I pulled down my paper mask and instantly felt the sweat on my face tingle in the cool breeze. 'Prepare yourself.' I pointed to the ground in front of me. 'Just there, see it?'

Stuart edged in front of me. He leaned closer. A little further forward then, 'Oh-my-fucking-god,' he stumbled backwards. He tripped over my feet. He landed on his arse on the cool compacted earth of the dig.

What had got Stuart so agitated? The same thing that made Uncle Bern shriek like a little girl when he first saw it. Poking out from under a thick concrete crust was a hand: a human hand attached to a wrist with about four inches of forearm visible before it disappeared under the as yet unbroken slab. It was neither skeletal nor fleshy: mummified probably the best word. I'm no scientist, but I'd hazard a guess that not much air would get to it under the solid concrete slab, which is why it hadn't rotted away. Any moisture had long since leeched out of it. The hand was clenched in a fist, the skin across the knuckles tight and leathery, the thumbnail clearly visible on top of the fist.

'I'm sorry Stuart, but I think we need to call the police now.'

-22-

'NEVER SEEN ANYTHING like it, not in all my puff,' Bern had been regaling his assembled audience in the Golden Lamb with the gruesome find all afternoon—so much for my telling him to keep things top secret. Adding to his very loose lips and inability to keep a secret, the increasing volumes of IPA made his account grow more and more lurid. By the time I'd walked in you'd think he was Indiana Jones or something.

'You know, I've always said I was a bit psychic. I often think of someone and then, next day, I'll bump into them. Anyway, we were down in this cellar and something doesn't feel right, like someone was calling my name,' Bern was loving the attention and getting into the story, I stood behind him, 'So I put the Kango down and start clearing away, and I can still hear this voice in my head calling my name and as I look down in the hole… there's this hand reaching out to me—'

'Bern,' I tapped him on the shoulder.

'Wah!' Bern sprang into the air, his audience ducked to avoid the tossed pint slopping in their direction, 'Oh it's you. Everything okay?'

'Come with me,' I said, and led him away to the other side of the bar. I explained what had happened in the past couple of hours since I let him and the demolition crew go at lunchtime. Stuart reported our find to the police, and a few uniforms were on site within minutes. A little later we were joined by a joyless lanky arsehole: grey hair, grey face, grey suit, calling himself DCI Paul Hutton. He took charge of the situation and chucked us out.

'So, what happens now?' asked Bern.

'I don't actually know. He took my witness statement, then told me to get out. I asked if he wanted to talk to you, he said it'd probably be no more than I'd already told him so he wouldn't bother. Of course, he didn't know about your psychic tendencies.'

'I knew you were going to bring that up.'

'I waited for them to finish with Stuart to see what was going on. They've taken the keys off him, made it a crime scene and are going to break out the rest of the floor, see what's there.'

'How long will that take?'

'According to Stuart—no idea. This DCI Hutton, he told him it'll take as long as it takes. Which is no help to anyone.'

Bern scratched his head and crinkled his nose to push his glasses back up. 'So, what's the plan then?'

'Well,' I began, 'there's possibly a few days left on the salon, but with the Admiral Guthrie closed off as a crime scene and the other Kidd properties in probate, I don't have anything else.'

Bern looked up at me with big helpless puppy dog eyes. I already hated myself for what I was about to say… 'Is there anywhere else you can find a few days' work? Until I sort stuff out? Someone who can keep you busy?'

An insect in the pit of my stomach gnawed at me. 'It's only for a few days,' I found myself saying, but I'd had this feeling before: many years ago, a raggedy old stray cat appeared under our shed, a half-bald, flea-ridden, tortoise-shell moggy. I wanted to keep him. As Bern looked at me now, all I could see was that cat sitting on my lap, wrapped in an old towel, my mum driving us to the animal shelter, *it's for the best Mark, he'll be much happier there.* The guilt ate through me as Uncle Bern kept those big helpless eyes fixed on mine. He turned without a word and returned to his friends. He didn't look back and my shame intensified: *it's for the best, he'll be okay, don't cry Mark.*

THE FOLLOWING DAY, I dropped back on to Hamlet's second salon, joining Disco and Fiery Jac who'd made terrific progress. It looked great, too good for somewhere that will never actually ever get used. But we were getting paid, so why complain? They both wanted a blow-by-blow account of the grim discovery, but I didn't have much to tell. Thankfully someone else did, because mid-morning a familiar voice called through from the street door. To my amazement, I found Nick Witham loitering there.

I'd known Nick since we were at school together. He'd always been as big and dopey as a bag of bollocks. He used to look like a toilet brush: long, skinny, mass of black curls. That was a long time ago and age had replaced it with a patchy, balding buzz cut and a belly full of beer. Other than that, he was still the same good-natured idiot.

'Detective Constable Witham,' I said in greeting; oh yeah, he's also police, but other than that he's alright. 'To what do we owe the pleasure.'

'Just passing,' he said. 'Saw the van outside so thought I'd pop in to say hello,' he swept a cursory glance around the shop and pursed his lips in a nod of approval. 'Looks nice.'

'Thanks.' I doubted he wanted to talk architecture. 'What's really up, Nick?'

'Okay, I'm here about the body you found in the pub,' he rubbed the back of his neck, then his chin.

'I'm guessing this isn't an official visit, Nick?'

'No. But I know you too well Mark,' a smirk had appeared, and the fidgeting stopped. 'I know you'll make a nuisance of yourself trying to find stuff out, and just like last year, you'll get in people's way, piss them off and land yourself in trouble. So, to save everyone the anguish I thought I'd give you the heads-up, but this is strictly off the record, okay?'

Nick summarised the events so far: good news, the police had excavated the cellar floor, so that's saved me a job, but bad news, they'd uncovered the body of a woman. Lots of tests to be done but initial assumptions were she'd been dead for at least thirty years, the body was naked, with no personal effects to identify her but thanks to the mummification, the experts estimated she was between seventeen and twenty-one years old. Nick got up to leave, when a thought occurred to me.

'Has there been any news on Danny Kidd's murder yet?'

'I honestly wouldn't know, mate. It's being handled by a different team, nothing to do with us. I can't go asking questions without raising suspicion. Sorry, can't help.'

TEN MINUTES LATER, my phone rang. Hamlet. He was angry. 'You need to get yourself down here right away, I want an explanation as to why the Old Bill's been snooping around my salon.'

Eyes and ears everywhere, nothing happens in the Medway Towns without Hamlet knowing. He's got informers all over the place, more grasses than Kew Gardens.

NICK'S WORDS RESONATED with me during my journey across town to Hamlet. I thought of the young girl dying alone, nothing to identify her, two feet of concrete in the hope she'd never be found. Is her family still out there? Thinking of her? Waiting for a phone call, or a card through the post: *this Christmas might be the one she comes back*. Never moving home. Never taking a holiday. It sounded familiar, far too like my dad's final years, waiting for Adam to return. Adam was still in my thoughts when I pulled up outside Hamlet's other salon. That was a mistake, I should have cleared my head first.

HAMLET WAITED FOR me behind the reception counter. His face didn't move and this time it wasn't the Botox, this time it was pent-up rage that he was struggling to keep under control.

'Took your fucking time, glad to see your time's more valuable than mine. I'll just sit here all day like a dickhead,' he said. He was wrong, I'd sailed through traffic, I defy anyone to have done it quicker, but I knew better than to argue with him in this mood so I left it. 'Now, suppose you tell me why my shop is crawling with filth.'

'It's not, it was only one guy, you know him, Nick Witham, and he's barely police.' As I spoke, I could see the recognition pass across Hamlet's face.

'Him? The one who can't find his arse with both hands,' a flicker of a smile.

I nodded. 'He'd swung by to tell me about the body we found in the Admiral Guthrie.'

'Yeah, I'd heard about that,' Hamlet rose up from his seat and placed both palms flat on the countertop, shoulder-width apart and got comfortable bearing down on his hands, like some old-fashioned genial shopkeeper from a bygone time. 'So, go on then, what about it?'

I shared everything Nick told me with Hamlet, knowing full well he could have gone directly to a dozen different people within that police station, all who were a lot closer to it than me. Whether this was some sort of test, or he just fancied a natter I can't say, but he listened closely and silently until I'd finished.

The edge of Hamlet's mouth turned upwards into a smile, 'So, where's your contract stand on the site being a murder scene? Do you get paid stoppage time?'

'Nobody's said it's murder yet,' I felt obliged to point out, just to shut down his gloating.

'What, she did it herself, did she? Poured a ton of concrete on top of herself then curled up for a nice kip?' Hamlet laughed at his own flippancy. 'Where are you going with that wheelbarrow? Just getting forty winks, mate!'

An unpleasant tingle shook through my neck. I knew my hackles were rising. It was obvious he was trying to bait me for no reason other than his own amusement.

'Here, it's a bit like that old joke…' Hamlet wore a massive grin, he'd thought of something and was so very pleased with himself. I shook my head, but he didn't care. 'This girl walks into the Admiral Guthrie pub with a bag of cement and a shovel, she says: "Pint for me… and one for the road!" Do you get it?'

The smug laugh, the self-satisfied smirk, it had got to me: treating this poor girl like it's a big joke, like the family who've been waiting forever for her are one big joke, like my dad is one big joke, like I'm one big joke…

'Think it's funny? Someone disappearing like that, deliberately hidden, never to be found?'

'Steady on, Marky Mark,' Hamlet slowly fluttered his hands. 'No need to get all lemony. It's only a bit of banter.'

'No, I've had enough of your bullshit. Where is he?'

'Who?'

'You know who. Adam.'

'Ah, touched a nerve, have I? I wondered when you'd bring up your soppy bollocks brother.' Hamlet slumped back in his seat, cupped his hands then kept them pressed together; he looked to be choosing his words carefully. And so he should be.

Adam: three years older than me, Hamlet's driver, fetcher, carrier and general dogsbody. He loved it. He thought being in Hamlet's orbit meant something, that it made you someone important. Then one day, seven years ago, he disappeared. Gone. Without a trace. His car rotted outside my house: the battery dead, the tyres soft and the fuel long since evaporated. My dad got sick, got terminal, died. When he didn't come back for the funeral, that's when I wrote him off for dead. Only he wasn't. I caught sight of him briefly, at a distance, last year. It was him, he was real, he wasn't a hallucination or a ghost. He was there, flesh and blood, in front of me. Then just as quickly as he appeared, he was gone again, vanished back where he came from. All of it thanks to Hamlet's shenanigans unleashing a horde of villains, hooligans and nutters on a manhunt.

'Where is he? Tell me.'

'Whoa, cool your jets, remember who you're talking to.' Hamlet slowly rose to his feet as he spoke, stepping in to close the gap between us.

'Mark, Mark, calm down son,' said a voice close by, its familiarity disarming by being so out of context. Uncle Bern stood beside me in socks, struggling to button his shirt. He dropped his shoes to the floor and slipped into them. 'I thought I heard your voice. No need to shout, son, all friends here.'

Hamlet eased himself back down into his seat, a smug smile emerged. 'I offered you his whereabouts, Marky, remember?'

'You offered me an impossible choice. You knew which way I'd go.'

'I gave you a fair choice.'

'Hardly. You—'

'How's my tan looking?' interrupted Bern. He stretched out his forearms, rolled them over, then back again. 'Coming on nicely, who needs Spain eh?'

Hamlet leaned back in the chair. His posture relaxed. I think Bern had just saved me from myself.

'Have you told him about the body in the cellar yet?' said Bern. Hamlet nodded, Bern continued, 'Thirty years they say she's been down there. Got me thinking, there was a few murders back then, you always remember because murder was something of a rarity back then. I tell you the one I always remember, it was around nineteen eighty or eighty-one. Some young lad got stabbed in Chatham town centre, in… oh what was it called… gah, I forget. Do you know the pub I'm talking about?'

'No idea,' said Hamlet, speaking for both of us. If Uncle Bern wanted an encyclopaedic knowledge of the pubs of the Medway Towns, then he should speak to Disco. I just hoped this story had a point, before Hamlet started getting annoyed again.

'Anyway, some fella got stabbed to death there, it was big news. No one ever got done for it. But everyone suspected it was a sailor in on shore leave.' Bern stood with both hands on the back of his hips, his elbows jutted behind him. He looked like some eccentric academic. 'The Navy got banned from Chatham Town Centre for a long while because of it.'

'So what?' Hamlet had started to get restless. Bern was losing his audience.

'I'm coming to that,' Bern wagged his finger professorially. 'Because they got banned from Chatham, they all came to Gillingham instead, and if your Admiral Guthrie is one of the first out of the gate and if it's offering girls, I can just imagine it would have been the matelots' favourite.'

'And?'

'Well, do you think it has anything to do with the girl we've found in the cellar?'

Now it was my time to get annoyed. 'What? Is a local fairy-tale you can barely remember linked to our girl? And you want a serious answer? Oh do shut up, you silly old fart.'

'It's worth a thought,' said Hamlet to my utter amazement. 'Look, you wanted to find out about that pub, now there's a way that you can.'

'Is there?'

'I've got something for you.' He slid a folded piece of paper across the table at me. 'There are the contact details for the landlord, nineteen seventy-nine to nineteen eighty-four inclusive. I know for a fact the police have traced him and been to see him already, but he's a tough old bastard, he won't have told them anything.'

'So why do you think he'd talk to me then?'

'Because the pub game runs in families, that's why,' said Hamlet. 'His darling beloved daughter now runs a pub with her husband. One of my pubs, in fact. So, if they want to keep on doing that, he'll talk to you, don't worry about that.'

As I looked at the piece of paper in the van afterwards, I couldn't shake the feeling that Hamlet had somehow once again duped me into something; trouble was, I just couldn't see what.

-23-

I RECOGNISED THE address Hamlet had given me right away. I'd done a bit of work there a few years ago for a main contractor who'd picked up a lot of healthcare work: a hospice in Rochester, God's waiting room, express checkout. When I was here last time it was gallows humour and sympathetic smiles, but that was before Dad became ill.

What do you think, Dad? Would you have wanted to have come to a place like this? It looks nice enough, it's clean. There're a few green spaces, plenty of birdsong—you'd have liked that. But it's just the knowing what the place is for, why everyone's there; sort of becomes a factory then, doesn't it?

Look at that woman over there, the younger one helping the older lady in the pink hat get comfortable on that garden bench, she's only my age, but I bet she feels twice that right now. I bet the older lady's her mum judging by how much fuss she's making of the younger one's hair, brushing her fringe out of her eyes. Still trying to take care of her when she's the one that needs it now. The daughter probably woke up this morning, looked in the mirror and thought 'Jeez, is that me?'. Probably took every ounce of effort to choose some nice clothes, do her hair, do her make-up—just to keep up appearances. Not for her though, thoughts of a love-life and looking good… couldn't be further, they've flown to the other side of Neptune and beyond. I bet what she wants to do is curl up in a ball and sob at the cruelty of it, I bet she wants to rip her clothes and shout and bellow and roar at the unfairness of it, I bet she wants to do it all, all at the same time. I know this, because I did. But you can't. Instead you—we—keep up appearance. Don't let them see you cry, don't let them see you panic, don't let them know it affects you. You think your fear is contagious, so you plaster on a smile, talk shit about work you've lost interest in and people you've lost contact with, and pretend everything is alright. Me and her, we're in the same club, Dad. I know exactly what she's going through, and more frighteningly, I know exactly what lies ahead.

A parp from the car behind woke me from my daydream to let me know I was blocking the entrance. With a friendly wave to the rear-view mirror, I rolled slowly towards a visitor's parking bay. The woman and her mother had gone by the time I'd locked the van and walked to the main reception.

'I'm looking for Mr McInally,' I said to the cheerful receptionist, who then relayed my request to a passing nurse in pristine navy-blue medical scrubs. She told me to follow her.

'Morning Brian,' she knocked on the open door and spoke with a pleasant sing-song in her voice. 'You've got another visitor, lucky you,' and with that she was gone, leaving me at the threshold.

The room was large and square, looking out over the front gardens. Every attempt had been made to make it cosy with nice furniture, carpets, photos on the side, shelves with knick-knacks from home. The big hospital bed looked out of place. Then on a closer look other medical paraphernalia began to emerge from their camouflage of normality: the red pull cord, the high-backed chair, the notices on the wall. Once seen they couldn't be unseen. The disguise had slipped. It was what it was: a hospital room for a long-term resident.

Sitting deep in the high-backed chair was Brian McInally. He looked like a big man deflated. I could imagine him heavyset and imposing, a former rottweiler of a man. Now, no more the tough guy; his skin hung from him in folds and jowls as though he'd sprung a leak. A yellow rubber facemask was in his lap, presumably within easy reach if needed. From it, a clear plastic hose snaked and coiled away to the floor then slithered out of sight behind the chair. A dark little joke played out in my head. I imagined him sucking on that facemask, refilling to his original size and popping up ready for fun like one of Del Boy's sex dolls. I forced back the twitch of a smile and entered the room.

'So, you're Hamlet's man, are you?' McInally's distaste for Hamlet was obvious from the acid in his tone. 'Come to interrogate me about a pub I worked at thirty, almost forty years ago. Worked in pubs all me life. Know how many I ran? Twelve. How's anyone expected to remember what happened one night in one of them that long ago? At my age they all start to blur into each other, happens when you get old, things seem distant.'

I didn't bother introducing myself, he already knew why I was there and didn't care who I was, so with niceties skipped by mutual agreement I launched straight into it: 'Surely if you'd buried a dead body, you'd remember where?'

'Course I'd fucking remember it. And I don't, so I can't help you.' McInally heaved a dry retching cough, then reached for a nearby cardboard bowl to spit out thick dark mucus. 'I've already told the police everything I know—which is nothing. Must have happened before my time.'

'Mr Hamlet thought you could help me, he—'

'*Mister* Hamlet, is it? Get you with your arse kissing. He's a pig, a fucking pig. My Donna's been good for him. Her pub, it's the highest barrelage pub he's got, did you know that?' He expected a response, he was that kind of man. I quietly mouthed I didn't to get him talking again. 'That's all down to Donna, it was a shithole when she took it on. And this is how he repays her, with threats. Man's a fucking pig.' McInally spat again, as if to emphasise his point. 'Don't look at me like that, I don't care if he hears me, what's he going to do? I'm dead before Christmas, anyway.'

I thought about muttering concerned pleasantries, but he didn't deserve my sympathy. He was a hard man with a hard attitude. It was easy to picture him in his pomp: six-foot tall and eighteen stone, keeping the peace in his pubs by taking the anti-social outside and cracking a few skulls. Afraid of no one, plain-speaking to the point of obnoxious, he would have bullied and battered his way through life. Then one day he'd find himself out of breath shifting a few crates, *just me age catching up with me*, then there'd be the cough that couldn't be shaken off, *colds nowadays seem to hang around forever don't they*, but the breathlessness and the cough wouldn't go away, *nothing to worry about I'm fine*, by the time the cough brought up blood he may have been persuaded to see a doctor, but by then the race was lost. The doctor would illuminate black and white x-rays then point to the lumpy little grey blob. All the hoodlums and hardmen he'd faced down over the years meant nothing, he'd been beaten by a little grey blob: *it looks like horseradish*—a clumsy punter's wayward splash of horseradish to wipe off the table top during Sunday service. But as the horseradish took over, his size and his stature diminished, leaving just his belligerence to echo around his empty chest. He didn't deserve my sympathy.

'Mr…' I paused, but then decided *fuck you*, 'Mr Hamlet tells me the pub had all sorts going on—stolen goods and contraband out the dockyard, hookers, the lot. Did you tell the police that?'

McInally stared straight at me for a moment before speaking, 'Think you fucking know it all, don't you? So, what do you want from me?'

'I'll take that as a yes, it's true, in that case,' I said. 'So, who ran it?'

'I did,' another spit, another point emphasised.

'No. Who really ran it. We're talking smuggled goods and prostitution; whose pub was it? Hamlet said it was the Flint family out of South East London.'

'Well, there you go, see, you don't need me at all.'

'And he says the pub had a pet copper,'

McInally rolled his eyes. He was losing patience. 'There was a few over the years, they'd like a late drink, have their handouts if anything nice came through the docks or a freebie upstairs with the girls. But yeah, there was one. He came as a fitted fixture with the pub when I took it over. Desk Sergeant. He made sure all attention was diverted from us, and we were left to manage things our own way. Name of Hutton. Sergeant Bob Hutton.'

'Hutton?' I knew a policeman by that name. 'Are you sure about that?'

McInally rolled his eyes again, 'Course I am. Hutton. Miserable bastard he was, too. Never saw him smile once.'

McInally pointed to a low-level bookcase behind me. I didn't react, so he pointed more vigorously. Eventually I relented, and stepped towards it. He guided me to a photograph album: a thin black faux leather volume with, I'd guess, two dozen flip over plastic sleeves. I handed it to him and he riffled through the sleeves, then with about a third of them flipped he gripped both edges of the album and turned it towards me.

'Nineteen eighty-three,' he said, pointing at the photo. It was packed full of people, taken in the dark using a cheap pocket camera with a crappy built-in flash. They were mostly fuzzy round the edges, their skin an unnatural shade of pink, and their eyes glowed red.

'What is it, a party?'

'No. Just a late drink for regulars. Lock in.' McInally pointed to a face more or less centre of the snap. A balding middle-aged man, not unlike Phil Collins, having the time of his life as two young women, teenagers probably, planted big red lipstick kisses on either side of his face. 'That's him, with the girls, Hutton.'

'He looks happy enough there.'

'Oh, well there you go then, he smiled… once.'

I reached for the album, but it was clear he didn't want to let go of it, forcing me to lean in closer to him. The back of my throat caught his powerful fragrance of antiseptic and piss. The closer I got to the photo, the more indistinct it became due to the poor focus, but this man, Hutton, front and centre remained the sharpest in the image. I didn't recognise him. My eyes passed across the partygoers' faces until they reached two young men on the side. They stood out as they were the only people staring directly at the camera. Slightly in shadow, slightly blurred, demonic red eyes but they interested me: one short, with long dark complicated hair, the other taller with thick ginger curls and a busted nose, I pressed my fingertip against them and asked, 'Who are they?'

McInally peered over the top of the album, looking at it upside down. 'No idea,' but he could tell I wasn't buying that as an answer. He turned the book around to himself, 'Them? The one trying to look like Spandau Ballet, he was the doorman for a while, didn't stay long, can't remember his name.'

'And the other one?'

'Carrot top? No idea. Probably his mate trying to blag a late drink, who knows,' replied McInally, closing the book with a snap.

'Speaking of redheads, do you know Clive Gordon? People called him Ginger. He was your pot man?'

McInally nodded and coughed a laugh that rattled inside him, 'Ginger? He was as useless as the day was long. Always hanging around but never doing much, more of a mascot than a pot man. Why?'

'No reason. And which one's the dead girl? Got a photo of her?'

'What? Who do you think you're talking to, I ought to kick your arse—' McInally pushed himself upright using the arms of his chair as support. I don't know why, but I didn't believe his explanations of the two herberts in the photo and Ginger had annoyed me, so I thought I'd provoke him to see what kind of response I'd get. I didn't expect anything quite so ferocious as this. McInally was shouting and swearing and coughing. He got to his feet but clattered into things. The spit-bowl of mucus fell tumbling to the ground to congeal on the carpet.

'Don't think I'm not capable of it…' McInally flailed his arms and struck out with his feet, but before he could reach me the same nurse who'd shown me in had flown through the doorway, followed by a male attendant.

'Brian, calm down, Brian,' she said in a soothing voice and took his hands in hers. She delicately sat him back in his seat and turned her head towards me, 'I think perhaps you should leave now.' No happy sing-song lilt for me.

I didn't need telling twice. The only problem was, in my hurry to get out, and with no one to direct me, I ended up taking the corridor the wrong way, coming out at the far end of the building. I didn't fancy going back inside, so I followed the footpath round the front perimeter of the building back to the car park.

Walking along, my inherent sense of nosiness took over. I couldn't help glancing in every window I passed. At a window about halfway along the path, I recognised the room I'd just been ejected from. I stopped. I stood dead still and hoped I'd be out of sight. I watched the male attendant return the photo album to the bookcase, then with a wave to McInally, he left the room and pulled the door closed behind him. McInally, satisfied the room was empty, reached to the cabinet beside his chair and pulled out a phone. I couldn't hear what he was saying through the closed window, but from his red face and fingers jabbing in time with every word he spoke, I got the impression it wasn't a friendly call.

I ducked down below the window ledge and scuttled past. I found the visitors' car park and got in the van, pulling Dad's address book from out of the door pocket. I dialled Ginger's number; it rang and rang without reply, then voicemail. I cut the call and tried again; the same: bloody hell Ginger, you're meant to be agoraphobic, where the bloody hell are you? It went to voicemail again and this time I left a message, 'Ginger, it's Mark Poynter, I'd like to talk to you about the Admiral Guthrie, I think you can help me. Can you call me back please?' then joined the traffic on City Way heading back towards town.

AS I WAITED to turn right at Jackson's Field with Rochester behind me, a crack of thunder exploded overhead. The air was charged and the hairs on my arms tingled with static, then the rain began to fall. At first it came in fat individual drops, leaving circles as big as half-crowns on my windscreen. The spots rapidly spread to full coverage as the rainfall increased. By the time I'd reached my destination, it had become torrential. My wipers struggled to lift. They flicked away the water, only for it to be replaced by even more as soon as the blade rose again.

It was on a whim I'd ended up at this second-hand car dealership. I was passing, I saw it, I decided to come in: it was as simple as that. It was a nice one, a second-tier dealer: the sort just below the main dealers in terms of newness; cars start at three years old, none older than six. It looked very smart with a lot of money sunk into the stock on the forecourt. Not a soul to be seen, any browsers kept away by the rain. I trundled the van across the yard almost all the way up to the door of the sales office and then sprinted the remaining short distance to get inside. Even still, my hair was stuck to my face and an icy chill rolled down my spine thanks to a wayward bead of rainwater that had crept into my collar.

'I'm looking for Phil Hopkins,' I said to a tall middle-aged man using a laptop. It was connected to a screen on an adjustable chrome arm, on an otherwise empty desk. He looked up and smiled at me. His hair was fast retreating back from his forehead, and I couldn't help noticing it was more brown than grey, whereas his neatly trimmed beard was more grey than brown—go figure.

'That's me,' he stood, buttoned his suit jacket and extended his hand to shake all in one fluid movement in that way salesman seem to do effortlessly. I looked around and saw he was the only person there; mid-week must be quiet in the motor trade if it's just the guv'nor on his own. 'Are you the gentleman that phoned about the Audi?' he asked.

He seemed unfazed when I said I wasn't, the professional salesman simply looked for the next opportunity. 'Do you have anything in mind? We've plenty to choose from, as you can see, and our stock's changing all the time. Anything you'd like to look at, Mr…?'

'No thanks,' I replied. 'And it's Poynter. Mark Poynter.'

'Oh,' he looked me up and down with suspicion, glancing over my shoulder at the van outside then back to me again. The pound signs fell away from his eyes. 'I'm sorry, I don't have time for sales pitches, you'd need to make an appointment, but I can tell you now, I've already got a contractor who takes care of my facilities and I'm very happy with them.'

'The Admiral Guthrie.'

'The…? I'm sorry, I don't know what you're talking about,' Hopkins wandered back to his desk and sat. I stood for a moment in silence, I sensed his awkwardness and let it fester. He tapped his keyboard to wake the screen and tried to look busy.

'The Admiral Guthrie,' I repeated. 'You had it up for auction. You sold it to Danny Kidd, the footballer.'

He didn't break his staring gaze from his screen, but I'm sure I saw a reaction, just the faintest of twitches flickered across his cheek, I'd scored a direct hit, he knew exactly what I was talking about. He exhaled a long breath, rubbed his nose, then looked back towards me. 'Yes. I sold it. And now it's gone. It's nothing to do with me anymore.'

I gave up waiting to be invited and plonked myself down in a customer seat on the opposite side of the desk. A soft, deep cradle of a chair fashionably designed in soft leather and chrome which told me Hopkins liked to get his customers relaxed before making the deal. The waft of fresh coffee added to the customer's comfort and my senses traced it back to its source: a fancy stainless-steel coffee maker and a glass jar of big golden cookies against the wall. He hadn't offered me a seat but, I admit, I hoped he'd offer me a coffee. Instead, he opened a spreadsheet of figures on his screen and pretended to study it, hoping I'd take the hint and go away. I needed to give him something to earn a little trust and make him meet me halfway. 'Look. I've been working on the Admiral Guthrie for Danny Kidd, it's been nothing but trouble, it's like the building's cursed.'

'Cursed,' he muttered as though trying the word on for size. He decided it fitted… 'Cursed. That's about right.'

'What made you sell it? It should have been a nice little conversion job, easy to do, tidy profit in it?'

Hopkins still hadn't looked at me again. 'I just didn't have the time,' he said to his screen.

'But you had time to get a full detailed design? And go through the full planning approval process? And judging by the stock out there on the forecourt, you can't have any problem getting finance?'

He ignored me and scratched his beard as if his spreadsheet required deep thought. I needed a reaction, 'Did you know about the dead girl buried in the cellar? Is that why you sold it?'

Showing amazing resolve that I know I couldn't have managed, still he ignored me. He pecked away at his keyboard. I realised it was time to throw in the hand-grenade question, 'Do you know a man called Donaldson? Scottish?'

Now he looked at me. Straight at me. An expression of fear and revulsion washed across his face. An inward gulp suggested he was holding back the urge to vomit.

'There's a man called Donaldson who's been making his presence known ever since I got involved with that pub, do you know him?' I said, and Hopkins gave a slow, gentle nod that I took to be confirmation. 'Tell me about it then.'

Hopkins glanced down at the table-top as if composing his thoughts, then exhaled through his nose. 'I bought the Admiral Guthrie six years ago. I'd done a few property developments in the past, done all right out of them, thought this'd be the same. If only I'd known.'

I shuffled in the comfy chair to lean forwards, rest my elbows on the edge of the desk. Hopkins in a subconscious reaction sat back in his own seat and steepled his fingertips across his stomach.

'A friend of mine worked for the brewery, so I got it for a good price before it went on the open market. It didn't take long before I got a visit from Donaldson offering to buy it off me, but that just convinced me it was a money maker.'

'Danny Kidd had the same thought,' I muttered. Hopkins closed his eyes and made a short, involuntary nod: a reflex response. No doubt he'd heard the news same as everyone else and was thanking his guardian angels for his near miss.

Hopkins held the silence for a couple of seconds, then: 'You get all sorts of threats and big mouths in this trade, you just learn to deal with them, so I ignored him. I got a scheme drawn up and it sailed through Planning, not a single query. But I couldn't get a quote from anyone. They'd all sound eager. They all came down to meet me there. But then they'd suddenly say they're too busy, those that bothered to respond, anyway.'

This all sounded startlingly familiar, I could see Donaldson' fingerprints all over it. 'So, what did you do?'

'I'd spent too much money on it to jack it in. This was going to be me and my wife's pension, couldn't just leave it,' his fingers remained steepled, but his thumbs had begun pawing at his tie, some sort of comforting gesture, I guessed, and waited for him continue. Sure enough, 'I'd try and revive it every six months or so. I'd meet someone new down there, they'd sound keen, then a day or two later they'd call and pull out. Every time.'

'And did you see Donaldson again?'

'Oh yeah. He'd come in here quite often, let me know he was around. Let me know he was behind the latest builder letting me down. But I still can't work out how he knew?'

'Knew what?'

'That I'd met with someone. I began doing it at different times, early mornings, evenings, summer, winter; I'd get firms from all over the county, South London, Essex; didn't matter, he always knew. It was as though he was always watching me.'

'Or the pub,' I added as a glimmer of a thought emerged.

'Maybe,' shrugged Hopkins, 'but out of sheer bloody-mindedness I kept on with it.'

He looked up at me in a way that made me think he was seeking my approval, and I found myself giving an appreciative nod to reassure him I was a friendly.

'But one day, it'd been a bad day generally, one thing and another, anyway he turns up here out of the blue again and tries his usual stuff. But as I say, it's been a bad day, I'm not in the mood, I start shouting back and then I shove him out the door. He doesn't like that.'

'I'll bet,' I leaned closer. 'What happened?'

'He came back about an hour later, with two goons. This is it, I thought, I'm going to get my head caved in. I told my salesman to get inside the back office,' with a flap of the hand he indicated a flush door, "staff only", at the rear of the room, 'and if anything violent happened to get straight on the phone to the police.'

'And did it?'

Hopkins gave a short, dry laugh full of contempt and frustration. 'Far from it. Donaldson sat right where you are now. He has this way of being polite yet threatening at the same time.'

I knew exactly what he meant, recalling the soft voice and the respectful bows, it made me think of a snake: quiet and serene, unmoving but laden with threat. My attention got pulled back into the here and now by Hopkins sobbing. 'He threatened my kids, man. He had photos. Put them on the table in front of me, here. Of my girls, at school, in the playground. He knew them, how to get to them.'

I could see that would have been a killer blow. 'So that's when you gave it up?'

'Yes. I promised him I'd give up any ideas to develop the pub. He seemed happy with that, and I never saw him again after. I waited a couple of years to let the planning approval lapse. I figured it'd take whoever bought it at least three or four months to reapply and go through the planning process all over again, and by then I'd be far enough away from it to make it someone else's problem. I stuck it in the auction. That was a bloody mistake.'

'Why? You offloaded it easily enough.'

'That's what I thought,' replied Hopkins, 'I got an offer straight away. It covered everything I was owed out of it and by then I was more than happy to walk away breaking even. And then the footballer wanted it and offered over the top for it. Better than that, he'd take it off my hands in forty-eight hours. Of course I accepted, I jumped at it.'

There was a 'but' coming, I was certain about that, and sure enough…

'Donaldson suddenly appeared again. He wasn't happy that I'd sold it to Danny Kidd, said I should have stuck with the first offer.'

'He was behind the first offer?'

'So it seems, but I didn't know that, I'd not seen hide nor hair of him for years. How was I to know? I was just given a company name, it didn't mean anything.'

'What was it?'

'Yellowbox Holdings Limited. I mean, seriously, how was I meant to know?'

I shrugged and shook my head as a sign of support. He was right, Yellowbox: as a name it meant nothing, but that was probably the intention.

'I told him he was too late, that the sale had gone through. He wasn't happy about it.'

'No?'

'Next morning, half the cars out there had their windows smashed. You don't win a prize for working out who was behind that.'

'No, I guess not,' I replied sympathetically. There wasn't any more to be learned here, and I got up to leave. I thanked him for his time, but got no response. He seemed lost in his own thoughts of what might have been, and I don't think he heard me.

-24-

THERE SEEMED TO be a party going on in my house. I pushed open the door and struggled to kick off my boots, confused by the sound of claps and cheers. Brain-freeze took over. Was it Perry's birthday? I edged into the living room, rapidly trying to concoct a plausible excuse, where I was met by a very excited looking Stuart and Perry.

'Isn't it great news?' asked Perry, only to realise from my befuddlement that I had absolutely no idea what was going on.

'Look,' said Stuart gesturing towards the muted TV. 'Look.' A man stood outside Downing Street mouthing silently about something important and boring, but then I noticed the rolling ribbon of text across the bottom of the screen… *'Grime hip-hop star Muzzkett arrested.'*

'See?' asked Perry, only to be interrupted by her phone ringing. She looked at the caller ID then walked into the kitchen to answer it.

In the meantime, the images on the screen had moved on to pictures of the Royal family doing something overseas. Stuart reached for the remote and increased the volume. He must have watched the rolling cycle of news several times over to know what was next, because thirty seconds later the newsreader began telling me what we were all waiting for:

'MOBO award winning Grime hip hop star Muzzkett has been arrested by police investigating the arson attack that occurred at footballer Danny Kidd's house just days before the former Premier League star was brutally murdered. Police have already detained a twenty-two-year-old who confessed to the crime on social media. The man describes himself as "one of Muzzkett's loyal army and a diehard Arsenal supporter" leading him to declare Danny Kidd as "the enemy". A police spokesperson said they were investigating whether Muzzkett

could be guilty of incitement through the use of social media. The police have yet to confirm whether the arson attack and Mr Kidd's murder are linked.'

The television cut away to a smarmy looking lawyer waffling about the charges being preposterous. He fully expected his client to be released within hours. It then returned to the studio where two middle-aged men were introduced: one an overweight sports journalist who looked as if he'd be out of breath blinking too much, and the other a fifty-year-old music journalist trying too hard to be current, with a teenage boy's haircut and badges on his lapel. When they started spouting their rent-a-gob opinions on Danny and Muzzkett, I switched the television off.

'Surely that's it,' Stuart couldn't keep the excitement out of his voice. 'I'm in the clear! This nutcase torched the garage when Danny was in the gym upstairs. Surely the police will be able prove when that failed, he went back a few days later to finish him off properly.'

The mention of the fire made me shudder. I'd managed to push it out of my mind all week, but now the dry choking stench of smoke filled my mouth again. I took a seat and inhaled deeply and slowly to clear my head and open my lungs. As my thoughts cleared, I realised Stuart was probably right and the party atmosphere when I arrived made sense.

'I can go home.'

'I wouldn't be so sure about that' said the re-emerging Perry, her phone held loosely to her ear. 'This is Rachel here…'

'Who's Rachel?' asked Stuart.

'My name is Rachel Ridder…' Perry had switched to speaker-phone and laid it on the coffee table in front of us, '…I'm an investigative journalist—'

'You! I remember you,' Stuart's mood had snapped from relief to anger in record quick time. The reality of the moment struck him. He looked at us like traitors, 'What…'

'You need to listen to her Stuart.' Perry had adopted her kind and sympathetic caregiving voice; she squatted in front of him and placed her hands on his. 'Please, just listen to what she says, it's very important that you do.'

Stuart looked at me with wide confused eyes, I gave a nod of agreement which he accepted with a mumbled 'Okay.'

'Thank you,' said Rachel's disembodied voice from the table. 'I'd be very happy to talk you through my interest in your brother at another time Stuart, but for now it's your safety I'm concerned about. I've been monitoring the social media feeds ever since the news of Muzzkett's arrest broke earlier today, do you have access to it?'

Perry had activated her laptop whilst Rachel was speaking, she twisted the screen towards us. 'Go ahead Rachel.'

'There's been significant online traffic all day, messages along the lines of *Muzzkett is innocent, Kidd's family know it.* And *No charges will be pressed.*'

I looked across and saw several similar messages.

'This is a popular tactic on social media nowadays, they call it a dogpile because it encourages all and sundry to join in, but it's basically witness intimidation. Once it begins to gather momentum online it could very possibly spill into the real world. If you've a safe place to stay, I'd stay there if I were you, just until this has blown over.'

Stuart's happy demeanour went the way of a landslide, I could actually see it roll away to be backfilled by fear and doubt. Perry picked the phone back up off the table and took it into the kitchen to finish the conversation, leaving just Stuart and myself in the room.

'Do you think she's right?' he asked, between bites on his fingernails.

'She seems to know what she's talking about,' I replied. 'It wouldn't hurt being a little cautious I suppose. Plus, I guess this arrest will reignite the press interest, and do you want them all camped out on your doorstep again?'

He murmured something I took to be a reluctant agreement, then turned to face the black surface of the dormant TV. Trying to make conversation, I asked if he knew when we could get back to work, but he muttered about probate then shut down again. I wasn't in the mood to play babysitter, so I went to find Perry.

PERRY WAS FINISHING up the call with Rachel Ridder when a thought occurred to me. I gestured to Perry that I'd like to speak to Rachel and she handed the phone across.

'Rachel, hi, it's Mark,' I gibbered, trying to get my thoughts in order. These were very long straws indeed that I was clutching for, but I managed to clarify my thinking and got to the point. 'Can you look into something for me?' I told her about the girl's remains we'd found in the excavations. 'What with you having access to newspaper archives and that, I was wondering whether there was anything from about thirty years ago featuring a man called Donaldson, or a policeman called Bob Hutton?' and then I remembered Uncle Bern's old urban myth, 'And maybe a stabbing involving a sailor, nineteen eighty-ish?'

I heard the soft, rapid clicking of a keyboard in the background that I took to be her noting everything down and found myself grateful that she was taking me seriously. Another niggling question surfaced. 'While you're at it, do you think you could find anything about a firm called Yellowbox Holdings Limited please?'

'I can take a quick look, but what is it you're hoping to find?'

What was I hoping to find? I honestly had no idea, whatever it was it wasn't any of my business, but something stank, and for reasons that were nothing to do with me, I was out of work and losing money again, so maybe it'd be useful to get an idea of what was going on before I ended up in too deep. I needed to finish my homework.

I FELT GUILTY about Bern, it'd been scratching away at me all day long like a restless cat with a chair leg. I've brought people on and I've let them go again as the workload swells and falls like the tide, it's the nature of this business, but I'd never felt bad about it before.

Why? He was a moaning old malingerer. It's not as if he added any value, in fact he probably cost more to employ than he ever earned for me. And it certainly wasn't for his company or his contacts.

He was family.

That's why. Plain and simple. He was blood. And the one thing I'm supposed to do is take care of my own. That's why I work the long hours. That's why I work weekends. That's why I haven't taken a holiday since I don't know when. Because my job is to take care of me and mine.

And I failed.

'HI, HOW'S IT going?' I hoped my words spoke breezy and conversational.

'Fine. I suppose,' Bern's words spoke betrayed and defensive.

'What are you up to? Keeping busy?'

'Yes.' A one-word answer. It had taken three calls before he decided to pick up and now it was clear he was going to make me work hard for it. I paused, letting him come to me, I waited, and waited, until, 'I've got a few days with Alfie Rubbers.'

I stifled a groan. Of all the people to get in with, he couldn't have picked anyone worse. Let's be clear, Rubhaus Home Improvements wasn't your rogue trader you'd see on TV getting chased down the road by an angry camera crew, but he'd help them out when they were busy. He wasn't cheap, but he was extremely nasty, the sort to scare old widows out of their life savings just to sweep their path. He cuts so many corners on a job, all you're left with is confetti. Strange name, Rubhaus. He'd said his grandfather came to Britain from Austria during the War; I always suspected it was to escape the Nuremberg Trials.

Bern interpreted my silence as disapproval. 'At least he appreciates me, doesn't boot me into touch at the first opportunity.'

'You be careful with him Bern, he's trouble.'

'Yeah, yeah, yeah,' murmured Bern, then a dead tone. He'd cut me off.

-25-

THE NEXT MORNING, I sat idly waiting for the traffic lights to change. For some reason I can't remember, Perry and I had woken up to another stupid squabble and being the grown-up, I'd pulled my boots on and stormed off to work, forgetting I didn't have any to go to. My empty stomach gave a harsh growl to match my bad mood.

All my eggs had been in the Kidd basket, and now with the pub sealed up as a crime scene and the properties awaiting probate, my luck was well and truly scrambled. I reached for the phone realising it was time to eat shit…

'Mr Unwin,' I said in my most polite tones, 'I hope you're keeping well—'

'What do you want?'

'I appreciate you're busy, but if you've five minutes I'd like to speak to you about that job.'

'Would you now? Too bad, you're too late.'

'But we only spoke two days ago. You couldn't have placed it already? Just send me the details and I'll get the prices back to you straight away, I'll make it my top priority.'

'No.'

'But… I thought Fielder's wanted me? Me in particular? What's happened?'

'You thought wrong. You're off the list. Don't need you anymore.'

'But…'

'Look, I'm very busy, there's nothing more to say, goodbye.'

The drone of a dead connection resonated through the van.

Bastard!

BORED. FED UP. Hungry. I took a seat in the corner of Dave the Manc's café and picked up a discarded newspaper to flick through while I waited for my order. The front-page headlines told me Muzzkett had been released without charge almost immediately. His smug lawyer gave snappy soundbites about it being a good result for the protection of free speech. I couldn't be bothered to read any further, so I folded it and flung it on the neighbouring table.

Speaking of free speech, five noisy fellas hunkered round a table in the opposite corner; I didn't recognise any of them. Otherwise there was no one else in and that suited me. I wanted to be alone. All I've tried to do is earn a living, make a few quid, keep myself afloat and through no fault of my own I've failed, again.

A soggy sausage and a grilled tomato was shoved in front of me. Comfort food, ideal for when you're feeling sorry for yourself. I intended savouring every last morsel. As I unwrapped the cutlery from the napkin wrapper, my phone rang: balls! Bern's name and photo displayed on the screen. I laid the phone face down on the table and ignored it, I could do without his nonsense this morning. I let it ring off. The breakfast was good, the toast just the right stiffness, the tea just the right brownness, but only a few minutes later the phone rang again. Bern—again. Ignored—again.

With a second round of toast ordered, I reached for the newspaper and scanned it with as little interest as before. The phone rang again. Bern—again. For God's sake Bern, leave me alone, I'm not in the mood today. It rang off.

The door opened, but only the slenderest slants of sunlight penetrated, eclipsed by the massive bulk of the Tombliboos. Seated on the other side of the cabin, I felt it rock and sway with a sickening surge as they both stepped inside, all three hundred kilograms of them, as big, dark and solid as bulls, muscles on top of their muscles. They saw me and nodded, I nodded back. One gave the other a nudge, a hint to go to the counter, then he headed my way. Oh joy, looks like I'm getting a serving of conversation I didn't order.

He pulled out the chair opposite and sat down without asking. His massive forearms dropped on the table-top like felled trees, circular ripples repeated across the surface of my mug: 'Alright Mark.'

'Yeah, all good, how you doing?' I had no idea which one he was, so I deliberately avoided using any names.

'Fine mate, fine,' and as he spoke, his brother slid a can of fizzy energy drink in front of him. 'Cheers, Wes,' he said to the giant sibling returning to the counter. By the powers of deduction, I took it that I was facing George.

'We heard about the pub, the surprise in the cellar and all that,' said George, ripping open the energy drink. A revolting smell of chemicals crawled up my nose and made me blink.

'Yeah, nasty business, and it's bolloxed me right up. The job's shut down and I've nowhere else to go.' I tried to speak and breathe through my mouth at the same time. 'You haven't got a couple of days work for a sparkie have you?' I added in jest, except it wasn't.

'Sorry mate,' he took a long gulp of the energy filth; when he spoke again, his tongue was coated green. I couldn't concentrate on anything else—it was like watching a newt popping in and out of its hole. His brother sat beside him, holding two plates. They were brimmed high with fried delights, and the sight of them shook me from the hypnotic newt's trance.

'Say that again?' I asked. I'd not been listening to him, but an alarm in the back of my head chimed to tell me I should have been.

By now he was eyes down, elbows out, ploughing through greasy bacon and slippery mushrooms. He looked up, sucked his fork clean, and started to speak: 'I said we'll be in the same boat as you in a couple of weeks. We'd been turning work away because of the big Fielder job, but they went and pulled it yesterday.'

'What, cancelled the development?'

'No, that's still going ahead. They told us they've changed their minds and are now going to go out to tender to get the best price.'

'You didn't tender for it in the first place?'

George by now was snout down again and shovelling, but they seemed to work as a tag team because Wesley looked up and spoke: 'No. In fact, we'd never done anything for Fielder Homes before, ever. We just got a call one day to say we'd been recommended, we were sent the paperwork with all the rates, good rates too, and that was that, given a start date and told to get ready for it.'

'No warning they were about to change their minds?'

'No, why?'

'Same thing happened to me, sort of. They were throwing work at me, refused to take no for an answer, but then when I wanted to talk with them about it, I was given the big eff ewe.'

'Funny firm,' said George.

'Funny firm,' agreed Wesley.

'Yeah, funny,' I chorused, but something gnawed away at me. 'When did they come to you, can you remember? What were you doing at the time?'

George blew out his cheeks as he considered the question, 'I don't know, it was about a month, six weeks ago probably, Wes?'

His brother took another gulp from his can, *ignore the newt, ignore the newt*, 'No. I tell you when it was, it was around the time we were looking at the Guthrie. Remember, we'd been to see it and were at home trying to work up the prices when we got the call.'

'That's right,' George confirmed. Wesley, clearly pleased with himself, dove head first into the remains of his meal with great gusto. 'Why'd you ask?'

'Just curious, that's all,' I replied getting to my feet. 'See you around, and bear me in mind if anything comes up.'

I SLID BACK behind the wheel of the van with the thought that this whole thing seemed very curious. My phone rang: Perry. I jabbed the decline button and realised my thoughts had seen the interruption as their chance to beat a swift retreat. Muttering swears, I leapt for them, grasping at them and pinned them down: the Tombliboos get the call shortly after looking at the Admiral Guthrie, so do I. The phone beeped, another interruption, my thoughts skittered off in all directions like woken butterflies. Perry had left a voicemail. I ignored it. I swung wildly to bring down my thoughts before they headed too far out of reach: today we've both been shunned with the same shitty stick treatment. Another chime, this time telling me a text message had arrived. Would this bloody phone not give me a second's peace? I retraced the footsteps in my head to glimpse the path I'd been following, it had become faint, but I managed to find it: strange way to do business, I thought, another excuse I can chalk up for not liking residential developers. Another chime, another text message, for God's sake. I had hoped to lay my thoughts out for quiet consideration: creating a map in which I could move from point to point to point, but these interruptions carpet bombed the landscape beyond recognition. I gave up and opened the text message: *'Stop ignoring me. You must call me at once. Uncle Bern had an accident. Heading to hospital. Call me. P.'*

Oh balls!

IT TOOK ABOUT fifteen minutes for me to reach Medway Hospital, then nearly the same again to find somewhere to park. Even though they'd bolted together a flat-pack multi-storey, there still weren't enough spaces, there never will be. In the end, I parked round the back by the Estates Office in the hope that it'd look like I was working there. Perry was at the main entrance to meet me; children's paintings of rainbows still decorated the foyer.

'They say they tried calling you with his phone because you were first in his list of emergency contacts, but when they couldn't reach you, they called me,' said Perry, as she walked quickly down long corridors. I struggled a little to keep pace with her. This was her domain; I could only follow. She pulled open a heavy-looking door. Unlike every other door around, this one had no signage. 'Staff shortcut,' she said. I followed her through and down a flight of stairs.

We came out in a drab empty space, below ground, no windows: claustrophobic and oppressive. A prickly heat clung to my skin, and the yellowy lights gave everything a sallow wash.

Perry could see my uncertainty about my surroundings: 'This is the recovery area. He's in theatre at the moment, when he's done they'll bring him out here for a little while until they can find a ward for him,' she explained. 'Normally we make relatives wait out in the casualty waiting rooms, but, well, this is more private. There's not many perks to this job, so I'm going to use them when I can.'

She guided me towards a row of brown hard plastic chairs and I obediently sat myself down, then she took herself to the nurses' station at the end of the area.

I looked around me, there was nothing here: no posters, no magazines to read, not even a clock on the wall; only lengths of high-level plastic track for the bunched-up floor-to-ceiling curtains there to be drawn as and when the big rolling beds get wheeled in after surgery.

Perry re-emerged a few minutes later and handed me a pale tea in a chunky mug, 'Here, drink this,' she said. 'The milk came out a bit too quick, I'm afraid, but at least it's real tea. Better than the vending machine slop.'

'Thanks,' I muttered, looking around for somewhere to put it down, only to find nothing suitable. I gently placed it on the floor between my feet.

'I've just made a couple of calls,' Perry began. 'I'm told he fell from height, off a ladder. He's in surgery right now. Mrs Abadiano is one of the best, so he's in good hands.'

A wave of warmth rushed over me as I looked at this woman I loved: so strong, so caring. I remembered how petty I'd been leaving the house, then ignoring the phone calls. A shiver of revulsion slicked over me. I've never been good at accepting compliments. I've always been embarrassed hearing any kind of praise. But I've never ever felt as uncomfortable as I did right then, receiving such kindness after being a total and utter selfish arse. I didn't deserve it. I wasn't a good person. I felt like a fraud. A phoney.

'From what I understand, he was up high and the ladder slipped. He banged his head on the road, and one arm got pinned under the ladder in the fall. They need to deal with any damage to his arm from the impact, but also they're being very wary of any trauma or bleeding to the brain.'

Bloody Alfie Rubbers. I warned Bern: slapdash and unsafe, that's bloody Alfie Rubbers. I bet the ladder wasn't tied, I bet no one was holding it. I could kill him, I could bloody strangle him.

Perry had her arm around my shoulder. The closeness: I wanted to cry. 'He's in the best place, Mark. We'll take care of him.'

The use of 'we' caught my attention, not 'they'. Who was 'we'? Was she talking on behalf of the hospital, or was 'we' Mark and Perry in it together? It didn't matter, either way it made me more aware I was such a phoney. I didn't deserve this woman.

'Are you meant to be here?' I asked. 'Won't you be missed? Are you meant to be somewhere?'

'No, it's fine,' she took my hand with a gentle squeeze. 'As soon as I told them he's family, they told me to take the shift off to be with him.'

Family. The F-word. I cried. She held me close. I apologised. She held me closer.

-26-

MY BACK HURT like a bitch. I stretched up. I pressed myself against the stiff plastic chair. I extended my arms as far as they could reach over my head. Anything to tease out those deep gnarly knots, but nothing worked.

Perry placed a hand on my knee, 'You okay?'

'Fine,' I stood and rolled my hips, chasing out the numbness. A glance at my watch told me two hours had passed, still no news.

'It won't be much longer, but you can go if you want, I'm happy to wait here, I'll call you as soon as anything happens,' said Perry, and I genuinely believed she meant it. I sat back down and failed abysmally to get comfortable in the seat. Perry took my hand and held it in her lap, I think to calm me down.

'I hate this place,' I said to break the silence.

'We can go back to the public waiting area if you like. I just thought you'd prefer the privacy of being in here.'

'No. I hate this place. Here. Medway bloody Hospital. Can't stand the place.'

Perry dropped my hand and let it fall. I saw hurt on her face. This was her home-ground; this was where she toiled the long, arduous hours, her ears bleeding from the permanent pull of the face mask, her only protection against the killer. She's rightfully very proud of the role she played, and no doubt also of the place she played it in. No wonder she looked offended. Well done, big mouth, you've done it again!

'Sorry. I just don't like it,' I began to explain, digging myself ever deeper, 'I'm still creeped out, the pandemic, the virus, the fear, it doesn't feel safe…'

'You did alright,' aggression tainted her voice. 'Or have you forgotten how we met? I can take you upstairs to A and E and show you where you were stitched back together if you want.'

Of course, it was only a year ago, assaulted on my own doorstep. The memories of coming round, battered and bewildered, to be greeted by the nurse with beautiful eyes were still vivid. I nodded a grudging apology; she was right. Again.

'And you were born here,' she seemed determined to hammer home her win, 'Even you'd have to admit that hospital visit brought a little happiness... for your parents at least... for a little while, anyway.'

'Oi!' I said in mock outrage, having spotted the grin creeping up towards her eyes. We both laughed, welcoming the thaw that was emerging, 'H'actually I was born at All Saints.'

'Course you were, you bloody would be. The famous, much-loved All Saints Hospital,' Perry's tone had a touch of sarcasm I found amusing. 'I've heard all about the dearly beloved All Saints. Usually when they're complaining about the waiting times, *shouldn't have closed All Saints should you, wouldn't have happened if we could have gone to All Saints,*' she said in a high-pitched, whiny voice.

'Used to be the old workhouse, All Saints, did you know that?' I told Perry, who gave a polite but disinterested uh-huh.

'You know Charles Dickens lived round here?'

'I've been here just over a year now, Mark, and you know what? I'm told at least once a week by someone or other that Charles Dickens lived round here. There's signs bloody everywhere!'

'Okay, chillax,' I said in a playful way knowing, it would annoy her, 'All I was going to say was that workhouse, that became All Saints, it's said Dickens based the story of Oliver Twist on it.'

'Really?'

'Not true though.'

Disappointment could be heard in Perry's one word, 'Oh.'

'No. I looked into it a few years back. Found out it was actually the second workhouse in Medway. The first one, Dickens' one, was down in Chatham town centre.'

'Oh, that's a shame' she said for reasons I didn't understand. 'What made you look into it?'

'Silly really,' a warm flush prickled my cheeks just below my eyes, 'I started doing my family tree.'

'There's nothing silly about that. It's great.'

'I didn't get far though,' I replied not feeling it necessary to explain it was my reaction to Dad's diagnosis, my way to face up to that sudden feeling of mortality. As his condition grew worse, he became my priority. I gave it up and never went back to it. 'But what I did find out was my dad's granddad, he was born there, in the workhouse and then exactly one hundred years later, same month, same date, four generations, I was born there too. When it was All Saints.'

A look of excitement sparkled in Perry's eyes, the sort of look that could persuade a man to do anything, 'Wow, that's the sort of thing you should write down, make a record of.'

'Why? Who cares?'

'It's interesting, people love family history. Imagine having a little nugget like that to pass down.'

'Pass down? Who've I got to pass anything down to? There's only me,' I said in the knowledge that like the Dodo, the dinosaurs and Gillingham's play-off hopes this year: after me the Poynter line is extinct.

'Doesn't have to be that way Mark,' Perry took my hand again, this time she cupped it in both of hers and rested her head on my shoulder. 'Doesn't have to be.'

Her words hung in the air in front of me for a moment, then all at once my brain absorbed what she was saying, I leapt to my feet, turning to face her.

'Are you…' the words were so desperate to be heard they all fell out in a jumble. 'What are you saying… are you… what?'

Perry understood my gibberish and laughed, 'Am I pregnant? No Mark I'm not, relax.' She patted the seat, indicating I should sit down again. As bashful as a schoolboy, I meekly sat beside her.

'But that's not saying I couldn't be, Mark,' Perry continued, 'if that's what we both wanted.'

Oh!

'I TAKE IT that's a no then,' said Perry, after the silence hung just long enough to become uncomfortable. I was so flustered I couldn't respond. Thankfully, I was saved by the sudden appearance of a tired-looking man in maroon medical scrubs who entered through a door at the far end. We both sat in silence, trying hard not to watch him. He tried hard not to show us he knew we were watching him. He slowly traipsed the length of the room and out through a door at the other end, his white rubber shoes squeaking with every step. The wide, heavy door flapped shut behind him and the silence resumed.

I didn't know what to say. I'd landed in a hole and didn't have the skills to clamber out again.

'I was just thinking Mark, you know, seeing as we don't have the cat any more…' Perry used a very deadpan voice, but there was mischief in her eye and I saw the beginnings of a smile twitch. Luckily Perry had the skills I lacked. She saw the confusion flickering around the edges of my mouth and took my hand again, laughing as she gave it a gentle squeeze.

'I just want to know what's going on, Mark, in there.' She gave my forehead a playful poke. 'Sometimes I think we've got the best thing ever going on, but other times I think you can't wait to get away from me. Where are we Marky Mark? Are we serious?'

'It's been a year…' I said.

'A year, yes. But is that *it's been a year* as in twelve months equals long-term relationship, or is that *it's been a year* as in it's *only* been a year?'

She'd cut right to the heart of it, exposed my uncertainty, and shown me up for the ditherer I'd become. I hesitated, she continued. 'A year, Mark. It's really time now to decide, to shit or get off the pot. If only for practical reasons—my lease is up on the house soon, do I renew it or are we living together? Do we take the plunge or knock it on the head?'

I hadn't expected that. An ultimatum. In my mind, we'd have just muddled on for the foreseeable, same as we had been doing, taking every day as it comes. I stood, but a giddiness took over me, I thrust out a hand seeking the wall for support. I buried my chin in my chest and took a series of deep breaths, my blood pressure balanced itself and the light-headed feeling swirled like a whirlpool down the drain. Within the blink of an eye I had my answer, I knew what I needed to say. I turned to face her, and began to speak '…'

Before I'd uttered a single word, a pair of doors crashed open, their thick plastic edges slapping against the wall. Reclining on pillows and a white mattress, a sleeping Uncle Bern floated into the room as though he was riding a magic carpet. Behind him followed a team of busy, harassed-looking people in varying shades of blue.

-27-

BERN WAS ROLLED into the recovery area and we spent a few minutes with him whilst they did whatever they had to do. Plum-coloured bruising flowered across one side of his face, and both arms were bandaged from wrist to elbow.

'It's good news in respect of his head,' explained a very thin, very tall doctor with kind eyes. As she spoke, I noticed a greying curl had broken free from the mass of hair captured beneath the paper-thin blue cap and spiralled loosely in front of her ear. 'He's suffered some concussion, but there's no bleeding on his brain.'

Bern would have a banging headache for the next few days, but no lasting damage. He'd been lucky.

'As regards his arms,' the doctor had noticed where my attention lay, and poked the stray tendril of hair back up under the cap's elasticated rim without breaking her delivery, 'they were pinned under him by the ladder when it fell. He has a spiral fracture to his left wrist. The X-Ray said his right was undamaged, but we've strapped it to keep it level and secure until the physio has properly seen him.'

A not unpleasant rolling sensation rumbled around my stomach and then bubbled away through my veins. Anxiety: it must have been worse than I'd allowed myself to believe. I thanked the doctor and sat beside Bern. Perry was deep in conversation with the doctor at the far end of the room, although she looked keen to follow her team who had vanished through the big wide doors.

Just me and Bern by ourselves, alone: 'You gave us all a fright there, you silly old sod,' I said. The machines attached to his sleeping body responded with hisses and beeps. 'What were you doing? I warned you about Alfie Rubbers. Stick with me in future, I'll look after you.'

At the far end of the room Perry was still in conversation with the doctor, although from her face I could see the status had changed: no longer colleague to colleague, she was now just another concerned family member looking for comforting news. The doctor placed her hand on Perry's forearm as she spoke, and they both smiled at each other.

Perry and I had needed today, we needed this enforced confinement to make me face a few truths and realise what was important. 'Thanks,' I whispered to Bern, and kissed his cheek.

PERRY HAD LEARNED Bern would be taken up to a general ward very soon and kept in for at least a couple of days, just to be sure. He'd been heavily sedated, and with the assurance from the other nurses that Perry would be kept informed of his progress, I suggested we leave, in the hope we could pick up where we were before Bern came out of theatre. I hoped to get another chance to lay my cards on the table.

On the way home, with phones back on after half a day incommunicado, the messages rolled in. Beeps and chimes every minute or so when, one by one, they were pushed down from wherever in space and time they'd been circulating all afternoon. Most were from concerned friends and acquaintances passing their best wishes on to Bern for a speedy recovery thanks to Disco spreading the news from the Golden Lamb. Then came a voicemail chime from a number I didn't recognise. With a press of the prompt it played through the speakers in the van: *'Hello… hello… this is Clive Gordon, Ginger… I got your message… about the Admiral Guthrie. I don't know anything about it. Nothing at all. I told you this already. Now, leave me alone. Please.'*

There was something about his tone I didn't like, something I didn't trust. It got me thinking, so much so it distracted me entirely from what I'd intended to say to Perry. In the end I couldn't haul my mind back, and the moment was lost. I left it unsaid.

WE'D ONLY BEEN home a few minutes when there was a knock on the door. It was Stuart. Perry let him in and told him about Bern. Stuart nodded along as she spoke and politely said some kind words to wish Bern well with his recovery, then got to the reason for his visit.

'I've had a call from the police, two things… Firstly, they've ruled out that bloke, the one who burned down the garage with Danny in it.'

'But he did it, he admitted it.'

'The fire, yes,' confirmed Stuart, 'but they couldn't get him for the murder.' Stuart sounded disappointed, annoyed even. 'Arsenal were in the Champion's League the night Danny was killed. Playing at home to Werder Bremen. Torchy's a season ticket holder, he was there, could even be seen behind the goal when Arsenal scored. Witnessed by millions. What a pain in the arse!'

Not for him, I imagined, but I could understand Stuart's frustration and thought it safest to change the subject: 'What was the second thing the police called about?'

'They've finished with the pub, it's no longer a crime scene. They say we can collect the keys in the morning.'

'Okay, leave it with me,' I said, 'By the way, have they said anything about the funeral?'

'Yes, it's all in hand. Danny's been released to the undertakers and we're just finalising the arrangements, you'll be coming, won't you?'

I replied I would of course be there, but it wasn't Danny's funeral I had meant.

-28-

I GOT UP early and left the house quietly. I had somewhere to be, someone to see, and the fewer people who knew about it the better. It was after lunch by the time I went to collect the keys from the police station, and what a drab, overcast afternoon it was. The lead-grey clouds hung low and motionless, a flotilla of battleships waiting for orders. A storm was coming.

A sarcastic desk sergeant made it perfectly clear how inconvenient it was to deal with me.

'Your job'd be so much easier if it wasn't for the public, wouldn't it?' I said to him, but he merely growled at me. Eventually I got the keys back. As I signed for them I made another request, much to his annoyance, but he'd given me the hump so I was beyond caring.

'Don't want much do you?' he grumbled, then pointed towards seats against the wall, which I took to mean I should sit and wait. I sat and waited. Neither of us speaking, him not even acknowledging I was there. He reached for the morning's red-top tabloid and turned to the back, starting at the sports pages.

A few minutes later my request was granted: an electronic lock clicked, a secure door opened and out walked Nick Witham.

'Marky, how you doing?' he shook my hand firmly. The desk sergeant looked up from his article with undisguised contempt.

'Fine, Nick, fine.' I raised a finger, spearing a silver ring. Three keys dangled below. 'Picking these up.'

The desk sergeant occupied himself by being a nuisance: deliberately flipping, then flattening the tabloid pages with more noise than was actually necessary.

'I just wondered if there's any news? About the body in the cellar?'

'Of course you did, Marky,' Nick replied. 'Well, there's not much to add, really. She was young, between seventeen and twenty-one, but there's nothing else there.'

'How do you mean?'

'No clothes, no personal effects, not even any jewellery.'

'But what about dental records?'

'You watch too much TV mate,' Nick snorted, loud enough that Officer Grumpy Git looked over at us again from his newspaper. 'This poor girl's been down there at least thirty years, the records don't go back that far.'

'So how are you going to identify her?'

'I've got a pile on my desk about three feet high of young missing women going back to nineteen seventy-two, and the thankless task of reviewing each and every one to see how they compare. And that's just the Medway Towns. It's going to take me forever.'

'Just you?'

'Just me,' replied Nick. 'Hutton, the guv'nor, thinks it's a waste of time: she's been dead over thirty years, no clues, no leads, no witnesses, no complaint, no nothing. He wants me to gallop through those files then put it back to bed, says we've got too much going on without chasing cold cases.'

That name chimed a bell. 'Hutton? Is he any relation to a Bob Hutton?'

'How do you know Bob Hutton?' asked Nick, but before I could answer, 'Bob was my boss Paul Hutton's dad. He was a legend here.'

'In what way?'

'Just was,' he replied, as if that was a good-enough answer. I waited. He realised it wasn't and started to fill in the details: 'He'd been on the force man-and-boy. His dad before him and his son Paul after him. His granddaughter, Paul's girl, is at university doing criminology with a view to joining the force when she graduates. I think that's the only reason Paul's hanging on in here, he's entitled to retire on full pension if he wanted to but we all think he's waiting until she joins so he can hand the baton on to her. If she does join, that family would have been policing the streets of Medway continuously since the fifties. That's quite something.'

'Fair enough.' I realised one word stood out, 'You said continuously? So, Paul and Bob served at the same time, did they?'

Nick's eyes flicked up towards the clock on the wall, I was losing his attention and he'd be making excuses to leave very soon, I needed him to concentrate.

'Yeah, they overlapped for a few years. Bob was the desk sergeant. Very popular he was at it too, not like that arsey git over there. He retired about fifteen years ago, I'd only just joined, but I heard the bitching.'

I gestured for Nick to go on, I knew he'd enjoy the chance to gossip and the clock now didn't seem so urgent to him. 'From what I recall, Paul was just a green on-the-beat bobby, but there were rumours of favouritism, being given easy shifts, mistakes overlooked, that kind of thing. Did okay out of it, he's now a detective chief inspector whereas I'm still a lowly detective constable.'

Between you and me, I'd suggest the only person preventing Nick's meteoric rise up the ranks was Nick himself; some people soar, some people plod. Starsky and Hutch he most definitely was not. No maverick thief-taker, just an ordinary guy going through the motions looking for a quiet life. He's been doing it almost twenty years and can't face the idea of learning to do anything else, so may as well string it out until he qualifies for his own full pension. One day someone won't make a movie about a copper like Nick Witham.

'So, Bob Hutton…' I tried steering the conversation back to where I wanted it, '…ever heard any rumours about him? Dodgy? Was he on the take?'

Officer Grumpy Git at the desk peered over the top of his newspaper at us. Nick grabbed me just below the shoulder, his grip tightened and he manoeuvred me to the furthest corner away from the desk.

'Mark,' his voice not much above a whisper, his face close to mine. 'You can't go throwing questions like that about. Not about a family like that. And definitely not in a police station. Anyone could be listening.' With a tilt of the chin he pointed back at the sergeant who was sucking on a biro as he contemplated a crossword.

-29-

THE RAIN HAD stopped by the time I reached the Admiral Guthrie, but the roads were slick and puddled. They'd stay that way for a few hours more because, despite the storm passing, it still wasn't that warm.

I parked up and walked the shortest route, across a grassy verge. It was overdue a mow and held a lot of water, the claggy river mud below didn't offer much drainage. The damp sucked into my trainers, drawn up with as much resistance as a sponge: wet feet, just what I need. Brilliant.

I twisted the long brass key in the escutcheon. The bolt slid back with a satisfying clunk, but before pushing the door open, I turned around to face the road.

Or rather, I turned to face the buildings across the road. I scanned the horizon until I saw it, halfway up the hill with its commanding viewpoint: the low-level, biscuit brown block of flats. I kept my eyes fixed on the upper level and began counting windows from the left inwards, thinking it should be the third or fourth. Sure enough, it was the third window. Even from this distance, I could make out the figure. A dark shirt and head of brilliant white hair on top, he was almost spherical, from this distance he resembled a Christmas pudding. I waved towards him and shouted, 'Hello Ginger, you snidey snake.' He saw me and ducked out of view. 'You silly old sod', I laughed to myself. I turned back, opened the door and stepped through.

INSIDE, THE PUB was largely as we'd left it, apart from all the discarded takeaway coffee cups the police had left all over the floor. I didn't want to spend too long here, it'd be getting dark soon. I hadn't rigged up any temporary power yet, so there was no point hanging around. I don't know why, but curiosity got the better of me—a morbid ghoulish kind of curiosity—and I found myself heading downstairs to the cellar. I'd no idea what I expected to find down there. Nick Witham had already told me the police had dug out and removed anything of interest, but still I descended the tight wooden staircase, ducking my head at the low beam.

It was dark in the cellar, but the last stragglers of natural daylight hung on in to let me see my way around. The police had indeed excavated the remainder of the floor to uncover the body, but hadn't bothered clearing it. Instead, broken boulders of concrete were piled in a heap below the grey steel cellar flaps, waiting for Muggins Poynter to hoik them up and out to the pavement later on: thanks!

I knelt down into the excavated area and ran a hand across the compacted earth, feeling the tiny stones abrade my fingertips. There was no trace of anything on the ground—unless you knew what had been found here, you'd never suspect a thing. It had been picked clean.

I realised then what had driven me downstairs, and it wasn't curiosity. It was sympathy. And it was solidarity. Any thought I had of this girl was linked inextricably to my brother, Adam.

Where are you, Adam? Are you safe? It breaks my heart to picture you like her: lost, hidden and forgotten by everyone except the one person you left behind, the one who loves and misses you?

I let the fine mix of sand and stone trickle through my fingers one last time, then stood. Time to go home. *Take care of yourself, brother.*

THE LIGHT HAD diminished even further—the sun still fell quite early this time of year. With great care, I walked slowly back to the staircase, seeking my way out. Much attention paid to every step—the last thing I wanted was a trip, fall or sprain, and it took a whole lot longer going this way than it did coming in.

Above my head, I heard a long creak. I stopped to let the flutter in my heart pass: you daft dingbat, all old buildings creak, especially when they start to cool off after the sun's gone down!

I found the bottom tread of the stairs. I gripped the handrail and stooped my head and shoulders. In the darkness I wasn't sure where exactly the low beam was and figured stooping all the way was the safest method. I began to climb. Another long yawn of a creak, this time no heart tremors: it's an old timber staircase, of course it'll twist and turn, come on calm down, let's go home.

At the head of the stairs, I came out of the narrow doorway in the main bar area. We'd grubbed everything out of there on the first day, and safe in the knowledge there was nothing in front of me, I straightened from my stoop. There was something in front of me.

A man. It was only because he was so close to me that I could see him in the darkness, any further away and his dark clothing would have rendered him invisible in the shadows. His face covered by a balaclava ski-mask. And there was a smell, a familiar smell, what was that smell? Surprise and confusion froze me to the spot. He shoved me firmly in the chest, my head smacked back against the low doorway and I lost my balance. I was about to fall. I tried to steady myself as I slipped off the top step, but without success, and I toppled down the stairs. I was unconscious before I reached the bottom.

I AWOKE. IT took a moment or two to remember where I was. My head hurt like a bastard, a bastard with a headache. A hand to the back of my head probed through the grit and sand in my hair until it felt a damp stickiness. I brought my hand around and looked at it, I was bleeding: how can I see so clearly down here, have I been here all night, is it morning already?

Then I became fully aware of the orange glow radiating from the doorway at the head of the stairs, and the dry warm air. The building was on fire. I instantly knew what the smell was, and why it seemed so out of context: petrol. The man in black had set this fire deliberately. And then it dawned on me, he set it after pushing me, he wanted me down here.

Fire, why fire? I'd not slept well at all since the arson attack at Danny Kidd's house. I hadn't said anything to Perry, not wanting to worry her. But every time I shut my eyes I could see the flames,

I could feel the smoke engulf me, wrapping me, choking me. And now it was back to claim me for certain this time.

The only way out was up the stairs but flames danced in and out of the doorway at the head of the stairs, taunting me: *we'll get you Poynter, we'll get you this time.*

We'd made it easy. We'd stripped away the ceilings, we'd removed any kind of fire resistance. Fingers of flame jabbed between the gaps in the floorboards above me until they finally took hold and within minutes large sections overhead were ablaze. The fire caught on to the thick joists: solid beams of timber that'd been drying out for over a century. The flames greedily devoured them and the heat became intense. Smoke began to gather in the cellar.

I moved away from the staircase, further towards the corner. My eyes streamed, and I couldn't breathe for coughing. I dropped to my knees against the excavated earth, where I'd been kneeling earlier. A robbed grave: *you can't cheat death Poynter, if you take one out you need to give one back.* A section of the floor above crashed down near the stairs, sending a flurry of sparks upwards as it struck the ground. I knew my time was up. The flames crept closer. Another section dropped, another incendiary payload cascading in all directions. Embers landed on and around me. I patted down a needle-sharp burn on my thigh to kill a fallen spark. The whole structure above me was on fire, any section anywhere could drop, to be under it would be certain death. I looked around and spotted the cellar flaps. Despite the dangers around me I was impressed by my logic: if I can get under the flaps I'll be protected, they won't drop on me.

Bent double, I moved as fast as I could, climbing over the rubble left behind by the police. It slipped and moved, my shin scraped across the rough concrete edges as I lost my footing, but I persevered and got refuge under the pavement flaps.

The cool evening breeze whistling through the flaps was refreshing on my face. Between the gaps around them I could see the deep blue twilight sky, maybe a star or two. That's nice, I thought, a nice thing to see before I die, good idea of mine to get under the flaps.

It wasn't until then I made the connection: the flaps open outwards on to the pavement, it's a route out. It hadn't occurred to me before then: maybe it was the bang on the nut, maybe it was lack of oxygen, maybe it was fear of the fire, or maybe I was simply dense in the head.

I twisted myself around on top of the rubble pile until the soles of both my feet were flat against one flap and my knees bent. Bearing down, my back against the concrete, I pushed with my legs. Every ounce of strength I had left, but nothing. It wouldn't budge.

Above me, over the roar of the fire around me, I heard the approaching wail of a siren: please, please be the fire brigade.

I contorted my body to reach for a loaf sized lump of concrete nearby. Taking it in both hands, I swung it against the steel flaps, then again, then again. My eyes were streaming, I could barely see, and I could only breathe through my mouth; my nostrils clogged with soot. I swung the rock again against the flap but I could tell it didn't carry the same force behind it, the next swing even less, the next even less—there wasn't a next after that, I'd passed out.

THE NEXT THING I remember is waking up frightened. My eyes opened, my consciousness switched on to full alert, but nothing made sense: where am I, how did I get here? I tried to move but felt someone physically holding me down and I heard some half-remembered voice murmuring assurances in my ear. My senses reached out, trying to understand my situation. I was lying flat on my back, my feet on the edge of my vision told me that, and I realised I was elevated off the ground when my elbow slipped off whatever was supporting me and sent my arm dropping straight down without resistance. I tried to speak but couldn't, only then discovering something was across my face, a mask. The stars and the moon looked sharp and close at hand, as though the earlier rainstorm had given the sky a much-needed hose down.

The soft murmured assurances resumed in my ear again, that familiar voice again. Then a face loomed above me, blocking out the moon with an infectious ear-to-ear grin: Fiery Jac.

'Marky Mark, fancy meeting you here,' she unclipped the mask from my face and passed me a bottle of water. 'Gently, just sip it.'

The water washed away the gritty taste of soot. The compulsion was to gulp it down in one, but I knew she was right. I didn't want to choke or vomit, so I took a few small sips. I tried to speak, but no words came out, my mouth dry and throat seized. I took a bigger sip and sloshed it around my mouth for a few seconds before spitting out on the ground, then tried again. 'Thanks,' I gasped.

'You were lucky,' said Jac, stating the obvious. 'It was only because I was standing on the flaps and felt a knocking that we found you.'

From where I lay I could see the Admiral Guthrie, or what was left of it. It must have gone up like a tinderbox. All that was left was a charred and blackened skeleton of what it once was.

'These guys are going to take you to hospital to get you properly checked over,' Jac indicated two paramedics that stepped into my vision as she spoke. One stood at my head the other my feet and I felt myself being lifted.

'I tried contacting Bern but couldn't get hold of him,' said Jac, 'so I called Disco and he said he'd get in touch with Perry. Okay?'

I gave a feeble nod and was lifted into the back of an awaiting ambulance. The doors closed, I watched one paramedic reaching up to a wall cabinet for something but don't remember anything else as I'd fallen back to sleep.

-30-

'MARK, MARK,' THE voice roused me from a sleep without dreams. 'Ah, good, you're awake. How are you, son?'

I let my head flop to the side, my cheek immediately enjoyed the cool touch of the pillow. Uncle Bern was sitting up in the next bed to mine, about six feet away, a fresh white plaster-cast on his left arm.

'Hello Bern, how long have I been here?'

'They brought you up here about half-eight last night. I've been earwigging the doctors. You're perfectly fine, they'll be letting you go later on this morning.'

I looked around for a clock but couldn't see one. Bern guessed what I was doing. 'It's just gone ten,' he told me. 'You've missed breakfast. Mind you, you didn't miss much.'

Food was the very last thing I craved. My stomach was raw and tender, my throat found it painful to talk, but I managed to croak a few words out: 'How... what...?' I said, rolling my hand back and forth between us.

Bern understood my gestures. 'Perry. She pulled a few strings, got us put together. She's a good girl, that one, priceless.'

I nodded, my eyes felt heavy, she was priceless, I slipped back into sleep, only this time with dreams.

I WOKE LATER to find Disco and Bern jabbering away about someone I didn't know who'd just been chucked out by his wife to make way for a toyboy she'd met on the internet. I lay still and listened for a few minutes before pushing myself up on my elbows to fully take in my surroundings.

'Is nobody at work today?' I asked the pair of them.

'You haven't got any work,' replied Disco. 'We've finished the tanning salon. The Kidd properties are on hold until he sorts out the legals. And the pub burnt down last night. We are now officially on furlough… again.'

I searched for something to say before one of them tried tapping me up for money—no-one had ever heard of furlough payments a year ago, now everyone's an expert. 'Is that why Jac was out last night?'

'Yep. She took a bit of overtime because we were done at Hamlet's shop,' Disco said, reaching behind him. As he brought it in to view, I realised he'd brought donuts. 'Want one of these?'

I hadn't noticed my appetite had returned until I saw them and took one with grateful thanks. My blood welcomed the sugar intake and I felt a tremor as it raced through me, jolting me fully awake.

'You just missed Perry,' said Bern. 'She was here a long time, but in the end had to go back to work. Says she'll look in on you as soon as she gets a chance.' Bern helped himself to one of Disco's donuts, took a bite, then sprayed crumbs all over his bedsheets by adding, 'She reckons you'll be out of here by lunchtime. Just waiting for the doctor to do his rounds, then he can give you the all-clear and you're off.'

'What about you?'

'I'm getting out today too, hopefully we can share a taxi.' Bern, it seemed, had already figured out how to save himself a few quid by piggybacking on my ride home.

'This might be him now,' Disco pointed at two men in suits. They strode with purpose towards us.

'That's no doctor,' I replied. I knew exactly who they were.

'Mr Poynter, good morning,' said Detective Chief Inspector Paul Hutton, for it was he, and still a joyless lanky arsehole. With his wire grey hair, sallow grey face and tight-fitting grey suit he resembled a spanner. Beside him was a face I recognised and wasn't overjoyed to see, Detective Constable Nwakobu: young, eager and ambitious. A visit from the police is never a good experience, but at least I was the victim this time, so I relaxed a little.

'You are a person of interest, Mr Poynter,' said Hutton. Oh dear, this hadn't begun as well as I'd hoped. It didn't get any better:

'There've been a few notable incidents of late, and what's the common denominator, do you think?'

'You,' said Nwakobu, keen to join in and deliver Hutton's punchlines.

'Yes, you, Mr Poynter. A valuable chandelier gets nicked and sold on, you're involved. A local celebrity gets murdered, you're involved. A body gets exhumed on a building site, you're involved. A local car dealer complains of intimidation, you're involved. Your uncle is injured in a building site accident, the following day the builder, a Mr Alphonse Rubhaus, gets assaulted… know anything about that?'

I glanced across at Bern in the neighbouring bed. It was news to him, but he knew it was time to zip lips in front of our visitors.

'And now you've burned down the Admiral Guthrie.'

'Say what?'

I couldn't believe what I was hearing. I was the victim here, Hutton had gone off-piste making me piste-off.

'You're having a laugh,' was the best response I could manage—pretty lame in hindsight, but to be fair I'd only just woken up.

'Do I look like I'm laughing, DC Nwakobu?'

'No sir,' replied Nwakobu. 'He's not laughing Poynter. He doesn't laugh.'

I found the truth in that comment funny, but knew better than to let it show on my face. Instead I reverted to the in-built response we'd all grown up with: say nothing, do nothing. Hutton quickly grew bored with the sullen silence and began to grandstand like I expected him to: no surprise, they always do in the end.

'Your sort are all the same, Poynter. I've lost count of the moody arseholes and their no-comment attitudes I've faced over the past twenty-five years, but I tell you this, I've nailed every single one of them. And I'm going to nail you.'

'Dear oh dear. Badgering the witness your honour,' said a deep, plummy voice from the back of the room. Hutton and Nwakobu both turned, and between them I spotted an expensive, tailor-made, chalk-stripe suit and silk mauve tie standing in the doorway.

'Who are you?' Hutton's anger at the stranger interrupting his best Sweeney moment was all too apparent.

'James Capel. I am Mr Poynter's lawyer, and I'm afraid I . rather concerned at your behaviour, gentlemen. I do fear we may be contacting the Police Complaints Commission unless you desist immediately. Kindly leave my client to recuperate from his serious ordeal in peace.'

On the edge of my field of vision I caught Bern staring at me with a stunned expression that I took to mean '*Where'd he come from?*' I returned a shrug of the shoulders and a wonky mouth that said, '*I've no idea, mate*', but I was mightily glad he had miraculously appeared all the same. Disco in the meantime tucked into the last of his donuts and enjoyed the floorshow, taking it all in so he could recount it later in the Golden Lamb many, many times.

Hutton leaned over the bed, and spoke directly to me, 'I know it was you, Poynter.'

'Chief Inspector, I'm warning you,' Capel used a soft, level tone, but it carried an air of authority with it.

Hutton broke his eye contact with me and took a step towards Capel. 'Your client…' his voice dripped with acidic sarcasm, '…was seen by a reliable witness outside the Admiral Guthrie right before the fire began. Fact. His vehicle is still parked outside the building. Fact. Accelerants have been proven to have started the fire making it arson. Fact. Mr Poynter was the only person present when the fire services arrived. Fact.'

'Yes, yes, yes, all very interesting,' said Capel, again in the soft level tones, only this time they held a patronising edge. 'But if you want to talk to my client this is neither the time nor the place. You will need to make an appointment, with me present, after he has fully recovered from his ordeal.'

Capel reached inside his suit jacket and withdrew a stiff white business card which he held out towards Hutton between two straight fingers. Hutton looked down his nose at it, then stormed off. Nwakobu watched, waited a beat, took the card with a nervous 'thank you' and scampered after Hutton down the corridor. A silence hung in the room until Hutton and Nwakobu disappeared and the double doors flapped back into place on their sprung closers.

'Thanks, but what are you doing here?' I asked Capel.

'Mr Hamlet sent me as soon as he heard what they were planning,' replied Capel, who had taken a more relaxed position propped up against the window ledge. So, Hamlet was my saviour, was he? Someone within his legion of inside men had tipped him off. I can't say I wasn't grateful, even though I knew it was a gesture that would come with conditions.

'I listened to everything the gentleman had to say before I joined in,' Capel had a distracted air about him, looking out the window as he spoke. 'Most of it sounded like he was flinging mud against the wall, hoping something might stick, I wouldn't worry.'

'It's all lies,' said Bern. 'Mark's the victim here, they should be doing their job properly and be looking for who did it.'

'I quite agree, sir.' Capel's use of the word *sir* was easily translatable as the posh version of '*and who the fuck are you?*' I introduced both Bern and Disco to him and explained their connection to me.

Capel greeted them both, then returned to the matter at hand. 'I must admit though, the one area that I'm a little concerned about was the reliable witness they claim puts you outside the property immediately before the fire started.'

'I know exactly who that is,' I said. 'Ginger. Clive Ginger Gordon. He spies on the Admiral Guthrie for someone, feeds them information as to who's been there and when.'

'For someone? Any idea who that might be?'

'A man called Donaldson,' I replied, voicing my suspicions aloud for the first time, trying them out, see how they fitted. 'He's a hired heavy. An enforcer, gets things sorted for people. But I don't know who yet.'

'Do you think this Donaldson character knew about the girl in the cellar?' asked Disco, delighted to be privy to this brand-new rumour.

'He must have,' I continued, rolling out my suspicions in full. 'He's been desperate to shut down anything happening at that pub for years, he's tried buying it, he's tried threats.'

'Do you think he set the fire last night?' asked Disco.

'I don't know,' was my honest reply. 'I mean, why would he? What would be the point now if he was trying to keep the girl a secret? She's been found, the Old Bill have been all over it, and that's after we stripped the place back to a bare shell. There's nothing left to hide, so why bother torching it?'

Bern and Disco both resembled nodding dogs as they considered my assessment. Capel added, 'I have to say I agree with Mark. It doesn't make sense if there's nothing to hide,' which only made them nod even faster.

'What was all that rubbish about intimidating car dealers? Did he mean Phil Hopkins? Because I bloody never,' an angry snap in my voice, but that allegation annoyed me. 'I did no such thing. Has he complained about me? I'm going to see him, give him something proper to complain about.'

'I'd suggest in the strongest of terms that you don't. In fact, I'd recommend you don't speak to him or go anywhere near him.' Capel had taken a small hardcover notebook and pen from his jacket, 'Leave it with me, I'll make contact and find out what's going on there,' he said and began to write.

'I reckon they've been following you,' said Bern, his eyes wide and voice high, excited by his own conspiracy theory.

'And who are *they*?' asked Disco.

Bern paused, he hadn't expected a challenge. 'I don't know. Whoever it is that's got it in for Mark. They've been keeping tabs on you, and either got to the car dealer, or told the police about him.' See, told you: conspiracy theorist, totally delusional. Capel, I was sure, would speak sense.

'Sounds entirely plausible,' said Capel. 'It could be that someone's targeting you, our previous experience with the chandelier being a perfect case in point.' I'd since learnt more about the chandelier, although it was only hearsay. I considered mentioning it to Capel but got interrupted by Uncle Bern:

'And what about Alfie Rubbers getting beaten up?' he asked. I kept quiet and ignored him. Bern's question was left hanging until Capel broke the momentary silence:

'I think we're done for now. I understand you'll be going home very soon, so I suggest you keep a low profile and don't do anything reckless. Have a day or two off, watch a bit of telly. The one-day international cricket starts soon, enjoy that. Like I say, leave things with me,' and with that he was gone as quickly and as quietly as he arrived.

The doctor discharged both Bern and me just before lunch, and Perry was there to drive us back to my house. The doctor, like Capel, advised taking a day or two off, but in my case, it was compulsory rather than advisory: with no work to go to, I had no choice. Thankfully, activities in the next couple of days kept me busy in my downtime.

-31-

PRISTINE COMMONWEALTH WAR Graves proudly stood to attention in their own corner, forever England. The white Portland stone shone under the overcast sky as they silently marked Gillingham's centuries-long naval association.

I had no map to navigate me around the sprawling expanse of the Woodlands Road cemetery, having decided on a whim at the last minute to come. I trod carefully through the war graves section to a different area, then stumbled my way through row upon row of assorted stones and crosses and arrived late. The vicar looked up and stopped muttering his quiet words, surprised by my approach. He'd wrapped up snuggly against the cold and damp. Nice to see he'd maintained a sense of decorum for the occasion by draping his purple and gold stole across the shoulders of his puffa jacket. From the few unzipped inches at his throat, I caught a glimpse of his stiff white collar.

'Can I help? Are you lost?' he looked beyond me as he spoke, seeking out a party of mourners that may have mislaid an idiot.

'No. I'm here for…' I began but didn't know how to finish. The vicar seemed to understand, gesturing to the ground in front of him.

'Yes,' I said.

'You knew the deceased?' his voice had lifted, taking on an inquisitive tone, no doubt hoping he could add a name to the interred.

'No,' I said.

'Are you from the council? Normally it's Janet.'

'No,' I said.

'It's just that Janet…' his rambling slowed to a halt. Either he'd run out of things to say or he'd realised I wasn't interested. I didn't care which. Both suited me. I took up a position at right angles to him, against the long edge of the rectangular patch of disturbed ground. I stood in silence, bowed my head and clasped my hands together behind my back. He took this as his cue and with a rustle of paper restarted the service from the beginning, presumably for my benefit: the sole attendee. His delivery was a quiet murmur, I didn't take in much of it, most was lost beneath the gentle rumble of the railway line in the distance, the rest was drowned out by my own thoughts:

I will never forget. I will never forget.
Wherever you are. Whatever you've done.
I will never forget.
I will never forget you, Adam.

His hand on my shoulder startled me out of my internal place, I gasped my surprise.

'I was saying, I'm done now. Is there anything you'd like me to do for you before I go? Would you like to pray together?'

'No.'

He was about to say something else but was interrupted by a flustered-looking woman: middle aged, long dark roots, big leather handbag, rasping voice.

'Alan. Alan,' she called.

'Ah, it's Janet,' he sounded grateful for the interruption and scurried towards her.

'Sorry I'm late, Alan. Traffic was horrendous,' she pulled a folder from her bag as she spoke, wrapping it back on itself to expose the form within. 'Who's that?'

They both glanced back at me. The vicar gave a silent shrug. They walked away, filling out the form as they went, recording where this poor girl with no name ended up should anyone ever care.

I stood there a moment or two longer, then realised what was missing. Making sure I couldn't be seen, I pulled free two stems from a nearby arrangement: a big GRANDDAD left against a glossy black stone with a recent date inscribed in gold carvings. I didn't know what I'd plucked: one was bright red with lots of petals like a sunburst, the other was white and yellow like a big daisy. It was only two flowers; Granddad wouldn't mind, I'm sure. I squatted on my haunches and laid them gently against the chopped earth. They contrasted nicely, bringing a bit of colour to the broken orange clay.

'God bless, sweetheart,' I felt the effect of the squat stretch across my thighs as I spoke to her. 'I don't know you and won't make pie in the sky promises about finding whoever did this to you, to be honest I probably won't ever think of you again after today. But it is today, and I'm here, as it's not fair you go through this alone.'

I stood, one final look at the grave as I shook the tightness from my knees then headed back to the van hoping I'd paid it forward, put credit in the Bank of Karma. If my brother gets found, God forbid, alone and unrecognisable I hope, wherever he may be, a stranger can give him the courtesy of a goodbye.

I SAT IN the van, waiting for the warm-air blowers to clear the misty windscreen and thaw my feet, and couldn't help comparing and contrasting that simple, unremarkable ceremony against the carnival of Danny Kidd's funeral the day before: Rochester Cathedral! Rochester fucking Cathedral! They said it was the only place big enough for Medway's famous son. Utter madness. It was grander than Princess Di's.

The police took over the adjoining Kings' School for the day to use its playgrounds for VIP parking. This created a short, protected walk to the Cathedral door for celebrities and dignitaries. I suspect the Council had a hand in it too: the historic Minor Canon Row, an elegant Georgian terrace with its multitude of symmetrical square sash windows, was extremely photogenic. They must have known it would make such a good advert for the area in papers, magazines and websites across the planet when used as the backdrop for the rich and the famous on their way to and from the service. Press photographers and TV crews set themselves up on the grassy island in front of the arched gothic Cathedral doors. Opposite, in the Castle moat garden, hundreds, possibly thousands of celebrity spotters arrived early to bag the best spot to gawk at the famous faces.

My invite from Stuart also extended to Bern, who loved the cheers of adoration from the crowds until they realised we were nobodies. We were seated far, far back behind a couple of glamour models who spent the entire service on their phones posting inane platitudes to the world at large, but to their credit they did smell nice. Everywhere you looked were sporting legends past, present and future; comedians; presenters and people off the telly. And Hamlet, up towards the front beside a couple of soap opera 'hardmen'.

I knew for a fact he didn't know Danny, but obviously a day rubbing shoulders with the stars was too much for him to resist. I still hadn't spoken with him about the encounter with Hutton at the hospital and Capel's intervention, and didn't really want to discuss it now. I sat low in my pew and tried to avoid his star-struck wandering eye. Who'd he blagged an invite from? And that's another thing: invites! This was the first, and hopefully only, time I'd ever needed to produce an invitation to get into a funeral. The whole thing was a circus.

'This is a bit odd,' Bern whispered to me. 'We should be outside.'

He didn't need to tell me that—I'd never felt more out of place in my life. The disgusted look the glamour models gave us when we sat down made that clear—it was either Bern's bottle green suit and grubby plaster cast with hand-drawn obscenities courtesy of the drinkers at the Golden Lamb or it was that they could tell we were nobodies of the worst kind—skint nobodies.

'No, what I mean is, normally at a funeral you wait outside for the car to arrive and then they carry the box—' someone nearby tutted at Bern's turn of phrase, so he tried again with a noticeably condescending tone, 'and then they carry the... *guest of honour* in first, and everyone follows on behind to take their seats. This is more like a wedding, waiting for them to arrive.' He had a point. It did feel back to front, but I guess when you've got the celebs coming to town they want to be inside safe and sound away from the proles as quickly as possible.

The sound of a helicopter overhead became louder. From outside we heard the battery of camera shutters firing away, and then voices: a dull, basic football chant, repetitive and primitive: 'There's only one Danny Kidd, one Danny Kidd, there's only one Danny Kidd,' over and over.

'I guess he's here then,' said Bern, just as speakers throughout the vast cathedral, and outside, began to carry the sound of Coldplay's 'Fix You'. Bern rolled his eyes at the choice of song, but it was one of Danny's favourites, apparently. Everyone rose to their feet. The pall bearers, all from the world of football, slowly marched up the central aisle with their fallen teammate carried above them. The glamour models paid their respects by tweeting off a series of sad face emojis.

For the next three quarters of an hour we heard from a '66 World Cup Winner who'd coached Danny as a youth, and an up-and-coming comedian who seemed to treat it as his prime-time big break opportunity. Stuart didn't get up to speak but sat in the front row comforting his distraught elderly relations, none of whom I'd ever met.

We weren't invited to the reception afterwards. It was just for stars and VIPs. From the pictures in the paper next morning, it looked like it had been a very swanky bash indeed.

Instead we wandered off to the nearby Coopers Arms, a cute little tumbledown pub in the shadow of the Castle. Supposedly Charles Dickens was a regular, but then I imagine you go anywhere in Rochester and they'll all say that, even the mobile phone shop and the fried Chicken takeaway.

A few reporters, who couldn't get into the 'after-show party' as they called it, had knocked off for the day and drifted in for a quick pint, then thought they'd won the jackpot meeting Bern. Under the low-beamed ceiling, refreshed by a never-ending supply of free beer, Bern regaled them with tales of his life with Danny Kidd and within a few pints he'd laced Danny's first boots, a few pints later he'd taught Jose Mourinho everything he knew, and another couple later he was Bobby Charlton's best mate. He was quite miffed when none of it appeared in the papers next morning.

-32-

I'D FALLEN INTO a bored depression. After the funerals I had literally nothing to do, no job to go to, no estimates to price up, no leads to chase. For two days I sat on the sofa; the lockdown blues all over again. Sometimes the TV was on, sometimes it was off, it didn't matter to me. I didn't have the motivation to watch anything, even bland daytime shows about antiques and holiday homes seemed too much like hard work to concentrate on.

Where did it all go wrong? I asked myself again and again. All I wanted to do was earn a living. All I've done is fail at it, yet again. Perhaps, I wondered, this was a sign. Perhaps I needed to jack it in and try something different? Why not, I was still young enough to begin a second career. But what? The thought of working in an office terrified me; doing the same thing every day, with the same people in the same place, no way. Maybe I should take some time off, go travelling, see the world like my friend Tim did, come back in a year's time and try again when my heart's back in it? But where? And how? No, I couldn't do that, I've got commitments, I've got Perry, and now I've got Uncle Bern to look after. Maybe I should get some exercise, use this time off to lose a bit of weight and get fit? I could go for a gentle run around the block to ease myself in to it: bollocks to that, bollocks to all of it!

And that was essentially the looped thoughts going around and round in my mind continuously, grinding me deeper and deeper into the safe refuge of the sofa.

I WAS WOKEN on the morning of the third day by the constant ring of the phone. It had been another fractured night for me. I'd become afraid of falling asleep: the flames waited for me as soon as my eyes closed, and then when I couldn't resist any longer and sleep took over, the smoke suffocated me, and I'd wake gasping for breath. The night before had been the worst to date, so to be torn from a much-needed peaceful bout of sleep by this persistent caller fair made my piss boil in anger. The ringing, I recognised, was the landline phone downstairs. I groped for the alarm clock to check the time so I could unleash my frustration for being woken at this ungodly hour. I couldn't find it but my mobile told me it was ten-thirty-two. It also told me I'd missed seven calls this morning. Still the landline rang.

I took my time shuffling downstairs. I hoped the caller would give up before I got there, then it wouldn't be my fault they never got through. Still the landline rang.

'About fucking time!' were the first words heard when I lifted the receiver to my ear, I hadn't even had the chance to speak and didn't get one because Hamlet continued, 'I was about to call out a search party. Where've you been Marky Mark, why haven't you been answering your phone?'

I tried to think of a flippant response. 'Don't know,' I muttered, failing to find one.

'I need you down here today. The holiday's over, you can stop tugging on your old chap, get off the sofa, get dressed, get your toolbox and be down here within the hour,' insisted Hamlet, I asked him where *here* was exactly and in a tone that implied I was stupid for not knowing already was told the Chatham salon. 'Come on, chop chop.'

UNABLE TO THINK of any reason or excuse not to, I arrived at the salon about forty minutes later. The massive structure of Luton Arches dominated the local skyline, standing at least five storeys high while the foot of Chatham Hill fell to its lowest point beneath it. Its sturdy brick abutments, as thick as a house, were cut into the chalk cliff faces and supported a mighty lattice of steel trusses that arched high over the roadway to carry the London to Dover trains between the higher ground either side: a beast of Victorian engineering in fading red and green. Vehicles flowed continuously through the arches, making it one of Medway's principal arteries.

They joined the many-tentacled roundabout tucked behind the massive structure, then were flung off in all directions. A footbridge, a colossal zig-zag of grey steel and concrete provided pedestrians with a safe walking route over the constant traffic: a behemoth as ugly as it was huge. The area had a constant buzz of movement, people hurried about their business all around and yet Hamlet's little salon stood silently unnoticed within the weathered greyness of its neighbours and their sheen of accumulated road grime.

I parked on the spalled concrete hardstanding at the side of the salon, blocking in Hamlet's very expensive, very shiny, brand new BMW X5 and I came in through the back-access door. Hamlet and his lackey, Dunlop, turned as they heard the door swing shut behind me.

'Thank the Lord, he's turned up,' Hamlet slow-clapped his hands and spoke very loudly, almost shouted. 'Call off the dogs, tell the helicopter to come back, he's been found.' Dunlop sniggered at his master's wit: a sneaky, self-serving laugh given to curry favour.

'I'm here. What do you want?' I dropped my toolbox at my feet with a surly clatter. I found my act of belligerence quite comforting.

'Just a few minor defects, Marky Mark, that's all.' Hamlet talked to me as though I was a stroppy teenager in need of placating. Dunlop slumped his skinny arse onto the receptionist's stool and wrapped his long limbs across one another like a spider monkey. Hamlet gestured towards the tanning booths, 'There's a buzzing noise coming from number one, and the fan next to number two isn't working.'

'Seriously? That's it?'

'Don't worry, I'll pay you for it,' said Hamlet misreading my mood. I wasn't worried about getting paid or not. I simply couldn't be arsed to find the motivation for such tiny problems.

'And, I wanted a chat Mark,' Hamlet looked over at Dunlop. 'You, make yourself useful and fuck off for ten minutes. Go and get us a coffee. Skinny lattes all round. Skinny latte good for you, Marky?' I shrugged my assent, and Hamlet handed a note across to Dunlop. 'And I want change!'

The street entrance door squawked an electronic chime as it opened and closed, and Dunlop sauntered off down the street. When satisfied he'd gone Hamlet beckoned me with a wave of the arm, 'Come in to the back room, it's more comfortable there.'

The back room certainly looked different to the bland magnolia staff room I'd decorated for him a week or so ago. Now a huge chunky safe, the size of a washing machine, dominated the corner. Countertops had been installed, on which sat two electronic money counters, and between them neatly lined up like parked cars in their bays were stacks of notes, sorted and piled by denomination.

I knew the rules: you see nothing, you hear nothing, you say nothing, but I still didn't want to be here. By being here I'd been presented with a secret, a confidence, I now owed Hamlet, again, and I didn't like it.

Two armchairs were pushed tight against a wall. They weren't a pair, they didn't match, they didn't even co-ordinate. They were probably salvaged from one or other of his many rental properties and brought here. He gestured to one and then sat in the other, I sat beside him.

'It's good to see you Marky Mark,' he reached across and squeezed my knee. 'Can I be frank with you about something?'

I knew he was going to be, regardless of what I wanted. 'Sure, go ahead.'

'I think you had your head turned by the footballer, you got stars in your eyes. You let the showbiz glitter cloud your judgement.'

Only a couple of days ago I'd watched him laughing like a goon with the soap actors at Danny's funeral. He was the one getting selfies with reality stars, not me—his words grated.

'I've been looking out for you, Marky, and I know you've been having a hard time of it lately. And it all begins and ends with the footballer.'

'I don't think that's true—'

'It is Mark, and you know it too.'

I did, he was right, and it irked me, 'So? What business is it of yours?'

'Because you're my friend,' replied Hamlet. 'Let's be honest. I know everybody of any influence or importance in these Towns, all of them, and there's hundreds if not thousands of them. You remember my brother, Benny?' I nodded, he continued, 'Since he's been gone, my actual proper friends, I can probably count them on one hand and here's you,' he'd extended his left hand and was gripping his thumb to illustrate his point.

I'd never seen him like this before. Hamlet: the bon viveur, the alpha-dog, the big man, always surrounded by hangers-on and worshippers. I'd never once considered that in amongst it all he might be lonely.

'You're one of my closest friends Marky Mark, I'm worried about you, okay. I'm worried you're getting out of your depth, I'm worried you're heading for trouble.'

'I'm fine,' I replied, then realising that it was necessary added, 'thanks.'

'You want to talk about anything?'

'No.'

'Okay. Get on with your work then.'

IT HAD STARTED to feel a little claustrophobic, so I was grateful to be dismissed. Hamlet stayed in the back room with calls to make. I went across to the tanning booth and tried to assess the problem.

I'd been there about ten minutes: almost finished. It wasn't a big deal, just an adjustment to the transformer. I gathered my things together and heard the electronic chime of the street door: must be Dunlop returning with the coffees, I thought.

As I packed the last of my tools away, I paused humming my happy little tune and became conscious of the silence in the salon. It was unusual, but I didn't think too much about it. Toolbox in one hand, I rose to a standing position—then I saw him.

In the highly reflective polished glass of the tanning booth I saw a man approach behind me: dressed in black, a ski mask hid his face. I closed my eyes in a slow, deliberate blink. Was I that tired and sleep deprived? Were my fears and fantasies from the fire now haunting my daytime too? But no, when I opened my eyes he was still there, only closer. I blinked once again to be sure. In the reflection he raised something black and club-like. He's going to cosh me, I thought. But no, he raised it to his shoulder and brought his eyeline down along the length of it. I recognised the two black holes pointing straight at me.

I swung round, the toolbox gathered its own momentum in the spin, arcing upwards and gaining speed. It struck the end of the shotgun, which erupted in a boom of blue smoke and the rich smell of cordite. The tanning booth behind me exploded into a million, billion glass fragments.

The office door flew open and Hamlet charged out, 'What the fuck—' The gunman turned to see where the noise was coming from. I swung the toolbox again. It was heavy in my hand until it reached its terminal velocity and began to soar. The gunman pre-empted it, stood back, and it sailed safely past.

Hamlet charged at the gunman. He sidestepped Hamlet, then drove the shotgun butt firmly into Hamlet's belly. Hamlet dropped to his knees, winded. The gunman looked through the opened door to the back room and within two steps was in there. He scooped up as many of the piled notes as he could, stuffing them inside his jacket, and then he ran.

'I'll have you,' called Hamlet after him, struggling to his feet. I helped him up and together we lunged towards the gunman. He was snatching at the door handle in his panic to escape, but he turned and raised the gun to us. The shop was too narrow and we were too close together, there was no way we could separate and force him to leave one of us uncovered. Hamlet and I both halted and ducked just as the gunman fired. Above and around us, more glass rained down in jagged little splinters. In the melee he yanked the door open and ran.

I got to my feet and ran to the door; the gunman was about eighteen feet ahead of me sprinting away. Walking towards him, oblivious to what had been happening, came Dunlop holding two takeaway coffee cups.

'Stop him. Stop him,' I shouted. I waved my arms and pointed at the man between us, 'Thief. Stop him.'

Dunlop understood and planted both feet firmly on the pavement, blocking the gunman's path. The gunman slowed but didn't stop. He did a shuffle, a dummy, bobbing one way only to turn the other and straight past Dunlop as easily as if it was a kids' game in a playground. Dunlop at least had the presence of mind to launch a full cup of coffee at him, hitting him squarely on the back of the head.

'Don't stop, get after him,' I called. Dunlop turned and raced after him. I watched them tearing down the road. The gunman made a sharp left down an alleyway. Dunlop followed closely behind. Once out of sight I looked back in to the salon, and only then noticed Hamlet hadn't moved from behind a fallen cabinet.

I went to him and saw the pool of blood on the floor, fragments of the highly polished glass glittered like crystal within it. I looked at Hamlet, seeking out the wound, and it was quickly found. There was no mistaking it. A spear of glass shaped like a lightning bolt was embedded in his back, just below his right shoulder. His shirt was stained maroon around the edges of the glass and his face had turned an unhealthy pale colour. He'd lost a lot of blood. I knew what I had to do. I got out my phone and dialled.

PERRY ARRIVED IN under fifteen minutes. She wasn't happy about it, but she heard the concern in my voice, realised the severity of it and decided to park the argument for another day. She'd brought a small medical kit with her, but after taking a good look at Hamlet, despatched Dunlop with a shopping list and told him to hurry. She gave Dunlop her keys, and he screeched off in her little white Fiat to the nearest pharmacy. I'd not had the chance to ask Dunlop what had happened with the gunman, it'd have to wait until he got back.

'I'd be a lot happier if we took him to the hospital,' Perry said, inspecting the wound. The shard still penetrated Hamlet's back but the blood flow seemed to have slowed.

'We can't.'

'But why?'

'You know why. Too much to explain.' I couldn't think of anything else to say. I went and stood by the window and waited for Dunlop's return. When he did come back he clutched a tall narrow white pharmacy bag. He handed it to Perry. She tipped the contents on the floor in front of her to inspect everything. On her instructions, Dunlop and I cleared a space and manhandled Hamlet into it. Perry tore open Hamlet's shirt to expose the wound then pulled on a pair of blue latex gloves.

'I need you to gently press down on his shoulders. Stop him wriggling around.'

I did as I was told. Firmly gripping the shard, Perry pulled. Slowly it emerged from within him, its faces shone red in the daylight: stained glass. The sound of tearing flesh made my stomach churn, but I had a job to do. I held him down and despite my better judgement watched as she withdrew the full length of the glass—about four inches—from him. She threw it to one side and quickly used wadding to stem the blood that bubbled to the surface from the void the glass once filled.

I watched in awe and wonder, there's something incredibly sexy about seeing the woman you love save a life. I wanted to take her there and then. Perry must have recognised my sudden lust. She turned and said: 'You're okay, you can go now. I'll call you if I need you.' My passion, immediately extinguished.

As a very poor consolation I went to the van and fetched a few rubble sacks, and began the tidy up whilst Perry stitched Hamlet back together.

-33-

I HAD TAKEN out a dozen sacks, each one jagged and lumpy with broken glass and chunks of plaster, when Perry shouted through to say she'd finished. I'd just about finished cleaning up too, but it would still need a thorough vacuum to dredge the smallest particles from the carpet.

Perry had Hamlet seated upright in one of the back room's mismatched armchairs. I'd found one of the salon's branded staff t-shirts in a cupboard and gave it to him to cover himself up with. It was a couple of sizes too small and looked comically ridiculous stretched across his massive chest and shoulders; any movement threatened a Hulk-effect bursting of the seams in every direction. At least his face had restored its normal complexion. A mug of water sat beside him. He took occasional sips while swallowing handful after handful of paracetamols direct from the bottle. Perry had given up asking him to take it easy with the painkillers after being ignored so many times before and let him get on with it.

The pills hadn't numbed his anger. 'I want whoever did this. I want their fucking heads.' I'd not seen him in such a fury before. The old streetfighter who'd fought his way to the top of the food chain had re-emerged. 'I want them,' he repeated, but I suspected they'd be lying very low by now. They may very well have been an opportunist with no idea whose money they'd stolen, but they'd find out soon enough and then if they had any sense they'd be on a very long, faraway holiday.

Turning on a dime, his demeanour changed entirely. Gone was the rage, in came the charm: 'She's a diamond, this girl, Marky Mark.' Perry immediately bristled with fury. Despite her feelings towards Hamlet, her first instincts were that of a care-giver, but now he was out of trouble her old animosity resurfaced.

'Thank you,' I said to her, knowing this wasn't her world, and it was wrong of me to have involved her, but at the same time I knew I had no alternative.

'But as for you, Marky, you're a Jonah,' Hamlet said. 'You must be the unluckiest man in the world.' He laughed at his own witticism, and I noticed the sparkle of tiny glass splinters in his hair catching the light as he moved. Hamlet hadn't finished, he wanted to share more of his wisdom. 'I mean, first you get caught up in someone's arson about, and then you get caught up in someone robbing me. Talk about always being the wrong man in the wrong place.'

I looked across to Perry. I'd hoped to exchange an '*ignore him, he's an idiot*' glance, but she appeared to be contemplating his words: 'I think Mark's the right man in the right place.'

'And what makes you say that?' Hamlet replied with a smirk, ready to take the piss.

'Look, someone burns down that pub. Why? It couldn't be to hide any secrets as they'd already been found. It was set on fire because you were in it.' Perry's eyes flashed, she was convinced by her theory and was determined to share it, 'And then look at today—'

'Yeah, somebody robbed me,' interrupted Hamlet.

'But did they?'

'Yes. They bloody well did.'

'No,' persisted Perry. 'Think back, think about what actually happened, like you explained it to me earlier.'

'Well,' I tried walking through the events step by step, 'The gunman started shooting the place up—'

'No, take it from the beginning, where did he start?'

'He came up behind me, and I saw him reflected…'

'Exactly.' Perry snapped her fingers, she had the bit between her teeth now. 'He came and sought you out first. Robbing the money came later, after he'd failed. You were the one he wanted.'

'Me?' I was astonished. If what she was saying was right, I'd been subject to two assassination attempts in the same week. I became light-headed at the realisation and needed to sit down. 'But why me? What have I done?'

'Been too nosey,' answered Hamlet. 'I have to say, I think she's right, Marky. And I'll bet it's because you've been sticking your beak in, asking too many questions.'

I thought back and agreed. I'd lifted too many stones and something nasty had crawled out from under one of them, only problem was I didn't know which one or what.

I PERCHED ON the arm of Perry's chair and tried to shake off the dizziness. Someone wanted me dead because someone wanted me to stop asking questions. But who? And what if they wanted to try for third time lucky.

A ringing phone made us all sit up and take notice. We all felt our pockets. It turned out to be Perry's. She read the name flashing on the screen, 'It's Rachel,' and stepped out of the office to answer the call, passing Dunlop lurking in the doorway.

'Now then Numbnuts, tell me some good news. What do you know?' demanded Hamlet of his red-faced underling.

Dunlop poured himself a cup of water from the cooler in the corner and gulped it down in one long swallow. 'When he ran out of here, I chased after him. He did a long loop round the block, almost a complete circle. He had a car waiting, more or less behind here,' he pointed towards the back of the salon, diametrically opposite to the direction which the gunman took off in.

'What kind of car? Driver or passenger?' demanded Hamlet.

'Driver, he was on his own for this,' replied Dunlop. 'And the car was a Range Rover. Black… or possibly a very dark blue. I couldn't get the registration number. When he was tidying up,' Dunlop indicated to me with a flick of the chin, 'I went outside again to see if any of the neighbours picked anything up on CCTV.' I'd noticed he'd gone AWOL when I was doing all the donkey work, so perhaps I should have been grateful he was at least doing something useful and wasn't just sloping off. 'Nobody had anything that was any good,' he continued, 'As far as I can tell he got in the car under the footbridge and sped off up Magpie Hall Road.'

'Who's that bloke we've got in Highways? Jagesh something? Maybe he can pull up off the traffic cameras?' said Hamlet to Dunlop.

'No need,' I replied, 'I've got an idea who it might be. Did you see his face?'

'No, not properly.' Dunlop reached into his pocket and pulled out his mobile phone, flicking through the menus to bring up a fuzzy image. 'This was the best I could do, he'd started to take his mask off but I was still some way away. I only had a second or two to take the photo, so I had to snatch at it, sorry.'

The image he held out before him showed the gunman in the process of pulling off the mask. It was so fuzzy and grainy, it was like looking through a net curtain. All that was exposed was his chin and jawline, but that was enough.

'It's Donaldson,' I said, taking the phone from Dunlop and passing it across to Hamlet.

'Are you sure?' Hamlet peered closely at the image, angling his head and bringing it closer as though that'd help him see up and under the mask.

'Positive, one hundred percent,' I replied.

Hamlet leaned forward in his chair, elbows on his knees, and dropped his face in his hands with a loud sigh. He held the pose then drew his face up, rubbing and slapping his cheeks, as though trying to chase out a weariness within.

'In that case,' he spoke slowly, picking his words for economy and impact, 'I have a problem.'

My immediate reaction was if it was '*I*' and not '*we*' that have a problem then that was fine by me, but coming up so close behind it was piggybacking on the first thought was the realisation that if I'm not already involved, I'm definitely going to be, so I should at least know what I'm getting into. 'Go on,' I said.

'This all comes down to that pub, the Admiral Guthrie,' said Hamlet. 'Remember I told you it was a Flint family business? And Donaldson doesn't want you anywhere near it? I'm starting to wonder if Donaldson still works for the Flints?' I nodded along. His logic seemed to work. 'The rule we've all abided by, the one rule, the golden rule, is that there's enough here for everyone as long as you don't interfere, and you stick to your own.'

Honour amongst thieves, I thought, but knew better than to say out loud.

'Honour amongst thieves?' said Dunlop. Hamlet swung and slapped Dunlop across the side of his face, 'Watch your mouth, dickhead!' Poor Dunlop, he'll learn.

'But if they've come here, to my business, destroyed it and stolen from me, then they've crossed the line, they've broken the rule, they've made it personal. And now I'm involved, I have to react.'

Hamlet had maintained a level of composure throughout, kept his emotions balanced, but I knew he was talking about a gang war. My head swam. A hurricane was about to rip through the Medway Towns and here I was in the eye of it. A warm bubbling sensation warned me I was in danger of vomiting, and I tried to force it down. I was saved by the reappearance of Perry in the doorway.

'It's Rachel,' she placed her phone on the countertop. 'She wants to talk to you. Go ahead, Rachel.'

'Hi Mark, can you hear me?'

'Hi Rachel, yes, you're on speakerphone. What's up?'

'I'm following up on those queries you asked about, are you ready?'

'Yep, go ahead.'

'Okay then. You asked about a man called Donaldson. I'm afraid that it's just too common a name, and without any context then it's an impossible task, so I drew a blank on that one, sorry.'

'No worries, thanks anyway, but I think we know enough about Mr Donaldson now,' I replied, at which Hamlet gave a laugh that was more of a grunt: a sarcastic response.

'Who's that?' asked Ridder, not recognising the owner of the sound.

'Ignore him, it's nobody important,' said Perry. Hamlet's reaction amused me, it must have been the first time anyone's ever called him an unimportant nobody to his face.

'I had a bit more success with your other queries,' Ridder continued. 'In nineteen eighty-three the body of a sailor on shore leave was found in an alleyway off Ordnance Street in Chatham. The newspaper report described it as a notoriously rough area—'

'Still is,' interrupted Hamlet, earning a 'shh' and a gentle slap on the arm from Perry, but the pause had given me a chance to think and assess Rachel's news.

'That's not the one I was thinking of,' I told her. 'The story my uncle told me was of a local getting stabbed, and the suspect was a sailor on shore leave, not the other way around like your story.'

'Are you sure?'

I glanced over at Hamlet for reassurance, he was there when Bern spun his yarn. 'Yes, sorry, I'm positive.'

'Oh,' Rachel's tone sounded disappointed. 'It's just that it marries up with another of your queries. You see, the newspaper report mentions the police officer that was first on the scene: PC Paul Hutton.'

I recalled that I'd asked her whether there was any information out there on Bob Hutton, but I found this interesting all the same, even though I had no use for it.

'I'll email you copies of the newspaper reports, okay?' said Rachel, and I thanked her for her time and her efforts. 'Oh, and before I forget, Yellowbox.'

Ah yes, Yellowbox, I'd forgotten about that myself. 'What did you find out?'

'Absolutely nothing,' she replied, and I noticed my lip tighten in disappointment. 'It's a bog standard, ready-made, off-the-shelf company bought from a website for a few pounds about three months ago. It has no share capital and is valued at one pound. It's so new that it's not submitted any accounts, and it doesn't even have any directors listed yet. There's nothing there at all.'

'It's a front,' said Hamlet. Perry and I turned to look at him, Rachel remained silent. Seeing as he was the only one that seemed to know what he was talking about, everyone let him speak. 'It's just a vehicle to pump money through and to hide behind. Probably one in a series of anonymous, faceless companies that nobody will ever be able to penetrate. The money gets funnelled from one to another to the next, out the country and back in again later.'

'What he said,' replied Rachel. 'That's pretty much word for word what I was about to say.'

'Are there no clues as to who's behind it?' I asked.

'Ask her what's the registered office?' said Hamlet.

'There is an address given, but it looks like an accountant's office,' replied Rachel. 'Let me check it out,' and we heard the soft clatter of keys being typed in the background. 'Here we go, I've done a quick cross-search using the term registered office and the address, and it's come up with a list of limited companies. I was right, it's just an accountant.'

'Who are the other firms listed?' asked Hamlet.

'There's all sorts, there must be at least a dozen,' said Rachel, and then she began to recite the list: 'Bramstone Limited; Corby and Corby Services; EASL Tutors Limited; Fielder Holdings Limited; Fielder Homes Limited; Garrick and Singh Limited—'

'Wait,' I said, 'Yellowbox has the same registered office as Fielder Homes?'

'Yes, and all the other Fielder companies,' Rachel replied.

'Ron Fielder,' Hamlet's two words were delivered in such a way that there was no mistaking exactly what his opinion of Ron Fielder was.

'I tell you what Rachel, would you be able to have a look into Ron Fielder for me please?' I asked.

'Okay, why, you think he's connected to Yellowbox?'

'I don't know,' I replied. I looked at Hamlet and considered the way he'd said his name. 'Just curious, that's all.'

Rachel promised to come back soon with whatever she found, and we thanked her for the call and said goodbye. Perry said she was leaving and looked amusingly uncomfortable when Hamlet squeezed her tight in a hug to say thank you for her medical assistance. I said I'd see her at home and kissed her on the cheek.

Just Hamlet, Dunlop, and I remained. I knew I wasn't going anywhere, Hamlet had plans.

-34-

'THERE, QUICK, follow her,' said Hamlet. Dunlop jumped out of the back of the car. We watched his abject failure to be discreet, walking on quick long legs to catch up with an elderly lady laden with shopping bags. She turned and looked at him. He had no choice but to keep striding on past her before she became suspicious and called for help. Hamlet fumed at his incompetence: 'Idiot.'

LESS THAN THIRTY minutes earlier, we were in Hamlet's salon where he'd made his plans clear: 'I want Donaldson. Where is he Marky Mark?'

'How the bloody hell should I know?'

'Well, how do you contact him, got a number?'

'No, he just pops up when you least expect him and least want him, like a cold sore.'

'Cold sore, that's funny,' said Hamlet, although he didn't sound amused. 'I doubt he lives like a bloody hermit, surely someone knows how to contact him?'

A thought occurred to me. 'Actually, there might be someone.' And that's why we were sitting outside Ginger's block of flats trying to find a way past the communal controlled-entry security door.

DUNLOP HAD FOUND a spot of wall to lean against. He smoked a cigarette in an attempt to look casual, but failed miserably. Instead, he had the look of the world's worst burglar about him. To make matters worse, the elderly lady wasn't even going in to the flats. She trudged past Dunlop and gave him a very distrustful stare with every slow, ponderous footstep. No doubt she'd be telling everyone she met about the shifty looking individual outside the flats, so time was now of the essence.

The stars must have been shining on us, because within an instant a young woman with a toddler in a pushchair arrived and struggled to exit through the heavy door. Acting the perfect gent and neighbour, Dunlop held the door open as wide as it could go, making it easy for her to manoeuvre her way out. She gave a cheery word of thanks over her shoulder as she walked away. Dunlop stepped inside, letting the door swing shut behind him just in case she looked back. Hamlet and I got out of the car and approached the door, Dunlop opened it for us, and we were in. Hamlet bounded up the stairs two at a time, Dunlop and I followed.

Dunlop and Hamlet dropped back, loitering outside the neighbouring flat, and left me to approach Ginger's door alone. I knocked and waited. I could hear the noise of the television but there was no response. I knocked again, louder this time. No response again. I thumped the flat of my hand against the door, as hard as I could and in a clear, loud voice said, 'Ginger, it's Mark Poynter, I need a word.'

'Go away,' came a reply from inside, muffled and indistinct on its travel through the thickness of the door.

'Ginger,' I called, thumping hard on the door again.

Sliding bolts rattled and the door opened—only an inch, but enough to release the warm, fetid vapour of a sealed-up sweaty flat and a bad diet. Ginger peered through the gap. 'I don't want to talk to you, I told you to leave me alone. Go away.'

His face disappeared from view and the door began to draw to a close, but it wasn't quick enough. Hamlet and Dunlop had appeared at my side, both had knees up and booted the door with an enormous force. It flew backwards at an alarming speed, knocking Ginger clean off his feet. Sprawled on the floor of the narrow hallway, a thin trickle of blood began wending its way across his forehead from where the edge of the door glanced against him in the impact.

'You know who I am?' said Hamlet, to the still flattened Ginger. Ginger nodded: a slow, wary nod. Hamlet smiled, 'Good, then this will be easy for us. Go and sit down.'

I helped Ginger to his feet, pulling him up, his hand damp and clammy as dough. He led us all into the living room and used a remote control to switch off the television.

'Nice new telly that,' Hamlet gestured towards it with a tilt of the head. 'How'd you afford that when you live like a fucking pig in shit?' Ginger blustered a ragged response that made very little sense and convinced no one, least of all Hamlet. 'Stop. You got it because you're a grass. You're a snide little snaky tell-tale, spying and selling information, aren't you? Aren't you?'

Ginger nodded, then looked straight at me. 'I didn't know about the fire, honest I didn't. All I did was call them when you arrived, tell them you were there. I didn't know they were going to torch it. Honest I didn't. I'd never have called them if I'd known—and it was me what called nine-nine-nine when the fire started, it was me what saved you.'

'Great, thanks.' I was unsure whether I should be grateful to him or not, but I wasn't going to let him know I was wavering, so I walked across to the window and stared out. From this viewpoint I could see the full aftermath of the fire at the Admiral Guthrie—pretty much the whole roof had gone: I knew I was lucky getting out when I did; the thought of being trapped and having several tonnes of slate and timber rain down on me made such a chill run through my blood I found myself rubbing my arm to relieve the goosepimples.

'I want Donaldson,' said Hamlet. 'Give him to me.'

Ginger looked around him, as though checking the surfaces, 'He's not here. I don't know where he is.'

'You have a number for him,' I said. 'You call him whenever anyone goes anywhere near that out there. Give him the telephone number.'

Ginger stood and, with a few nimble steps that were surprising for such a big man, picked up a mobile phone from a dropleaf table in the corner of the room. His fat fingers prodded the keys, then he turned the screen to Hamlet. It displayed an unnamed phone number.

'Prove it,' said Hamlet. 'Talk to him now,' and he pressed the dial button. We heard the ringing tone as the call tried to connect.

Ginger panicked. He asked me what he should say. I shrugged to show I didn't care, it wasn't my problem.

The ringing stopped. 'Hello,' came a voice: Donaldson.

Ginger looked at me, his eyes desperate for my help, I turned away from him and looked again at the burnt-out shell below me.

'There's someone looking at the pub,' said Ginger. His voice wobbled a little, but he managed to keep it together on the whole.

Donaldson' disembodied voice carried menace towards Ginger, 'Who is it?'

'I don't know,' said Ginger. 'A man in a suit, got a folder with him. Looks like he could be from the insurance.'

'Alright. Keep an eye on him. Let me know when he's gone,' said Donaldson and killed the call.

Hamlet took the phone, passed it to Dunlop and told him to write down the number he'd just dialled. Hamlet looked at Ginger with utter contempt.

'You want to hit him?' he asked me. Much to Ginger's relief, I replied I didn't. Much to my relief, Hamlet hit him anyway. Then we left.

As I pulled the door shut behind me, I called out to Ginger, 'You should bolt this door. You can't be too careful any more, know what I'm saying.'

BACK ON THE street, Hamlet gunned the BMW X5 into life and roared away from the kerb. He drove too fast around the winding estate roads, and even faster when we connected back on to the public roads. My knuckles tightened around the arm rest, I didn't react well to Hamlet's impulsive and reckless driving. I asked, 'Are you not going to call Donaldson?' but he just shook his head.

Eventually, after about fifteen minutes of taking his aggression out on the road, he calmed his driving and shared his plans, 'I'm not going to call him yet. I want all the facts first. We're going to see someone. Almost there.'

By the time we were driving through Rochester, I had a fair idea where we were headed, and I was right: the hospice. Hamlet parked in an empty disabled space right outside the entrance doors and told us to get out.

We entered, striding to keep up with Hamlet. The receptionist tried to engage but Hamlet put her down without even breaking pace, 'It's alright, he knows the way.' He shoved me in the back, 'Lead on.' I retraced my steps along the corridor to McInally's room. The door was closed but, with a heavy hand, Hamlet threw it open and again I was shoved from behind: I entered, whether I wanted to or not.

McInally sat in the oversized armchair beside the bed, or rather he was propped up in it. Pillows and cushions were wedged around and behind him, holding him upright and in place. He appeared to be dozing, his eyes were shut, and his feet raised on a footstool in the same pale green vinyl as the chair. His face looked gaunter than last time, his skin waxy. I looked along the length of him. His ankles were swollen, the same thickness all the way down: thigh, knee and ankle. Exposed skin, as dry and red as brick dust, looked stretched to bursting. His socks were now too tight; the elastic dug in as though clinging on by a stranglehold and created a deep depression around his calves. It made his ankles look even softer—puddingy, my dad would say. I've no idea what it meant medically, perhaps I should ask Perry, but I'd bet it wasn't good.

I tapped a loud knock on the door jamb to rouse him. 'Brian.' He sputtered awake with a snort and rubbed his nose with the back of his hand: an odd gesture, one I've only ever seen gloved-up boxers do, old habits die hard I suppose.

McInally studied me with bleary eyes until the connection was made. 'You. I thought they'd slung you out. What're you doing here? More of that bastard Hamlet's donkey work?'

'Actually, I'm quite capable of doing that myself,' said Hamlet, taking that as his cue to enter the room. With a gesture he told Dunlop to guard the door and using far greater care than he opened it with Hamlet pushed the door closed behind him. 'Hello Brian, how you are doing?'

McInally's face changed at the sight of Hamlet: the frail waxy death-mask was gone, replaced by fierce eyes and flared nostrils. Like I say, old habits...

'I'm dying, what the fuck's it got to do with you?'

Hamlet laughed, but not in the antagonistic way I was used to. He wasn't demeaning McInally. He respected him and the fire still inside him. Hamlet saw it as sparring between two old fighters.

'Still a grumpy old git Brian,' said Hamlet. 'The big C's not changed that then?'

McInally choked out a laugh that rattled with mucus and pain, 'Nope. Just about alive, but still bloody well kicking.'

Hamlet sat close to him, perched on the edge of the bed, and reached out to tap a hand on McInally's knee, 'Well do me a favour, hold on for at least another half hour as we need to talk to you, alright?'

McInally tried to speak, but a retching cough overwhelmed him. It shook through his entire body. Spotting a small plastic jug of water beside the bed, I poured some into a matching plastic beaker and handed it to him. The coughing eased, and the maroon face faded back to the sallow yellow of the long-term hospital patient. He nodded his thanks and returned the empty beaker to me.

'Finished?' asked Hamlet, unable to resist taking the piss. 'Now then Brian. I don't think you were entirely truthful with my friend here when he came to see you. So, what have you been holding back?'

Any fight in McInally had been flattened by the coughing fit. But he didn't seem meek or cowed by Hamlet, he just seemed like he didn't give a shit any more. 'What do you want to know?'

'Let's get to the nitty gritty. Who was the girl in the cellar?' asked Hamlet.

'I don't know,' McInally said through another cough. He looked up from his handkerchief into Hamlet's unimpressed face. 'She said her name was Caroline. She hadn't been there long, from up north somewhere. I didn't have much to do with her. She was upstairs.'

'On the game?'

McInally's expression showed he found Hamlet's turn of phrase distasteful. He didn't pick him up on it, but his tone made it clear in just one short word, 'Yes.' He held eye contact with Hamlet for a few seconds to make his point, then added, 'She worked upstairs. And as you know I had nothing to do with that, I just ran the pub.'

McInally, whether on purpose or not, had revealed Hamlet knew more than he'd let on. He'd cheated me, yet again. I cast a curious glance towards Hamlet, but he deliberately avoided me. I raised a question of my own, 'How old was she?'

'I don't know. Young. Eighteen. Nineteen. I don't know. I didn't ask,' McInally raised a fresh tissue to his lips and hacked another cough. 'She had a look about her, vulnerable, I got the feeling she was a runaway. She didn't talk much but when she did, there was an accent, northern. But she was only there a couple of weeks. If that.'

I pushed a little further, I didn't think it relevant, but I wanted to know for my own peace of mind, 'Where northern?'

McInally looked at his slippered feet on the stool in front of him. He gave no impression of having heard me and sat in silence. I was about to repeat myself when in a quiet voice he answered, 'Liverpool. Pretty little thing she was,' and then drifted back to wherever his thoughts had taken him before.

Hamlet leaned in closer. Even though there was only the three of us in the closed room, it felt as though Hamlet wanted to create an extra level of secrecy before asking, 'So who ran the upstairs?'

Disbelief was plain on McInally's face. He couldn't believe Hamlet had asked such a dumb question. 'The Flint family.'

Hamlet snapped back, his turn for disbelief at the dumb response, 'Tony Flint is a multi-millionaire and Ken, the old man, was even richer. He wouldn't have hopped in the Roller down to Gillingham every day for a crappy little knocking shop. Who ran the day-to-day?'

McInally gave a very slow short nod, up and down just once, his chin barely moving, just enough to say he understood.

'Photos,' he said, looking at me, pointing towards the bookcase behind us. As I did last time, I fetched the slim plastic album over to him and he flicked through the pockets until he reached the same one as before. He stretched forwards to peer over the top of the album. The veins and tendons in his neck stood out against his leathery old skin as he did so, giving him the look of a tortoise.

Hamlet studied the party scene, the revellers' demon red eyes glowed from the print at him.

'What am I looking at?' asked Hamlet. McInally pointed at two faces looking directly out of the photo: one short, with the long, complicated Spandau Ballet haircut; the other taller with thick ginger curls and a flattened nose.

I remembered them from when I saw the photo on my last visit, 'The doorman?' Hamlet and McInally both laughed, and I suspected I'd been too gullible. A heat blossomed on my cheeks, 'Who is it then?'

'He was brought in by the Flints to run the girls, and everything else for them,' McInally replied. 'I just pulled pints. He took care of it all, and he was brutal with it.'

'And he did the girl in the cellar, did he?'

McInally gestured for some more water. I poured him some. He took a sip and sloshed it around his mouth then spat a thick brown glob of mucus into his handkerchief then looked at it with curious interest, 'It'll be blood soon. I'm dying, you know. It'll be days, that's all.'

'I'm sorry to hear that Brian,' said Hamlet, he sounded genuine.

'That's why I'm helping you. You get that? Because I've so little time left, what have I got to lose? But you promise me, you promise you'll look after my Donna.'

'Of course, Brian, she's got a job as long as she wants one. She's one of my best. I always take care of my own,' Hamlet again sounded genuine.

McInally seemed reassured, took a deep breath and then answered my question, 'No. He didn't kill the girl in the cellar. He'd been dropped on us by the Flints to look after their interests, and he brought in his best mate Ginger Nut there,' McInally tapped the face in the photo. 'I forget his name. Rod, Ray, Roy, Ron, something like that but he was an animal, a fucking animal. He was the one hired as the doorman, but he ended up starting more fights than he ever broke up.'

'And he killed her?'

'No,' McInally spoke to me as though he was growing impatient with a naughty child. On the edge of my vision, I saw Hamlet smirk. I decided I'd stay quiet and let McInally tell it his own way. 'The Animal, he was quite sweet on her, she'd only been there a week or two, but he seemed quite struck by her. Anyway, one night the Navy was in town, the pub was full of sailors on shore leave. One of them takes a fancy to her and takes her upstairs. After a while the Animal thinks they've been up there too long and goes to investigate, I suppose shake down the sailor for more money or chuck him out. He walks in, finds the sailor had got kinky with her, been choking her and gone too far. Killed her.'

McInally turned the album towards himself and looked at the two faces staring back as if seeking their approval to confess. He paused, dabbed the end of his nose again with the back of his hand, and at that point decided to continue, knowing there'd be no going back from this point. 'The Animal flew into a rage. He went mental. He battered that sailor to a pulp and then next thing, he's pulled a knife from somewhere and is sticking him with it, again and again and again.'

Hamlet and I turned at the sound of a commotion. Through the door's glazed panel, we saw Dunlop arguing with a nurse in navy blue scrubs, the same one I'd met before, the one with the sing-song voice. She barged past Dunlop and came into the room, not breaking her stare on me. 'Everything okay, Brian?'

McInally nodded and made a small smile for her. 'I'm fine, dear. Just catching up with my friends, almost finished.'

'Okay,' she said in two parts: oh-kay, sing-song, high-low. The sort of response that said I don't believe you, but it'll do… for now. She backed out of the room, still eyeing me with suspicion which gave me the hump to be honest. I'm sitting here next to the area's leading villain and someone about to confess to their part in a murder, and I'm the one getting the stink-eye.

McInally maintained the sweet smile of a harmless old grandfather until she had gone, then went back to his tale, 'So now there's two dead bodies and they drag me into it,' he must have read our minds screaming *'how?'*, because he explained: 'They threatened my Donna. She was only a little girl at the time, they threatened to hurt her. Look after her, promise me you'll look after her.'

Hamlet reached across and squeezed his hand, 'Of course I will. I promise.'

McInally reached for a fresh tissue and dabbed at a tear welling in his eye before wiping his nose, 'It's almost closing time and I'm told to get everyone out, no late drinks nothing. The even got their pet copper, Hutton, to clear the place out.'

'So, he was aware of what happened?' I asked.

'Oh yeah, he knew,' replied McInally. 'Then I'm set to work: me and the Animal in the cellar. We begin breaking out a hole in the floor but it's solid concrete, it took ages just to make a hole about three-foot square. In the end they have an idea, as she's the smallest they'll put her in the hole. So that's what we do, we fold her up and squash her in. Me and the Animal then knocked up some concrete to fill her in with. In the meantime, the other one takes my car, sticks the sailor in it, and then drives to the other side of Chatham. This was before cameras everywhere, so he just sails through as it's the middle of the night, dumps him in an alley behind some shithouse rough-as-arseholes pub and is back within forty minutes.'

'Ordnance Street?' I asked, dumbfounding McInally, who looked at me as though I'd suddenly revealed the gift of second sight.

'Yes. Ordnance Street. So that's that. One buried in the cellar, the other dumped across town,' he said, his story concluded.

'Not quite,' added Hamlet. 'Where's the police in all this?'

'Hutton was in on it, like I say they had him shooing everybody out. I knew he had a few dirty coppers working for him, they must have done something behind the scenes as I never heard any more about it: The Navy accepted their boy had got into a fight over that side of town and it quickly got swept under the carpet. No one ever came looking for the girl, like I say I think she was a runaway anyway.'

'And what happened to the brothers Grimm in your photo?'

'The Animal: I never saw him again after that night, he'd only been working there a couple of weeks anyway but he never came back. I always assumed Donaldson sent him packing.'

Hamlet and I both sat forwards as though we'd been stung. 'Donaldson?' I asked.

McInally looked from me to Hamlet and back to me again, 'Yes, Donaldson. With the silly boy haircut in the photo. The one brought in by the Flint family, Donaldson.'

'Scottish?'

Again, McInally looked dumbfounded at my sudden clairvoyance, 'Yes.'

'Do you still see him?' asked Hamlet, only to receive a sullen shake of the head. 'But you know how to contact him, don't you? I bet you spoke to him right after Mark came to see you last time.'

McInally looked to the floor, a gesture that cried out with shame, 'They threatened my Donna. Those threats never go away. Ever.'

McInally began to sob quietly. I didn't think we'd get any more out of him. Hamlet had obviously reached that conclusion before me, as he was already on his feet heading to the door. I got up and followed but as he left the room Hamlet turned and said, 'I promise you Brian, I'll make sure she's looked after.'

As we walked the corridor towards the exit, the sobs from the room grew louder. The nurse passed in the corridor and stared at me with utter contempt.

-35-

OUTSIDE HAMLET DELEGATED driving duties to Dunlop and took the passenger seat. Stuck in the back, I was glad to find Dunlop was a safer driver than Hamlet, who currently seemed preoccupied with thinking aloud: 'It seems like I was right about Donaldson working for the Flints. I'm guessing Donaldson didn't want anyone developing the Admiral Guthrie because of the girl's body in the cellar.'

'But he didn't kill her.'

'No. But he knew about her. He helped hide her, and he covered up the sailor's death, so that certainly gives him skin in the game.'

'But it was thirty odd years ago,' I protested, 'If he'd just left it all alone, there couldn't have been anything to connect him to it this far on. Especially as McInally, who he must know hasn't got long left, has been too terrified of him to ever say anything. And the only other man who knew—the Animal—he disappeared into the wide blue yonder.'

'Did he?' replied Hamlet. 'All McInally said was *he* never saw him again.'

I thought about Hamlet's remark, he'd made a good point, one I hadn't previously considered. 'You think he's doing all this to protect him, the Animal?'

Hamlet nodded. He reached into his jacket pocket and pulled out McInally's photo.

'I can't believe you stole that.'

Hamlet gave a dismissive 'pah' and held the photo at arm's length between finger and thumb. 'You need to find out who he is.' The hard work passed to me again, I noticed. He looked back and read my pissed-off expression. 'Oh shush. He's got no more use for it, you heard him, they'll be re-letting that room by the end of the week.' I have to say that didn't appease me and he knew it. 'Tell you what, if it gets that lemony look off your face, I'll give it back to Donna when we're done, okay?'

We drove on for a while and nobody spoke. An old Paul Simon song came on the radio that I'd not heard in ages. I was rather enjoying it, but then Dunlop surprised us by having a sensible thought to share: 'I get that this Donaldson bloke helped with the two deaths back in the day, and I get that he tried scaring off everyone from the pub ever since to hide it. And I get that he wanted you to stop sticking your nose in, so he was behind the shooting and the fire to try to get rid of you… but who killed Danny Kidd?'

Oh! That foxed me. I must admit I hadn't thought things through that far and, judging by the chin-scratching going on, I assumed Hamlet hadn't either.

Dunlop hadn't finished, 'Because the papers say it was his brother—'

I leaned forward between the two front headrests to make sure I was heard, 'It wasn't Stuart.'

'How'd you know that?' asked Hamlet, not bothering to turn his head towards me, his eyes fixed on the horizon outside.

'I just do,' I insisted. I trusted my gut instinct. I couldn't be bothered explaining and watched the world zip past the window instead.

'Of course, the papers said he also had that thing going on with that rapper, could have been him or one of his lot,' said Dunlop.

'Maybe,' I said, although I didn't think it likely. 'But I'm beginning to think it was Donaldson. Danny nicked the pub off him, then he insulted him when he tried to buy it back. Danny was pretty gung-ho about getting the development going, which Donaldson didn't like. I think it was Donaldson.'

Hamlet turned in his seat, looking over his shoulder straight at me, '*Thinking* and *proving* are two completely different things. Anyone can tell you that. And we don't know yet whether the Flint family are involved or not, so that's exactly the sort of thinking you keep to yourself,' he jabbed a finger at both me and Dunlop. 'Those words don't go any further than this car, understand?'

We both agreed, Hamlet seemed satisfied and his shoulders, as massive as a mountain range, relaxed. 'Good. So, now we know what you think, it's up to you to prove it.'

I sprung up between the seats again, a demented jack-in-the-box.

'Me? Why's it my job?'

Hamlet threw me a belittling laugh to say such a question was beneath him, 'Because you can get your best-bud Stuart off the hook for one. And two, whose job do you think it is: the police? Donaldson, via the Flint's, has had them in his pocket for decades. In case you've forgotten, they're already trying to fit you up for whatever they can make stick. You really think they're any help?'

I fell back against the seat, knowing how the cat in the sack feels when it hears the splash of the river. Hamlet was right, again. I'd made too much of a nuisance of myself. Donaldson wanted me silenced, and he was either going to do it himself or get his tame policemen to do it for him. If I was going to get out of this mess, it was down to me to do it.

WITH BERN STILL recovering under Perry's watchful eye at my house and wanting somewhere safe from prying eyes and beaky noses, I asked Nick Witham to meet me at Bern's flat. I set about tidying it, gathering up the post, packing him a change of clothes, that sort of thing, while I waited for Nick to come. He arrived ten minutes later than we'd arranged, blaming it on work.

'Sit down Nick, I've something to talk with you about, I need your help.'

I didn't really know how to begin. I'd rehearsed a few different opening lines before he got there but, in the end, I let it come out in a rambling mind dump. He listened, didn't interrupt, in fact didn't say a word, and after I'd finished sat in silence for a few moments considering it all.

'Let's get this straight: you want me to re-open a thirty-five-year-old cold case? Some dead sailor that everybody's forgotten and no one cares about?'

I replied that in a nutshell, yes, I did.

'And how exactly do I get the authority to do that?'

'I've no idea, that's for you to work out.'

'Thanks. And what possible justification do I give for resurrecting this case after so long?'

'I told you, say you noticed it happened around the same time as the girl's body in the cellar and you'd like to see if there's any connection.'

'And I told you, Hutton's already instructed the cellar girl's case be closed and archived as a matter of urgency.'

I don't think Nick understood, so I spoke very slowly and chose my words with great care, 'Hutton wants it closed because Hutton's involved. His father was key in covering up the girl's death in the first place—'

'Yes, the father but—'

'But,' I countered, 'read the newspaper report I got from Rachel Ridder. The sole officer on the scene at the sailor's death was PC Paul Hutton, the son, your boss. No doubt to squish any interest in it and block any progress. He's in on it. He's followed his old man straight down the Flints' pocket. No wonder he wants any mention of it shut down.'

Nick looked more bewildered than usual. I felt sorry for him, it was a lot to take in, it's not every day you find your boss and mentor is dirty.

'You said yourself Nick, he's due a full pension retirement. He'll do everything he possibly can to keep a lid on it now, he'll want to sail quietly off into the well-paid sunset. You'll need to find a way to work around Hutton.'

'But… how?' Poor old Nick looked as though he was about to soil himself. 'How do I do that? I can't just waltz up to the chief superintendent and ask for permission because I think a highly respected officer from a highly respected family is bent. And do you know how they treat grasses in the police force, Mark? You're asking me to put my job on the line. Why?'

'Because it's the right thing to do, Nick, the right thing.'

He rose from the chair, and without saying a word headed to the door. At the threshold he turned, his eyes looked sorrowful, 'I'll see you later,' he murmured.

'Her name was Caroline, Nick.'
He looked about to speak but didn't, then he was gone.

-36-

PERRY WAS STANDING in the window, looking out, when I arrived home. I don't know how, but I knew she'd been standing, waiting, there for a long time. I walked up the path and caught her eye. She smiled, but I could tell it wasn't real. It didn't ignite in the same way as they usually do.

Inside she fussed about me, she avoided asking direct questions, but I knew she was keen to hear what we'd found out. I told her everything and watched the conflicting emotions battle within her. On the one hand, she seemed pleased to be proven right that I was the target of bad people's attention for snooping about, but on the other, she was concerned that I was the target of bad people's attention for snooping about.

I shared with her all that McInally told us, and she nodded along to every new revelation, trying to take in the enormity of it. On the table in front of us, I laid Hamlet's stolen photo and pointed to the doorman—the Animal. 'I need to find out who this fella is.'

'And then what?' Perry's tone was sharp, her words snapped and stabbed in an angry question. 'You've already been told: there's a world of difference between thinking and proving something.'

'But what do you suggest I do then?'

'I don't know. Can't you just leave things be?'

'No. I'm in this too far now, I can't.'

'Why not? Can't you just walk away and forget about it? That's what everyone else wants to do, why can't you?'

It was a good question, one I'd been contemplating myself, but I kept coming back to the same conclusion. In a voice not much more than a whisper: 'Adam.'

'Adam? Your brother? What in God's name has it got to do with him?' Perry walked to the other side of the room as she spoke. She kept her back to me.

'Someone died, Perry,' I said, not knowing whether to follow or stay where I was. 'Somewhere a family might still be thinking of her. Still waiting for that phone call or that knock on the door, still waiting to see her again.'

Perry turned to face me, her eyes looked damp and heavy with welling tears, she understood now that this had become personal to me, that I'd projected my loss and my grief on this poor young girl, this Caroline. Perry came towards me, arms outstretched, and wrapped them around me in a tight squeeze.

'Please, be careful,' she murmured against my chest.

'What's all this bloody noise?' came Uncle Bern's unwelcome voice. 'You two bloody squabbling again?'

We turned to face the interruption himself descending the stairs, his bandaged arm held out at right angles in front of him like an old-fashioned waiter in a seaside postcard. Late afternoon and still wearing pyjamas. My pyjamas. He realised I'd clocked them, 'I found these in the airing cupboard. I need to recuperate, remember? Anyway, I'm making a cup of tea before the cricket starts, anyone want one?'

Before either of us could answer, Perry's phone rang. Recognising the number, she accepted the call and switched it to speakerphone.

'Hi, it's Rachel Ridder, have you got a moment to talk?'

She replied that we did and sat back down on the sofa, I joined her. Bern gave a shrug, muttered to himself, then shuffled in to the kitchen where I swear he deliberately made as much clattering and banging as he possibly could just to be bloody awkward.

'I've got some info about Ron Fielder,' said Rachel. I'd forgotten I'd asked her for that and in fact my reasons for asking, but seeing as she'd put herself out and gone to the trouble, I felt obliged to listen. 'Lots and lots of stuff about his housebuilding business: great successes, impending knighthood, blah blah blah. But I'm guessing you know enough about that and it's not what you're looking for.'

I made no comment, too distracted by the sound of something smashing in the kitchen.

'So, I dug a little further. There's nothing official on the record, but I suspect he's a bit feisty.'

That intrigued me; something I hadn't expected. I recalled the roguish face from the property listings pages with his hair as white as Father Christmas, his wonky nose and his cheeky chappie smile: Uncle Ronnie is here for you, Uncle Ronnie will help you buy. 'Go on,' I asked.

'The official press mentions all portray Fielder as a fine upstanding citizen: a working-class lad from very humble origins, self-made multi-millionaire, now in line for a New Year's Honour. However, I spoke with a friend who sometimes writes for the financial gossip and scandal sections. There's been a number of rumours over the years of violent altercations with sub-contractors, mostly to do with missed deadlines and payment disputes.'

'Really?' I found myself asking aloud.

'Yes. They all led nowhere, though. Any allegations were withdrawn very quickly. That usually means a private settlement.'

That made sense to me: resolve any problem privately, throw money at it, make it go away before it becomes public.

'Also, some people have found it a little more than curious that every single scheme he's ever developed has sailed through planning, no matter the location or how contentious aspects may have been.' She didn't say it, but I understood she was implying corruption and bungs may have been used.

'So that's the rumours,' said Ridder, 'but I also found that several business columnists have had a bit of fun at his expense: they like to point out how awkward and uncomfortable he is in financial circles, amongst the old money and Oxbridge investors. The impression they give is he's got a massive chip on his shoulder about those people, thinking they're all looking down on him no matter how rich he is. He's one of those who likes to make it plain he's working-class and proud of it, made his money the hard way. Supposedly overjoyed about getting knighted, he thinks it'll stick in the posh boys' throats to have to call him Sir Ronald—and he'll make damned sure they do.'

'He'd have hated Danny Kidd then.'

'Why do you say that?'

'From what you've said, he sounds like everything Fielder hates: too rich, too young, too cocky and too flash.'

Rachel paused, presumably thinking it over, adding only, 'Probably.'

I thanked her, and she ended the call. Like Bern in my pyjamas, something didn't hang comfortably. I thought back to a conversation with Stuart. He said Danny and Ron Fielder were laughing and joking all night, the best of friends. Why would Fielder hang up his prejudices for the night to be the butt of Danny's jokes? Too much wine? The celebrity stardust? Neither sounded likely, but what do I know, I'm an electrician not a PHD in psychology.

'WHAT ARE YOU thinking?' Perry asked, but I didn't answer, I couldn't, I didn't know what to think. I didn't know whether Rachel's call was any help or was simply a distraction from the matter in hand. I tried to assemble my thoughts into some kind of order and opened my mouth to speak, but:

'I told you he was a bastard.'

I looked round to find Uncle Bern leaning against the kitchen door jamb blowing across the surface of his mug: *I love Belgrade.*

'Fielder. I said he was a bastard. None of you wanted to listen though, did you?'

'When did you say anything of the sort?' I asked.

Bern shuffled lazily across the room, his slippers carving shadowy lines across the carpet as they skimmed the nap. He flopped into the armchair opposite and used his working hand for a good, long scratch and forage around his nethers; I decided there and then I'd rather burn those pyjamas than see them back in my wardrobe. Bern had, by now, got everything arranged how he liked it and returned to my question. 'In the Golden Lamb. You, me and Disco. I said he was a nasty bastard, and you said he'd have to be to be successful.'

That triggered something. I half-remembered the conversation. 'But I thought you meant…' the sentence remained hanging, unfinished, I trailed off, not knowing what to say.

'What do you know about Ron Fielder, Bern?' asked Perry, managing to put into words what I was thinking but unable to express.

'Every bugger and his brother knows about Ron Fielder,' he replied. 'Everyone my age at least. Anyone who worked in the Dockyard would remember the real Ron Fielder.'

Perry looked at me, I didn't know if she was seeking my input so I shrugged a gesture to say I had nothing to add.

'One of the Towns' dirty secrets,' continued Bern. 'Anyone old enough to know him knows it's in their own best interests to keep schtum, and anyone younger only knows him as the face of the housing developments. It all gets hushed up and forgotten about until only the respectable image remains.'

'So, what was he like?' asked Perry.

Bern took a mouthful of tea and relaxed back in the armchair, crossing one leg across the opposite knee, settling in as if he was some great raconteur about to captivate a cocktail party with his sparkling anecdotes. He was milking the attention and it was giving me the hump: 'Get on with it, you old fart.'

'Alright, alright, calm down,' he used a slow patting gesture as he spoke, which annoyed me even more. 'Let me tell you about Fielder. He was a proper nasty piece of work. He kept popping up in the Dockyard, casual work for various different firms, never lasted long. He was normally sacked for starting fights, or nicking stuff.'

Perry laid her hand over mine. The warmth it created cupped over my fingers was quite pleasant and the gentle squeeze she gave me nicely intimate.

'Everyone knew he was a volatile nutter, best given a wide berth. This was the early eighties I'm talking about. Football hooliganism was at its worst and guess who was leading the charge, the Great Ronaldo. I don't think he actually followed any particular team, he was just there for the tear-ups. He started appearing around town as a bouncer, working the doors. I guess they thought they'd rather have him inside the tent pissing out, know what I mean?'

Perry and I nodded. So, I thought, it looks like genial Uncle Ron has a dark side and there may be substance to the rumours Rachel Ridder had unearthed after all.

'This is all very well, but it's just gossip, that's all,' I said.

Perry looked from me to Bern, then asked, 'Would Hamlet have known this about Fielder?'

'For sure,' said Bern.

'That'd explain why he sounded so contemptuous when Fielder's name came up in conversation then,' said Perry. 'I guess that answers that little query, but it doesn't get us any further in sorting out the problem surrounding the pub.'

'Doesn't it?' Bern sounded genuinely confused. 'Why did you want to know about Ron Fielder then? When I heard you talking about him, I assumed you were talking about that!'

Perry and I both followed the invisible line from Bern's extended finger to its target: McInally's photograph on the table.

I leant forward to get a closer look at the picture, and in particular at 'the Animal': his busted nose, his buck teeth and his full head of copper curls. What was it Ginger had said? *The curse of the redheaded man. We never go bald, instead we go pure white.*

Ron Fielder—soon to be Sir Ronald—was 'the Animal'. Ron Fielder was a killer.

-37-

THE GOLDEN LAMB was busy. I should have expected it. Ever since a misguided happy hour promotion intended to attract the homecoming London commuters actually hooked the trades' knocking-off shift, it's always been a builders' pub. Between four and six the place is usually full of dirty boots unwinding after a long day of fixing, sawing, nailing, drilling and lugging, and today was no exception.

Wanting a bit of privacy, I took one look at the near-filled car park and decided we should pass straight on, less than quarter of a mile down the road just past the train station to the Sutton: a small little pub, not much bigger than the flat-fronted terrace houses it stands between. I hadn't been in here since I was at school when I had a brief dabble with a girl in the year above who lived nearby—funny, I've not thought about her for years. In fact, I can't remember anything about her now, apart from she was convinced she'd be a star someday despite having the worst singing voice I've ever heard. Pretty girl ,too: looked like a screen siren, sounded like an air-raid siren.

Anyway, it hadn't changed at all, it still looked like someone's front room: reprints of old Victorian watercolours depicting local scenes in heavy, cheap gold frames, a pile of used paperback books to borrow and swap beside the fruit machine, dark painted wooden panelling and heavy brown furniture. The few heads that were in there snapped round to scrutinise those who dared step into their hallowed inner sanctum. Plenty of tables stood empty, but my eyes followed a young woman with an unlit cigarette between two duck-like pursed lips; she pushed open a door at the back of the room with one hand whilst the other repeatedly sparked a disposable lighter in impatient anticipation. Through the open door, I glimpsed a small garden and I ushered Stuart towards it.

AFTER REALISING WHO and what Ron Fielder was, Perry, Bern and I had sat looking at each other, nobody quite sure what there was left to say. We sat in still silence for at least a couple of minutes until Uncle Bern leaned across and switched the television on, 'Cricket's starting.'

As it happened, the cricket was exactly what was needed. Trance-like, we disengaged from what was going on around us whilst Sri Lanka took to bat. Half an hour of zoning out and parking any worries did me the world of good. A tap on the window followed by the ring of the bell brought my attention back to the room. I got up and found a very happy Stuart on the doorstep.

The reason for his happy state, he explained, was that he'd just come off the phone from his lawyers. Everything had gone through probate and been released. 'We can get back to work,' he said, before rattling off a list of properties and jobs required, all of which flashed past me like darts, none of them sticking.

'Tell you what,' I managed to say when he finally took a breath, 'let's go for a drink. We can celebrate your good news, then work out where to begin getting things started back up.'

And that's how we ended up in the Sutton.

YEARS OF EXPOSURE to all weathers had turned the wooden picnic table silver, and it rocked with a seasick lurch as we sat down. A tall gas heater nearby took the edge off the early evening chill that was trying to take root. Small pointed petal-shaped flames glowed a pale orange below the umbrella head of the heater. My blood pumped cold at the sight of it. It didn't matter how small the flames were, I could see them and that was enough to trigger some primeval warning deep within me: *the fire has an appetite for you Poynter, it's had two tasters, now it will come for you.* I turned my back to it. I shuffled as far along the bench as I could, unsure what was more uncomfortable: the chill air gnawing into my lower back, or the sight of the flames and the thought of them reaching out for me again.

'So as of one p.m. today,' said Stuart, 'I am officially a millionaire. Cheers,' Stuart tapped his lager bottle against mine. 'Here's to new beginnings.'

'How's it feel?' I asked.

'Bloody amazing.'

'But money's not everything.'

'True, but it's a whole load of something.'

'It doesn't buy what you really want though, does it?'

Stuart gave me a quizzical look. I expanded, 'Wouldn't you give it all away if it got your brother back? I know I would for one more day with my dad. An hour, even.'

Stuart didn't answer. All at once I felt embarrassed and couldn't think of a way to change the subject without being obvious. I kept quiet and tore a long, thin strip of label. There're two kinds of people when it comes to drinking beer from bottles: those that pick and strip the labels, and those that don't. I've always been a picker.

I sensed a touch of bravado when Stuart finally said, 'Yes, sure, of course.' His response came more out of politeness than any other reason, perhaps I'd been too honest and direct, making him feel awkward. I decided to let him direct the conversation in whichever way he wanted. I scraped a thumbnail across my bottle, carving through the white gummy backing left on the green glass, and waited for him to speak. A familiar face loomed up towards our table.

'Ahoy there,' said Disco, for it was he, 'I popped down to say hello as I heard you were in here.'

How? Who could have possibly known I was there? Even I didn't know I was going there until three minutes before I walked through the door. But as I've said before, if Disco doesn't know about it, then it's not worth knowing. The local building trade thrives on gossip and rumours, and Disco is right at the beating heart of it. Want to know the word on the street? Disco probably wrote most of it. Who needs Facebook when you've got Disco? I invited him to sit with us and asked what he'd been up to over the past few days during my unexpected shutdown.

'Nothing special,' he replied, waving towards the door where a woman I recognised as the barmaid was holding a pint. She saw him and brought it over, which he gratefully accepted, 'Thanks Jo.' She gave him a kind smile and a cigarette, then lit one for herself and walked between the tables around the small garden, smoking with one hand and plucking dead glasses in bunches of three with the other.

'Disco has this magic skill,' I explained to Stuart. 'As well as knowing every pub landlord in a five-mile radius—'

'At least,' agreed Disco with a smile.

'Every pub landlord in *at least* a five-mile radius,' I said, 'he also has the knack of becoming the bar staff's best mate within seconds of meeting them. That's why he's the only bloke in this pub to have ever got table service and the full VIP treatment.'

Disco grinned and put his hands on either side of his face giving a dopey faux embarrassed, '*Shucks, me?*' gesture making Stuart laugh. I pushed him again, interested to find out what he'd been working on.

'Just some board-outs for Lofty Nige,' he said, meaning he'd been tacking floorboards for Nigel Larkin's loft conversions. It was easy, straightforward work that was below someone of Disco's pedigree. He should have been too good for work like that, but in the absence of a wife he'd taken the booze as the great love of his life. It had been a long and successful union as far as they were both concerned and providing he was in the pub no later than four they were both happy. So, something on a price he could bang out quickly with little effort suited him down to the ground. Hopefully Larkin didn't have much on, otherwise I knew I'd have trouble luring Disco back to work for me. He must have read my mind; 'He's only got enough to keep me busy until Friday, so I should be free next week if you've got anything?'

'There you go, Stuart,' I said. 'You and me can work out an action list, I'll get materials and everything else sorted, and then we can start in earnest next week, how's that sound?'

Stuart agreed that sounded like a plan, and with that rose to his feet offering to buy the next round. Disco eagerly accepted another drink despite having a full one in front of him, as we all knew it'd be long gone by the time Stuart came back from the bar, in fact it'd probably be gone by the time he got to the bar.

As soon as Stuart was inside, Disco pressed me for any news about the Admiral Guthrie. I knew anything I said would be shared to the world in seconds, immediately bringing to mind one of those viruses in a zombie movie. It'd take on a life of its own, multiplying and spreading without control, evolving and contorting out of all proportion but always traceable back to Patient Zero: me. Cautious, I avoided his question by fudging a response that even to my ears sounded unconvincing.

The garden door swung open. We both looked up expecting to see Stuart returning. I certainly didn't expect who was framed in the doorway: Hamlet. He stepped into the garden, sniffing the air as he did so, as though he'd just touched down in a totally foreign country. He walked straight over and sat at the table without any word or invitation. It gave another see-saw swing as it took his weight, then rocked once or twice back to resting. Disco decided at that point to make himself scarce—gripping his glass, he headed inside without a word. Glancing around, I noticed the few other people that had been out here had suddenly vanished. We were alone.

'Evening Marky Mark. I heard you were here.'

What? Him as well? What's going on, am I being tracked by satellite or something? Has everyone got an app that I don't know about?

'What do you want now?' I asked.

'Nothing. Honest. I thought you looked a bit glum this afternoon in the car, thought I'd buy you a drink, cheer you up. We're mates, aren't we?' he sounded genuine; I looked closely, trying to get the measure of him. 'Honest,' he protested.

'Oh, right, thanks,' I said, knowing I shouldn't be churlish. I might be suspicious, but there was no need to be a dick about it.

'I also wanted to give you a warning, a friendly heads-up as it were,' he leaned forwards and spoke in a low voice despite no one else being around, 'Have you been lifting more stones? This time asking very specific questions? About a plod called Inspector Hutton in particular?'

I gave a slow nod but didn't speak.

'He knows,' said Hamlet, he paused for so long I thought that was him done, lesson over, but then, 'Whatever you've been up to, word's got back to him. And he doesn't like it.'

I leaned back on the bench and watched the clouds overhead, hoping to find inspiration for something to say up there.

The same barmaid as before brought out a clear drink—knowing Hamlet, I knew it was vodka, and a bottle of a fancy tonic water. 'Lovely, thanks Jo.' I began to wonder if I was the butt of a joke I hadn't yet worked out, as it seemed the whole world and his wife now knew where I was any time of day, and everybody in the Medway Towns apart from me now got preferential table service.

'In my line of work it helps to have a few pet policemen, and I've had it confirmed from a reliable source… Hutton wants to send you a warning, he wants you to back off and walk away.'

The expression on his face told me he was serious, I nodded to say the message had been received, and Hamlet's face relaxed. He tipped the pink-tinged tonic into the glass, picked it up by the rim, and gently shook it to mix the solution. He raised it to his lips and took a sip.

'Did you know Ron Fielder was McInally's Animal? That he killed the sailor?' From the wide eyes bulging above the rim of the glass and the coughing fit that followed, I was convinced he didn't. I let him recover before I asked, 'Well, if you didn't, why were you so scornful of him when his name got mentioned?'

'Let me tell you about Ron Fielder,' said Hamlet. 'He was a nutter. One of those blokes that live for a punch-up. He could start a fight in an empty room. He got in to door security. Through that he got jobs as muscle for all sorts of lowlife: loan sharks, tenant evictions, you name it he was up for it. But never ever would I have had him down as a life-taker.'

'Our local success story? The Medway boy done good?'

'Is he fuck.' Hamlet clearly disagreed with who Her Majesty wanted to dob with her sword. 'What pisses me off most of all about Ron bloody Fielder is how he bangs on and on about his humble roots and how hard he had to work. But it's all with someone else's money, they never talk about that do they?'

'I see,' I said, but I didn't.

'It was luck. Right place, right time,' continued Hamlet. 'We could all be property magnates if we had someone bankrolling us.'

Now I began to get it, Hamlet had a touch of the green-eyed jealousy, maybe he felt he'd missed his opportunity and blamed Fielder personally for it.

'I knew he was a nutter,' said Hamlet, 'but like I say, I never saw him as a killer. But him and Donaldson together, makes sense now.'

Hamlet had lost me. I told him so. He looked at me with pity, as though I was a slow, dim-witted step-child, then took a long breath up through his nose, pause, then back down again. He was ready to continue.

'Fielder, despite being a vicious lunatic, has somehow managed to avoid getting a record. As far as I know, he's never ever been pulled for anything. Donaldson on the other hand has been charged, more than once. So, put them together, what have you got?'

'A pair of nutters?'

'No. Well, yes. But no, you've got a respectable clean face of the business and you've got Donaldson behind the scenes solving any problems.'

I thought back to what Rachel Ridder had said about Fielder's schemes sailing through the approval process and it made sense: if bribes didn't work, Donaldson could pay them a visit and threaten their children: the car dealer Hopkins, a case in point. And as for subcontractor disputes being settled privately, of course Fielder would throw money to make them go away, and if that failed then Donaldson was there to sort things out the hard way. Any means necessary to keep the real him hidden from view.

'The only thing I still need to find out,' said Hamlet, 'is whether or not the Flints are involved. If this whole pub business has just been Donaldson protecting his mate Fielder, then that's one thing… but if he's working for the Flints, then that's a whole new level of complicated. I need to make some calls.'

Hamlet took out a mobile phone. From the way he jabbed in a long sequence of numbers from memory, I suspected it was a burner phone with a lifespan of less than twenty-four hours before it's broken up and tossed. He stared at me with a look that I immediately knew the meaning of. I left him at the table and went inside.

I found Stuart and Disco face-to-face at a small drum table barely wide enough for two blokes to rest their nuts on—so Disco tipped his greedily into his wide maw of a mouth and chomped. Stuart dragged across a chair from a vacant table, expecting me to join them.

'To be honest, I'm not in the mood any more, sorry,' I said to them. 'I'm going to head home. Do you want a lift back, or are you okay?'

Stuart assured me he was happy to have a few more with Disco. I told them both I'd see them later and felt the nosey parker regulars' eyes burning my shoulders as I headed on my way.

I'd parked in the vast railway station car park opposite, which at this time in the evening stood two-thirds empty, the many commuters by now comfortable at home in their slippers looking forward to steak and chips for tea. I'd no sooner twisted the key in the ignition and rolled the van forward a few feet when blue lights set alight the dusk and a peal of a siren shocked me from behind. I hadn't noticed the police car parked a row or two back in the shadows, but they'd made sure I noticed it now. I rolled back into the parking bay I'd just left, switched off the engine and waited.

-38-

IF YOU'RE GETTING older when the police start looking younger, I must be getting prettier. A beast in a stab vest loomed over me. The little embroidered patch on his tunic said Constable Oates. Oates commanded me to get out of the van; I suspected I may be some time.

'I've told you once already, get out the vehicle,' said Oates, arms crossed against his barrel chest. I looked him up and down, then obeyed and stepped out. He had one of those mugs that was the same stubble all over: hair buzzed down and chin grown out; a reddish fuzz smothered his big round head, making him look like one giant testicle. I leant back. My bodyweight pushed the door closed behind me with a soft click, and I rested against the van. The old instinct kicked in: stay passive, say nothing, do nothing.

'You know why I stopped you, sir?' he said, spitting out the sour taste of the last word. I didn't speak, I remained expressionless, the Great Stone Face that's me. He continued, 'I believe you to be driving under the influence of alcohol.'

What nonsense was this? First, I'd only had one small beer, and secondly—driving? I'd only put the van into first, I doubt the tyres had turned more than twice over. Is this what Hamlet had warned me about? Police harassment everywhere I went from now on?

With a smirk twitching below the gingery stubble, the policeman asked, 'Are you denying this, sir? Perhaps you'd care to take a breathalyser test?'

I didn't respond. I looked at his boots, at the ground, anything to avoid eye contact with him. I considered what was happening. Obviously not quick enough for his liking. 'You are refusing to provide a breath test? Noted. In that case, you will need to come with me to the station to give a blood sample.'

'Say what? Are you out of your mind? What are you talking about?'

'No need for that kind of attitude, sir, please come with me,' his paw squeezed my upper arm in a tight and painful grip. My elbow jerked in an upward arc to try to throw him off—a reflex reaction. Bad move. I felt the baton strike before I saw it. It happened so fast he must have already it had it drawn, itching for an excuse to swing it. A belt of pain right across my thigh, my knees collapsed, and I fell to the ground and looked skyward to see him over me, baton raised.

'Hey!' cried a voice in the distance, 'Hey!'

'Stand back please,' shouted Oates without glancing back. 'This man's assaulted a police officer and is resisting arrest.'

The onlooker had drawn closer. I thought I'd recognised the voice and had never been so grateful to be proven right: 'Constable,' said Hamlet, the first syllable deliberately over-emphasised. 'Let him up.'

Oates was clearly annoyed by the interruption; another do-gooder getting in the way of a spot of light police brutality. He turned, ready to shoo them away with a well-rehearsed threat when he recognised who was behind him.

'Constable Oates,' Hamlet's tone was loaded with derision, 'I don't think you want to be doing that to my friend. Marky, get yourself up off the floor.'

Oates looked at me with undisguised hatred as I rolled over and stood up. I held on to the van, not wanting to give him the satisfaction of seeing me struggle. A damp heat radiated from within and I knew it meant a nasty black bruise was blossoming across my thigh.

Oates turned on the spot and started to walk away with the rolling gait of a bulldog. Hamlet kept step with him, I couldn't hear words spoken but I knew from their stances and Hamlet's gestures with his hands that they were talking. They reached the nose of Oates' car and continued to talk: their backs to me, their words private and clandestine.

Hamlet slapped Oates on the back; a matey hearty and hale gesture but also loaded with authority, even from my distant position, I could tell he'd taken the high status from Oates and reduced him to nothing. Hamlet sauntered back towards me, only pausing to add, 'You and me will be having words later, Philip.' Oates halted what he was doing, only for a moment, a split second, but long enough for Hamlet to claim victory. Oates gave a shrug as if to say 'whatever' but I could tell his heart wasn't in it. He climbed into his car and revved it back to life. Hamlet called out to him, 'You know we will, Philip.' Oates pulled away in fury, leaving black tyre smears across the road surface.

Hamlet broke into a loud, filthy laugh. Adrenalin sluiced through me and mixed with the relief that it was over: a fizzy concoction. I found myself laughing too. We stood in the last dying moments of daylight laughing uncontrollably until we couldn't breathe any more.

SIX MINUTES LATER the adrenalin wore off, the laughing stopped, and the hurting started. Hamlet suggested it'd be better if I stretched myself out rather than letting all the muscles contract and tighten. I guess if anyone knew how to recover from a beating, it was him. An evening commuter train discharged dozens of weary office workers, all trying to remember where exactly they'd parked twelve hours earlier. They milled around the parking bays hunting for their ride home. We didn't talk much as he marched me briskly around the perimeter of the car park until we were back at the van, 'I warned you, do you believe me now? He'd been sent to sort you out, mate. He was waiting for you. You're lucky I was there. He was going to turn you over simply to prove that they can.'

'Who can?' I asked. 'Hutton, you mean?'

'Chief Inspector Hutton, the very man,' said Hamlet, 'Like I say, you've been poking around. It didn't take very long for it to trickle back to him. And if Hutton's embedded in there, second generation bent, you can bet your life he's got a legion of them keen to take his cash, and that Oates is as dirty as they come. He's got two kids in private school and a daughter just started university, how'd you think he affords that? Because he's got his grubby mitt held open for every bung going.'

I heard what Hamlet said. It was all too clear I'd got in deep, far too deep, I was drowning.

-39-

'YOU SCARED ME half to death,' laughed Perry. She'd walked into the darkened bedroom and found me, unexpected, sitting upright on the bed. I hadn't noticed the night falling, I'd been too lost in my thoughts. Perry clicked on the lamp beside the bed and clambered up to join me.

We sat on the bed, holding each other, saying nothing. Our bodies lay half in half out of the soft buttery glow from the bedside lamp that fought a losing battle to hold back the cold black night pouring through the open curtains. Occasionally a random water pipe expanded or contracted and clunked noisily. We'd snap our heads round seeking the source of the sound, the both of us too jumpy by far.

Perry's cheek had been resting on my chest for some time, I liked it: the feel of her, the smell of her hair—a freshly showered clean floral tang. She struggled against drowsiness. I assumed it must have been a difficult shift in accident and emergency, but I didn't ask. This period of quiet had given me room to think: 'I can't do this anymore.'

Perry murmured a soft soothing pleasantry and rubbed my chest.

'I want out. It's none of my business, not my battle, I should never have got involved.'

Perry continued stroking my chest, a pacifying gesture, cooing in a gentle voice, 'Good. Good,' and then the thought struck her, 'How?'

I hadn't planned that far ahead. I suppose I'd assumed if I went home and took my ball with me everybody else would walk away too, game over, forget it ever happened and we'd all live happily ever after. Perry's questioning made me realise the only way to let them know I'm out would be to announce it, which meant admitting I was involved in the first place: man alive, what a mess I'd got myself into.

'I'm glad,' said Perry. 'It's for the best, you realise that don't you?' I assured her that I did, and knew she was right, 'What were you hoping the outcome would be, anyway?'

'Outcome?'

Perry moved off me and sat up. She raised her knees to her chest and wrapped her arms under them, 'Yes, outcome. What'd you hope to achieve?'

What had I hoped to achieve? Had I hoped to achieve anything? I began to worry I'd set myself the noble quest of finding the truth with no plan what to do with it once I'd found it.

Perry nudged her bare feet under a nearby pillow to keep warm. 'What was the plan, Mark? You've found out this Donaldson man and his friend Ron Fielder killed and buried someone in the pub, which is why they scared people away from it for years and used the police to cover it up. What did you hope to do with that kind of information?'

I propped myself up on my elbows and caught a glimpse of my reflection in the wardrobe mirror as I did so. I looked so tired, so old. I knew a toll had been taken on me mentally, but now I saw its physical effect.

'I don't know,' I replied in absolute honesty, because I didn't. Perry reached an arm out around my shoulder and pulled us close, a nice gesture, but I don't know if it was done in appreciation of my honesty or out of sympathy for my naivety.

'These are dangerous people. They've power and influence,' said Perry. 'It's not like the movies, you're not a vigilante. You can't topple them, bring them to justice, not on your own. Anyone trying to do that would be hurt, probably killed, long before they got anywhere close.'

She'd summed up my thoughts exactly. She was one hundred percent right again, 'I'm not Clint Eastwood,' I muttered in agreement.

'I always preferred Schwarzenegger anyway,' she quipped. 'Come on, Muscles.' Perry stretched her legs out straight, and stepped off the bed, 'I'm hungry, let's get something to eat. Brand new start tomorrow.'

As I followed her downstairs she suggested, 'We could go on holiday, get away from all of this. Listen, one of the consultants at the hospital, she recently retired, opened a B&B in the New Forest, I could call her, I'm due a few days leave. Think about it.'

Now there was a nice idea: a few days away, chance to create a bit of distance, opportunity to clear my head, time to be alone with the person I care about. I admit I was sorely tempted.

'Okay, you're on. Let's do it.'

Perry spun on the spot and squeezed me in a tight bear hug. A bolt of pain shot up from my bruised thigh, but I found it oddly pleasurable when I saw how happy she was. Holibobs here we come.

I made a phone call to order us a pizza. When told it'd be delivered in the next half hour, Perry switched on one of the soaps she likes to watch and got comfortable on the sofa. I sat next to her and attempted to follow along, but it held no interest for me, besides there was something I needed to do first if I was ever to get closure.

'MARK, HOW ARE you?' said a surprised Nick Witham, picking up on only the second ring. In the background I heard the clatter of home life and felt a pang of guilt interrupting his dinner. 'Spencer says hi.' I responded with a hello back to Spencer and Nick relayed it, that seemed to satisfy the small talk and pleasantries.

'Nick, I need to tell you something,' and so I proceeded to tell him all about his boss Hutton and the roles of Donaldson and Fielder. 'As I say, that's all I know, I've nothing concrete, no smoking gun, but there you go, do with it what you will, I'm done.'

Nick went quiet for a moment, and down the line I heard the same dialogue from the same soap as Perry was watching in the other room, clearly Spencer was also a fan. I'd known Spencer nearly as long as I'd known Nick, way back when we were all at school together, and I liked him a lot—a very funny guy. I guess we always knew Nick and Spencer were an item, even before we knew what that meant. Two big happy bears, still together all these years later.

Nick was still processing his thoughts. 'Okay Mark,' he said slowly, as though buying time before committing to anything. 'Thanks for letting me know.'

'Sorry to dump it all on you, mate, but I've had enough of it. Whatever you do with it, it's up to you, I don't care.'

'Fair enough,' although Nick didn't sound as though he thought it fair. 'And what do you want me to do with all the sailor's stuff?'

'The what?'

'For fuck's sake Mark,' yep, Nick wasn't finding it fair. 'You asked me—no, you pleaded with me to get that dead sailor's case re-opened, and what? You've forgotten all about it?'

Oh! The sailor stabbed and dumped in an alley, he was right I had forgotten all about that, but only because he'd told me it'd be impossible for him to get it re-opened, so I did the only decent thing: I blamed him.

'Thanks to you, Mark,' the raised volume of his voice suggested that telling him it was his fault hadn't worked, 'I've now got a boot full of manky old clothes, my car smells like a jumble sale.'

That, I admit, took me by surprise. Nick was more than willing to explain; no doubt having wanted to vent at me for the past couple of days. 'Because by going to the archive to pull out the old file, I was also given bundles of evidence. All his clothes and personal possessions, sitting there for thirty-five years, unloved and unwanted. No record of any of it on the file, but that's not unusual considering how many moves and reorganisations there's been since then, they've probably been moved on more often than a homeless dog.'

'I don't know what to say, Nick. Keep it, bin it, give it back. Do what you like with it, I don't care anymore.'

'Thanks. Thanks a fucking lot. Mate.' Nick spat out the last word and cut the call before I could respond. I couldn't leave it like that, not with one of my oldest friends. I dialled his number again. It rang and rang before clicking over to voicemail. I dialled again, this time it picked up on the first half ring. A voice that wasn't Nick's answered:

'Hello Mark,' said Spencer, 'Nick doesn't want to talk to you, says you've pissed him right off.'

'I have, yes,' I admitted. 'Will you tell him I'm sorry please?'

'Sure,' said Spencer. 'As it happens, we're off for a week in Tenerife at the weekend anyway, so give him a little time and it'll all have blown over I'm sure.'

'I expect you're right,' I said. 'Funnily enough I'm away too, me and Perry are having a little holiday.'

'Well there you are then, give us a call when you're back and I'm sure it'll all be right as rain again, okay?' suggested Spencer, and with that we both said our goodbyes.

The closing theme tune of the soap began to play and then fell silent, followed by Perry calling out from the other room a second later, 'Any sign of that pizza yet? I'm starving.' I promised to chase it up, I just needed to make one more call. Perry released the mute button and noise returned, this time the jangly synthesised theme tune to some godawful reality nonsense she liked full of people so desperate to be famous at any cost shouting and hollering at each other in semi-scripted arguments.

I reached out to pull the door closed, wanting to mask out the sound of women screeching, but something on the screen made me stop dead. A young woman cursed and threatened her love rival. Her straightened hair was so smooth and so glossy it looked metallic, see it close-up and you'd think it was from the panel of a new car. She was the same one Danny Kidd had been fighting over in the infamous tabloid nightclub photos. That all seemed like such a long time ago now, back then I was happy doing landlord tests and the occasional rewire. How did it all come to this? Unable to answer because there was no answer, I pulled the door closed and made my second call and again downloaded everything I knew to the recipient.

'That's explosive stuff,' said Rachel Ridder, once I'd finished sharing all I had. 'Police cover-ups, corruption, murders. This could be massive.'

'Yeah, yeah, Watergate all over again,' I said. 'I'm giving you all I know, but what you choose to do with it is up to you, do whatever you want, just keep my name out of it, okay? Please?'

'Sure, sure,' Ridder replied, but her tone gave the impression her thoughts were elsewhere, no doubt wondering how to turn this into the biggest story of her career.

'If you want to dig deeper, then that's entirely up to you,' I said, 'but be warned, they're not nice people. Tread carefully.' I ended the call and returned to the living room feeling oddly jubilant. I was officially out. We could sleep safely in our beds tonight and dream of holiday tomorrow.

The motion-activated lamp outside flashed on: its stark, brilliant light illuminated the frosted glass panel in the front door and bled in around the edges of the curtains. A second or two later the doorbell rang. 'Pizza, at last,' Perry squealed with excitement, giving one of those ladies' claps—three or four rapid beats using dead-straight fingers. 'You can get it, as you're up already.'

Ever the gentleman, I obliged and released the latch. The door swung inwards and open while I sunk my hands deep in my pockets. I trawled for loose change and looked down to my palms, hoping there'd be enough to make a decent tip for the pizza-boy. It was only when I looked up that I saw the gun aimed directly at my face, point-blank.

The muzzle of the pistol twitched, beckoning me to follow it outside. My mind, still expecting to see a pizza delivery boy, was scrambled at the sight facing me. It spun through a whirl of random thoughts like a ball on a roulette wheel before landing on the one which stuck: 'But I'm going on holiday tomorrow.'

-40-

THE GUN BECKONED me outside a second time, I feared there wouldn't be a third. I raised my hands to shoulder height. I don't know why I did that, I wasn't asked to. Fair play and good sportsmanship I suppose: if I'm no threat maybe he'd reconsider shooting me. Soft-lad thinking, I know, but I was still new to this having-guns-pulled-on-me malarkey. The loose change tumbled from my palms, the gun jabbed forward a couple of inches, reacting in case it was a ruse before a bold act of heroism—as if. The sight of the gun had already turned my insides to liquid and they felt ready to seep. You can forget any bravery. There was absolutely no chance of me becoming Captain America, not when it was all I could do not to cough for fear of soiling myself.

I gave a lingering downward glance to my bare feet, the gun followed my eyes, and in measured, deliberate motions, I slid and twisted and nuzzled my toes into a nearby pair of Nikes. As I did so, my eyes to the floor, I noticed his trainers looked brand new, like they were straight out of the box: a vivid blue, the same blue as Chelsea play in. Funny the things that go through your head when a gun's pointed at it, isn't it? Shoes on, I nodded, I was ready to go. I stepped outside using wide slow movements—the last thing I wanted was a barrage of bullets in the back just because tripping over trailing laces gets mistaken for an escape attempt.

In the brightness of the floodlight I got a good look at the bearer of the gun and the Chelsea-blue shoes. He was mid-twenties, of mixed race, and despite the padded puffa jacket wrapping him up, I could tell he was in the same sort of good shape as a sportsman, or a soldier. Also, he'd never once wavered or trembled—he knew how to handle a weapon and had done so many times. He was a professional.

Without a word spoken, just through flicks of the pistol's barrel, he directed me to a nearby car, a big fat Porsche SUV, nice. The rear door opened as we approached, then everything went dark. He'd dropped something over my head, a bag or a hood of some kind. Total darkness and the warm dry taste of my own breath. A strong hand on the base of my neck pushed me forwards and downwards in the same motion, and I was blindly fed into the back seat of the car.

'But I'm going on holiday tomorrow.'

THE HOOD CAME off and I blinked against the harsh lighting. White diffusers, two-foot square, set within a suspended ceiling grid: one lamp at every fourth square in all directions. The standard layout. Office layout. I was in an office—a meeting room, to be exact. I'd been placed beside a large square table: smooth brilliant white, with sockets and data ports sunk into the surface. A speaker phone sat at the centre of the table, its bulbous centre and several arms extending from it resembled an octopus. Twelve matching chrome and leather chairs ringed the table, three to each side. A gleaming smart board took up an eight-foot span across one wall, and arty pen and ink prints hung on another depicting famous landmark buildings from around the world. So far, so fancy. This was a swanky place.

A large oblong window in the wall opposite faced me, showing jet-black sky beyond the silver slats of the blind. The window had curved corners, edged in a narrow white plastic framing. A modern slim air-conditioning unit hung above the window. From the look and feel of the room, I had an idea of where I was, but not *where* I was.

The journey had been smooth—you'd expect nothing less from a nice car like that—but from under my shroud it gave no clues as to the direction of travel. All I knew was there were two of them in the car. I knew whoever opened the rear door from inside had stayed put, as our shoulders bumped when I got into the car. Once in, their fingers were all over me until they located my phone, which was taken off me without a word. I assumed my friend, Chelsea-blue, doubled up as the driver, but they didn't speak to each other for the entire journey. In fact there was no sound inside the car, no radio, no sat-nav giving directions, nothing. It didn't take long before I'd lost all track of time.

When the car stopped, I heard the electronic door locks whirr, the driver's door yawn open, then a second or two later the door beside me was opened too. A tight grip around my elbow pulled me out and pushed me forwards.

I started walking. The ground felt firm and solid underfoot. Deep inside me a pang of relief celebrated the fact I hadn't been dragged out to the-arse-end-of-nowhere-countryside where in a fortnight's time an old man and his dog would follow the stench of my rotting corpse to find me shot and dumped in a ditch. I was on a road or pavement of some sort, it was a hard-finished surface. The pang of relief immediately evaporated, replaced by the realisation that situations a whole lot nastier than dark ditches existed in factories, industrial estates and scrap yards. I walked on blindly, listening out for big machines that could crush me, squash me or shred me into tiny little pieces.

The ground had solidity without scuffing: it was a tight, hard surface, not compacted earth or concrete. Tarmac was my guess, but then it changed to an uneven, rough surface that felt hollow and gave a metallic clatter: some kind of grating? A jerk on my elbow brought me to a halt. Ahead of me I heard the jangle of keys, then bolts turning in their locks. A door opened. An internal alarm woke up and gave its introductory pulsing beeps. There followed a few electronic pips from code being punched in to a keypad. The alarm went back to sleep.

Things were beginning to come together in my mind: I'd joined a few jigsaw pieces but still couldn't quite see the whole picture. I slid my feet back and forth, I was certain I'd come from a parking bay and now stood on a matwell, the sort used to scrape boots clean. I responded to a nudge in the back and stepped up through the open door. A hand on my shoulder steered me forwards. The floor didn't have the hard, unforgiving feel of a concrete slab, or the echoey vibration of a timber floor, it had a bounce to it, spongy almost.

There's only one type of floor I knew that flexes like that and combined with the style of the window before me, I knew I was right. I was in a portable building. Judging by the room I was in and its fancy décor, I knew it wasn't Dave the Manc's greasy spoon canteen. I figured it must have been a sales office or marketing suite. The only problem was I had no idea where. Or why.

I was alone. Chelsea-blue played sentry outside, his back to the door. My thoughts went to Perry: what must she be thinking, what's she going through, she must be scared stiff. I pulled the speakerphone towards me by one of its tentacles: there must be a way to get a message to her. I jabbed at the buttons hoping for an outside line but nothing. The digital display was dark and blank, dead: dead as any hope of contacting her.

THE DOOR OPENED. Chelsea-blue, my gun-toting amigo, leaned in. 'Don't,' he said, using his chin to point at the speakerphone, then leaned back.

The door began to close, 'Wait, what's going on?' I asked, 'What do you want?'

'They'll be here in a minute.'

'But you—'

'Ssshhh,' he said. The door closed. Who? Who'll be here? Where is here? It was clear he wasn't going to tell me anything. He knew his role and he wasn't going to deviate from it.

I looked around the room again for clues, but yet again came away with nothing. I rose from the seat. Chelsea-blue gave a cursory glance in my direction, but there was nowhere for me to go without getting past him. He knew I'd never attempt that, so he quickly turned back, satisfied there was no threat. I walked across to the window and used finger and thumb to widen the gap between the slats of the blind. I peered out. As my eyes took in the view before me, a freezing cold lightning bolt crackled down my spine, and that liquified feeling grumbled deep inside. I knew where I was. And I knew who *they* were.

From the window I saw the Porsche SUV—I'd been right, I'd come from a parking bay. A newly created parking bay with crisp, unspoilt white lines within neat and tidy landscaping: planting beds created from freshly laid bricks with perfectly perpendicular joints and populated with shiny new shrubs and bushes. The area was lit by expensive, low-level stainless-steel bollards. It was lined on two sides by a hoarding two metres high. Clad in a glossy black laminate, the hoarding was pristine, not a mark or scuff visible. This whole area—the parking bays, the landscaping, the shiny hoarding, the swanky office building—had been designed for the sole purpose of enticing the public; it was a sales and marketing hub. I was certain of this because mounted on the hoarding, facing the road and spot-lit for twenty-four-hour visibility, were artists impressions of aspirational living beneath large red logos and letters bearing the words *'Fielder Homes'*. I was in the Animal's den.

I DROPPED INTO the seat nearest the window and waited for the chill in my blood to subside. Outside, the hoardings showed graphics of young families on a lawn playing games in the sunshine, while sexy modern apartment blocks stood in the background looking reassuringly solid and luxurious. Would I get the chance to play ball with my kids? That's what Perry was getting at, and realising I was probably never going to have that made me realise how much I actually wanted it.

The door opened, and I turned to see another visitor being escorted in the same way I was. Once inside the room, he had his hood yanked off in a violent snatch, jerking his head back: Hamlet. Hamlet? As if things could have got any worse, they'd just taken it up a level. If they can get to Hamlet, then who could possibly stop them?

Hamlet's escort was quick on his toes getting out of the room. He'd locked the door behind him before Hamlet had a chance to react. Blood had crusted all around Hamlet's nose and his eyebrow was split and swollen; clearly, he'd put up more of a fight than me when they came to get him. Hamlet hammered on the door with both fists, then started kicking. The veneer began to crack and splinter. 'You fucking cocksucker, I'm going to have you. I'll have your carcass, you hear me.'

Chelsea-blue, still on sentry duty, appeared at the glazed panel and pointed his gun straight at Hamlet. Hamlet took a half-step back, keeping eye contact locked on and jabbed an angry middle finger salute at him, then dropped himself into the closest seat. It was then and only then that he noticed me in the room with him. 'Marky, what the fuck? Do you know what's going on? Where are we?'

I beckoned him over to the window. 'It looks like we're guests of Ron Fielder.'

'Fuck,' Hamlet dabbed at his nose with the back of his hand and studied the bloody smears it left. 'I think this might be my fault, Marky, sorry.'

Before I could find out why, the door swung open and in walked Chelsea-blue, followed by the one who'd escorted Hamlet. They took a corner each, strategic positions, facing Hamlet and me. They had a military bearing in the way they stood. Both had their guns in their right hands, their left hands clasped their right wrist, held low at groin level. The sweater sleeves of Hamlet's escort had been pulled halfway up his forearms, exposing finely detailed tattoos of feathers beautifully rendered in black and white ink, almost photo-realistic: sheer works of art.

Feathers, the same as Chelsea-blue, stood as still and unmoving as bookends at either end of the wall. They watched us and didn't utter a single word.

After they'd taken their positions, confident the room was secure, a man followed them in, and took a seat across the table from us. He looked in his fifties but he was trendy with it, not gaudy logo-heavy stuff for teenagers that Hamlet wears, but in a classic, groomed way: smart black jeans, a fitted black sweater beneath a short sandy-coloured Burberry mac. His silver hair was styled, and silver beard trimmed with sharp, precise edges. He sat opposite us, fiddling with his cuffs as though killing time before a business meeting, waiting for the last attendees to arrive.

Hamlet opened his mouth, about to speak, but the man raised a finger. 'Uh-uh, save whatever you're going to say until everyone's here. I'm not going through all this twice.'

Hamlet, to my amazement, did as commanded. He fell silent and stayed that way. Beside me, I saw Hamlet's fists clench the moment Donaldson walked into the room. He had an escort, another lean tough guy of the military bearing, but no bag on the head for him. It seemed Donaldson was an invited guest, but he looked just as surprised to see us as we him. The man pointed to a seat, Donaldson obediently sat. Hamlet glared at Donaldson, poised ready to spring across the table at him. Donaldson glared back. Neither spoke.

All heads turned when the door opened again, and there we saw Ron Fielder, alone, no escort required for him. He was dressed immaculately in a crisp dinner suit, with what appeared to be a hand-tied silk bow tie around his collar. Fielder looked to the man at the table.

'What the bloody hell is this all about? I'm meant to be hosting a charity event.'

'Shut up Ron and sit down,' he pointed to a chair beside Donaldson. Fielder walked around the table. He gave Donaldson a friendly squeeze on the shoulder in greeting, then sat beside him, obeying the man's instruction to the letter.

'Right gentlemen, we're all here. Let's begin.'

He gave a signal: Donaldson' escort left the room and gently pulled the door closed behind him, then took up sentry duty in front of it. The other two, Feathers and Chelsea-blue, remained rooted to the spot and watched the room. Everyone assembled around this table, these hard men, these dangerous men, every single one of them had become meek little lambs before this man in the Burberry mac. This was a man who commanded respect and authority, and now he was looking directly at me, red veins standing out against the whites of his eyes.

'You're Mark Poynter, are you?' I nodded that I was. 'You know who I am, do you?'

'This,' said Hamlet, coming to my aid, 'is Tony Flint.'

-41-

A NAME EVERYONE'S familiar with. Everyone knows the stories. Never in my lifetime did I think I'd ever meet Tony Flint, any more than I thought I might sit down for tea one day with Jack the Ripper. A legend often whispered about, but no one ever meets the man himself. He was the crown prince among crime lords, no wonder everyone in this room was so deferential to him. And now, somehow, he's got his sights on me.

'Yes, I'm Mark Poynter,' I said to him, aware my disappointment at being so very close to have put all of this behind me had added a heaviness to my tone.

Flint flicked his chin up, as though mentally ticking my name off his list of attendees at this meeting. 'This is yours,' he pulled my phone from his mac pocket. It wasn't a question but a statement of fact, and I guess it answered any lingering query about who sat next to me on the drive here. He placed my phone on the table in front of him, then turned to Feathers, his man in the corner, and jerked a thumb towards Hamlet. 'Got his?' Feathers pulled a phone from the back pocket of his jeans and handed it to Flint, who laid it side by side against mine, 'Now yours,' he said, looking at Fielder and Donaldson.

Donaldson hesitated, then, with a shrug, slid his across the table to Flint. Fielder didn't move, Flint fixed a stare on Fielder. 'Tony, what's this all about?' protested Fielder.

'Phone. Here. Now.' Flint jabbed the tip of an extended finger against the table top in time with every word spoken as though tapping out a code. Fielder maintained the stare right back at him and held it for a few moments before muttering, 'Fine.' He opened up his tuxedo, a flash of a peacock blue silk lining, and pulled a phone from the inside pocket. He flung it over to Flint.

Flint gathered the phones together and handed them to Chelsea-blue with the words 'Take these outside.' He dutifully obeyed and was back in the room seconds later.

'Right, now we're all happy no one's recording, and no one's got any outside contact we can talk freely,' said Flint. 'So, who wants to go first?'

Hamlet sat at the edge of my vision. I'd never seen him so subdued. There was a story from when I was a kid that came to mind: the superior forces overpower Aslan the mighty lion. They declaw him, muzzle him, hack off his noble mane. Hamlet was like that fallen king. In the story, good triumphs over evil and the lion roars proudly again. But that's just a kid's fairy tale, this is real life, Hamlet's certainly not a noble leader—in fact I'd question if he's ever been on the side of good before, but at that moment him and me were on the same team and it felt like we were going to lose.

Fielder was agitated, 'Tony, will you tell me what the bloody hell this is all about?' Flint's eyes walked the room, landing on each of us in turn before moving to the next in the same way a crocodile scans the river bank looking for an easy lunch. After two slow circuits he said just two words, 'Admiral Guthrie.'

Fielder slumped back against his chair. He exchanged a conspirator's moment of eye contact with Donaldson, 'Oh.'

'Oh? Is that all you have to say: oh?'

'What more do you want me to say?' a touch of irritation had crept into Fielder's voice.

'Murders? Fires?' Flint sounded irritated too. 'We had that pub over fifty years, since before the War. Until the nineties. Why's this the first I'm hearing about it?'

'It's old news, Tony. Over thirty years ago.

Donaldson leant forward on his elbows. 'It's dealt with. Forget about it.'

'Dealt with? By destroying my shop, by robbing me? Forget about it?' Hamlet was incensed. Donaldson smirked at Hamlet's rage, not a wise move, Hamlet had got his roar back. The claws and fangs would follow. This could get messy.

Flint patted the air in front of him, an instruction for Hamlet to calm down, then he turned towards Donaldson. 'Did you bring his money, like I asked?'

Donaldson like a stroppy kid shrugged and puffed out a sigh. Flint wasn't impressed with that as a response, but despite Donaldson' attitude, he didn't need to repeat the question a second time.

'In the car,' replied Donaldson.

With just a movement of a finger, Flint instructed Feathers to step across to Donaldson. As if carved from rock, he stood solid and immense beside Donaldson until Donaldson relented and handed him his car key. Feathers took it and left the room. Another awkward silence trapped us for a few minutes until Feathers returned. He dropped a sports holdall on the table. Flint unzipped it, peered inside, then held it wide open so that we could see the contents, 'All there?' he asked. Donaldson nodded. Flint zipped the bag closed, then pushed it across the table to Hamlet.

Hamlet hugged the bag close to him. He wasn't going to let it get away from him again. 'Thanks. Are we done, can we go now?'

'Soon, soon,' laughed Flint. 'Let me show you something first. Come on, follow me.' He walked to the door. 'Come on.'

The four of us—Donaldson, Fielder, Hamlet and me—paused in a confused stupor, then rose as one, and followed Flint to the main marketing suite outside of our room. Flint stood with a miniature scale model on a table before him: a giant towering over the perfect housing development. The apartment blocks, the road layouts, mature trees, bench seating, statues and public art were all perfectly created down to the finest detail, even the teeny-weeny phones and books in the hands of the half-inch high people. Flint gazed fondly upon the tiny world in front of him. 'Doesn't this look great?' Hamlet and I leaned in for a closer look and nodded politely.

Fielder felt the need to assert himself, it was his name above the door after all. He spoke as if addressing a press conference: 'Eleven-acre former brownfield site. All contamination properly cleared offsite, any inert spoil taken to the estuary to form new habitats for bird and wildlife sanctuaries. There will be over twelve hundred new dwellings, thirty retail units including a major national supermarket chain taking the anchor store, ten units for food and beverage, four restaurants and a medical centre. It's going to be a proper, fully formed and integrated community. We're working with the council to refurb and overhaul the nearby primary school in readiness for the additional new residents, and we've pumped a fortune into upgrading the road network.'

'Very nice,' said Hamlet directly to Flint, deliberately ignoring Fielder. 'But, so what? What's it got to do with us?'

'Come on, I'll explain,' said Flint, 'Ron, go and open upstairs.'

Fielder disappeared through a door at the end and in the quiet of the evening we heard his footsteps bouncing up a staircase then striding over our heads. Flint then ushered us in the same direction, up to the level above.

WE CAME OUT in a large open room, glazed floor to ceiling the length of one wall. 'Go on, go on,' Flint urged us to move closer to the glazing. At Flint's instruction, Fielder flicked a switch, and a network of floodlights outside bleached the dark night sky with brilliant white beams. The shiny black hoarding had been erected to hide the grubby realities of a live building site from passers-by and maintain Uncle Ronnie's façade of aspirational living: *like it? You too can live here, low deposit, stamp duty paid, help to buy, Uncle Ronnie will make all your dreams come true.*

From this higher level we could see over the hoarding. The whole site was laid out before us: skeletal cages of rusty brown steel rods poked up out of white concrete footings that criss-crossed the flattened earth like scars; huge machines were silent, sleeping off their hard day's graft; a large red and white cement silo stood half in the shadows, and the base of tower crane could be seen at the far end of the site, ready to grow tall and fast, like a sunflower, in the coming days. Dotted all over the site were huge concrete rings. Fielder noticed they'd caught my attention. 'Foul drainage,' he said. 'Because of the high volumes of occupancy, we need to run in new sewage. Twelve hundred flats, two and a half thousand people, that's a lot of shit to shift. Those are three-metre rings, and to make sure all that shit rolls the right way the trenching is nine metres deep by the time it reaches that point,' he pressed his finger against the glass and I followed it to an area near us at the front of the site that had been protected with road plates—heavy sheets of steel an inch thick—to cover open excavations.

'Nine metres deep?'

'Nine metres,' confirmed Fielder, and then added for the benefit of Hamlet, 'That's about thirty feet in old money.' Hamlet gave a small whistle, but I doubt he could picture a trench of thirty feet deep any more than he could one of thirty fathoms.

Fielder looked directly at me. 'You're the electrician, right?' I nodded. 'We're having to pull in brand new utilities, the HV main comes in under the pavement there and a new substation's going over there,' he said pointing at different locations across the site. I must admit, despite the situation, I was enjoying the view and the chat, but Hamlet had had enough:

'This is all very nice, but so what? What's it got to do with me?'

'Because it's been twenty years in the making, that's what,' Flint said. He stood close to the glazed wall. The darkness of the night combined with the contrasting piercing white of the floodlights' beam gave a cold blue-ish hue to his reflection. He looked outwards, but his mirrored face hung on the glass like a ghostly apparition and stared straight at us. 'Twenty years' hard work. And I'm not having some nosey parker, too curious by half, jumped up bloody sparky come in and ruin it!'

'Hold on—' I began, but Hamlet's elbow jabbed me in the side, a signal that a degree of tact and diplomacy was required. I paused to compose myself, then, 'Mr Flint. I'm sorry, I really have no idea what you're talking about. But if you want someone to blame, blame him, he started it.' I pointed my finger. Donaldson looked taken aback to be its target. He tried to speak, but Flint told him to shush before he'd even begun.

'Fielder Homes has become one of the UK's biggest property developers. I've done that. Sunk fortunes into it. Into him.' Fielder gave a slight twitch of the neck but it was enough, I saw it and I bet Hamlet did too. Flint continued, 'This is the first of four schemes being rolled out in the next two years. By the end of it, Fielder Homes will have built almost ten thousand new units. This is my exit strategy, this is my retirement plan, my investment gets paid out and I become an extremely, and I mean extremely, wealthy man.'

Hamlet gave an appreciative nod of respect to show he was impressed. To be honest, so was I, but there was something that bugged me. 'So why did you offer me a job then, if you're saying I'm upsetting things, why offer me work?'

Flint's head spun round in the way of a cat's sensing danger. He didn't know about them throwing offers at me. He looked to Fielder and Donaldson for an explanation. Donaldson offered it.

'Because we thought it would distract you. It worked for everyone else that'd been sniffing round the Admiral Guthrie: offer them a nice job for more money than it's worth and they soon forget about that shitty little pub. But for some reason you didn't go for it. Preferred to stay in with the footballer. Some would say you're a man of morals, Mr Poynter.' I could feel all their eyes on me, all judging me, weighing me up. Hamlet gave another appreciative nod, as did Flint, suggesting loyalty meant something to them.

'I, however,' continued Donaldson, 'say you're a fucking idiot!' Even now he was trying to goad me. 'Your pig-headedness got the pub burned down. Got his shop shot up,' he was definitely trying to coax me into retaliating. 'Got your uncle in the hospital. Up the ladder, whoops.' It worked… I lunged for him, only to be hauled back by Hamlet before I reached him.

Flint took up a position between Donaldson and me. 'Stop it, the pair of you, pipe down.' Flint turned his attention back outside. 'Twenty years I've spent cultivating his image, building his brand.'

'That was why we did what we did, Tony,' said Donaldson, 'to protect Ron's image.' Flint didn't give any response, just a thoughtful 'hmm' which only he knew the meaning of. He watched trance-like as an ambulance sped along the near deserted street, its blue beacon lights flickered against the glossy black hoarding and for a moment the whole scene before us was electric blue. I blinked away bright stars from my eyes for several seconds after it passed.

'We've created the ultimate local boy done good success story. You'll never have a clue how many strings I've had to pull, palms

I've had to grease and bungs I've had to make over the years. But it's worked, and in a few months' time he's going to the Palace. Sir Ronald Fielder.'

'Yeah, I don't get it,' said Hamlet.

Flint threw a quizzical look at Hamlet, the same as a dog gives another dog it sees on television, the look that asks, '*are you for real?*'. Flint puffed out an exasperated sigh, and then explained with a weary tone that suggested he felt obliged to:

'No one can get enough of UK property, especially property in London and the South East. Half the units here, they're already sold. But it's China and Hong Kong, they're the markets we want. There's developments up in London where they don't even bother with a sales office on site, they set one up in Hong Kong or Macau instead.'

Another ambulance tore through the quiet night. It made me remember I still didn't know where I was. Was it going to the same place as the first one? Had there been a major incident up ahead, or were we on the approach road to a hospital? I had absolutely no idea, and that scared me.

'I want investors from Hong Kong buying without even seeing the scheme, buying an entire floor at a time.' Flint was warming to his subject now, his cool façade was thawing, 'And you know what they love overseas? A bit of British class. *Sir* Ronald Fielder, they love it, ever since the news of the honours list broke they've been fighting to buy from Fielder Homes. They hear Sir Ronald Fielder and they think he's aristocracy. They're thinking he's Downton Abbey. Never mind he's only a divvy off the White Road Estate, to them he's royalty.'

Now I understood. Image was everything. Flint had every penny he'd ever earnt and every penny he'll ever earn sunk into the earth and steel outside. He needed Fielder to get his title if he was to make a quick profit.

Flint scratched his well-manicured beard. In the stillness of the room, I could hear the rasping as he did so, and then he began to speak again. 'I'm sorry about what happened to your uncle. That wasn't anything to do with me or on my instruction, someone had gone rogue.'

Donaldson' pockmarked face curled into a sneer—he felt cornered and I knew he wanted to lash out, but one look from Flint sent him meekly away. Flint turned to Fielder and in stern tones said, 'You'll compensate the man for his injuries. I don't care how you do it, but Fielder Homes will pay him a weekly wage for the next twelve months. Does that satisfy you, Poynter?'

I confirmed it sounded like a very generous arrangement, and I thanked him, but I wasn't satisfied, it didn't clear up everything. 'People have been killed over this,' I said.

'That was thirty years ago,' responded Donaldson. 'No one cared then, they care even less now.'

'Only because you bought the police off to smother it,' I said.

'You've been very nosey,' Donaldson said to me. 'I hear you've made Chief Inspector Hutton a bit anxious. I daresay he'll be wanting words with you sooner or later, Poynter.'

Hamlet turned and faced Donaldson, he wanted to see Donaldson' face when he scored his point, 'Hutton's nothing. He tried flexing his muscles and failed. Any bent copper in my town belongs to me, Hutton knows that now.'

Flint considered his thoughts then delivered them with the placid tones of a diplomat, 'To be absolutely honest with you Hutton's long outlived his usefulness to me. He's what, just a senior officer in a regional plod? That doesn't count for much nowadays,' he said, I'm sure to chip a little off of Hamlet, to put him back in his place. Flint continued, 'I've got commissioners and ministers on speed dial. I'd been thinking of chopping away some of the dead wood, now's as good a time as any. He's all yours, do what you like with him.'

'I wasn't talking about thirty-five years ago,' I said, 'I'm talking about Danny Kidd. You killed him.'

'No, I bloody didn't!' said Donaldson, his face flushed red with rage.

Fielder was beside him, he too full of fury and rage. 'That was nothing to do with us. You be very careful throwing accusations about like that, you hear me?'

'Well, if it wasn't you, who was it?'

'How the bloody hell do I know?'

'Because according to his brother, you were the last one seen with him. Laughing and joking, instant best mates, love at first sight, at some gala dinner.'

Fielder paused, his eyes flashed up and right, as though intently thinking about something, before coming back to the conversation. 'I remember that night. He was being an arrogant prick, but he was famous. Premier League footballers are big news right across Asia. I wanted him on my team, so to speak. I thought I could sweet talk him, get him attached to the firm somehow: I don't know, maybe cutting a ribbon somewhere or presenting a local school with new playground equipment on behalf of Fielder Homes. It's all good publicity, it'll sell units.'

'You wanted the pub off him, he'd already knocked you back, so you killed him for it.'

'Oh, do shut up! Tony, must we listen to this?' protested Fielder, but Flint turned his back to him and gazed upon the dark streets outside. Fielder filled the silence. 'I told you, I wanted him working for me. We came to an agreement, only his brother got the hump with that and stormed off in a pissy fit. End of story.'

'Look, tensions have run a bit high tonight,' said Hamlet, 'but what happens now? Do we put it all behind us, bygones be bygones? I've got my dough back. Your uncle's compensated for his injuries…' Hamlet paused for dramatic effect, then looked at Donaldson adding, 'and that ratfink weasel there overstepped his authority and nearly brought war when there's been peace in Medway for decades.'

Flint turned to face the room, one finger held upright, gently tapping against his lips while he considered what he'd just heard. His mind made up, he announced, 'I'm going for a smoke.'

-42-

FROM OUR GLAZED eyrie above, we watched Tony Flint lean against the bonnet of his Porsche SUV and smoke his cigarette. Chelsea-blue had accompanied him, and we observed him getting his instructions. Flint was one of those people that holds a cigarette between his first two fingers but still uses that same hand to illustrate his instructions. The glowing red tip of his cigarette bounced and bobbed like a firefly as he gave directions in the dim puddled light of the street lamps. Chelsea-blue looked up at us and brought a phone to his ear. Inside our viewing gallery a ringtone played out, we looked around. Feathers took the message without speaking. He looked at our expectant faces, 'All of you, outside. Now.'

WE ASSEMBLED OUTSIDE, close to Flint's Porsche. Behind it sat the black Range Rover I'd seen Donaldson driving, and slightly apart from that was a sparkling new Mercedes saloon, which I deduced must be Fielder's. Flint had taken refuge from the gloom of the night by sitting inside his car, and he spoke to us through the open window:

'I've given it some thought,' he said. 'You, Hamlet, you called me today to ask if what had been going on had been in my name. I hope you're satisfied now that it wasn't?' Hamlet responded that he was.

'As for the other matters: you've got your money back, the old man gets compensated for his injuries, and I've no qualms whatsoever about whatever you choose to do with Hutton,' said Flint. 'Is that everything?'

Hamlet nodded, confirming it was. I noticed the sports holdall strapped across his back. I was still unsure how this night would pan out, but of one thing I was certain—he wasn't letting that money go again, they'd have to prise it out of his cold dead fingers if they wanted to take it back.

'And you, Nosey,' Flint said, looking directly at me, 'I hope you appreciate now this is how the big boys play, and why some things you keep your beak out of.'

A nudge from Hamlet prompted me to confirm that I did, and that he had my assurance I'd walk away and forget everything. But I knew he wasn't Santa Claus and I wasn't going to get what I wanted, which was something close to a satisfactory resolution. To these people everything came down to money, if it didn't have a pound note value it didn't matter. So, any hope of giving peace to the family of that poor girl, that Caroline, had to be put aside for now. All I wanted was to get home, so I humbly bowed and scraped and said thank you very much, sir.

'Good, I'll be off then,' said Flint. 'Just one more thing,' and he pointed at Chelsea-blue, circling his extended finger before flicking it to his right. I don't know how I knew its meaning, but I wasn't mistaken—it was sign-language for '*wrap it up and get on with it*'.

Chelsea-blue grabbed Donaldson from behind, pinning him by both elbows. Feathers took up a position in front of him, his gun pointed straight at his face. Donaldson looked on with wide, moist eyes. He struggled, but Chelsea-blue held him tight. He jerked Donaldson suddenly to the left, pulling him off balance and propelled him forwards. Between Chelsea-blue and Feathers, he was manhandled through a gate in the glossy black hoarding to the building site beyond.

Silence. Not even any passing traffic to create a noise. The night was quiet. Nothing stirred. The loud, fast bang of a gunshot ripped through the air with the sudden drama of a thunderbolt. Silence fell again.

The gate in the hoarding opened, only two men came back: Chelsea-blue and Feathers. Feathers clambered into the back of the Porsche and Chelsea-blue climbed into the driver's seat. He started up the engine.

Flint leaned forwards. 'Nine metre trenches,' he said, then the window rose and blacked out any visibility inside the vehicle. The car drove away.

-43-

03:51. THE RED numbers glowed from the alarm clock by the bed, taunting me *'Almost four in the morning and still no rest'.* Small bright spots pierced the darkness of the room: various gadgets created little red and green fairy lights while they charged, from which I could make out the shapes of bottles and boxes on the dressing table. Not bright enough to read by, but bright enough to become annoying when sleep refuses to come. The room was quiet apart from Perry breathing softly on the pillow beside me. I hoped she was safe in her own happy dream-space, far away from all tonight's worries.

I'd got home a little after midnight. Hamlet had driven me. He'd claimed Donaldson' Range Rover as his prize: to the victor the spoils. 'He's got no more use for it,' his justification. He liked it and was confident that he could get it a new birth certificate from Polish Mick—whoever he might be. I didn't know and didn't want to know, my head already too full of secrets I never wanted.

Perry and Uncle Bern were still up, waiting, when I got home. They both looked like they'd been crying, but I didn't ask, and they didn't tell. Instead, we all hugged each other tight, I told them I loved them, and they told me back. A cold pizza sat untouched in its box, and I fell upon it ravenously. They didn't ask where I'd been, and I didn't offer, other than to say, 'It's done. I'm out. It's over.' They both hugged me again, and we all cried happy tears of relief. But awake and alone in the night, there's no relief to rid me of my conscience.

Dad, was that you? There was an angel on my shoulder tonight protecting me, was it you? I'm pretty sure it could quite easily be me at the bottom of that trench if things had taken a different turn. Thank you. But what did I witness? What did I become part of? What have I become? Am I now accessory to murder? How did it come to this? But if I'm really honest, if I look deep into my soul and pinpoint exactly what my problem is, the truth is I couldn't care less about Donaldson. In a way, I'm glad—live by the sword and all that. He wasn't a good person. He'd bullied and hurt people all his life; vulnerable, weaker people like Ginger or McInally and his Donna, or Hopkins and his kids. Threats and violence were his trade. People like that, it always catches up with them in the end. So, no, I won't shed any tears for him. But I'll tell you my issue, what's really eating away inside of me: Adam. Adam was the reason behind all of this. Not knowing how he is, or where he is. When we found that girl, that Caroline, hidden in the floor, all I could think of was her family. Were they like me, still hanging on to the faintest glimmer of hope that one day they might see her again, or were they like you Dad, destined to go to their graves never finding out what happened to their child? And what's shredding my sanity now, what's making me hate myself, is not knowing whether Donaldson had a family. Did he have a wife? Children? Will they be waiting for the rest of their days for the phone call that never rings and the door that never opens? This... this... 'situation' tonight, I didn't agree to be part of it, but it's instantly made me everything I loathe, everything I was trying to resolve. All I wanted was to bring a family some closure, instead another family's got a lifetime of the same suffering and anguish. I don't know how I'm going to fix this Dad.

Perry murmured something, then rolled onto her other side, taking most of the duvet with her. For want of anything else to do, I navigated my way through the darkness to the bathroom and emptied my bladder. Perry still slept soundly, and across the landing through the spare room's flimsy door I heard Bern snoring like a constipated elephant. Lucky them, but there wasn't much point in me going back to bed if I couldn't sleep.

I headed downstairs and settled into an armchair. I found a movie on the planner I'd not seen before. I turned the volume down as low as it could possibly go: quiet enough not to wake anyone up, but loud enough that I could hear it. I got comfortable, and the movie began.

I can't tell you a single thing about that movie, I don't remember any of it. Sleep must have crept up on me at some stage, tiptoeing silently behind me and catching me unawares. When I lifted my head, it was broad daylight. Quarter past eleven according to my watch, and a blanket had appeared from somewhere to cover me.

A thumping noise made me turn in surprise. Perry, the source and creator of the thumps, manhandled a large suitcase down the stairs, one tread at a time: bump bump bump. I met her halfway up, halfway down the stairs, and carried the case the rest of the way down.

'I thought I'd let you rest,' she said. 'You looked like you needed it. And while you were asleep, I've packed for us. Everything we need for a few days away.'

No one had ever packed for me before, I wasn't sure how I felt about it. Part of it felt like a nice gesture, part like an invasion of privacy and part like *what's in there, it's bound to be wrong.*

'Everything?' I asked.

'Everything. Chillax,' she replied, her tone playful, 'and if I've forgotten anything, where we're going they've got these great things, they're called shops.'

And so, an hour later, we were on the road. Perry driving her little white Fiat, me in the passenger seat and the large suitcase across the back seat packed with everything we needed for a few days away. Except for shampoo. And deodorant. And razors. But there was a shop for that.

IT TOOK ABOUT three hours to reach the New Forest and our hosts, both former doctors taken early retirement, were waiting at the door of their cottage for our arrival. It was near a village called Sway, and the cottage was picture-postcard perfect: its honey-coloured stone complimented by box hung sash windows and wisteria around the door. They greeted Perry fondly, and over tea and homemade cakes they spoke of mutual friends and acquaintances from the hospital. Normally such conversations give me the right hump: people I don't know talking about people I don't know doing things I wasn't at; but this time I didn't mind. Sure, I felt a bit left out, but their little dog, an excitable, happy Border Terrier called Barney kept me company and decided I was his new best friend.

Barney accompanied Perry and me on long meandering walks through the forest and enjoyed sprawling across my feet under the shade of tables in the most glorious country pub gardens whenever we stopped for lunch. The days felt like Summer, with clear blue skies and warm southern winds breezing up fresh from the continent.

We had an agreement: no phones. There was something liberating about being out in the country, the sun on our faces, just ourselves for company and no connection to the outside world. It was the best distraction I could have hoped for. The tension in my body dissolved away and my conscience began to scab over—if I didn't think about things, they would go away. I'd never forget, and knew I'd carry it forever, but one day maybe it would get pushed far back enough that it doesn't become the first thing I think about all the time, that was what I hoped. And what could be a better way to fill your head with happiness than having a bouncy little dog to play with.

To say the four nights we spent in the New Forest was lovely would be an understatement, things were brilliant between us. Perry was funny and beautiful and kind. It had taken recent events to make me realise she was all my dreams come true. On our last night, we spoke properly and truthfully about us. In the corner of a candle-lit pub under dried hops and flowers hung from hefty blackened timber beams and on a leather sofa so old the red hide had worn to the soft scuffed patina of a well-travelled cricket ball, we agreed she'd quit her tenancy on the house next door and we would live together. Officially. Permanently.

'Does that mean we're engaged?' Perry asked, then snorted back a giggle at the sight of my face. 'Relax, I'm joking. This is a major step for you Marky Mark, I appreciate that. So, let's celebrate. Then, who knows? Let's see where it leads.' We clinked our glasses together, then topped them up with the last of the Pinot Noir.

'We need a couple's name,' said Perry. 'You know, like Brangelina or Kimye. How about Merry? Merky Park? I've got it… Perky.'

'Perky?'

'Perky. Team Perky, that's us. Team Perky against the world.'

Next day I said a sad farewell to Barney, although I suspect I was more upset than he was seeing as I'd caught him in flagrante, lying belly-up and seeking tickles from a family of Canadians who'd had arrived that morning. So much for man's best friend—Judas more like. I'd miss him though, the soppy little thing.

We headed home, ready to tell friends and family our news about Team Perky. We weren't expecting the news that waited at home for us.

-44-

'IT WAS ON the telly last night…' Uncle Bern couldn't wait to tell us, we'd barely set foot inside the door when he swooped down to fill us in, 'and it's in the papers today.'

Perry passed me her phone, having run a search on Bern's claims. 'He's right, take a look at this.'

In bold typeface the banner headline simply said: '*Decades of A Dirty Cop: Police Cover Up Medway Double Murder*'. Perry flicked through various searches and confirmed that most of the major newspapers and media channels were running the same story—our story.

RACHEL RIDDER HAD been very clever in pitching it, knowing it would propel her career into the big time. Taking all the information I'd given her, she'd assessed it for herself and then focussed on the role the police took. The golden nugget in her story that caught the public's attention was when a young woman was buried in concrete thirty years ago and a sailor was murdered on the same night the police officer on the scene was a Paul Hutton, and now thirty-five years later the young woman has been exhumed and the scene destroyed by arson, and the police officer in charge of the investigation with no leads, suspects or arrests is the same Paul Hutton. A 'career of corruption' she called it. She'd also been good to her word and kept me out of it entirely, for which I was grateful, especially after how it escalated.

Rachel's story was printed online to begin with and got picked up by one news channel during the course of the first day.

On the second day, it made all the newspapers and became a subject of intense debate and discussion on television and radio by the third.

On the fourth, Hutton faced the cameras and gave a statement. By then he must have realised he'd been cast adrift by both sets of patrons: the police and the Flints, the cops and the robbers. We watched him on the evening news, he looked nervous, even greyer than normal if such a thing were possible. He delivered a carefully worded, but ultimately bland, statement in which he denied any wrongdoing and in a tetchy tone added that his family had served the people of the Medway Towns for half a century, which was a wrong move. It sounded as though he expected everyone to give him a pass just because he thought he deserved it. Anyway, it backfired massively because:

On the fifth day they took aim at his father and why not, the dead can't sue for slander. One of the TV news programmes had it *'on good authority'* that Bob Hutton, deceased, orchestrated any corruption within Medway police from the Sixties through to his retirement in the mid Nineties. A few silhouetted heads with overdubbed electronic voices recounted their experiences serving with the Huttons. I didn't doubt for a minute they'd been put up to it by Tony Flint, keen to deflect any attention away from him, and I had a solid guess where they'd got the photo of Bob Hutton they'd been using in all the bulletins: his leering face, smeared by red lipstick kisses, ogling the teenage girls partying around him.

On the sixth day Hutton came out swinging, determined if he was going down he'd take as many as he could with him. A Police Federation rep stood at his side whilst he gave his statement to the media. Under the flickering strobe of constant flash photography, he announced he would fully co-operate with any investigation.

On the seventh day his employers cut him loose and the Chief Constable announced he'd been suspended.

On the eighth day he was dead. Hutton hanged himself. His daughter found him strung up from the banister rail of his staircase landing. His note apologised for *'betraying my fellow officers'* and *'my deep regret at abusing my position of authority and trust within the community'*. His daughter didn't believe it and told any reporter that would listen that she thought he'd been silenced: I did too, but seeing as nobody asked me, I was happy to keep my own counsel.

THE POLICE CAME under pressure to show a clean face and make some progress on the Admiral Guthrie. A new team was appointed, led by Detective Chief Inspector Michael Senia. I'd come across Senia before, we hadn't played nice together, but in a strange way I was glad he'd taken over. I knew he'd do a proper job.

After a week or so, Senia appeared at the back end of the TV evening news as the fourth or fifth segment of the programme, a new and more thrilling story having bumped the case down the pecking order. Senia announced he'd like to interview a Mr Neale Donaldson. The following day's papers carried Donaldson' photo saying he was a person of interest, but he was far from the front pages and tucked low in a corner, way behind Danny Kidd's reality TV bimbo's carefully staged photos frolicking on a foreign beach somewhere in her skimpy swimwear. Poor old Danny Kidd however didn't even warrant a mention, had his murder gone into the 'too difficult' box: out of sight, out of mind. The thought that the perpetrator was walking free angered me, and I hoped and prayed my gut instinct was right, that it was them lying in the bottom of a nine-metre trench.

As regards the Admiral Guthrie killings, thanks to Rachel's intervention, Donaldson and Hutton had been identified as the villains and perpetrators of these horrible events. Case closed. The general public moved on to the next big scandal dominating the headlines, satisfied with the guilty verdict proven by media. Did it matter that they weren't getting the whole story? Part of me resented Fielder getting away with it, but part of me (if truth be told, a much bigger part of me) was just glad it was all over and life could go back to normal.

HOW EXACTLY COULD life to go back to normal? Answer: life finds a way. The sun still rose, the rain still fell, the grass still grew, and the moon still shone—and in between all that my old routine soon found its way back to becoming routine once again. I had Disco and Fiery Jac, and we picked up where we left off. We were back doing Kidd Properties repairs and maintenance. Jobs had backed up during our downtime, so much so I needed to bring in a couple of guys on a casual basis to lend a hand, seeing as I couldn't rely on Uncle Bern for a while. His arm was still in plaster, and being the old malingerer he was, I anticipated it would stay in plaster for some time still to come. Plus, he was now on the Fielder payroll and happy to sit around watching cricket all day long earning free money.

After a few weeks, it felt safe to breathe out again. The danger had passed. Perry had quit her lease on the house next door and moved in permanently with me. Stuart had gone back home, the media circus had trundled on to the next town, work was busy again and the money had begun coming in once more. Happy days. What could possibly go wrong?

-45-

DISCO, FIERY JAC and I were working in a small house for Stuart in Lordswood, a newish modern village just outside of Chatham town centre. It was a pleasant enough terraced house in a pleasant enough cul-de-sac. Unfortunately, there was an unpleasant enough tenant, with an unpleasant enough attitude and four months' rent owing, who trashed the place and scarpered the day before the bailiffs were due. The place needed emptying out, a deep clean, and then a full redec before it could be re-let. Amazingly, demand was so strong Stuart had already got someone lined up. Great news for him, but it meant time was of the essence for us.

The whole house stunk of piss. Whose? Who can say? Cat, dog, human, all of the above? They'd used their home as a toilet. Every carpet needed ripping up. They'd shredded the kitchen: doors ripped from their hinges, electrical sockets torn from the walls. The bathroom had come off worst: huge swathes of tiles hacked from the walls, taps bent and twisted, and a massive hole booted through the bathtub. As for the garden, you don't want to know.

It was dirty, filthy work but, by the end of the third day, all that was left was for Fiery Jac to take care of the decorations, and Disco's second fix carpentry in the kitchen and bathroom. Stuart had his own carpet guy he liked to use for all their properties, and he'd asked me to make a measure of all the rooms. I was to give it to him, he'd give it to the carpet guy, then the carpet guy could lay next week, and the new tenant could move in. Easy peasy.

STINKING OF PISS and feeling itchy, I went home first to shower and change. Perry arrived just as I was about to leave. When I told her I was popping over to Stuart's to drop in the measurements, she suggested tagging along and then she and I could go for dinner and a drink afterwards. Sounded like an ideal evening to me, what's not to like. On went my best going-out shirt.

We got to Danny's house—sorry, Stuart's house—a little after five. Stuart moved straight into Danny's big house after leaving us. I don't think he even transferred anything across from his cottage on the grounds, he went straight to the big house. The old barn that used to house Danny's cars and his gym above still stood as a burnt-out carcass. The scrap metal that was once tens of thousands of pounds of luxury motoring had been removed, but the building remained. The sight of the hollowed-out structure and the smell of ash made the hairs on my arms stand on end and my heart hammer. The back of my head pressed deep into the headrest, as though I was subconsciously trying to get as much distance from it as possible. Perry must have read my panic, as I felt a reassuring hand touch my forearm, I smiled and pretended it was nothing, but I realised my fire anxiety was far from gone.

I understood from Stuart that the barn would stay like that for the foreseeable. It'd fallen under the property's historic building listing as well as the property itself being within a conservation zone. The insurers and the local council locked themselves into a battle as to whether the barn could be demolished and replaced with a new building, or whether it had to be rebuilt to its former glory. The difference between option one and option two was very big bucks, meaning for Stuart this was an argument likely to run for some time and meaning for me this was an anxiety I needed to get over if I was to keep working for Kidd Properties.

Clutching my handwritten measurements, we approached the office suite: a delight in orangey-red, as warm and welcoming as a bowl of tomato soup for a January lunch. Its two-hundred-year-old bricks oozed with wavy mustard-coloured mortar, thick in parts and thin in others. In front of it stood a line of cardboard boxes and black bin bags. Perry noticed them too, 'Looks like he's having a clear out.'

We neared the French doors and saw Stuart had company. The visitor stood with his back to us. All we could see was the silver hair finishing neatly above a crisp white shirt collar and navy-blue suit jacket. As we grew closer, we could see the stiff white double cuff of the shirt, the sparkle of a gleaming silver cufflink and the faintest pinstriping design to the jacket sleeve. Closer still: the toe of his smart black brogue, highly polished to a mirror shine. One step closer, Perry reached for the door handle, I tried to stop her, I knew who the visitor was. Too late, my heart sank:

'Mr Senia, what a lovely surprise, fancy meeting you here,' I'd mustered as much sincerity as I could, which from the way he raised his eyebrow at me I knew wasn't a lot.

'Mr Poynter, we meet again.'

Stuart looked surprised, 'You two know each other?'

'Oh yes,' Senia eyed me up and down in the way some people decide: keeper, charity shop or bin? I couldn't tell which I was. 'Mr Poynter helped me with my enquiries on one of my first cases when I transferred to Medway.' He could have made that sound a lot worse, especially as I was his one and only suspect for the murder of a good friend, so I guess that meant I wasn't binned—yet.

'So, what brings you here then, Mr Senia?' I asked.

'Funny, I was just about to ask you the very same thing,' he replied. His sharp, pointed features were loaded with fox-like curiosity and cunning. He stared at me with his dark eyes.

'Mark does the repairs and maintenance for all our properties,' offered Stuart as a response.

Senia didn't react, he hadn't stopped staring at me. 'Of course. The main contractor.'

'Something like that,' I answered without feeling the need to explain my business to him. 'So why are you here?'

'A man called Neale Donaldson,' Senia replied, his senses twitching, seeking any kind of reaction, 'do you know him?'

'Why? Does he say he knows me?'

Senia held his eyes on me, then looked back across to Stuart. 'He's not said anything yet. I'm looking for him.'

'And you thought he was here, did you?'

Stuart rose from his seat, a gesture that said he'd nominated himself as the self-appointed mediator between Senia and me. We both paused and waited for him to speak: 'Mr Senia came here to see me, Mark.' Senia bobbed his head in agreement. 'He'd heard that Donaldson had been involved with the Admiral Guthrie and also that policeman who killed himself, Hutton.' Stuart's face was pale and washed out, in the drabness of the room he looked ill. I was about to ask how Senia knew about Donaldson, but Stuart spoke first, cutting me off:

'I told Mr Senia that Donaldson had been threatening and intimidating towards me and Danny. On account of that pub we bought.'

'So, once more Mr Poynter, do you know Neale Donaldson? And tell me about this pub.'

I pulled over a seat and sat without waiting to be asked. I crossed one leg over the opposite knee and immediately regretted it. It was a classic Hamlet move: an attempt to gain the higher status by looking casual and relaxed. I forced myself to stay like that—it was too late to change position without looking fidgety and shifty.

I took a wide look across the room. It felt dark and barren, as though Senia had sucked any sparkle out of it, as though his very presence had made it dank and colourless. I took a dramatic intake of breath through my nose, then, 'I've told your lot about the pub already.' Senia took a half step back and perched against the edge of Stuart's desk. He crossed his arms and gave me a look that was one part quizzical two parts pissed off.

'Your predecessor, Mr Hutton. He interviewed me. In my hospital bed, I'd add. Straight out of casualty, doped up on painkillers, no appointment, no lawyer. He turns up firing his questions and accusations at me.'

Senia's expression had remixed, it was now three parts quizzical to three parts pissed off. He didn't know anything about it, Hutton must have been acting off-book, naughty-naughty.

'Your lad Nwakobu was there too,' I added for no other reason than to cause a little mischief, knowing there'll be hell to pay back at the station for the young officer.

Senia looked at the ceiling. Shadows formed in the hollows around his impressively straight jawline, and I noticed one or two tiny crimson splashes where he'd nicked himself shaving that morning. A second or two later he faced me again, his thoughts composed and re-strategized, 'So, please tell me what you told them.'

'There's not a lot. I met him once or twice. He made it clear he was interested in the pub—'

'The Admiral Guthrie?' Senia asked seeking clarification, I nodded, 'And when you say interested, what does that mean?'

'Okay. I first met him shortly after our original visit to the Admiral Guthrie when we met the auctioneer, he tried warning me off buying it, got up close to me, a bit intimidating. Then he showed up a couple or three times after Danny bought it, offering the chance to sell it on.'

'Intimidating again?'

'I suppose.'

'You suppose?'

'I didn't own the pub, and it wasn't my money funding the development scheme. It wasn't anything to do with me, so yes, he came and made a nuisance of himself, but that was for Danny and Stuart's benefit. I just happened to be an onlooker,' I said, hoping it was enough to satisfy him and make him leave me alone.

'And then the pub burned down?' asked Senia, already knowing that it did. 'With you in it. That was rather unlucky, don't you think?'

'Yes, I bloody well do think so. You found anyone for that yet?' I wanted to deflect and push it all back to him; if he couldn't answer the big questions, perhaps he'd stop asking me. Senia tightened his arms across his chest, he knew what I was doing. Stuart however didn't:

'Donaldson did it. He set the fire.'

Senia and I both looked at Stuart with interest—he sounded very strong in his assertion and we waited to see if there was more. There was:

'The girl in the cellar. He knew about her, he must have, that's why he wanted to scare us off, then when that failed he tried to buy us off. And then when that failed, he burnt the place down to get rid of the evidence.'

Senia tilted his head and gave a sideways glance at Stuart, judging him. Then he turned his attention back to me, 'And do you share this theory, Mr Poynter?'

'I don't know anything,' I replied. 'Like I say, I'm just the hired help. None of it is anything to do with me.'

Senia gave a small nod, as though mentally ticking off the answer he'd expected me to give. Thankfully Perry had the sense not to get involved and kept quiet. Senia waited patiently for me to say something, anything to fill the gap. I'd played this game with him before, I knew how to keep my mouth shut. The silence grew, sucking the oxygen out of the room, pumping it full of nervous tension. Senia held his nerve. So did I. So did Perry. Stuart didn't: 'Donaldson killed Danny.'

Well, it's fair to say nobody was expecting that. Senia, Perry and I all turned and looked at Stuart agog. A mask of raspberry pink spread across Stuart's face at the realisation he was centre of our joint attention. He dropped to his chair with the grace of a punched drunk and raised both hands to his head. His fingers fossicked through his hair and left untidy little clumps sticking up in their wake.

'He must have,' Stuart didn't sound quite so convinced now, 'I mean, who else could it have been?'

Senia stared at Stuart intensely. Then he stood up and shot out his arms, straightening his sleeves. He gave a gentle tug to his shirt cuff, followed by a little twist to level his shiny cufflinks while he considered Stuart's claim.

Stuart reminded us, 'You ruled out that nutter, the one who tried to set fire to Danny in the gym.'

'Bearing in mind he was seen by millions on *Match of the Day* when your brother was murdered, it's reasonable to say he had a pretty solid alibi,' replied Senia, showing he was already up to speed and familiar with all of Hutton's cases.

Stuart continued to push Senia, 'And that rapper, Muzzkett? You ruled him out?'

'He was performing in Manchester that night, sir, as I think you've already been informed.'

'And his scumbag friends?'

'If you're referring to Mr Ketay—Muzzkett's—friends and associates, they travel as his entourage. Their social media accounts all have corresponding photos and status updates of each other at the Manchester arena.'

'There you are then,' Stuart felt his point proven and slapped a hand against the desk top as emphasis. 'There's nobody else. There can't be. It had to be Donaldson. He wanted Danny away from the pub. He tried money, he tried threats and when all failed, he killed him.'

I have to admit, it did sound plausible. From my experiences with Donaldson I knew he was capable of acts of extreme violence, but I also knew that getting involved was more trouble than I needed right now—no matter how much I wanted it to be proven true—so I kept quiet. I sunk low in my seat and hoped I'd become as anonymous as part of the furniture while Stuart and Senia talked things through.

'Did he ever make you fear for your safety? Did you ever worry he would act in such a way?'

Stuart looked at his hands as though they held the answer, before he replied, 'Yes. If I'm truthful, yes. He kept popping up all over the place. He's got a nasty way about him, he'll needle you until you go mad and react.'

'An example would be the golf club incident?' Senia read the question on Stuart's face and answered, 'I saw the video online. You and your brother both looked pretty angry in that exchange. Donaldson, however, he looked calmer than the Dalai Lama on holiday.'

Stuart sat back, his mouth twitched with a smug curl. He thought Senia had proven his point for him. Neither of us expected what Senia said next, 'You and your brother, both got a bit of a temper? Have you got a temper, Mr Kidd?'

Stuart opened his mouth, but no words came. He sat upright in his chair, his forearms flat across the desk top as though relying on it for support. His hair still stuck up in odd clumps, giving him a slightly deranged look with his wide-open eyes and even wider open mouth.

Senia lost patience waiting for an answer, 'I think you do. Every report I've seen about you Mr Kidd has had you losing your temper, the golf club being a perfect example. The newspapers picked up on it too, didn't they. How was it they described you? Bitter and twisted? Jealous? Mentally ill?'

'Hey! Whoa, that's uncalled for,' said Perry, jumping to Stuart's defence.

Senia looked at her, properly, as though it was the first time he'd noticed she was there. 'And you are?'

'Parminder Grewal,' she replied. 'I'm a friend of Stuart's.' Senia nodded, storing that away for future reference.

The interruption had given Stuart time to calm his emotions; if Senia's intention had been to provoke Stuart, then Perry's intervention had scuppered that. I knew from my own experience if Senia gets you in his sights it's nigh on impossible to shake yourself out again, I'd have to help Perry keep her cool if she wasn't to fall foul of Senia.

'That was one course of anti-depressants over twenty years ago,' Stuart's voice was level and rational. 'And I flushed half of them down the toilet.' Senia's nostrils flared in annoyance. I wondered if he had a theory he had been keen to try out before we'd blundered in and spoilt the moment.

'It was only a suggestion,' added Stuart, his voice meek and pathetic.

Senia fiddled with his shiny cufflinks once again and considered Stuart's comment before: 'Yes. A suggestion. Thank you for that, Mr Kidd, I'll add that to our casefile. Thank you for your time. I'll be in touch.' Senia left, pulling the door gently closed behind him.

IN THE SILENCE that fell afterwards Stuart looked shell-shocked, I knew from personal experience that being under scrutiny from Senia would do that to the best of men, but it felt a bit awkward lingering. Perry and I made our excuses and left. As we drove, my mind wandered: how had Donaldson ended up on Senia's radar? Then I remembered Flint's boast, "*I've got commissioners and ministers on speed dial*". Had he made a couple of calls to the higher-ups, redeemed a few favours? Had Flint's influence behind the scenes dropped Donaldson' name as a lead, or more likely a lure, to divert attention away from Fielder? Perry's voice shook me from my daydream, 'I said, you forgot to give him the measurements for the carpet!'

PERRY AND I found a nice pub on Bearsted Green, an ancient old inn made to look older still with modern Farrow & Ball colours. Lots of chalk feelgood slogans of the eat, drink and be merry variety. The sort of place that has glass jars of fancy nuts behind the bar to scoop out into little bowls, rather than packets of dry roasted tugged off a card. Perry ordered a bottle of wine then headed off in search of a table, leaving me to pay for it—a wise move, considering. After paying for the wine and worrying I'd need to take out a mortgage if she wanted another one, I joined her at the table she'd found. It gave a nice view out across the village green where I could see several people in lycra congregating to bend and stretch. I poured us both some wine, and the herd outside stampeded away into the distance.

'That was very unexpected,' said Perry.

'Not really,' I replied. 'Probably just a running club.'

Perry paused with her glass halfway to her lips and gave me a quizzical look, before she said, 'I was talking about Stuart.'

'Yes. I knew that,' I lied. 'Don't worry about it, probably just Senia on a fishing trip.'

'I don't know Mark, it sounded quite plausible.'

'What, that Danny and Stuart had arguments? All brothers and sisters do. I've heard you go into one with your sisters more than once, doesn't mean you'll actually kill them.'

'True, I accept that,' Perry took a sip then peered into her glass and slowly rotated it by the stem, as though seeking wisdom within the Pinot Noir, 'Look, I know he's your mate and everything, but do you think…?'

She didn't need to finish the question, I knew what she was implying, and I knew she was wrong. 'No way. Absolutely not.'

Perry didn't speak, her eyes caught mine in an expression that said 'okay', and her hand crept across the table to hold on to mine—we were both in unison, a team. I could have stayed like that all day, but we both gave a little startled jump, then giggled at how easily spooked we both were by the people next to us breaking into song.

The caterwauling of 'Happy Birthday' rang out loud and proud from a choir of women at varying stages of sobriety. A large ice cream sundae fizzing with sparklers and foil streamers was brought out from the kitchen. The recipient, a young lady with a sparkly pink '21' badge, looked so giddy with excitement that Perry and I couldn't help but smile. There's always something there to remind you, no matter how bad you feel, that a little human connection makes it all right again. And everyone loves a bit of a sparkle, don't they—which got me asking: 'Seemed a bit dark and dingy in the office today, didn't you think?'

'I don't know about that, but I thought it felt a bit sparse and… what's the word… unfinished.'

'How do you mean?'

Perry watched with an amused smile as the Birthday Girl struggled to get the wire cage off a champagne bottle. 'Had they only just moved into that office building?'

'No, it was one of the first things we finished for them,' I replied.

'Oh. It just seemed empty. Bare walls, bare shelves, no pictures, nothing.'

A loud pop followed by cheering and whoop-whoops. The Birthday Girl had uncorked her champagne and was clumsily pouring it into a dozen flutes lined up along the table. White foamy spumes billowed over the rim of each glass. I thought about what Perry said, and watched the bubbles fizz and twinkle under the lights. Mobile phones and flash photography captured the moment for posterity. Then it came to me:

'It had all been cleared out.'

'What had?'

'Danny's trophies, his memorabilia. The silverware, the champagne bottles. All the sparkly shiny stuff. It had all gone.'

'It's probably all in those boxes we saw outside,' said Perry, pulling her jacket back on. 'Come on, let's go.' She gulped down her wine in one and gripping the bottle by the neck headed towards the exit.

She stopped at the next table, plonked the three quarters full bottle down, 'Happy birthday, my darling, have a drink on us.' The Birthday Girl looked bewildered, but her friend snatched up the bottle and raucously swigged from the neck to more cheering and whoop-whoops from the sisterhood.

Perry stood, holding the door open. 'You,' she called out to me and for her own amusement beckoned me with a come-hither finger. 'Let's go. I'm waiting,' cue even more raucous cheers and whoop-whoops from the women, who took Perry's command and sly wink to mean that if I'm lucky it could be my birthday too. I'd never done a walk of shame, but that short distance across the quarry tiles to the chorus of a dozen party girls came very close.

'I CAN'T BELIEVE you talked me into this,' my voice not much above a whisper, my body crouched. Perry strolled behind fully upright, her voice loud and proud, bold as brass, 'Get over yourself. Look around you, you can see he's not here. And if he does turn up, just tell him you're back because you forgot to give him the carpet measurements. Get up.'

She was right, but I couldn't help myself from casting a cautious, searching gaze all around before slowly straightening up. We were back at Kidd Properties' office. Like the big house, and the rest of the estate, it was locked up and in darkness: the master was away. We approached the boxes lined up against the wall, and Perry lifted the lid of the first one. Inside sparkled cut crystal dishes and trophies, all engraved *Awarded to Danny Kidd...*

The next box contained two enormous bottles of champagne, both very expensive brands with a TV company logo embossed on them and the words, '*Man of the Match*'. And beneath them framed magazine covers, some fashion, some sporting, some lifestyle, all Danny Kidd. Perry closed the lid down, firmly pushing it back on. Now she was the one who whispered, 'He's getting rid of Danny.'

-46-

11:09 READ THE dashboard clock. My mental arithmetic told me we'd been sitting there for two hundred and nineteen minutes. That's two hundred and nineteen minutes without even getting out for a wee, but I had beaten both players on the radio's Pop Master quiz, so it wasn't a complete waste of time. I was ready to give up and drive away when our patience paid off. A shiny black Mercedes, as sleek and smooth as a manta ray, glided past into its reserved parking spot. We got out of the van and ran across to the Mercedes. I knew that if he got into the building, his building, then the security, his security, would make sure we were kept well away from him.

'Ron. Ron Fielder,' I called. He pushed the car door closed and looked over to where the noise was coming from. He gave the sort of smile that suggested he found this amusing in a curious way.

'Mark Poynter, I never expected to see you again. And who's this with you? Your bodyguard.'

I moved myself in front of Perry, blocking her from his view, 'Never you mind. Listen, I just want a minute of your time, please.'

'I thought we was done. That's what Tony Flint said. It's all done and over with. So, no, I don't have any time for you.' Fielder walked away towards the entrance doors of his building. He'd got near enough to activate the automatic eye, the doors slid open gracefully and waited for him to enter. The attractive young receptionist within smiled towards Sir Ron, as she must do every morning whether she wants to or not.

I grabbed him by the sleeve, he spun on the spot, 'Get your fucking hands off me,' his lip curled, his eyes wild—the Animal not hiding far below the hand-tailored pinstripe suit. The young receptionist looked on, her mouth an O-shape of surprise. I had to act quick, or she'd have security down here in double quick time.

'We just want to talk to you about Danny Kidd. That's all. Please. Then we're gone.'

He paused. In the doorway, people began to gather and gawp. He tried shoo-ing them away with a flap of the hand, but nobody moved. 'Okay,' he said, 'but be quick'.

Behind me, his Mercedes blipped. Fielder reached across to pull the driver's door open and told me to get in the passenger side. Once in, with doors closed, 'Tell me what you want, then fuck off, I never want to see you again.'

THE NIGHT BEFORE, Perry and I had talked at length about Stuart. He was my friend. He'd helped me out when I was in trouble. He'd got me out of a jam when no one else would. I felt I owed it to him to find out what happened to Danny, and whether Donaldson was involved.

However, Perry had, with a level head and rational voice, played Devil's Advocate and raised questions I couldn't answer: why had Stuart cleared out the office so thoroughly of Danny's things? And so soon? And how about the fact he'd moved straight into the big house at the first opportunity? Or his jubilation on the day he was granted probate of Danny's estate? We could both put up arguments and equally sound counter-arguments to support our position for all those queries, and more.

Whichever way up I looked at it, I kept reaching the same conclusion—Ron Fielder held the answers, and that was why we had to speak with him.

SHORTLY AFTER LUNCH, Perry and I were back at Stuart's office. He looked surprised to see us but was welcoming, nonetheless.

'Sorry about popping by unannounced,' I said by way of apology, and pulled a folded piece of paper from the back pocket of my jeans, 'I forgot to give you this yesterday. The carpet measurements.'

Stuart took it from me, unfolded it, and lay it flat on the desk in front of him, 'Thanks, I'll pass it on to the floor-layer. Got time for a coffee?'

'No thanks,' I replied, and Perry shook her head with a smile in a polite refusal, 'We're not stopping.'

Perry turned and opened the door, about to step outside, then stopped. She turned her face back to Stuart, 'By the way, we ran into Ron Fielder this morning. He said to say hello.'

Stuart looked confused, 'Ron Fielder?'

'Yes, you know, Ron?' pressed Perry, 'You met him at the Cantium Invicta Awards gala dinner. He remembers you.'

WE SAT IN FIELDER'S Mercedes, in his personal parking bay outside the office building with his name written large across it: a modern three-storey structure that was wider than it was high. There was nothing feminine about the building at all: the bricks, the colour of mud, were smooth wire-cuts with recessed brown pointing; the doors and windows all solely functional, no design fripperies, in red powder coated aluminium. It was as if the building was constructed entirely from testosterone and aggression.

'Tell me about the night Danny Kidd died,' I said. 'I've heard you and he became best buddies. And you said you wanted him on your team. So, what happened?'

Fielder puffed a breath through his cheeks to signify this was all too inconvenient, he even tilted his watch towards him in case we didn't get the point. I'd asked the question and had nothing further to add. We waited for a response. Eventually, 'Alright,' conceded Fielder.

I saw a couple of men in black security ties and pullovers loitering around the reception desk. Those two goons had no authority, I wasn't worried about them, but I didn't fancy my chances if one of them decided to call the police. I needed Fielder to get a move on, 'And?'

'Well, we were talking,' began Fielder. 'Like I've already told you, I wanted to get him to work for me, be a spokesman, a public face, attract the Asian investors. We got on to the Admiral Guthrie. He didn't know I had history with it,' Fielder gave me a sideways glance, not understanding my smirk, but I'd found his bland euphemism darkly comic. However, the way he fixed his gaze on me, as if trying to read my mind, made me realise: he didn't know I'd discovered he was the Animal. As far as he was aware, Hamlet had a grievance about his business being affected, and he'd been dragged into it as he was the link between Donaldson and Flint. My smirk became a snort as I tried to contain myself. He broke his gaze with a shake of the head. He didn't ask for an explanation and I couldn't be bothered to give him one, so I waited until he continued.

'He told me he thought the pub conversion was more aggro than it was worth, that he was worried about losing money on it and he was getting nothing but grief from his brother because of it. I offered him a way out. A joint venture. I said if he put up the property, I'd provide the construction. He only needed to show up to be the public face, and we could share the profits.'

'And?'

'He was well up for it. It was a good deal for him.' Fielder scratched his nose, making his rabbit teeth twitch, 'And I was very happy. I thought it'd solve the problem with the cellar as I could manage that. And it was also the first step at getting him on the firm.'

'So, what happened next?'

'His dipshit brother came over, asked what we were celebrating, he told him, and the brother didn't like it. Threw all the toys out and began kicking off.'

I tried picturing it in my mind, playing out the scene, but couldn't quite catch the mood. Something felt wrong. 'Why would Stuart kick off? He was the one that wanted shot of the Admiral Guthrie.'

'Because,' Fielder had a lilt in his voice, the sort that knows it's got a secret too good to keep, 'Danny Kidd cut his brother out of the deal. At first, I thought he was being a wind-up merchant, jerking him around. But turns out he was serious. He told him he was going into partnership with me, just the two of us. He told his brother he could do one. The brother didn't like that one little bit.

He started ranting and raving. It all got a bit embarrassing, to be honest. In the end, the staff had to ask the brother to go home.'

Outside the reception doors, the security guys hovered, watching.

PERRY FINISHED RECOUNTING our meeting with Fielder and looked to Stuart for a response, 'Well, is it true?'

'That I got chucked out?' he snapped, 'I was drunk and loud and obnoxious, I admit it, yes it's true.'

That wasn't what Perry meant, and he clearly knew it as his eye contact with her simmered with hostility.

'Why did you rant and rave?'

'Because he annoyed me. Danny was a master at it, he knew exactly what buttons to press to wind me up.'

'But this sounds a lot more than a silly squabble,' I said to divert his attention, his angry eyes were still fixed on Perry and I wanted them away. 'He was cutting you out. Dropping you. What did he say? His money, his choice?'

Stuart stared at me, a flicker of a sneer twitched at the corner of his lip, we'd tapped a nerve and got him ready to explode. I poked a little further. 'He threatened to kick you out, didn't he? Now he had time on his hands, he didn't need you to handle things for him anymore, he could make his own deals, be a proper businessman, is that what he said?'

A loud boom made Perry and I blink in surprise: Stuart had slammed both palms against the table top in force and fury.

'That ungrateful, selfish…' Stuart's words lost momentum as he went on, as though he was losing power, winding down, '…All I did for him.'

Stuart sniffed away a tear and continued, his voice soft and rational now—the fury had gone. 'It should have been me, he only had a chance at the big time because of me. No one wanted him: he was too small, too lightweight, couldn't stay on the ball, just blow on him, and he'd fall over. They only took him on because they wanted me. And then he made it, and I didn't. But did he appreciate it? Was he grateful?'

Perry had moved around the desk, she recognised a soul in distress and gently placed a hand on his shoulder.

'And then, as he progressed, who looked after him? Who gave up their life to see him right? Me! That's who. Have you got any idea how many players end their careers skint? Bad investments. Greedy relations and ex-wives fleecing them, agents and lawyers robbing them. But I looked after him, I made him a very rich man.'

I looked at his dropped head, face down to the table top, and put the question: 'You resented him coming into the business, didn't you?'

He scoffed a derisory laugh, 'That's putting it mildly. We'd agreed. I'd carry on with the business, he'd go off and be a TV star. But when that failed, he went back on his word. He expected me to stand aside and let him take over. He was going to throw me out… of the business I built. My business!' The anger had returned, his face flared red and his teeth bared, spitting out his words like acid.

'In a matter of days, he'd taken us to the verge of bankruptcy, and then… then… when a rescue plan was found he wanted to chuck me away, like rubbish.'

'But what happened, Stuart?' Perry asked in a gentle, kind voice, trying to coax the truth. 'Please tell us.'

'The security, they chucked me out of the dinner, said I was making a scene, and bundled me into a taxi. I got home and waited. The longer I waited, the angrier I got; the angrier I got, the more I drank; the more I drank, the angrier I got. Eventually I saw Danny come home, and I went to confront him, found him in the kitchen. We had words, he was his cocky arrogant self, laughing at me.' Stuart had only been looking at Perry, talking directly to her as though he'd forgotten I was there. She gave a reassuring pat to the back of his hand and he exhaled. A long, deep sigh. All the air seemed to seep out of Stuart's body and he sank into his chair:

'I was in tears, crying my heart out. He laughed and walked off. I grabbed a knife from the block on the side and went after him. We fought, and it went too far. I woke late the next morning, too much to drink, no excuse I know that now, but when I woke the place was swarming with police. I was already a no-show, I figured another twenty minutes wouldn't matter, so I showered and scrubbed myself clean, my clothes going in the wood-burner. I came up to the house, they took me into custody, I figured that was that, I was ready to confess, but my lawyer did all the talking and got me off. By then the knife had been through the dishwasher and my clothes were burnt. When that idiot admitted to burning down the garage, and then after him came Donaldson and his bullyboy tactics, I don't know, somehow it just seemed easier to let someone else take the blame.'

Perry and I exchanged a look—we knew what we had to do. I turned towards the open door, 'Have you heard enough, Mr Senia?'

'Indeed I have, thank you,' said Senia, entering the office. Stuart didn't protest as Senia arrested him, and more surprisingly didn't seem to hold any resentment towards Perry and me as he was led away. In fact, he looked relieved.

-47-

THE REST OF the day moved glacially slow, Perry and I spent most of it in silence, unable to find words to capture the enormity of it all.

As I sat in still contemplation, something Fielder had said to me kept rolling around my quiet empty head. When we'd learned all there was to know, we made to get out of his car. I had one foot on the tarmac when Fielder called me back:

'Can I ask you, why did you stand by him, the footballer? Despite everything crashing around your ears, why stick with him?'

I leaned back in to the cabin of the car and chewed my cheek for a second or two whilst I collected my thoughts. 'Because he was good to me.'

'What's that meant to mean?'

'First of all, they were the only ones willing to let me earn a living when no one else would, that counts for a lot,' I told him, thinking back to last year when my name and reputation was in tatters, and then my memories jumped to a more recent time, sitting on the grass watching a dwindling grey column of smoke. 'I got an unexpected surprise. A nasty tax bill. After I saved him from his garage fire, Danny Kidd paid it for me, said we'd sort out a way to pay it back, but he never lived that long. I felt loyal to him, that I owed it to him.'

'So, it all comes down to the money,' snapped Fielder. 'Don't kid yourself about loyalty, it's all about the money. You're a whore just like all the rest of us, it's just that he bought you first.'

'Yeah. Great. Bye.' I slammed the door and walked away. Maybe he was right, maybe he was wrong. I don't know. I don't care. I didn't want a long philosophical debate with him, I just wanted to get the last word.

AS I WATCHED the evening news, I wondered whether Fielder had a point after all. The top story was, of course, that Stuart had confessed. Senia appeared on the steps of the police station and announced Stuart had been charged with the manslaughter of his brother Danny Kidd. Disco, Uncle Bern, Perry and I sat by the TV and watched it all in silence.

'Goes to show, you never can tell,' said Bern. It was a quip to break the ice, we all knew that, but it stung me. I should have known, if anyone should it was me, but I was totally blind to it. But Perry knew—she'd seen through all the sentimentality and misplaced loyalty. When she laid all the pieces in front of me, when she assembled the jigsaw, it was obvious: the more talented player as a schoolboy, robbed of a career by a cruel injury, always resentful of Danny's success, underappreciated for safeguarding Danny's fortune, feeling cast aside in the business he'd created when Danny retired, and then finally attempting to put right the mess created by Danny only to be callously bumped out of the lucrative solution. It was always a festering hotbed of sibling rivalry, only I was too dumb to see it and needed a blunt instrument like Fielder to make it clear. Maybe Fielder was right, maybe the easy money dazzled me to what was really going on.

To Perry it made absolute sense for Stuart to blame Danny's murder on Donaldson because he'd already been connected to the deaths at the Admiral Guthrie. Stuart knew he could rely on me as his witness to Donaldson' intimidation of the Kidds. The only problem was, he hadn't been aware of Donaldson' connection to Fielder, or that Tony Flint was behind the scenes performing an industrial deep clean on Fielder's reputation.

I HEARD THE next day from Nick Witham that Fielder had voluntarily arrived at the police station, fully lawyered-up, to co-operate and provide a full and detailed account of what went on at the Cantium Invicta Awards dinner. Apparently he said he was there "under advice", I had a pretty good idea who'd advised him to be seen as the co-operative citizen—and it wasn't his fancy legal team.

Nick also told me about the sailor cold-case. With Hutton out of the way, and keen to avoid any more accusations of cover-ups, Nick now found resources being thrown at him to keep the case open.

'It's ridiculous,' he said, 'I've been given access to anything I want: labs, forensics, an enquiry room, even had the Press Officer on to me asking if I wanted to do a TV spot.'

'And?'

'No, not for me, I'm not the TV type. But I did get the sailor's clothes and personal effects tested in the lab,' a quiver of excitement had crept into Nick's voice. 'Due to its being so long ago it had never been DNA tested, it simply didn't exist back then. And guess what… two types of DNA found in and around the wound areas on the clothing?'

'Whose?'

'One belongs to the sailor.'

'And?'

'Because of the locations and the volumes, the other must belong to the attacker.'

'Yes?' Even though I was speaking to him on the phone I'd stood up at this news, desperate to hear the name I was expecting, 'Whose is it?'

'No idea,' said Nick. 'There's no matching record in the database.'

I sat back down, that'd put the kybosh on my good mood.

WHAT CAME NEXT, however, nobody could have predicted.

Three weeks of torrential rain. Storms. Winds. Out in the Atlantic, Hurricane Oliver had battered the east coast of America and still hungry for more headed our way. Flooding up and down the country; roads became rivers; rivers became oceans; bridge abutments got swept away, and swollen culverts rose up to dissolve railway lines washing their ballast out to sea. Elsewhere, amidst all this devastation of biblical proportions, something unexpected happened.

One of the most commonly known facts of science is that water always finds its own level. You never see water stacked up, you never see water sloping. Water will always find the lowest point and fill it. And out there, when we were hit by four months' worth of rain in as many days, waiting like a big hungry mouth was a nine-metre trench. The water found it, and the water filled it. The more the water came, the more the trench devoured, taking everything the Heavens could throw at it. The swirls and the eddies of the never-ceasing water churned up the edges of the trench. The sheet piles, driven in when the ground was still firm, were weakened by the swollen waterlogged earth. They were as decorative as a foil pie-tin and offered about as much resistance. The trench collapsed in on itself.

When the rains finally passed, when the sun remembered how to shine, when the men came back to work grateful to be earning again, their first job was to secure the nine-metre trench. The big crane plucked out the mangled sheet piles and the big yellow excavator, its wheels taller than its driver, carved out the trench again. Its jagged-toothed bucket scooped away tonnes of loamy, sodden crap until a solid clay bed was found. The bucket transferred the load to a muck-away lorry, but where was the lorry to tip? With the rivers still swollen it couldn't muck away to the estuary and the bird sanctuaries, so to make up the lost time on the programme it tipped the load at the back of the site as a temporary fix. The following night, the security guard's dog chased a smell and dug out a hand from the spoil heap. The day after, the police identified the remains of Donaldson. For the next three days the men were kept from the site and couldn't earn again. Resentment began to grow against Fielder Homes.

Sometime later, the newspapers reported Donaldson had been shot once in the head, a fatal blow, from an untraced gun believed to be a semi-automatic nine-millimetre pistol. I read that and my eyes watered, just a little but enough, because it meant if there was anyone out there that the bastard cared about at least they could now get some closure and some solace.

RON FIELDER APPEARED in the news: he was outraged. Who would dare defile one of his developments in this way? The bleaching of his reputation was relentless, he would shine like a saint, especially when he announced that none of his workforce would lose money through the site being closed as a crime scene, they'd all be recompensed. No doubt such a grand gesture won favour with his Asian investors, proving him a man of honour. With only a month until he was due at the palace to get his gong, it looked like it was the final push at keeping him squeaky clean.

Fielder was so desperate to maintain his glowing reputation he even appeared on appeals asking anyone that knew anything to come forwards, to volunteer some information. I was starting to find the whole charade nauseating—seeing Fielder cropping up all over the news, acting the shining knight in armour made me angry. I longed to see him exposed for the animal he was, but Perry's warning still echoed in my thoughts: you can't bring down someone so powerful and protected as him alone—the influence is too deeply embedded into everything.

-48-

JUMP FORWARD A month or so: I'd been watching the cricket with Bern when I was called by a number I didn't recognise. England were trailing and I was losing heart, so I picked up our empty mugs, headed to the kitchen and answered the call.

The caller gave their name, but it was lost in the thunder of the kettle's boil. I've no idea why, but the bright red kettle Perry had bought sounded like a jumbo jet engine taking off every single time. 'Say again, who is it?' I demanded.

'Mark, can you hear me, it's James Capel.' It took me a second or two to put a face to the drawling posh voice, then it came to me: Hamlet's lawyer. Behind me, the kettle reached its crescendo. 'I can hear you're busy on site,' said Capel. 'Sounds like a lot of heavy machinery working away there.'

'Something like that,' I muttered and moved away from the kettle. 'Is that better?'

'Perfect. Mark, I've had a call from a chap by the name of Senia, from the police.'

My soul slumped to my knees at the mention of his name. 'What's he want?'

'He'd like you to help with an enquiry,' replied Capel, 'I don't think it's anything to worry about.'

'Do I have to? He's like a pit-bull, once he gets his teeth locked on you, he doesn't let go. I'd rather not.'

'No, you don't have to. But it would look disadvantageous to you if you were to refuse,' Capel spoke with great patience and clarity, I expect he was used to having this same conversation regularly with Hamlet. 'I also think it's significant he came to me to arrange the meeting as he could quite easily have turned up at your doorstep. So, I think he actually needs your help properly.'

'Fine, alright then.'

I MET CAPEL as instructed outside Medway Police Station at eleven o'clock. When I was a kid growing up there was a police station in every town across Medway: Chatham, Gillingham, Rainham, the one at Rochester was a huge big intimidating black and silver tower block I seem to recall. They were all closed now, most demolished to make way for new housing. They'd all been replaced by this place, a regional headquarters on the indistinct boundary between Gillingham and Chatham, close to the old Admiralty buildings that had been refurbished to host the university campus. Despite it being emblazoned in police logos, the traffic hurtled past at great speed, all day long, every day of the week, using the dual carriageway in front of it to dip under the river through the tunnel to pick up the A2 straight to London on the other side.

Capel was waiting for me when I arrived. He raised an arm above his head in case I'd missed him, which I hadn't because he was the only person there. He flicked his cigarette to the gutter then stuck out his arm to give me a strong, firm handshake. 'Are you ready, shall we do this?' in the authoritative public-school tone of voice that spurred working-class Tommies like me to clamber over the trenches a century earlier.

Senia was in the reception lobby waiting for us, the grumpy desk sergeant from before wasn't. Senia offered another firm handshake, just after my fingers had regained feeling after the first, brilliant. Behind my back, I flexed and wriggled my fingers to chase away the numbness.

'Thank you for coming in, Mr Poynter,' I noticed the mister was said with no edge or attitude, I began to think perhaps he really did need my help after all.

Senia led us into a pleasant meeting room. Its large window gave a nice green leafy view of trees outside, far nicer than the oppressive interview room he'd had me in last time I was here a year ago. He then offered us both coffees, or water if we preferred. I'd had the coffee here before and that was enough for me, I declined both. Capel took a water. With the pleasantries dealt with, Senia got down to business. 'Mr Poynter, as you must be already be aware, we are charging Stuart Kidd with the death of his brother Danny.'

'No comment,' I replied.

'You're not under caution,' said Senia, 'I'm not asking you to say or do anything in the case against Stuart Kidd.'

Capel arched an inquisitive eyebrow in that way only posh men can do. 'What do you want from my client then, Chief Inspector?'

Senia leant back in his chair, crossed one knee over the other and extended an arm across the top of the chair beside him, 'I'd like you to provide a swab please.'

Capel arched an eyebrow again, only this one carried the message '*what the fuck are you talking about?*' another talent only the poshest of men can do, making the school fees well worth the money for that alone in my opinion.

Senia read the message and understood it loud and clear. 'When our investigators examined the body and effects of Mr Danny Kidd, five different DNA traces were found. One of course belongs to the victim, another to his brother. But the remainder are currently unidentified and in need of elimination. Mr Poynter, you discovered and reported Mr Kidd's murder. It is reasonable therefore to assume one strand may be yours, do you agree Mr Capel?'

Capel didn't respond with words but bobbed his head and pursed his lips, which I read to mean '*Maybe. Maybe not.*' Senia, however, wasn't thrown by Capel's non-committal response. 'We could always apply for a warrant that would compel you to provide a sample, but I would prefer to be civil about this if we can.'

I watched the treetops sway in the breeze outside against the dappled grey sky and thought about what I was being asked. Senia fiddled with his cufflinks and waited for an answer. I had one for him, 'Can I have a few minutes to consult with my lawyer please?'

TEN MINUTES LATER there was a soft knock on the door. It opened. Senia peered in, 'Well? Are you ready for me yet?' Capel beckoned him in, he had that overbearing force of character, a sense of entitlement that expects control in every situation, and I was amused to see Senia suppress his annoyance at being made to feel beholden in his own house.

'So, will you provide a DNA swab, please?'

'My client,' began Capel, 'is only willing to provide a DNA swab if you can confirm that Sir Ron Fielder will be providing one too.'

Senia looked stunned—this was clearly the last thing he'd expected to hear. 'What?'

'We know that Sir Ron Fielder was one of the last people to be with Danny Kidd before his murder,' said Capel. 'We know they were in high spirits, with a degree of larking about. Mr Kidd, like many sportsmen, was a very tactile person. It is therefore reasonable to assume some of Sir Ron Fielder's DNA may have transferred to Danny Kidd in that time, is it not Chief Inspector?'

'I guess so, yes, it's possible,' conceded Senia, then after a pause for thought, 'Don't go trying to blame him for Kidd's murder. I've already got a confession.'

Capel chuckled a rich, plummy laugh, 'Certainly not. We're not suggesting any such thing.'

Senia was confused, 'Then why?

'Because, Chief Inspector,' Capel's voice suddenly took on a stiffer tone, 'your remit is to expel any allegations of corruption and deceit. How do you think it would play in the newspapers if it was found that you've deliberately chosen to not trouble a person seen in close contact with the victim in their final hours and not upload them to the national DNA database simply because they are rich and influential? And add to that, you have threatened to issue a warrant to extract the DNA of an ordinary working man, one who has already been subject to prejudice from your predecessor. I'll tell you how it will play, it will smack of corruption and abuse of privilege. So, let me ask you again, will you be seeking the DNA of Sir Ron Fielder?'

Senia was fuming. The expansive body language was gone, no draped arms or lounging in his seat. He sat upright, his jaw tight and defined. He didn't say a word but stared straight at us, holding his glare until we looked away. The thing is, I could tell he knew Capel was right and had outfoxed him.

'Okay, if it makes you happy, I'll do it,' said Senia, much to my amazement. I hadn't actually expected him to agree to it.

'In that case, please contact me with the time and date he will be providing his swab and Mr Poynter will be at the same appointment. Thank you.'

THE FOLLOWING AFTERNOON I returned to the police station by appointment. Capel was already there seated in the lobby, engrossed in his phone screen. An officer behind the desk got me to sign the visitors' book. He was an older man, his heft long since turned to fat, his head shaved smooth back to the skin, combining with his round face and fat neck to give him the look of a big baby. The grumpy desk sergeant wasn't there again today: time off or removed, I wondered. I made a note to ask Nick, as I was curious whether he was one of Hutton's dirty brigade.

Capel looked up from his device and noticed me, and with a grand magnanimous sweep of the arm beckoned me to sit beside him, which I did, but he didn't speak and returned to the messages on his screen.

A few minutes later Fielder entered, followed by his lawyer. Fielder looked sharp in a blue suit with a crisp pink shirt unbuttoned at the collar. He didn't wear a tie, but instead wore a face of angry resentment. He didn't want to be here, but if he's to maintain his public persona, he would have been told he needed to show he was cleaner than clean with nothing to hide.

Capel looked up from his screen again. 'Sebastian,' he called and rose to his feet, trousering the phone. Fielder's lawyer looked around, then threw out a hand to accept Capel's handshake. They greeted each other warmly and began chatting in the way of old friends. Fielder gave a look of contempt, reminding me how Rachel said he had an ingrained dislike for the old school tie network. Then he noticed me, 'We meet again.'

'So it seems,' I replied. I couldn't think of anything else to say and remained in my seat.

'What are you here for?'

I didn't know whether I should respond. I looked to my lawyer for a steer, but he was lost in light-hearted gossip with Fielder's lawyer, so I offered, 'I've been asked to come in about the Danny Kidd murder.'

'Me too,' replied Fielder with an undertone that said he had a million other places to be rather than waste his time here.

I hoped I'd sounded on the right side of surprised meets curious when I answered, 'Oh, right, is that so?' and to my great relief was spared any more difficult conversation by the arrival of Senia, followed closely by a female officer in a charcoal grey suit.

Senia greeted us and thanked us for attending. I waved my hello from the opposite side of the room, smug that I'd managed to dodge any bone-snapping handshakes this visit. Senia addressed the female officer, 'Leigh, will you please take our guests upstairs to the interview suites so we can take their samples?'

As we followed Leigh through the building, I wondered whether Leigh was her first name or surname, but not enough to ever find out.

The swab of a cotton bud on the inside of my cheek was all that was required to extract all the DNA they needed. It took only a matter of seconds. It took far, far longer for the lawyers to go through the paperwork and processes, but we were informed we were free to go within half an hour with the advice that our DNA would be uploaded to the national database by the end of the day.

I'd sent a text message to Nick to say I was there, and on the way out he caught up with me and walked me off the premises. Apparently, the grumpy desk sergeant was having a week in Majorca, Nick seemed surprised by my question and I didn't think it worth explaining any further, that was a sleeping dog that could lie snug and sound where it was.

It came as a total surprise to me, probably to Nick too, but Nick had shown a bit of initiative and proved he's no slouch after all. He'd got in touch with Merseyside Police to ask about missing persons called Caroline, Carolina, Carol or similar variations from between nineteen eighty and eighty-three and that they'd come back with thirteen possible. He said he was in the process of following them all up. It occurred to me that if our girl was a runaway, she could have very possibly made up a name to prevent herself from being traced, but what Nick had was a start and I hoped something good might come of it.

As he began to return to the police station, I called him back. He paused mid-step and gave an expectant look over his shoulder in my direction.

'The sailor's clothes, did anyone know you had them?'

Nick used the handrail to steady himself, 'No. I thought I told you. Nobody knew they were in the archive, they didn't appear in any database, just on the original old paper docket. Unless anyone pulled the docket, like Muggins here, they'd never have known about his belongings. And seeing as my name was the only one on the docket since it was first archived, I'd guess everyone forgot all about them years ago.'

'Yeah, that's right, I remember you saying now.'

Nick shuddered, he was getting cold outside. He'd come out without a jacket and wanted to get back in to his cosy warm office and bad coffee, 'So why are you asking?'

'No reason,' I replied. 'Just an idea, though. You might want to run your DNA test on it again tomorrow morning. You might have a nice surprise.'

I walked off and let his shouted questions get blown away in the breeze.

-49-

PERRY AND I stood before the unmarked grave. The panels of turf laid across it hadn't knitted together yet, their joints curled at the edges like the pages of old books. They gaped open, exposing the broken earth beneath. Perry had stopped to buy a small bouquet of spring flowers at the supermarket and spent the entire journey trying to pick the sticky label price tag off the cellophane wrap, as though anyone would judge her cheap for her purchase. She laid them with respect and reverence, then slipped a small white card beneath the cellophane wrap, *'For Caroline'* was all that was written on it.

I'd not heard from Nick recently, he'd been a bit busy in the past two or three weeks. He'd made a high-profile arrest—a knight of the realm no less, who'd have thought it? His star, previously of the dimmest wattage imaginable, suddenly shone bright. Nick had gone from backroom boy to golden boy. I was really pleased for him. Last I heard, he was still following up his missing person leads; no success yet, but he remained hopeful.

The clatter from the railway tracks far away carried on the soft wind. It reminded me of the old Paul Simon song I heard in Hamlet's car that day we learned the truth, the one about everyone loving the sound of a train in the distance.

The sound rattled rhythmically, unlocking a freeflow of thoughts, and as the sound began to fade into the distance, I realised I'd had my heart and my brain back to front and upside down. I'd been led by my heart in the pursuit of finding the truth, and by my brain in considering how my life could be better. I understood now I had it the wrong way around. I should have listened to my heart sooner and accepted Perry made my life better, as did Bern, I suppose. And I should have used my brain and realised sooner that the truth was sometimes better left alone.

I hoped we'd soon have a name for Caroline, that we'd be able to get her home, and wondered where my brother was and what he was doing. Before my thoughts became too maudlin, I was saved by Perry taking my hand in a warm, tight clasp. She reached around to place her other hand on top of our joined hands and tapped it, 'Come on, let's go home. We don't want to miss the party.'

WE DIDN'T MISS the party, we couldn't—we were the hosts. Thirty or so friends filled our small house, friends from my work, Perry's friends from the hospital, a nice blend of people all getting along nicely, and all to celebrate the same thing:

Our engagement.

That's right. I'd decided enough with the prevarication and procrastination, I'd never find anyone as perfect for me as Perry and so before she saw me for all my flaws—or perhaps because she saw all my flaws—I asked her to make it permanent.

It got to around ten p.m. and the party was in full swing. I'd borrowed an electric piano for the occasion, and Uncle Bern was persuaded to come out of retirement to play for us. Not that he was reluctant about it, a few claps and cheers soon got him banging away. A few duff notes to begin with—he blamed it on his arm still being a little stiff since the cast had come off, but it wasn't long before he was entertaining everyone and loving the attention.

Around midnight people began to fade away. Perry stood by the door saying goodbyes, thanking them and accepting their best wishes with the brightest most glorious smile—she was so happy. Bern saw me watching her, 'Well done son, you've got a good one there,' he said.

'I know. She's the best.'

'Your mum would absolutely adore her,' Bern had draped his arm across my shoulder. 'You know that, don't you?'

'I do Bern, thanks.'

He realised he'd become a little oversentimental, the occasion and the drink had got to him, as he very rarely spoke of his sister, my mum. With a sniff he wiggled his glasses back up to the bridge of his nose and tried changing the subject, never a good idea after a drink's been taken.

'I spoke to Alfie Rubbers today.'

'Oh yeah,' I replied. 'Must have been nice for you.'

'He said they caught the fella that beat him up.'

'Gave him a medal, did they?'

Bern looked askance at me, then, 'You know what…' Bern's level of tact at the best of times was very low, with the beers to soften him, it was now virtually non-existent, 'I thought you done it.' He added a slight laugh at the end, as though suggesting it was all a big joke. I didn't respond. It dawned on him he may have misjudged his moment and his topic and he tried to backtrack, 'Just because… well… you know… I knew you never liked him, and on account of how you just disappeared for a morning, completely dropped off the radar, that day you were meant to pick up the keys from the police station.'

Typical Bern, when in a hole, rather than apologise or drop it, blame me instead.

'You want to know where I was?' I asked. He looked sheepish and muttered that he didn't, I told him anyway, 'I was paying off my tax bill. If it's any of your business, Danny had written me a cheque that then got frozen when he died. It was released by the executors the same morning my tax demand was due, so I needed to go in there to sort it all out before I got hit with fines… or worse.'

'Course son, yeah, yeah, no offence meant.' Bern patted me on the back and shuffled towards the corner where Disco and Harpo sang in sozzled harmony.

'What was that all about?'

I was pleased to find Perry beside me and slipped my arm around her waist. I assured her it was only Bern being Bern. She smiled, cradled my face in her hand and stepped up on tiptoe to plant a long, lovely kiss.

'Not interrupting, am I?'

We broke off and turned towards the voice. Hamlet stood in front of us. He thrust a magnum of champagne towards Perry, a fancy brand too: hand painted art-nouveau flowers decorated the bottle. With grace and generosity, she thanked him, and took it.

'I'm not stopping, I only popped in to wish you both congratulations,' he said, 'I'm sure you'll be very happy together.' Perry gave him a peck on the cheek. Hamlet giggled like a schoolboy. I liked this side of him.

'Quick one for you, Marky. The Admiral Guthrie. I bought it off the administrator. Very good price too, but that's not important,' he informed me. 'I'm getting a scheme together to knock what's left of it down, clear the site and build a new apartment block, nine flats.'

'Nice,' I replied. 'Best of luck with it.'

A line of confusion wrinkled Hamlet's shiny, smooth forehead. 'No, you aren't getting it,' he said, 'I want you to do it for me, to be my builder.'

I was lost for words, but only because I didn't know what the right answer was. Luckily Perry was there to tell me.

'You may as well do it, you haven't got any other work on. Go for it. But you…' she pointed her finger at Hamlet, '…you keep him out of trouble, okay?'

Hamlet roared with laughter and assured her it would be best behaviour only from now on. He draped a heavy arm around me. His massive bicep, almost the size of my head, lay across my shoulder. It pushed my neck forward, but I didn't mind, it created a huddle, it felt matey. With our heads almost touching Hamlet dropped the volume of his voice, 'Marky, I've been meaning to talk to you about something.' Gone was the life-and-soul party animal, replaced by a serious tone that started to trouble me, 'It's about your brother.'

Adam. My veins froze, the anticipation of bad news caused my body to close down, my fingers trembled, the edges of my vision began to darken. I didn't want to hear bad news, not here, not at my party. Perry immediately spotted the change in me and guided me to a seat. Aside from Bern, Harpo and Disco, everyone else had left. I became aware the three amigos had quietened down and knew they were watching my humiliation, but I tried to rationalise it—if I was to get the worst news imaginable at least I had some close friends with me.

Hamlet realised he had an audience, but he also realised I was on the verge of an emotional collapse. He rasped his hand over his chin, then broke his lifetime rule and discussed his business in public: 'Don't panic Marky Mark, it's nothing terrible.'

The darkness around the edges of my vision began to fade and return to colour. Perry's comforting hand on my back helped my breathing slow and normalise.

'What I wanted to tell you…' Hamlet paused, then rolled his index fingers around each other as though trying to rewind his thoughts back to the beginning, '…You asked me where Adam is. But the fact is, I can't tell you, mate. And I can't tell you because, I honestly don't know.'

Bern had approached on my other side, I felt his hand on my shoulder, 'That's a mean trick to play on the lad. Why'd you want to do something like that on tonight of all nights?'

Hamlet was shaken and took half a step back. He raised both hands up at his sides, symbolising he'd come in peace, 'No trick Bern. Look Marky Mark, I'm sorry, I haven't explained myself very well. I don't know where he is because it's for his own safety. If I don't know where he is, they can't get to him through me.'

'They? Who's they?' asked Perry, but Hamlet ignored the question and carried on talking directly to me:

'For his safety. If I need to get hold of him, or him me, it's all handled through intermediaries. I don't know them, and I don't know where he is. I don't have a number for him. I wish I could help you Marky.'

I didn't have a clue what was happening any more. I looked to Perry for guidance, but her attention was fixed on Hamlet, her eyes dark and hostile.

'I used to have contact details for him, I wasn't meant to have it, it came to me through a mutual friend,' continued Hamlet. 'But I've lost it. I've looked everywhere, thought it was on my desk at home but… oh well. If I had it, I'd give it to you, I promise. But I can tell you this… he's fine.'

I nodded, more to say I was listening than for any other reason. Part of my head was still reeling at the concept of Adam being in hiding for his own protection, but another part was glad beyond belief to learn he was well.

'Intermediaries, Marky,' he repeated. 'It's all through intermediaries. Sorry. And I'm sorry if I spoilt your party, it wasn't my intention. I'll go now.'

He sounded genuinely apologetic. The big alpha male, the king of the jungle: he looked like a lost little boy standing in front of me. He'd come with good intentions, I realised, slightly misjudged but good intentions, nonetheless. I muttered something, neither positive nor negative, just something. Then he removed an envelope from inside his jacket, a daffodil yellow rectangular envelope. 'I almost forgot, this is for you, too.' Looking at it, I guessed it was a greeting card to go with his gift of the champagne. He still looked awkward and embarrassed. He gripped the envelope in one hand and flicked it against the palm of the other hand.

'Anyway, I'll call you sometime next week about the new apartments. Night.'

He walked slowly towards the front door, Perry followed and held it open for him. He wished her goodnight. He leant down to whisper in her ear, followed by a peck on the cheek and then he stepped out into the night, handing her the yellow envelope as he did. Perry closed the door behind him and returned to where I still sat. She crossed the room and handed the envelope to me, 'Here.'

I let the envelope fall from my fingers to the floor, I wasn't in the mood for the fake pleasantries of greeting cards, I'd have been happier if everyone just went home and left me alone.

Perry stooped and picked the envelope up, then prodded it back in my direction, 'He told me to make sure you opened it.'

Just to keep the peace, I took it and tore it open. Inside, a greeting card, *'You're Engaged'*, in curly gold foil letters, surrounded by gold and silver balloons and love hearts, 'Nice,' I muttered with sheer indifference.

I opened it and read the message of congratulations and best wishes he'd written. A faint tickle brushed across my knuckles. I looked and saw something hanging off the back of the card. I pulled it and came away with a small square of neon yellow paper, a post-it note. I held it before me and studied it.

'What's that, son?' asked Bern.

'An email address,' I replied, 'Adam's.'

ABOUT THE AUTHOR

Matthew Ross was born and raised in the Medway Towns, England. He still lives in Kent with his Kiwi wife, his children, a very old cat and a bouncy young puppy.

He was immersed in the building industry from a very early age helping out on his father's sites during school holidays before launching into his own career at 17. He's worked on projects ranging from the smallest domestic repair to £billion+ infrastructure, and probably everything in between.

A lifelong comedy nerd, he ticked off a bucket-list ambition and tried his hand at stand-up comedy. Whilst being an experience probably best forgotten (for both him and audiences alike) it ignited a love for writing, leading to various commissions including for material broadcast on BBC Radio 4 comedy shows.

Matthew moved into the longer format of novel writing after graduating from the Faber Academy in London in 2017.

'The Red Admiral's Secret' is his second novel in the planned series of stories featuring Mark Poynter and his associates.

Matthew enjoys reading all manner of books - especially crime and mystery; 80s music; and travelling and can't wait for the next trip to New Zealand to spend time with family and friends.

AUTHOR'S NOTES AND ACKNOWLEDGEMENTS

Thank you for reading this book. If you've followed Marky Mark and the gang from the previous book, *'Death Of A Painter'*, then welcome back – thank you for your support and your encouragement, it's so very greatly appreciated!
And if you came fresh and green to us this adventure, welcome too, we're glad you joined us. It may very well be the case that it was the amazing cover that drew you to it, and thanks should go to Sean at Red Dog for leading the design process with verve and passion.
From the very outset, I should make clear that none of my characters are based on real people. Similarly, the Medway Towns in this story is my Medway Towns of fantasy and fiction so I apologise for dropping dead bodies and a crowd of reprobates on it. I'd like to reassure anyone thinking of visiting that in real-life it's very lovely. I'm proud that it's my hometown, and to be a Man of Kent.
I'd like to thank everyone at Red Dog Press for giving me this wonderful opportunity and having faith in me a second time. The encouragement, guidance and support from Sean, Richard and Meggy has been there in abundance from the very beginning, and I realise I've been very lucky to be in their safe hands. The Red Dog Kennel is a very happy home with some wonderful writers, and the spirit of collaboration and mutual support within it is uplifting and rewarding.
I feel I need to address the use of the C-word in the book … Coronavirus! Ordinarily I hate anything that firmly anchors a story in one specific place and time, and I gave it a lot of thought and consideration but ultimately I felt I needed to refer to the Pandemic of 2020. The lead characters would have witnessed the effects at close hand – with one a nurse manning the front line full-time, the

other a self-employed construction worker shut down and unable to work – and it would have been wrong to have to ignored the effects it had on them. So I would like to take this opportunity to thank all of our medical professionals, our first responders, our key workers and our essential operatives who took care of us and kept the country going during lockdown – they are all amazing, and on behalf of myself and my family we are truly grateful and I hope within the story I've treated the matter with the appropriate respect.
I'm grateful to my wife, Rebecca, and our children for their love and support at all times – thank you, I'm so very lucky to share my life with you.
And finally, thank you for taking the time and trouble to read this book, it's more appreciated than you may ever realise. If you enjoyed it please do leave a review, your feedback would be great.
I'd love to hear from you so please do feel free to get in touch with me. You can find me on Twitter @mattwross and contact me via Red Dog Press.

Lightning Source UK Ltd.
Milton Keynes UK
UKHW010719210121
377439UK00001B/81

9 781913 331481